A Century
of South African
Short Stories

A Century
of South African
Short Stories

*Revised edition
edited by
Martin Trump*

*Based on the first edition
edited by
Jean Marquard*

AD. DONKER PUBLISHER

AD. DONKER (PTY) LTD
A subsidiary of Jonathan Ball Publishers (Pty) Ltd
PO Box 2105
Parklands
2121

Original selection published by Ad. Donker Publisher 1978
Revised edition first published 1993

ISBN 0 86852 192 2 (Paperbook edition)
ISBN 0 86852 194 9 (Hardcover edition)

Typesetting and reproduction by Book Productions, Pretoria
Cover design by Michael Barnett, Johannesburg
Printed and bound by National Book Printers, Goodwood, Cape

Contents

Introduction

Reading a country's literary works is arguably one of the best ways of learning about the private and public history of that country, and the short story is one of the most accessible and attractive of all literary forms. This book consists of South African short stories of the past hundred years. From the 1890s, the short story has become a brilliant vehicle of literary expression in South Africa.

As one reads these stories – arranged chronologically – one gets a fine sense of South African history. The large public events and epochs are discernible in the stories. Colonialism is an element in virtually all of the early stories and the shift towards an industrialised and racially-divided society looms large in many later works. Yet there is what I called earlier a 'private history' in these stories as well. The great personages of South African history are rarely named in the stories and are not their central characters. Instead, the short stories describe the lives of people most usually outside the grand spotlight of national history. Yet their history is the country's history. What happens to these 'little people' – these fictionalised characters – is really emblematic of a wider public history. Fiction takes one far into the personalised history of the country, where frequently family relationships and areas of subjective experience receive the key focus. This is a history with which most of us can identify. The institutionalised record gives way to a more personal and subjective one.

Here is a brief set of comments about the stories in this volume and the history they traverse. Right from the first story, William Scully's *Umtagati* (1895) to Maureen Isaacson's *Holding Back Midnight* (1992), the interaction of black and white people in South Africa forms the subject-matter of many of the works. And a very wide range of human relations between black and white characters is presented in these stories. One also finds in stories which deal exclusively with one or other of these groups that the presence of 'the other' is felt.

The opening stories by Scully, FitzPatrick and Glanville – all written in the last decade of the nineteenth-century – deal with colonialism in South Africa. By colonialism, I mean the seizure of land from and the political subjugation of indigenous people by an alien conqueror. Scully's *Umtagati* is an illustrative fable of how colonialism works. After the forcible annexation of land, the native population is cajoled into submission. The story is full of wry humour and pathos. The FitzPatrick and Glanville stories touch on some of the popular, colourful features of colonialism. Africa is a place of adventure. White people view the region as foreign and exotic. Here we have 'curious tales of man and beast in darkest Africa'. Later in this volume we read stories that describe the souring of colonial optimism. The excitement of the hunt in *Uncle Abe's Big Shoot* (1897) for example, gives way to a bitter reflection about hunting people in Africa in Ernst Havemann's story *A Farm at Raraba* (1987), written nearly a century later.

Olive Schreiner's monumental tale of Boer suffering in the nineteenth-century, *Eighteen-Ninety-Nine* (1906), indicates the dark face of colonialism, and the story, notable in so many ways, highlights in particular the plight of the Boer woman. The mania about colour or 'racial' differences between people is the subject of the next two stories by Perceval Gibbon and Arthur Cripps. This distorting obsession becomes the subject of a large number of later stories as well. William Plomer's *The Child of Queen Victoria* (1933), is one example among many. Pauline Smith's *Desolation* (1925) describes the hardship of a poor white family and is rare in dealing with this subject.

Rolfes Dhlomo's *Murder on the Mine Dumps* (1930) is one of the early stories in English by a black South African, and touches on a number of issues that also preoccupy later black writers. The violence of the system of colour and labour exploitation becomes an inescapable part of the ethos of black life in South Africa. With it there is a profound sense of alienation among many of the black characters. In many stories, black people are outsiders, fugitives and outlaws. Pressured at every turn by a system of colour discrimination, the black person lives on the edge of legality, constantly having to forge meaning beyond the confines of the system. Frank Brownlee's *The Cannibal's Bird* (1938) offers what is palpably an outsider's view of black society, and it is worth comparing this with A.C. Jordan's insider's view in *The Turban* (1973). Peter Abrahams's *One of the Three* (1942) offers a good example of an insider's view of black alienation and cruel social entrapment.

Herman Charles Bosman is among South Africa's most popular story writers and his fiction is an established and familiar part of the local cultural fabric. What is frequently not recognised about Bosman's work is that much of it was extremely topical and controversial. Throughout his life Bosman was a rebel and his Marico stories offer no complacent view of South African society. Bosman is a satirist *par excellence* and he is unerring in holding traditionalist Afrikaner values up to close scrutiny. The story I have chosen to represent Bosman's work – *Birth Certificate* (1950) – is one of his most bold and direct social satires. His small contemporary readership would have been in little doubt about the author's social views and the targets of his satire. In the story, Bosman brilliantly satirises and connects two extremely topical South African events of his day. The first was Professors Dart and Broom's paleaontological discoveries near Johannesburg of the *Australopithecus africanus* man. It was suggested that this discovery offered clear proof of an evolutionary connection between ape and man. The second was the Afrikaner government's imposition of the Population Registration Act in 1950. Bosman holds both up to derision. The theory of the evolution of ape to man and the closely analagous notion that on the evolutionary scale black people were inferior to white people are the underlying subjects of *Birth Certificate*.

In many ways Bosman's stories, or what I would call his political fables, offer a bridge to the contemporary short story. Bosman's Marico stories suggest the complex, often acrimonious interaction between different groups of people in the country. And this becomes the central, overwhelming subject of much South African short story writing since the 1940s.

Uys Krige's *Death of the Zulu* (1953) is a rarity, taking as its subject the experiences of South African soldiers in the North African campaign during the Second World War. The meeting of a white and a black South African soldier is the central episode of the story and the nature of their meeting suggests that this encounter stands for the wider pattern of black and white South African interaction. The story reads as a bittersweet allegory.

Many key stories of the 1950s and 1960s deal with the tormented relations between black and white South Africans and give a sense of how much is being lost in terms of productive human intercourse as a result of the society's discriminatory practices and mental attitudes. There is an edge of revolt and anger in stories of this period by the black writers James Matthews, Can Themba, Ezekiel Mphahlele and Ahmed Essop.

Nadine Gordimer, along with Herman Charles Bosman, is one of South Africa's most accomplished short story writers. She has been a prolific story writer since the 1940s, and her works deal with a very wide range of subjects. I suspect, however, that the fictional subject for which she would best like to be remembered is her treatment of people who have opposed the system of apartheid in South Africa. *A Chip of Glass Ruby* (1965) is one such work. Here personal and public history are intimately linked. Similarly, Njabulo Ndebele's later story *Death of a Son* (1987) celebrates the courage and resilience of people opposed to the violence of the society. In both of these stories, the authors focus on personal responses to hardship and suggest that a better future in South Africa is possible.

Many of the stories since the 1970s have dealt with the last tired phase of apartheid. Peter Wilhelm's *Lion* (1975) could well be read as a despairing fable about black aspirations being crushed. Bessie Head's *Life* (1977) is an equally sad reflection about the failures of urban and rural cultures to co-exist harmoniously in Southern Africa. Gcina Mhlope and Zoë Wicomb's stories deal with loneliness and take up the theme of black hopes being distorted and defeated. Joel Matlou and E.M. Macphail's stories describe the lives of two very different kinds of South African migrants. In Matlou's *Man Against Himself* (1979), the experiences of an impoverished black migrant worker are graphically described: the passages dealing with his work on the platinum mine conjure up a portrait of a terrestial hell. In a very different social class, but not dissimilarly disorientated and cast adrift, is the central character of Macphail's *Annual Migration* (1991). Here, Esther is a well-to-do white South African whose children have left to settle in the USA. Each year, Esther wanders North America, finding herself spurned by her children.

In stories of the 1980s and 1990s, several writers look beyond the travails of the present situation. Christopher Hope's *Learning to Fly* (1980) is a witty, predictive fable about what might happen in a future South Africa. Hope's story sourly suggests that little will really change when power shifts from white to black. Deena Padayachee's *The Finishing Touch* (1992) also offers a wry view of social attitudes and moves in its sphere of concern from the past into the future. The last story in the volume, Maureen Isaacson's *Holding Back Midnight* (1992) humorously deals with the irresistable nature of change in South Africa. The old guard find themselves overwhelmed by the changes in the country, and the author seems to be joyfully ushering in a new, albeit unpredictable order of things. We have, indeed, moved a long way from the colonial adventures described in the stories of a hundred years ago.

Notes About the Second Edition

This anthology has been built on Jean Marquard's pioneering first edition which appeared in 1978. Marquard's untimely death in the early 1980s meant that the book has not been revised. The second edition updates the first and introduces a number of changes. I have not followed Marquard's convention of giving more than one story per author – each writer is represented by a single work. Moreover, I have introduced several new authors into the earlier section of the book – Dhlomo, Boetie, La Guma, Mphahlele and Adams – and there are some story changes here as well, involving stories by Plomer, Krige, Jacobson, Cope, Paton, Themba, Wilhelm and Head. The last thirteen stories – since 1979 – are new to the volume. My introduction departs markedly from that of the first edition.

It is difficult to be an equal opportunities/affirmative action editor. Of the forty two stories in this book eleven are by women and sixteen by black writers, with the proportions increasing markedly as one approaches the present. Finally, all of the stories were written in English and one needs remark not only about the cornucopia of work in this language by black and white South African writers, but also to note that the short story has also been finely handled in the indigenous African languages and in Afrikaans. I would hope that readers are not misled into believing that English has been the only language of literary excellence in South Africa!

I would like to offer warm thanks to Denis Hirson, with whom I collaborated on *The Heinemann Book of Contemporary South African Short Stories*. Several of the stories included here in *A Century of South African Short Stories* were brought to my attention by him.

I would like to thank Craig Mackenzie of Rand Afrikaans University's English Department for his generous assistance.

Martin Trump

William Charles Scully

Umtagati

from *Kafir Stories* (1895)

'The great witch-doctor has come, and all
    Sit trembling with cold and fear
As they list to the words from his lips that fall, –
    The words all shrink to hear.
Lo! Look at the seer as he whirls and leaps
    The awestruck circle within,
Where each one shudders, and silence keeps
    As he thinks of the untold sin.

'On his head is a cap of dark brown hair, –
    The skin of a bear-baboon,
And the tigers' teeth on his throat, else bare,
    Jangle a horrible tune;
The serpents' skins and the jackals' tails,
    Hang full around his hips,
And a living snake from his girdle trails,
    And around each bare limb slips.'

                                                            The Witch-Doctor

I

The motive and controlling factors of great issues are not always recognised by those most interested, neither does honour nor yet reward always fall to those who best deserve or earn them. In proof of the foregoing propositions the following narrative is adduced.

Teddy's full name was Edmund Mortimer Morton. He was a Government official holding the appointment of clerk to the Resident Magistrate of Mount Loch, which district, as everybody knows, is situated in the territory of Bantuland East, and just on the border of Pondoland.

Vooda was a native Police Constable attached to the Mount Loch establishment.

Teddy's age was twenty-six, but he looked several years younger. He was a pleasant-looking little chap, about five feet four inches in height, slightly built, with blue eyes, yellow hair and an incipient moustache upon which he bestowed a great deal of attention. His hobby was popular chemistry. This he indulged in, greatly to the entertainment of his friends and the detriment of his hands, which were generally discoloured in a manner that defied soap. He lived in a little hut just outside the village. This hut consisted of one room, and was shaped like a round pagoda. It had a pointed roof and projecting eaves made of Tambookie grass. The walls were of sod-work, plastered over and whitewashed. Here Teddy dwelt – taking his meals elsewhere – and experimented in parlour-magic to his heart's content.

Vooda was a constable. He was a short, stout man, with a deep, although not wide knowledge of human nature; not wide only for lack of experience. He had dwelt all his life amongst the natives surrounding Mount Loch, and he could read them like so many books of Standard I. He could, moreover, tell by looking at a witness in court, whether that witness were speaking truth or lying, and the magistrate recognised and utilised this faculty. Vooda and Teddy were great friends, Vooda taking a lively and intelligent interest in Teddy's experiments.

Everyone knows that in the early part of 1894, Pondoland, the last independent native State south of Natal, was annexed to Cape Colony. Much to the general surprise, the annexation was effected peacefully, but for some months afterwards the greatest care had to be exercised in dealing with the Pondos. The people generally were glad of the change from the harsh arbitrary, and irresponsible rule of the native chiefs to the settled and equitable conditions of civilised government; but the chiefs gave trouble. They naturally would not, without struggling and agitating, submit to the loss of power and prestige which they sustained, and they bitterly resented being no longer permitted to 'eat up' those who annoyed them. Now, the instincts of clannishness and loyalty are so strong amongst the Kaffirs, that even against what they well know to be their own vital interests, they will follow the most cruel and rapacious tyrant, so long as he is their hereditary tribal chieftain, into rebellion.

Now, the Kwesa clan of Pondos dwelt just on the boundary of Mount Loch, and within thirty miles of the Magistracy. The head of this clan, a chief named Sololo, had not objected to the annexation, and was consequently looked upon as well-affected towards the Government. But within a few months after the annexation, a serious difficulty arose between the authorities and this man. One of his followers quarrelled with another, and after the time-honoured local custom, assuaged his feelings by means of a spear-thrust, which had a fatal result. The murdered man was one whom Sololo disliked, whereas, on the other hand, the murderer was one whom the chief delighted to honour. Consequently, when the magistrate demanded the surrender of the culprit for the purpose of dealing with him according to law, Sololo refused delivery, and couched his refusal in an extremely insolent and rebellious message.

Cajolements, remonstrances, and threats were of no avail; Sololo remained obstinate. His tone, however, somewhat changed; he sent polite, but evasive and unsatisfactory replies to all messages on the subject. The Chief Magistrate was at his wits' end. Of course the law had to be vindicated, but were an armed force to be sent against Sololo, the odds were ten to one that within twenty-four hours signal fires would be blazing on every hill, and the war-cry sounding from one end of Pondoland to the other. The Chief Magistrate's native name was 'Indabeni', which means 'The one of counsel'. He was a man of vast experience in respect of the natives, and moreover, he did not belong to that highly moral, but sometimes inconvenient class of officials who are known as 'the hide-bound'; that is to say, his ideas ranged beyond the length of the longest piece of red tape in his office, and he knew for a certainty that things existed which could not conveniently be wrapped up in foolscap paper. He was, moreover, one who trusted much to the effect of his own considerable personal influence, and he believed in utilising the talents of such of his subordinates as possessed faculties similar to his own in this respect.

Indabeni had taken Vooda's measure accurately. He knew the Constable to have a persuasive tongue, to be honest, loyal, and discreet, and, above all, to possess that nameless and almost indescribable quality of imparting trustfulness in those with whom he came in contact.

One afternoon a telegram marked 'confidential' came from Indabeni to the Resident Magistrate of Mount Loch. The purport of the message was that Vooda should go to Sololo and talk quietly to him, endeavouring by means of persuasion to effect a compliance with the reasonable demands of Government. Teddy, being in the fullest confidence of his Chief, was present when instructions were accordingly given to Vooda, who was directed to start early next morning for the kraal of the Chief of the Kwesas, in Pondoland.

When the offices were closed for the day, Teddy went home to his hut, and it was noticed by one who met him on the road that his manner was very preoccupied, and his walk unusually slow. Shortly afterwards he was seen to stroll over to the police camp, and go straight to Vooda's hut.

At eight o'clock that evening Vooda visited Teddy's dwelling, and a long and serious conversation ensued. This was varied by a series of experiments of a nature so striking that even Vooda was startled. At about ten o'clock a stranger passing noticed strange flashes lighting up the back

of the hut behind the reed fence. Shortly before eleven Vooda returned
to camp, carrying a small satchel which contained a packet of lycopodium
powder, a piece of potassium about as large as a walnut, and a number of
whitish lumps about an inch in diameter, such as are known amongst
practitioners of parlour magic variously as 'serpents' eggs' or 'Pharaoh's
serpents'.

II

At daylight next morning Vooda left the police camp, but it was late in
the afternoon when he reached the kraal of Sololo. He found a number
of strangers there, including Shasha, the 'inyanga', or war-doctor. The
men, all of whom were armed, were sitting on the ground in a half-circle.
Before them stood a number of large earthen pots of beer. Vooda, being
an old friend of the Chief, was invited to sit down and drink, so, after
removing the saddle from his horse, he joined the party. He soon saw,
however, that his presence had imported an element of restraint. He was
careful as yet not to allude to the business upon which he had come. Later
on others began to arrive, some carrying guns, some spears, and some
assegais. It was plain that an important discussion was on hand, and that
Vooda's presence was unwelcome. The beer was not in sufficient quantities to cause intoxication, but nevertheless all were somewhat mellow
when the sun went down.

Shortly afterwards, Sololo asked the visitor point blank 'where he was
thinking of'. This was an unusual thing to do under the circumstances,
such a question to a visitor being held amongst natives to be discourteous
and suggestive of inhospitality.

Vooda replied to the effect that he had an important matter to discuss
with the Chief, and asked Sololo to grant him a private interview.

Now Sololo, having had experience of Vooda's persuasive tongue and
knack of casuistry, did not wish to argue the point – knowing, as he did
full well, the object of Vooda's visit – and at once made up his mind that
he would not see the glib-tongued constable alone.

'Son of my father,' he said, 'what you have to say, let it be said before
these my councillors and friends.'

Vooda saw there was no chance of a private discussion, and determined
therefore to play his game boldly and in public. The dusk of evening was
just setting in, and some women had kindled a bright fire.

'My Chief,' he said, 'I come with the words of Indabeni, who has
chosen me because he knows I am your younger brother' (figurative).

'Indabeni is a great man,' said Sololo; 'he has eyes all round his head.
His words are good to hear – speak them, son of my father.'

'Indabeni's heart is heavy, my Chief, because you, the leopard, are placing yourself in the path of the buffalo, which is the Government. Men have told Indabeni that you refuse to deliver to the Magistrate one who has done wrong.'

'The leopard may stand on one side and tear the flank of the buffalo as he passes. He may then hide in the caves of the rocks where the buffalo cannot follow,' said Sololo, sententiously.

'The buffalo may call the wolves to his aid to drive the leopard from his cave,' rejoined Vooda, developing the allegory further; 'but why will you not give up the wrong-doer to the Magistrate?'

'Why must I give up my friend to be choked with a rope?' said Sololo, excitedly. 'He has not slain a white man, but one of my own people. Government must leave him to be punished according to the law of the native. If one of my tribe slays a white man, I will deliver up the slayer.'

'But you know what the Government is, my Chief – it is over all of us. Even Indabeni himself has to do as it tells him.'

'Indabeni is not a Pondo, neither am I Indabeni,' said Sololo, appealing, with a look, to the audience.

'Yebo, Yebo, Ewe – E-hea,' shouted all the men.

'I did not ask Government for its laws,' continued the Chief. 'U-Sessellodes [the native attempt at pronouncing the name of Mr Cecil Rhodes, Premier of the Cape Colony] came here and said in a loud voice that we all belonged to him. We were surprised, and could not think or speak. Besides, who listens to the bleating of a goat when an angry bull bellows? Now we have thought and spoken together, and we can also fight. I will never give up my friend to be choked with a rope.'

'E-hea,' shouted the audience.

'My Chief,' said Vooda, 'your words are like milk flowing from a great black cow ten days after she has calved, but there is one thing you have not seen, but which I have seen and trembled at.'

'What is this thing that frightens a man who is the father of children?'

'The magic (umtagati) of U-Sessellodes, which he has taught to Indabeni – the terrible magic wherewith he overthrew Lo Bengula and the Matabele.'

'We, also, have our magic,' said Sololo, glancing at Shasha, the war-doctor.

Shasha came forward in a half-crouching attitude, and approached Vooda, who appeared to be very much impressed. The war-doctor's appearance was startling enough. He was an elderly man of hideous aspect. On his head he wore a high cap of baboon skin. Slung around his neck, waist, elbows, wrists, knees, and ankles were all sorts of extraordinary things – cowrie and tortoise-shells, teeth and claws of various beasts of prey, strips of skin from all kinds of animals, inflated gall bladders, bones, and pieces of wood. In his hand he carried a bag made by cutting the skin of a wild cat around the neck, and then tearing it off the body as one skins an eel. Out of this he drew a long, living, green snake (inushwa, the boomslang), which he hung over his shoulder, where it began to coil about, darting out its forked tongue. As Shasha advanced quivering towards Vooda in short, abrupt, springs, all the things hanging about him clashed and rattled together. He bent down and beat the ground with the palms of his hands and the soles of his feet, making the while a low rumbling in his throat, the apple of which worked up and down. His eyes glared and his nostrils dilated. The snake hissed, and wound itself round his neck and limbs. The whole audience appeared to be struck with superstitious dread.

Shasha suddenly drew himself straight up, and chanted in a sing-song voice, rattling his charms at every period:

'I am the ruler of the baboons and the master of the owls. I talk to the wild cat in the bush. I call Tikoloshe (a water spirit) out of the river in the night-time and ask him questions. I make sickness do my bidding on men and cattle. I drive it away when I like. I can bring blight to the crops, and stop the milk of cows. I can, by my magic medicines, find out the wicked ones who do these things. I alone can look upon Icanti (a fabulous serpent) and not die. I know the mountain where Impandulu (the Lightning Bird) builds its nest. I can make men invulnerable in battle with my medicines, and I can cause the enemies of my Chief to run like a bushbuck pursued by dogs.'

The speech ended, Shasha again bowed down, quivering and contorting, beat the ground with his hands and the soles of his feet, and then sprang aside into the darkness.

Sololo looked at Vooda as though he would say, 'What do you think of that: is he not a most terribly potent war-doctor?' All the other men looked extremely terrified.

Dead silence reigned for a few moments, and then Vooda spoke:

'O Chief, the magic of your war-doctor is indeed dreadful to behold, but, believe me, the magic of U-Sessellodes and Indabeni is stronger, and I can prove it.'

This caused a murmur of incredulity and indignation. The magic paraphernalia of the war-doctor rattled ominously in the gloom.

'U-Sessellodes,' continued Vooda, 'has found the Lightning Bird sitting upon its nest, and plucked its feathers; he has discovered how to make water burn, and he has robbed the cave of Icanti of its eggs, which he can strew over the land to hatch in the sun, and produce snakes that will kill all who see them. These secrets he has taught to Indabeni, and

Indabeni has taught them to me so that I might warn you, and having warned, prove the truth of my words.'

At this a loud 'ho, ho,' accompanied by a rattling noise, was heard from the war-doctor. Sololo laughed sarcastically. Several of the audience did the same. Then Sololo said:

'Are we children, to believe these things?'

'My Chief,' said Vooda, impressively, 'you are not a child, neither is Indabeni; as you know – nor is the potent war-doctor, nor are any of these great men (madoda makulu) that I see around me. For that matter, neither am I a child. I have said that I can prove my words, and I say so again.'

'Prove them, then,' said Sololo.

'Three things will I do to show the magic of U-Sessellodes, which he has traught to Indabeni – I will show you a feather of the Lightning Bird, I will make water burn like dry wood, and I will produce some of the eggs of Icanti and make them, when touched with fire, hatch into young serpents before your eyes.'

There was not a breath of wind. Vooda seized a small firebrand, and stepped a few yards away from the fire. He held the firebrand in his left hand, and put his right into one of the pockets of his tunic. This pocket contained a quantity of loose lycopodium powder. He filled his hand with this, waved it over his head several times, and then projected the handful of powder high into the air with a sweeping throw. Then he slowly lifted the firebrand, and as the cloud of powder descended, it ignited with a silent, blinding flash. A loud 'Mawo' from the spectators greeted the success of the experiment.

The war-doctor gave a harsh laugh and shouted that there was no magic in the business, and that the Lightning Bird's plumage was still intact so far as Vooda was concerned; he, the war-doctor, knew how the thing was done, and would presently explain. Sololo and the others murmured amongst themselves.

'Now,' said Vooda, 'I will make water burn with a bright flame like dry wood.'

'You have, no doubt, brought the water with you in a bottle,' said Shasha, the war-doctor, with a sneer in his voice. He was evidently thinking of paraffin.

'No, O most potent controller of baboons,' said Vooda, 'I will, on the contrary, ask you to get me some water for the purpose, in a vessel of your own choice.'

Shasha went to one of the huts and returned with a small earthen pot full of water, which he placed on the ground near the fire.

Vooda took the lump of potassium which he had cut into the form of a large conical bullet, from his pocket, and advanced to where the chief was sitting. He beckoned to the war-doctor to approach, and then said:

'This, O chief, and O Discourser-with-the-wild-cat, is a new and wonderful kind of lead which U-Sessellodes has dug out of a hole in the ground far deeper than any other hole that was ever made. You will observe that my knife is sharp, and therefore I cut the lead easily. You may see how the metal shines when newly cut. Now, if a bullet such as this be shot into a river, the water blazes up and consumes the land.'

'Give it to me that I may examine it,' said Shasha.

Vooda handed a small paring of the potassium to the war-doctor, saying: 'Be very careful, O You-whom-the-owls-obey-in-the-dark, because it is dangerous stuff.'

Shasha did exactly what Vooda anticipated – he looked carefully at the shred of metal, and lifted it to his mouth, meaning to test it with his teeth. When, however, the potassium touched the saliva, it blazed up, and the unhappy war-doctor spat it out with a fearful yell. His lips and tongue were severely burnt. Sololo and the men, who had seen the flame issuing from Shasha's mouth, were terror-stricken.

Vooda now cut the lump of potassium into several pieces, and these he dropped into the pot of water. The lumps began to flame brilliantly, dancing on the top of the water and gyrating across and around. All the spectators were horribly frightened, and shrank back, their eye-balls starting, and their lips wide apart.

'Now,' said Vooda, who felt that he had practically won the game, 'I will produce the eggs of Icanti, the terrible serpent, and make them hatch out live snakes. Were I to do this without having other greater magic ready wherewith to overcome them, the snakes would kill us all. The only magic stronger than that of Icanti is the magic of the Lightning Bird, so I will drop a feather plucked by U-Sessellodes from the tail of Impandulu upon the snakes as they come out of the eggs, and that will cause them to turn into dust.'

Vooda took five large Pharaoh's serpent-eggs out of his pocket and placed them on a flat stone about a yard from the fire. He then asked Shasha to approach, warning him to be very careful, as the serpents might be dangerous. After the experience with the potassium, such a warning to Shasha was quite a work of supererogation. He came forward with hesitating steps, and stood behind Vooda, watching.

Vooda had a small quantity of lycopodium powder in his left hand. With his right he seized a flaming firebrand, and with this he touched each of the eggs in turn. At once five horrible-looking snakes began uncoiling, blue flame surrounding the spot at which each emerged from its egg. Vooda then shouted loudly, calling on the name of Impandulu, and making mystic passes over the coiling horror with his firebrand. Stretching forth his left hand, he liberated a small cloud of lycopodium powder, which ignited with a brilliant flash. At this, all the spectators leaped to their feet, wildly yelling, and, with the exception of Sololo, who stood still – although the picture of terror – disappeared into the surrounding darkness. For some seconds after the sound of the last footfall had died away, the rattle of Shasha's charms, as he fled, could be heard.

Vooda approached Sololo:

'My Chief, what word am I to carry to Indabeni?'

'Tell Indabeni that the wrong-doer will be given up to the Magistrate to choke with a rope. Yet you need not tell him, because the man will be in the Magistrate's hand before your voice can reach Indabeni's ear.'

And so he was.

Thus was a war averted, and yet neither Vooda nor Teddy Morton ever received any reward for their distinguished services.

Sir Percy FitzPatrick

The Pool

from *The Outspan: Tales of South Africa* (1897)

Everyone remembers the rush to De Kaap some years ago. How everyone said that everyone else would make fortunes in half no time, and the country would be saved! Well, my brother Jim and I thought we would like to make fortunes too; so we packed our boxes, donned flannel shirts, felt hats and moleskin trousers, with a revolver each carelessly slung at our sides, and started. We intended to dig for about a year or so, and then sell out and live on the interest of our money – £30 000 each would do. It was all cut and dried. I often almost wished it wasn't so certain, as now one hadn't a chance of coming back suddenly and *surprising* the loved ones at home with the news of a grand fortune.

Full of excitement (certainties notwithstanding) we went down to Kent's Forwarding Store, and met there Mr Harding, whose waggons were loaded for the gold-fields. This was our chance, and we took it.

On November 10, 1883, we crossed Little Sunday's River and outspanned at the foot of Knight's Cutting. The day was close and sultry, and Harding thought it best to lie by until the cool of the evening before attempting the hill. It wasn't much of a cool evening we got after all; except that we had not the scorching rays of the sun beating down upon us, it was no cooler at 10 p.m. than at midday. We were outspanned above the cutting, and the oppressive heat of the day and the sultriness of the evening seemed to have told on our party, and we were all squatted about on the long soft grass, smoking or thinking. Besides my brother and myself there were two young Scotchmen (just out from home) and a little Frenchman. He was a general favourite on account of his inexhaustible good-nature and unflagging high spirits.

We were, as I have said, stretched out on the grass smoking in silence, watching the puffs and rings of smoke melt quietly away, so still was the air. How long we had lain thus I don't know, but I was the first to break the silence by exclaiming:

'What a grand night for a bathe!'

There was no reply to this for some seconds, and then Jim gave an apathetic grunt in courteous recognition of the fact that I had spoken. I subsided again, and there was another long silence – evidently no one wanted to talk; but I had become restless and fidgety under the heat and stillness, and presently I returned to the charge.

'Who's for a bathe?' I asked.

Someone grunted out something about 'no place'.

'Oh yes, there is,' said I, glad of even so much encouragement; and then, turning to Harding, I said:

'I hear the water in the kloof. There is a place, isn't there?'

'Yes,' he answered slowly, 'there is *one* place, but you wouldn't care to dip there ... It's the Murderer's Pool.'

'The what?' we asked in a breath.

'The Murderer's Pool,' he repeated with such slow seriousness that we at once became interested – the name sent an odd tingle through one. I was already all attention, and during the pause that followed the others closed around and settled themselves to hear the yarn. When he had tantalised us enough with his provoking slowness, Harding began:

'About this time last year – By-the-by, what is the date?' he asked, breaking off.

'The tenth!' exclaimed two or three together.

'By Jove! it's the very day. Yes, that's queer. This very day last year I was outspanned on this spot, as we are now. I had a lady and gentleman with me as passengers that trip. They were pleasant, accommodating people, and gave us no trouble at all; they used to spend all their time botanizing and sketching. On this afternoon Mrs Allan went down to the ravine below to sketch some peculiar bit of rock scenery. I think all ladies sketch when they travel, some more and some less. But Mrs Allan could sketch and paint really well, and often went off alone short distances while her husband stayed to chat with me. She had been gone about twenty minutes when we were startled by a most awful piercing shriek – another, another, and another – and then all was still again. Before the first had died away Allan and I were running at full speed towards where we judged the shrieks to have come from. Fortunately we were right. Down there, a bit to the right, we came upon a fair-sized pool, on the surface of which Mrs Allan was still floating. In a few seconds we had her out and were trying restoratives; and on detecting signs of returning life we carried her up to the waggons. When she became conscious she started up with oh! such a look of horror and fright. I'll never forget it! Seeing her husband, however, and holding his hand, she became calm again, and told us all about it.

'It seems she had been sitting by the side of the stream sketching the pool and the great perpendicular cliff rising out of it. The sunlight was playing on the water, silvering every ripple, and bringing out every detail of the rocks and foliage above. Feathery mosses festooned from cliff to cliff; maidenhair ferns clustered in every nook and crevice; the drops on every leaf and tendril glistened in the setting sun like a thousand diamonds. That's what she told us.

'She sat a few minutes before beginning, watching the varying shades and hues, when, glancing idly into the water, she saw deep, deep down, a sight that horrified her.

'On the rocks at the bottom of the pool lay the body of a gigantic Kaffir, his throat cut from ear to ear, and the white teeth gleaming and grinning at her.

'Instinctively she screamed and ran, and in trying to pass along the narrow ledge she slipped and fell into the water. Had her clothes not buoyed her up she would have been drowned, as when the cold water closed round her it seemed like the clasp of death, and she lost consciousness.'

'Well, what about the nigger?' I asked, for Harding had stopped with the air of one whose tale was told.

'Oh, he was dead right enough – throat cut and assegai through the heart. A fight, I expect.'

'What did you do?' I asked.

'Raked him out and planted him up here somewhere. Let's see – yes that's the place' – indicating the pile of stones my brother was sitting on.

Jim got up hurriedly; perhaps, as he said, he wanted to look at the place. Yet there was a general laugh at him.

'Did you think he had you, Jim?' I asked innocently.

'Don't you gas, old chap! How about the bathe you were so bent on?'

Merciful heavens! The words fell like a bucket of ice-water on me. I made a ghastly attempt at a laugh, but it was a failure – an utter failure – and of course brought all the others down on me at once.

'The nigger seems to have taken all the bathe out of you, old man,' said one.

'Not at all!' I answered loftily. 'It would take more than that to frighten *me*.'

Now, why on earth didn't I hold my tongue and let the remark pass? I must needs make an ass of myself by bravado, and now I was in for it. There was a perfect chorus of, 'Go it, old man!' 'Now, isn't that *real* pluck?' 'Six to four on the nigger!' 'I pet fife pound you not swim agross and dife two times.' This last came from the little French demon, and, being applauded by the company, I took up the bet. The fact is I was nettled by the chaff, and in the heat of the moment did what I regretted a minute later.

As I rose to get my towel I said with cutting sarcasm:

'I don't care about the bet, but I'll just show you that *everyone* isn't afraid of his own shadow; though,' I added forgetfully, 'it's rather an unreasonable time to bathe.'

Here Frenchy struck a stage attitude, and said innocently:

'Ah! vat a night foor ze bade!'

The shout of laughter that greeted this sally was more than enough to decide me, and I went off in search of a towel.

Harding, I could see, did not like the idea, and tried to persuade me to give it up; but that was out of the question.

'Mind,' said he, 'I'm no believer in ghosts; yet,' he added, with rather a forced laugh, 'this is the anniversary, and you know it's uncanny.'

I quite agreed with him, but dared not say so, and I pretended to laugh it off. I was ready in a few moments, and then a rather happy idea, as I thought, struck me, and I called out:

'Who's coming to see that I win my bet?'

'Oh, we know we can trust you, old chap!' said Jim with exaggerated politeness. 'It'd be a pity, you know, to outnumber the ghost.'

'Very well; it's all the same to me. Good-bye! Two dives and a swim across – is that it?'

'Yes, and look out for the nigger!'

'Mind you fish him up!'

'Watch his teeth, Jack!'

'Feel for his throat, you know!'

This latter exclamation came from Jim; it was yelled out as I disappeared down the slope. Jim had not forgotten the incident of the grave, evidently.

I had a half-moon to go by, and a ghostly sort of light it shed. Everything seemed more shadowy and fantastic than usual. Besides this, I had not gone a hundred yards from the waggons before every sound was stilled; not the faintest whisper stirred the air. The crunching of my heavy boots on the gravel was echoed across the creek, and every step grated on my nerves and went like a sword-stab through me.

However, I walked along briskly until the descent became more steep and I was obliged to go more carefully. Down I went, step by step, lower and lower, till I felt the light grow dimmer and dimmer, and then quite suddenly I stepped into gloom and darkness.

This startled me. The suddenness of the change made me shiver a bit and fancy it was cold; but it couldn't have been that, for a moment later the chill had gone and the air was close and sultry. It must have been something else. Still I went down, down, down, along the winding path, and the further I went the more intense seemed the stillness and the deeper the gloom.

Once I stood still to listen; there was not a stir or sound save the trickling of the water below. My heart began to beat rather fast, and my breath seemed heavy. What was it? Surely, I thought, it is not fright? I tried to whistle now as I strode along, but the death-like silence mocked me and choked the breath in my throat.

At last I reached the stream. The path ran along the side of the water among the rocks and ferns. I looked for the pool, but could not see a sign of it. Still I followed the path until it wound along a very narrow ledge of rock.

I was so engrossed picking my steps along there that, when I had got round and saw the pool lying black and silent at my feet, I fairly staggered back with the shock. There was no mistaking the place. The pool was surrounded by high rocks; on the opposite side they ran up quite perpendicularly to a good height. Nowhere, except the ledge at my feet, would a man have been able to get out of the water alone. The black surface of the water was as smooth as glass; not a ripple or bubble or straw broke its awful monotony.

It fascinated me; but it was a ghostly spot. I don't know how long I stood there watching it. It seemed hours. A sickening feeling had crept over me, and I *knew I was afraid*.

I looked all round, but there was nothing to break the horrid spell. Behind me there was a face of rock twenty feet high with ferns and creepers falling from every crevice. But it looked black, too. I turned silently again towards the water, almost hoping to see something there; but there was still the same unbroken surface, the same oppressive deadly silence as before. What was the use of delaying? It had to be done; so I might as well face it at once. I own I was frightened. I would have lost the bet with pleasure, but to stand the laughter, chaff, and jeers of the others! No! that I could never do. My mind was made up to it, so I threw off my clothes quickly and came up to the water's edge. I walked out on the one low ledge and looked down. I was trembling then, I know.

I tried to think it was cold, but I *knew* it was not that. I stooped low down to search the very depths of the pool, but I could see nothing; all was uniformly dark. And yet – good God! what was that? Right down at the bottom lay a long black object. With starting eyes I looked again. It was only a rock. I drew back a pace and sat down. The perspiration was in beads on my forehead. I shook in every limb; sick and faint, my breath went and came in the merest whispers. So I sat for a minute or two with my head resting on my hands, and then the thought struck me, 'What if the others are watching me above?'

I jumped up to make a running plunge of it, but, somehow, the run slackened into a walk, and the walk ended in a pause near the ledge, and there I stood to have another look into the dark, still pool.

Suddenly there was a rustling behind me. I jumped round, tingling, quivering all over, and a pebble rolled at my feet from the rocks above. I called out in a shaky voice, 'Now then, you chaps! none of that: I can see you.' But really I could see nothing, and the echo of my voice had such a weird, awful sound that I began to lose my head altogether. There was no use now pretending that I was not frightened, for I was. My nerves were completely unstrung, my head was splitting, and my legs could hardly bear me. I preferred to face any ridicule rather than endure this for another minute, and I commenced dressing. Then I pictured to myself Jim's grinning face, Frenchy's pantomime of the whole affair, Harding's quiet smile, and the chaff and laughter of them all, and I paused. A sudden rush, a plunge and souse, and I was in. Breathless and gasping I struck out, only twenty yards across; madly I swam. The cold water made my flesh creep. On and on, faster and faster; would I never reach it? At last I touched the rocks and turned to come back. Then all their chaff recurred to me. Every stroke seemed to hiss the words at me, 'Feel for his throat! Feel for his throat!' I fancied the dead nigger was on me, and every moment expected to feel his hand on my shoulder. On I sped, faster and faster, mad with the dread of being entangled by the legs and pulled down – I swam for life. When I scrambled on the ledge I felt I was *saved*! Then all at once I began to feel my body tingling with a most exhilarating sense of relief after an absurd fright, a sense of power restored, of self-respect and triumph and an insane desire to laugh. I did laugh, but the sepulchral echoes of my hilarious cackle rather chilled me, and I began to dress.

Then for the first time occurred to me the conditions of the bet: 'Two dives and a swim across.' Now, this would have been quite natural in ordinary pools – a plunge, a scramble on the opposite bank, another plunge, and back. But here, with the precipitous face of rock opposite, it meant *two* swims across and *two dives* from the same spot. But I did not mind; in fact, I was enjoying it now, and I thought with a glow of pride how I would rub it into Jim about fishing up his darned old nigger with the cut throat.

I walked to the edge smiling.

'Yes, my boy,' I murmured, 'I'll fish you up if you're there, or a fistful

of gravel for Jim and Frenchy – little devil! It'll be change for his fiver;'
and I chuckled at my joke.

I drew a long breath and dropped quietly into the water, head first;
down, down, down – gently, softly. A couple of easy strokes and I glided
along the bottom. Then something touched me. God in heaven! how it
all burst on me at once! I felt four rigid fingers laid on my shoulder and
drawn down my chest, the finger-nails scratching me. Instantly I made a
grasp with both hands; my left fastened on the neck of a human body,
and my right, just above, closed, and the *fingers met* through the ragged
flesh of a gashed throat.

I tried to scream – the water choked me. I let go and swam on, and then
up. I shot out of the water waist high, gasping and glaring wildly, and
then soused under again. As I again came up I dashed the water from my
eyes. I saw the surface of the pool break, and a head rose slowly. Kind
Heaven! *there were two*! Slowly the two bodies rose across the black
margin where the shadow ceased, full in the moonlit portion of the pool
– cold, clear and horrible in their ghastly nakedness. And as they rose
the murderous wounds appeared. The dank hair hung over their
foreheads; the glazed and sightless eyeballs were fixed with the vacant
stare of death on *me*. One bore a terrible gash from temple to eye, and
lower down the bluish red slit of an assegai on the left breast.

On the other was one wound only; but how awful! The throat was cut
from ear to ear; the bluish lips of the great gash hung wide apart where
my hand had torn them. I could even see the severed windpipe. The head
was thrown slightly back, but the eyes glared down at me with an awful
stony glare, while through the parted lips the teeth gleamed and grinned
cold and bright as they caught the light of the moon. One glance – half
an instant – showed me all this, and then, as the figures rose waist-high,
I saw one arm rigid at right angles to the body from the elbow, and the
stiff hand that had clawed me. For one instant they poised, balancing;
then bowing slowly over, they came down on the top of me.

Then indeed my brain seemed to go. I struggled under them. I fought
and shrieked; but I suppose the bubbles came up in silence. The dead stiff
hand was laid on my head and pressed me down – down, down! Then the
hand of death slipped, and I was free. Once I kicked them as I struggled to
the surface, and gasping, frantic, mad, made for the bank. On, on, on! O
God! would I never reach it? One more effort, a wrench, and I was out.
Never a pause now. One bound, and I had passed the ledge; then up and
up, past the cliffs, over the rocks, cut and bleeding, on I dashed as fast as
mortal man ever raced. Up, up the stony path, till, with torn feet and
shaking in every limb, I reached the waggon. There was an exclamation,
a pause, and then a perfect yell of laughter. The laugh saved me; the

heartless cruelty of it did what nothing else could have done – it roused my temper; but for that, I believe I should have gone mad.

Harding alone came forward anxiously towards me.

'What's the matter?' he asked. 'For God's sake, what is it?'

The laugh had sobered me, and I answered quietly that it was nothing much – just a thing I would like him to see down at the pool. There were a score of questions in anxious and half-apologetic tones, for they soon realised that something was wrong; but I answered nothing, and so they followed me in silence, and there, on the oily, unbroken surface of the silent pool, floated in grim relief the two bodies. We pulled them out and found the corpses lashed together. At the end of the rope was an empty loop, the stone out of which I must in my stuggle have dislodged. Close to the nigger we laid them, with another pile of stones to mark the spot; but who they were and where they came from none of us ever knew for certain.

The week before this two lucky diggers had passed through Newcastle from the fields, going home. Four years have now passed, letters have come, friends have inquired, but there is no news of them, and I think, poor chaps! they must have 'gone home' by another route.

Ernest Glanville

Uncle Abe's Big Shoot

from *Tales from the Veld ...* (1897)

I had ridden out one day to the outpost, where a troop of young cattle were running, when the horse rode into a covey of red-wing partridges, a brace of which I accounted for by a right and left. Picking up the birds, and feeling rather proud of the shot, I continued on to Uncle Pike's to crow over the matter.

The old man was seated outside the door 'braiding' a thong of forslag or whip-lash.

'Hitch the reins over the pole. Ef the shed was ready I'd ask yer to stable the hoss, but there's a powerful heap o' work yet to finish it off nice an' shipshape – me being one o' those who like to see a job well done. None o' yer rough and ready sheds for me, with a hole in the roof after the fust rain. A plump brace o' birds – you got 'em up by the Round Kopje.'

'Yes, Uncle; a right and left from the saddle. Good shooting,eh!'

'Fair to middling, sonny – fair to middling – but with a handful o' shot an' a light gun what can yer expect but to hit. Now, ef you'd bagged 'em with one ball outer an ole muzzle-loader, why I'd up an' admit it was praisable.'

'Why Uncle, where's the man who would knock over two birds with a ball? It couldn't be done.'

'Is that so? Well, now yer s'prise me.'

'You're not going to tell my you have seen that done!'

'Something better. That's small potatoes.'

He rose up, went indoors, and returned with an ancient single muzzle-loader, the stock bound round with snake skin. 'Jes yer handle that wepin.'

I handled it, and returned it without a word. It was ill-balanced, and came up awkwardly to the shoulder.

'That wepin saved my life.'

'In the war?'

'In the big drought. You remember the time. The country was that dry, you could hear the grass crackle like tinder when the wind moved, an' every breath stirred up columes of sand which went cavorting over the veld round and round, their tops bending over to each other an' the bottoms stirring up everything movable, and the whole length of the funells dotted about with snakes, an' lizards, an' bits of wood. Why, I see one o' em whip up a dead sheep, an' shed the wool off o' the carcase as it went twisting round an' round.'

'And the gun?'

'The gun was on the wall over my bed. Don't you mind the gun. Well, it was that dry the pumpkins withered up where they lay on the hard ground – an' one day there was nought in the larder, not so much as a smell. There was no breakfast for ole Abe Pike, nor dinner nor yet tea, an' the next morning 'twas the same story o' emptiness. I took down the old gun from the wall an' cleaned her up. There was one full charge o' powder in the horn, an' one bullet in the bag. All that morning I considered whether 'twould be wiser to divide that charge inter three, or to pour the whole lot of it in 't once. When dinner-time came an' there was no dinner, I solumnly poured the whole bang of it inter the big barrel, an' listened to the music of the black grains as they rattled on their way down to their last dooty. I cut a good thick wad from a buck-hide and rammed it down, "Plunk, plenk, plank plonk, ploonk," until the rod jumped clean out o' the muzzle. Then I polished up that lone bullet, wrapped him round in a piece o' oil rag, an' sent him down gently. "Squish, squish, squash, squoosh." I put the cap on the nipple, an' sent him home with the pressure o' the hammer. Then I took a look over the country to 'cide on a plan o' campaign. What I wanted was a big ram with meat on him ter last for a month, if 'twas made inter biltong. There was one down by the hoek, but it warnt full grown. He was nearest, but there was one I'd seen over yonder off by the river, beyond the kloof, an' I reckoned 'twas worthwhile going a couple o' mile extra to get him.'

'You were sure of him?'

'He was as good as dead when I shouldered the gun an' stepped off out on that wilderness o' burnt land. The wind came like a breath from a furnance, an' the hair on my head split an' curled up under the heat. Whenever I came across a rock with a breadth of shade I sot there to cool off, panting like a fowl, an' also to cool off the gun for fear 'twould explode. By reason o' this resting the dark came down when I reached the ridge above the river, an' I jest camped where it found me, after digging up some *insange* root to chew. The fast had been with me for two days, an' the gnawing pain inside was terrible, so that I kept awake looking up at the stars an' listening to the plovers.'

'It must have been lonesome!'

' 'Twas not the lonesomeness so much as the emptiness that troubled me. Before the morning came, lighting up the valley, I was going down to the river on the last hunt. 'Twas do or die that trip – an' it seemed to me I could see the gleam o' my bones away down there through the mist that hung over the sick river. I made straight for the river, knowing there was a comfort an' fellowship in the water which would draw game there, an' the big black ram, too, 'fore he marched off inter the thick o' the kloof for his sleep. By-and-by, as I went down among the rocks an' trees, I pitched head first – ker smash – in a sudden fit o' dizziness, but the shock did me good. It rattled up my brain – an' instead o' jest plunging ahead I went slow – slow an' soft as a cat on the trail – pushing aside a branch here, shoving away a twig there, an' glaring around with hungry eyes. I spotted him!'

'The ram?'

'Aye, the ram. The very buck I'd had in my mind when I loaded the old gun. He stood away off the other side o' the river, moving his ears, but still as a rock, and black as the bowl of this pipe, except where the white showed along his side. He seemed to be looking straight at me – an' I sank by inches to the ground with my legs all o' a shake. Then, on my falling, he stepped down to the water, and stood there admiring hisself – his sharp horns an' fine legs – an' on my belly, all empty as 'twas, I crawled, an' crawled, an' crawled. There was a bush this side the river, an' I got it in line. At last I reached it, the sweat pouring off me, an' slowly I rose up. The water was dripping from his muzzle as he threw his head up, an' he turned to spring back, when, half-kneeling, I fired, an' the next moment the old gun kicked me flat as a pancake.'

'And you missed him?'

'Never! I got him. I said I would, an' I did. I got him an' a 9 pound barbel.'

'Uncle Abe!'

'I say a 9 pound barbel, tho' he might a been 8½ pound, an' a brace of pheasants.'

'Uncle Abe!'

'I zed so – an' a hare an', an',' he went on quickly, 'a porkipine.'

'Uncle Abe!'

'Well – what are you Abeing me for?'

'You got all those with one shot. Never!'

'I was there – you weren't. 'Tis easy accounted for. When I pulled the trigger the fish leapt from the water in the line, and the bullet passed through him inter the buck. I tole you the gun kicked. Well, it flew out o' my hands, an' hit the hare square on the nose. To recover myself, I threw up my hands, an' caught hold o' the two pheasants jest startled outer the bush.'

'And the porcupine?'

'I sot down on the porkipine, an' if you'd like to 'xamine my pants you'll find where his quills went in. I was mighty sore, an' I could ha' spared him well from the bag. But 'twas a wonderful good shot. You're not going?'

'Yes, I am. I'm afraid to stay with you.'

'Well, so long! I cut this yere forslag from the skin o' that same buck.'

'Let me see- it's nine years to the big drought.'

'That's it.'

'That skin has kept well.'

'Oh, yes; 'twas a mighty tough skin.'

'Not so tough as your yarn, Uncle. So long!'

Olive Schreiner

Eighteen-Ninety-Nine

from *Stories, Dreams and Allegories* (1923, written circa 1906)

'Thou fool, that which thou sowest is not quickened unless it die.'

I

It was a warm night: the stars shone down through the thick soft air of the Northern Transvaal into the dark earth, where a little daub-and-wattle house of two rooms lay among the long, grassy slopes.

A light shone through the small window of the house, though it was past midnight. Presently the upper half of the door opened and then the lower, and the tall figure of a woman stepped out into the darkness. She closed the door behind her and walked towards the back of the house where a large round hut stood; beside it lay a pile of stumps and branches quite visible when once the eyes grew accustomed to the darkness. The woman stooped and broke off twigs till she had her apron full, and then returned slowly, and went into the house.

The room to which she returned was a small, bare room, with brown earthen walls and a mud floor; a naked deal table stood in the centre, and a few dark wooden chairs, home-made, with seats of undressed leather, stood round the walls. In the corner opposite the door was an open fire-place, and on the earthen hearth stood an iron three-foot, on which stood a large black kettle, under which coals were smouldering, though the night was hot and close. Against the wall on the left side of the room hung a gun-rack with three guns upon it, and below it a large hunting-watch hung from two nails by its silver chain.

In the corner by the fireplace was a little table with a coffee-pot upon it and a dish containing cups and saucers covered with water, and above it were a few shelves with crockery and a large Bible; but the dim light of the tallow candle which burnt on the table, with its wick of twisted rag, hardly made the corners visible. Beside the table sat a young woman, her head resting on her folded arms, the light of the tallow candle falling full on her head of pale flaxen hair, a little tumbled, and drawn behind into a large knot. The arms crossed on the table, from which the cotton sleeves had fallen back, were the full, rounded arms of one very young.

The older woman, who had just entered, walked to the fireplace, and kneeling down before it took from her apron the twigs and sticks she had gathered and heaped them under the kettle till a blaze sprang up which illumined the whole room. Then she rose up and sat down on a chair before the fire, but facing the table, with her hands crossed on her brown apron.

She was a woman of fifty, spare and broad-shouldered, with black hair, already slightly streaked with grey; from below high, arched eyebrows, and a high forehead, full dark eyes looked keenly, and a sharply cut aquiline nose gave strength to the face; but the mouth below was somewhat sensitive, and not over-full. She crossed and recrossed her knotted hands on her brown apron.

The woman at the table moaned and moved her head from side to side.

'What time is it?' she asked.

The older woman crossed the room to where the hunting-watch hung on the wall.

It showed a quarter-past one, she said, and went back to her seat before the fire, and sat watching the figure beside the table, the firelight bathing her strong upright form and sharp aquiline profile.

Nearly fifty years before her parents had left the Cape Colony, and had set out on the long trek northward, and she, a young child, had been brought with them. She had no remembrance of the colonial home. Her first dim memories were of travelling in an ox-wagon; of dark nights when a fire was lighted in the open air, and people sat round it on the ground, and some faces seemed to stand out more than others in her memory which she thought must be those of her father and mother and of an old grandmother; she could remember lying awake in the back of the wagon while it was moving on, and the stars were shining down on her; and she had a vague memory of great wide plains with buck on them, which she thought must have been in the Free State. But the first thing which sprang out sharp and clear from the past was a day when she and another child, a little boy cousin of her own age, were playing among the bushes on the bank of a stream; she remembered how suddenly, as they looked through the bushes, they saw black men leap out, and mount the ox-wagon outspanned under the trees; she remembered how they shouted and dragged people along, and stabbed them; she remembered how the blood gushed, and how they, the two young children among the bushes, lay flat on their stomachs and did not move or breathe, with that strange self-preserving instinct found in the young of animals or men who grow up in the open.

She remembered how black smoke came out at the back of the wagon and then red tongues of flame through the top; and even that some of the branches of the tree under which the wagon stood caught fire. She remembered later, when the black men had gone, and it was dark, that they were very hungry, and crept out to where the wagon had stood, and that they looked about on the ground for any scraps of food they might pick up, and that when they could not find any they cried. She remembered nothing clearly after that till some men with large beards and large hats rode up on horseback: it might have been next day or the day after. She remembered how they jumped off their horses and took them up in their arms, and how they cried; but that they, the children, did not cry, they only asked for food. She remembered how one man took a bit of thick, cold roaster-cake out of his pocket, and gave it to her, and how nice it tasted. And she remembered that the men took them up before them on their horses, and that one man tied her close to him with a large red handkerchief.

In the years that came she learnt to know that that which she remembered so clearly was the great and terrible day when, at Weenen, and in the country round, hundreds of women and children and youths and old men fell before the Zulus, and the assegais of Dingaan's braves drank blood.

She learnt that on that day all of her house and name, from the grandmother to the baby in arms, fell, and that she only and the boy cousin, who had hidden with her among the bushes, were left of all her kin in that northern world. She learnt, too, that the man who tied her to him with the red handkerchief took them back to his wagon, and that he and his wife adopted them, and brought them up among their own children.

She remembered, though less clearly than the day of the fire, how a few years later they trekked away from Natal, and went through great mountain ranges, ranges in and near which lay those places the world was to know later as Laings Nek, and Amajuba, and Ingogo; Elandslaagte, Nicholson Nek, and Spion Kop. She remembered how at last after many wanderings they settled down near the Witwaters Rand where game was plentiful and wild beasts were dangerous, but there were no natives, and they were far from the English rule.

There the two children grew up among the children of those who had adopted them, and were kindly treated by them as though they were their own; it yet was but natural that these two of the same name and blood should grow up with a peculiar tenderness for each other. And so it came to pass that when they were both eighteen years old they asked consent of the old people, who gave it gladly, that they should marry. For a time the young couple lived on in the house with the old, but after three years they gathered together all their few goods and in their wagon, with their guns and ammunition and a few sheep and cattle, they moved away northwards to found their own home.

For a time they travelled here and travelled there, but at last they settled on a spot where game was plentiful and the soil good, and there among the low undulating slopes, near the bank of a dry sloot, the young man built at last, with his own hands, a little house of two rooms.

On the long slope across the sloot before the house, he ploughed a piece of land and enclosed it, and he built kraals for his stock and so struck root in the land and wandered no more. Those were brave, glad, free days to the young couple. They lived largely on the game which the gun brought down, antelope and wildebeest that wandered even past the doors at night; and now and again a lion was killed: one no farther than the door of the round hut behind the house where the meat and the milk was stored, and two were killed at the kraals. Sometimes, too, traders came with their wagons and in exchange for skins and fine horns sold sugar and coffee and print and tan-cord, and such things as the little household had need of. The lands yielded richly to them, in maize, and pumpkins, and sweet-cane, and melons; and they had nothing to wish for. Then in time three little sons were born to them, who grew as strong and vigorous in the free life of the open veld as the young lions in the long grass and scrub near the river four miles away. Those were joyous, free years for the man and woman, in which disease, and carking care, and anxiety played no part.

Then came a day when their eldest son was ten years old, and the father went out a-hunting with his Kaffir servants: in the evening they brought him home with a wound eight inches long in his side where a lioness had torn him; they brought back her skin also, as he had shot her at last in the hand-to-throat struggle. He lingered for three days and then died. His wife buried him on the low slope to the left of the house; she and her Kaffir servants alone made the grave and put him in it, for there were no white men near. Then she and her sons lived on there; a new root driven deep into the soil and binding them to it through the grave on the hill-side. She hung her husband's large hunting-watch up on the wall, and put three of his guns over it on the rack, and the gun he had in his hand when he met his death she took down and polished up every day; but one gun she always kept loaded at the head of her bed in the inner room. She counted the stock every night and saw that the Kaffirs ploughed the lands, and she saw to the planting and watering of them herself.

Often as the years passed men of the countryside, and even from far off, heard of the young handsome widow who lived alone with her children and saw to her own stock and lands; and they came a-courting. But many of them were afraid to say anything when once they had come, and those who had spoken to her, when once she had answered them, never came again. About this time too the countryside began to fill in; and people came and settled as near as eight and ten miles away; and as people increased the game began to vanish, and with the game the lions, so that the one her husband killed was almost the last ever seen there. But there was still game enough for food, and when her eldest son was twelve years old, and she gave him his father's smallest gun to go out hunting with, he returned home almost every day with meat enough for the household tied behind his saddle. And as time passed she came also to be known through the countryside as a 'wise woman'. People came to her to ask advice about their illnesses, or to ask her to dress old wounds that would not heal; and when they questioned her whether she thought the rains would be early, or the game plentiful that year, she was nearly always right. So they called her a 'wise woman' because neither she nor they knew any word in that up-country speech of theirs for the thing called 'genius'. So all things went well till the eldest son was eighteen, and the dark beard was beginning to sprout on his face, and his mother began to think that soon there might be a daughter in the house; for on Saturday evenings, when his work was done, he put on his best clothes and rode off to the next farm eight miles away, where was a young daughter. His mother always saw that he had a freshly ironed shirt waiting for him on his bed, when he came home from the kraals on Saturday nights, and she made plans as to how they would build on two rooms for the new daughter. At this time he was training young horses to have them ready to sell when the traders came round: he was a fine rider and it was always his work. One afternoon he mounted a young horse before the door and it bucked and threw him. He had often fallen before, but this time his neck was broken. He lay dead with his head two feet from his mother's doorstep. They took up his tall, strong body and the next day the neighbours came from the next farm and they buried him beside his father, on the hill-side, and another root was struck into the soil. Then the three who were left in the little farm-house lived and worked on as before, for a year and more.

Then a small native war broke out and the young burghers of the district were called out to help. The second son was very young, but he was the best shot in the district, so he went away with the others. Three months after the men came back, but among the few who did not return was her son. On a hot sunny afternoon, walking through a mealie field which they thought was deserted and where the dried yellow stalks stood thick, an assegai thrown from an unseen hand found him, and he fell there. His comrades took him and buried him under a large thorn tree, and scraped the earth smooth over him, that his grave might not be found by others. So he was not laid on the rise to the left of the house with his kindred, but his mother's heart went often to that thorn tree in the far north.

And now again there were only two in the little mud-house; as there had been years before when the young man and wife first settled there. She and her young lad were always together night and day, and did all that they did together, as though they were mother and daughter. He was a fair lad, tall and gentle as his father had been before him, not huge and dark as his two elder brothers; but he seemed to ripen towards manhood early. When he was only sixteen the thick white down was already gathering heavy on his upper lip; his mother watched him narrowly, and had many thoughts in her heart. One evening as they sat twisting wicks for the candles together, she said to him, 'You will be eighteen on your next birthday, my son, that was your father's age when he married me.' He said, 'Yes,' and they spoke no more then. But later in the evening when they sat before the door she said to him: 'We are very lonely here. I often long to hear the feet of a little child about the house, and to see one with your father's blood in it play before the door as you and your brothers played. Have you ever thought that you are the last of your father's name and blood left here in the north; that if you died there would be none left?' He said he had thought of it. Then she told him she thought it would be well if he went away, to the part of the country where the people lived who had brought her up: several of the sons and daughters who had grown up with her had now grown-up children. He might go down and from among them seek out a young girl whom he liked and who liked him; and if he found her, bring her back as a wife. The lad thought very well of his mother's plan. And when three months were passed, and the ploughing season was over, he rode away one day, on the best black horse they had, his Kaffir boy riding behind him on another, and his mother stood at the gable watching them ride away. For three months she heard nothing of him, for trains were not in those days, and letters came rarely and by chance, and neither he nor she could read or write. One afternoon she stood at the gable end as she always stood when her work was done, looking out along the road that came over the rise, and she saw a large tent-wagon coming along it, and her son walking beside it. She walked to meet it. When she had greeted her son and climbed into the wagon she found there a girl of fifteen with pale flaxen hair and large blue eyes whom he had brought home as his wife. Her father had given her the wagon and oxen as her wedding portion. The older woman's heart wrapt itself about the girl as though she had been the daughter she had dreamed to bear of her own body, and had never borne.

The three lived joyfully at the little house as though they were one person. The young wife had been accustomed to live in a larger house, and down south, where they had things they had not here. She had been to school, and learned to read and write, and she could even talk a little English; but she longed for none of the things which she had had; the little brown house was home enough for her.

After a year a child came, but whether it were that the mother was too young, it only opened its eyes for an hour on the world and closed them again. The young mother wept bitterly, but her husband folded his arms about her, and the mother comforted both. 'You are young, my children, but we shall yet hear the sound of children's voices in the house,' she said; and after a little while the young mother was well again and things went on peacefully as before in the little home.

But in the land things were not going on peacefully. That was the time that the flag to escape from which the people had left their old homes in the Colony, and had again left Natal when it followed them there, and had chosen to face the spear of the savage, and the conflict with wild beasts, and death by hunger and thirst in the wilderness rather than live under, had by force and fraud unfurled itself over them again. For the moment a great sullen silence brooded over the land. The people, slow of thought, slow of speech, determined in action, and unforgetting, sat still and waited. It was like the silence that rests over the land before an up-country thunderstorm breaks.

Then words came, 'They have not even given us the free government they promised' – then acts – the people rose. Even in that remote countryside the men began to mount their horses, and with their guns ride away to help. In the little mud-house the young wife wept much when he said that he too was going. But when his mother helped him pack his saddle-bags she helped too; and on the day when the men from the next farm went, he rode away also with his gun by his side.

No direct news of the one they had sent away came to the waiting women at the farmhouse; then came fleet reports of the victories of Ingogo and Amajuba. Then came an afternoon after he had been gone two months. They had both been to the gable end to look out at the road, as they did continually amid their work, and they had just come in to drink their afternoon coffee when the Kaffir maid ran in to say she saw someone coming along the road who looked like her master. The women ran out. It was the white horse on which he had ridden away, but they almost doubted if it were he. He rode bending on his saddle, with his chin on his breast and his arm hanging at his side. At first they thought he had been wounded, but when they had helped him from his horse and brought him into the house they found it was only a deadly fever which was upon him. He had crept home to them by small stages. Hardly had he any spirit left to tell them of Ingogo, Laings Nek, and Amajuba. For fourteen days he grew worse and on the fifteenth day he died. And the two women buried him where the rest of his kin lay on the hill-side.

And so it came to pass that on that warm starlight night the two women were alone in the little mud-house with the stillness of the veld about them; even their Kaffir servants asleep in their huts beyond the kraal; and the very sheep lying silent in the starlight. They two were alone in the little house, but they knew that before morning they would not be alone, they were awaiting the coming of the dead man's child.

The young woman with her head on the table groaned. 'If only my husband were here still,' she wailed. The old woman rose and stood beside her, passing her hard, work-worn hand gently over her shoulder as if she were a little child. At last she induced her to go and lie down in the inner room. When she had grown quieter and seemed to have fallen into a light sleep the old woman came to the front room again. It was almost two o'clock and the fire had burned low under the large kettle. She scraped the coals together and went out of the front door to fetch more wood, and closed the door behind her. The night air struck cool and fresh upon her face after the close air of the house, the stars seemed to be growing lighter as the night advanced, they shot down their light as from a million polished steel points. She walked to the back of the house where, beyond the round hut that served as a store-room, the wood-pile lay. She bent down gathering sticks and chips till her apron was full, then slowly she raised herself and stood still. She looked upwards. It was a wonderful night. The white band of the Milky Way crossed the sky over-head, and from every side stars threw down their light, sharp as barbed spears, from the velvety blue-black of the sky. The woman raised her hand to her forehead as if pushing the hair farther off it, and stood mo-tionless, looking up. After a long time she dropped her hand and began walking slowly towards the house. Yet once or twice on the way she paused and stood looking up. When she went into the house the woman in the inner room was again moving and moaning. She laid the sticks down before the fire and went into the next room. She bent down over the bed where the younger woman lay, and put her hand upon her. 'My daughter,' she said slowly, 'be comforted. A wonderful thing has hap-pened to me. As I stood out in the starlight it was as though a voice came down to me and spoke. The child which will be born of you tonight will be a man-child and he will live to do great things for his land and for his people.'

Before morning there was the sound of a little wail in the mud-house:
and the child who was to do great things for his land and for his people
was born.

II

Six years passed; and all was as it had been at the little house among the
slopes. Only a new piece of land had been ploughed up and added to the
land before the house, so that the ploughed land now almost reached to
the ridge.

The young mother had grown stouter, and lost her pink and white;
she had become a working-woman, but she still had the large knot of
flaxen hair behind her head and the large wondering eyes. She had many
suitors in those six years, but she sent them all away. She said the old
woman looked after the farm as well as any man might, and her son
would be grown up by and by. The grandmother's hair was a little more
streaked with grey, but it was as thick as ever, and her shoulders as upright; only some of her front teeth had fallen out, which made her lips
close more softly.

The great change was that wherever the women went there was the
flaxen-haired child to walk beside them holding on to their skirts or
clasping their hands.

The neighbours said they were ruining the child: they let his hair
grow long, like a girl's, because it curled; and they never let him wear
velschoens like other children but always shop boots; and his mother sat
up at night to iron his pinafores as if the next day were always a Sunday.

But the women cared nothing for what was said; to them he was not as
any other child. He asked them strange questions they could not answer,
and he never troubled them by wishing to go and play with the little
Kaffirs as other children trouble. When neighbours came over and
brought their children with them he ran away and hid in the sloot to play
by himself till they were gone. No, he was not like other children!

When the women went to lie down on hot days after dinner sometimes, he would say that he did not want to sleep; but he would not run
about and make a noise like other children – he would go and sit outside
in the shade of the house, on the front doorstep, quite still, with his little
hands resting on his knees, and stare far away at the ploughed lands on
the slope, or the shadows nearer; the women would open the bedroom
window, and peep out to look at him as he sat there.

The child loved his mother and followed her about to the milk house,
and to the kraals; but he loved his grandmother best.

She told him stories.

When she went to the lands to see how the Kaffirs were ploughing he would run at her side holding her dress; when they had gone a short way he would tug gently at it and say, 'Grandmother, tell me things!'

And long before day broke, when it was yet quite dark, he would often creep from the bed where he slept with his mother into his grandmother's bed in the corner; he would put his arms round her neck and stroke her face till she woke, and then whisper softly, 'Tell me stories!' and she would tell them to him in a low voice not to wake the mother, till the cock crowed and it was time to get up and light the candle and the fire.

But what he liked best of all were the hot, still summer nights, when the women put their chairs before the door because it was too warm to go to sleep; and he would sit on the stoof at his grandmother's feet and lean his head against her knees, and she would tell him on and on of the things he liked to hear; and he would watch the stars as they slowly set along the ridge, or the moonlight, casting bright-edged shadows from the gable as she talked. Often after the mother had got sleepy and gone in to bed the two sat there together.

The stories she told him were always true stories of the things she had seen or of things she had heard. Sometimes they were stories of her own childhood: of the day when she and his grandfather hid among the bushes, and saw the wagon burnt; sometimes they were of the long trek from Natal to the Transvaal; sometimes of the things which happened to her and his grandfather when first they came to that spot among the ridges, of how there was no house there nor lands, only two bare grassy slopes when they outspanned their wagon there the first night; she told of a lion she once found when she opened the door in the morning, sitting, with paws crossed, upon the threshold, and how the grandfather jumped out of bed and reopened the door two inches, and shot it through the opening; the skin was kept in the round storehouse still, very old and mangy.

Sometimes she told him of the two uncles who were dead, and of his own father, and of all they had been and done. But sometimes she told him of things much farther off: of the old Colony where she had been born, but which she could not remember, and of the things which happened there in the old days. She told him of how the British had taken the Cape over, and of how the English had hanged their men at the 'Slachters Nek' for resisting the English Government, and of how the friends and relations had been made to stand round to see them hanged whether they would or no, and of how the scaffold broke down as they were being hanged, and the people looking on cried aloud, 'It is the finger of God! They are saved!' but how the British hanged them up again. She told him of the great trek in which her parents had taken part to escape from under the British flag; of the great battles with Moselikatse; and of the murder of Retief and his men by Dingaan, and of Dingaan's Day. She told him how the British Government followed them into Natal, and of how they trekked north and east to escape from it again; and she told him of the later things, of the fight at Laings Nek, and Ingogo, and Amajuba, where his father had been. Always she told the same story in exactly the same words over and over again, till the child knew them all by heart, and would ask for this and then that.

The story he loved best, and asked for more often than all the others, made his grandmother wonder, because it did not seem to her the story a child would best like; it was not a story of lion-hunting, or wars, or adventures. Continually when she asked what she should tell him, he said, 'About the mountains!'

It was the story of how the Boer women in Natal when the English Commissioner came to annex their country, collected to meet him and pointing toward the Drakens Berg Mountains said, 'We go across those mountains to freedom or to death!'

More than once, when she was telling him the story, she saw him stretch out his little arm and raise his hand, as though he were speaking.

One evening as he and his mother were coming home from the milking kraals, and it was getting dark, and he was very tired, having romped about shouting among the young calves and kids all the evening, he held her hand tightly.

'Mother,' he said suddenly, 'when I am grown up, I am going to Natal.'

'Why, my child?' she asked him; 'there are none of our family living there now.'

He waited a little, then said, very slowly, 'I am going to go and try to get our land back!'

His mother started; if there were one thing she was more firmly resolved on in her own mind than any other it was that he should never go to the wars. She began to talk quickly of the old white cow who had kicked the pail over as she was milked, and when she got to the house she did not even mention to the grandmother what had happened; it seemed better to forget.

One night in the rainy season when it was damp and chilly they sat round the large fireplace in the front room.

Outside the rain was pouring in torrents and you could hear the water rushing in the great dry sloot before the door. His grandmother, to amuse him, had sprung some dried mealies in the great black pot and sprinkled them with sugar, and now he sat on the stoof at her feet with a large lump of the sticky sweetmeat in his hand, watching the fire. His grandmother from above him was watching it also, and his mother in her elbow-chair on the other side of the fire had her eyes half closed and was nodding already with the warmth of the room and her long day's work. The child sat so quiet, the hand with the lump of sweetmeat resting on his knee, that his grandmother thought he had gone to sleep too. Suddenly he said without looking up, 'Grandmother?'

'Yes.'

He waited rather a long time, then said slowly, 'Grandmother, did God make the English too?'

She also waited for a while, then she said, 'Yes, my child; He made all things.'

They were silent again, and there was no sound but of the rain falling and the fire cracking and the sloot rushing outside. Then he threw his head backwards on to his grandmother's knee and looking up into her face, said, 'But, grandmother, why did He make them?'

Then she too was silent for a long time. 'My child,' at last she said, 'we cannot judge the ways of the Almighty. He does that which seems good in His own eyes.'

The child sat up and looked back at the fire. Slowly he tapped his knee with the lump of sweetmeat once or twice; then he began to munch it; and soon the mother started wide awake and said it was time for all to go to bed.

The next morning his grandmother sat on the front doorstep cutting beans in an iron basin; he sat beside her on the step pretending to cut too, with a short, broken knife. Presently he left off and rested his hands on his knees, looking away at the hedge beyond, with his small forehead knit tight between the eyes.

'Grandmother,' he said suddenly, in a small, almost shrill voice, 'do the English want *all* the lands of *all* the people?'

The handle of his grandmother's knife as she cut clinked against the iron side of the basin. 'All they can get,' she said.

After a while he made a little movement almost like a sigh, and took up his little knife again and went on cutting.

Some time after that, when a trader came by, his grandmother bought him a spelling-book and a slate and pencils, and his mother began to teach him to read and write. When she had taught him for a year he knew all she did. Sometimes when she was setting him a copy and left a letter out in a word, he would quietly take the pencil when she set it down and put the letter in, not with any idea of correcting her, but simply because it must be there.

Often at night when the child had gone to bed early, tired out with his long day's play, and the two women were left in the front room with the tallow candle burning on the table between them, then they talked of his future.

Ever since he had been born everything they had earned had been put away in the wagon chest under the grandmother's bed. When the traders with their wagons came round the women bought nothing except a few groceries and clothes for the child; even before they bought a yard of cotton print for a new apron they talked long and solemnly as to whether the old one might not be made to do by repatching; and they mixed much more dry pumpkin and corn with their coffee than before he was born. It was to earn more money that the large new piece of land had been added to the lands before the house.

They were going to have him educated. First he was to be taught all they could at home, then to be sent away to a great school in the old Colony, and then he was to go over the sea to Europe and come back an advocate or doctor or a parson. The grandmother had made a long journey to the next town, to find out from the minister just how much it would cost to do it all.

In the evenings when they sat talking it over the mother generally inclined to his becoming a parson. She never told the grandmother why, but the real reason was because parsons do not go to the war. The grandmother generally favoured his becoming an advocate, because he might become a judge. Sometimes they sat discussing these matters till the candle almost burnt out.

'Perhaps, one day,' the mother would at last say, 'he may yet become President!'

Then the grandmother would slowly refold her hands across her apron and say softly, 'Who knows? – who knows?'

Often they would get the box out from under the bed (looking carefully across the corner to see he was fast asleep) and would count out all the money, though each knew to a farthing how much was there; then they would make it into little heaps, so much for this, so much for that, and then they would count on their fingers how many good seasons it would take to make the rest, and how old he would be.

When he was eight and had learnt all his mother could teach him, they sent him to school every day on an adjoining farm six miles off, where the people had a schoolmaster. Every day he rode over on the great white horse his father went to the wars with; his mother was afraid to let him ride alone at first, but his grandmother said he must learn to do everything alone. At four o'clock when he came back one or other of the women was always looking out to see the little figure on the tall horse coming over the ridge.

When he was eleven they gave him his father's smallest gun; and one day not long after he came back with his first small buck. His mother had the skin dressed and bound with red, and she laid it as a mat under the table, and even the horns she did not throw away, and saved them in the round house, because it was his first.

When he was fourteen the schoolmaster said he could teach him no more; that he ought to go to some larger school where they taught Latin and difficult things; they had not yet money enough and he was not quite old enough to go to the old Colony, so they sent him first to the High-veld, where his mother's relations lived and where there were good schools, where they taught the difficult things; he could live with his mother's relations and come back once a year for the holidays.

They were great times when he came.

His mother made him koekies and sasarties and nice things every day; and he used to sit on the stoof at her feet and let her play with his hair like when he was quite small. With his grandmother he talked. He tried to explain to her all he was learning, and he read the English newspapers to her (she could neither read in English nor Dutch), translating them. Most of all she liked his atlas. They would sometimes sit over it for half an hour in the evening tracing the different lands and talking of them. On the warm nights he used still to sit outside on the stoof at her feet with his head against her knee, and they used to discuss things that were happening in other lands and in South Africa; and sometimes they sat there quite still together.

It was now he who had the most stories to tell; he had seen Krugersdorp and Johannesburg, and Pretoria; he knew the world; he was at Krugersdorp when Dr Jameson made his raid. Sometimes he sat for an hour, telling her of things, and she sat quietly listening.

When he was seventeen, nearly eighteen, there was money enough in the box to pay for his going to the Colony and then to Europe; and he came home to spend a few months with them before he went.

He was very handsome now; not tall, and very slight, but with fair hair that curled close to his head, and white hands like a town's man. All the girls in the countryside were in love with him. They all wished he would come and see them. But he seldom rode from home except to go to the next farm where he had been at school. There lived little Aletta, who was the daughter of the woman his uncle had loved before he went to the Kaffir war and got killed. She was only fifteen years old, but they had always been great friends. She netted him a purse of green silk. He said he would take it with him to Europe, and would show it her when he came back and was an advocate; and he gave her a book with her name written in it, which she was to show to him.

These were the days when the land was full of talk; it was said the

English were landing troops in South Africa, and wanted to have war. Often the neighbours from the nearest farms would come to talk about it (there were more farms now, the country was filling in, and the nearest railway station was only a day's journey off), and they discussed matters. Some said they thought there would be war; others again laughed, and said it would be only Jameson and his white flag again. But the grandmother shook her head, and if they asked her, 'Why,' she said, 'it will not be the war of a week, nor a month; if it comes it will be the war of years,' but she would say nothing more.

Yet sometimes when she and her grandson were walking along together in the lands she would talk.

Once she said: 'It is as if a great heavy cloud hung just above my head, as though I wished to press it back with my hands and could not. It will be a great war – a great war. Perhaps the English government will take the land for a time, but they will not keep it. The gold they have fought for will divide them, till they slay one another over it.'

Another day she said: 'This land will be a great land one day with one people from the sea to the north – but we shall not live to see it.'

He said to her: 'But how can that be when we are all of different races?'

She said: 'The land will make us one. Were not our fathers of more than one race?'

Another day, when she and he were sitting by the table after dinner, she pointed to a sheet of exercise paper, on which he had been working out a problem and which was covered with algebraical symbols, and said, 'In fifteen years' time the Government of England will not have one piece of land in all South Africa as large as that sheet of paper.'

One night when the milking had been late and she and he were walking down together from the kraals in the starlight she said to him: 'If this war comes let no man go to it lightly, thinking he will surely return home, nor let him go expecting victory on the next day. It will come at last, but not at first.

'Sometimes,' she said, 'I wake at night and it is as though the whole house were filled with smoke – and I have to get up and go outside to breathe. It is as though I saw my whole land blackened and desolate. But when I look up it is as though a voice cried out to me, "Have no fear!"'

They were getting his things ready for him to go away after Christmas. His mother was making him shirts and his grandmother was having a kaross of jackals' skins made that he might take it with him to Europe where it was so cold. But his mother noticed that whenever the grandmother was in the room with him and he was not looking at her, her eyes were always curiously fixed on him as though they were questioning something. The hair was growing white and a little thin over her temples now, but her eyes were as bright as ever, and she could do a day's work with any man.

One day when the youth was at the kraals helping the Kaffir boys to mend a wall, and the mother was kneading bread in the front room, and the grandmother washing up the breakfast things, the son of the Field-Cornet came riding over from his father's farm, which was about twelve miles off. He stopped at the kraal and Jan and he stood talking for some time, then they walked down to the farmhouse, the Kaffir boy leading the horse behind them. Jan stopped at the round store, but the Field-Cornet's son went to the front door. The grandmother asked him in, and handed him some coffee, and the mother, her hands still in the dough, asked him how things were going at his father's farm, and if his mother's young turkeys had come out well, and she asked if he had met Jan at the kraals. He answered the questions slowly, and sipped his coffee. Then he put the cup down on the table; and said suddenly in the same measured voice, staring at the wall in front of him, that war had broken out, and his father had sent him round to call out all fighting burghers.

The mother took her hands out of the dough and stood upright beside the trough as though paralysed. Then she cried in a high, hard voice, unlike her own, 'Yes, but Jan cannot go! He is hardly eighteen! He's got to go and be educated in other lands! You can't take the only son of a widow!'

'Aunt,' said the young man slowly, 'no one will make him go.'

The grandmother stood resting the knuckles of both hands on the table, her eyes fixed on the young man. 'He shall decide himself,' she said.

The mother wiped her hands from the dough and rushed past them and out at the door; the grandmother followed slowly.

They found him in the shade at the back of the house, sitting on a stump; he was cleaning the belt of his new Mauser which lay across his knees.

'Jan,' his mother cried, grasping his shoulder, 'you are not going away? You can't go! You must stay. You can go by Delagoa Bay if there is fighting on the other side! There is plenty of money!'

He looked softly up into her face with his blue eyes. 'We have all to be at the Field-Cornet's at nine o'clock tomorrow morning,' he said. She wept aloud and argued.

His grandmother turned slowly without speaking, and went back into the house. When she had given the Field-Cornet's son another cup of coffe and shaken hands with him, she went into the bedroom and opened the box in which her grandson's clothes were kept, to see which things he should take with him. After a time the mother came back too. He had kissed her and talked to her until she too had at last said it was right he should go.

All the day they were busy. His mother baked him biscuits to take in his bag, and his grandmother made a belt of two strips of leather; she sewed them together herself and put a few sovereigns between the stitchings. She said some of his comrades might need the money if he did not.

The next morning early he was ready. There were two saddle-bags tied to his saddle and before it was strapped the kaross his grandmother had made; she said it would be useful when he had to sleep on damp ground. When he had greeted them, he rode away towards the rise: and the women stood at the gable of the house to watch him.

When he had gone a little way he turned in his saddle, and they could see he was smiling; he took off his hat and waved it in the air; the early morning sunshine made his hair as yellow as the tassels that hang from the head of ripening mealies. His mother covered her face with the sides of her kappie and wept aloud; but the grandmother shaded her eyes with both her hands and stood watching him till the figure passed out of sight over the ridge; and when it was gone and the mother returned to the house crying, she still stood watching the line against the sky.

The two women were very quiet during the next days, they worked hard, and seldom spoke. After eight days there came a long letter from him (there was now a post once a week from the station to the Field-Cornet's). He said he was well and in very good spirits. He had been to Krugersdorp and Johannesburg, and Pretoria; all the family living there were well and sent greetings. He had joined a corps that was leaving for the front the next day. He sent also a long message to Aletta, asking them to tell her he was sorry to go away without saying goodbye; and he told his mother how good the biscuits and biltong were she had put into his saddle-bag; and he sent her a piece of 'vierkleur' ribbon in the letter, to wear on her breast.

The women talked a great deal for a day or two after this letter came. Eight days after there was a short note from him, written in pencil in the train on his way to the front. He said all was going well, and if he did not write soon they were not to be anxious; he would write as often as he could.

For some days the women discussed the note too.

Then came two weeks without a letter, the two women became very silent. Every day they sent the Kaffir boy over to the Field-Cornet's, even on the days when there was no post, to hear if there was any news.

Many reports were flying about the country-side. Some said that an English armoured train had been taken on the western border; that there had been fighting at Albertina, and in Natal. But nothing seemed quite certain.

Another week passed ... Then the two women became very quiet.

The grandmother, when she saw her daughter-in-law left the food untouched on her plate, said there was no need to be anxious; men at the front could not always find paper and pencils to write with and might be far from any post office. Yet night after night she herself would rise from her bed saying she felt the house close, and go and walk up and down outside.

Then one day suddenly all their servants left them except one Kaffir and his wife, whom they had had for years, and the servants from the farms about went also, which was a sign there had been news of much fighting; for the Kaffirs hear things long before the white man knows them.

Three days after, as the women were clearing off the breakfast things, the youngest son of the Field-Cornet, who was only fifteen and had not gone to the war with the others, rode up. He hitched his horse to the post, and came towards the door. The mother stepped forward to meet him and shook hands in the doorway.

'I suppose you have come for the carrot seed I promised your mother? I was not able to send it, as our servants ran away,' she said, as she shook his hand. 'There isn't a letter from Jan, is there?' The lad said no, there was no letter from him, and shook hands with the grandmother. He stood by the table instead of sitting down.

The mother turned to the fireplace to get coals to put under the coffee to rewarm it; but the grandmother stood leaning forward with her eyes fixed on him from across the table. He felt uneasily in his breast pocket.

'Is there no news?' the mother said without looking round, as she bent over the fire.

'Yes, there is news, Aunt.'

She rose quickly and turned towards him, putting down the brazier on the table. He took a letter out of his breast pocket. 'Aunt, my father said I must bring this to you. It came inside one to him and they asked him to send one of us over with it.'

The mother took the letter; she held it, examining the address.

'It looks to me like the writing of Sister Annie's Paul,' she said. 'Perhaps there is news of Jan in it' – she turned to them with a half-nervous smile – 'they were always such friends.'

'All is as God wills, Aunt,' the young man said, looking down fixedly at the top of his riding-whip.

But the grandmother leaned forward motionless, watching her daughter-in-law as she opened the letter.

She began to read to herself, her lips moving slowly as she deciphered it word by word.

Then a piercing cry rang through the roof of the little mud-farm-house.

'He is dead! My boy is dead!'

She flung the letter on the table and ran out at the front door.

Far out across the quiet ploughed lands and over the veld to where the kraals lay the cry rang. The Kaffir woman who sat outside her hut beyond the kraals nursing her baby heard it and came down with her child across her hip to see what was the matter. At the side of the round house she stood motionless and open-mouthed, watching the woman, who paced up and down behind the house with her apron thrown over her head and her hands folded above it, crying aloud.

In the front room the grandmother, who had not spoken since he came, took up the letter and put it in the lad's hands. 'Read', she whispered.

And slowly the lad spelled it out.

'My Dear Aunt,

'I hope this letter finds you well. The Commandant has asked me to write it.

'We had a great fight four days ago, and Jan is dead. The Commandant says I must tell you how it happened. Aunt, there were five of us first in a position on that koppie, but two got killed, and then there were only three of us – Jan, and I, and Uncle Peter's Frikkie. Aunt, the khakies were coming on all round just like locusts, and the bullets were coming just like hail. It was bare on that side of the koppie where we were, but we had plenty of cartridges. We three took up a position where there were some small stones and we fought, Aunt; we had to. One bullet took off the top of my ear, and Jan got two bullets, one through the flesh in the left leg and one through his arm, but he could still fire his gun. Then we three meant to go to the top of the koppie, but a bullet took Jan right through his chest. We knew he couldn't go any farther. The khakies were right at the foot of the koppie just coming up. He told us to lay him down, Aunt. We said we would stay by him, but he said we must go. I put my jacket under his head and Frikkie put his over his feet. We threw his gun far away from him that they might see how it was with him. He said he hadn't much pain, Aunt. He was full of blood from his arm, but there wasn't much from his chest, only a little out of the corners of his mouth. He said we must make haste or the khakies would catch us; he said he wasn't afraid to be left there.

'Aunt, when we got to the top, it was all full of khakies like the sea on the other side, all among the koppies and on our koppie too. We were surrounded, Aunt; the last I saw of Frikkie he was sitting on a stone with blood running down his face, but he got under a rock and hid there; some of our men found him next morning and brought him to camp. Aunt there was a khakie's horse standing just below where I was, with no one on it. I jumped on and rode. The bullets went this way and the bullets went that, but I rode! Aunt, the khakies were sometimes as near me as that tentpole, only the Grace of God saved me. It was dark in the night when I got back to where our people were, because I had to go round all the koppies to get away from the khakies.

'Aunt, the next day we went to look for him. We found him where we left him; but he was turned over on to his face; they had taken all his things, his belt and his watch, and the pugaree from his hat, even his boots. The little green silk purse he used to carry we found on the ground by him, but nothing it it. I will send it back to you whenever I get an opportunity.

'Aunt, when we turned him over on his back there were four bayonet stabs in his body. The doctor says it was only the first three while he was alive; the last one was through his heart and killed him at once.

'We gave him Christian burial, Aunt; we took him to the camp.

'The Commandant was there, and all of the family who are with the Commando were there, and they all said they hoped God would comfort you' ...

The old woman leaned forward and grasped the boy's arm. 'Read it over again,' she said, 'from where they found him.' He turned back and re-read slowly. She gazed at the page as though she were reading also. Then, suddenly, she slipped out at the front door.

At the back of the house she found her daughter-in-law still walking up and down, and the Kaffir woman with a red handkerchief bound round her head and the child sitting across her hip, sucking from her long, pendulous breast, looking on.

The old woman walked up to her daughter-in-law and grasped her firmly by the arm.

'He's dead! You know, my boy's dead!' she cried, drawing the apron down with her right hand and disclosing her swollen and bleared face. 'Oh, his beautiful hair – Oh, his beautiful hair!'

The old woman held her arm tighter with both hands; the younger opened her half-closed eyes, and looked into the keen, clear eyes fixed on hers, and stood arrested.

The old woman drew her face closer to hers. 'You ... do ... not ... know ... what ... has ... happened!' she spoke slowly, her tongue striking her front gum, the jaw moving stiffly, as though partly paralysed. She loosed her left hand and held up the curved work-worn fingers before her daughter-in-law's face. 'Was it not told me ... the night he was born ... here ... at this spot ... that he would do great things ... great things ... for his land and his people?' She bent forward till her lips almost touched the other's. 'Three ... bullet ... wounds ... and four ... bayonet ... stabs!' She raised her left hand high in the air. 'Three ... bullet ... wounds ... and four ... bayonet ... stabs! ... Is it given to many to die so for their land and their people!'

The younger woman gazed into her eyes, her own growing larger and larger. She let the old woman lead her by the arm in silence into the house.

The Field-Cornet's son was gone, feeling there was nothing more to be done; and the Kaffir woman went back with her baby to her hut beyond the kraals. All day the house was very silent. The Kaffir woman wondered that no smoke rose from the farmhouse chimney, and that she was not called to churn, or wash the pots. At three o'clock she went down to the house. As she passed the grated window of the round out-house she saw the buckets of milk still standing unsifted on the floor as they had been set down at breakfast time, and under the great soap-pot beside the wood pile the fire had died out. She went round to the front of the house and saw the door and window shutters still closed, as though her mistresses were still sleeping. So she rebuilt the fire under the soap-pot and went back to her hut.

It was four o'clock when the grandmother came out from the dark inner room where she and her daughter-in-law had been lying down; she opened the top of the front door, and lit the fire with twigs, and set the large black kettle over it. When it boiled she made coffee, and poured out two cups and set them on the table with a plate of biscuits, and then called her daughter-in-law from the inner room.

The two women sat down one on each side of the table, with their coffee cups before them, and the biscuits between them, but for a time they said nothing, but sat silent, looking out through the open door at the shadow of the house and the afternoon sunshine beyond it. At last the older woman motioned that the younger should drink her coffee. She took a little, and then folding her arms on the table rested her head on them, and sat motionless as if asleep.

The older woman broke up a biscuit into her own cup, and stirred it round and round; and then, without tasting, sat gazing out into the afternoon's sunshine till it grew cold beside her.

It was five, and the heat was quickly dying; the glorious golden colouring of the later afternoon was creeping over everything when she rose from her chair. She moved to the door and took from behind it two large white calico bags hanging there, and from nails on the wall she took down two large brown cotton kappies. She walked round the table and laid her hand gently on her daughter-in-law's arm. The younger woman raised her head slowly and looked up into her mother-in-law's face; and then, suddenly, she knew that her mother-in-law was an old, old, woman. The little shrivelled face that looked down at her was hardly larger than a child's, the eyelids were half closed and the lips worked at the corners and the bones cut out through the skin in the temples.

'I am going out to sow – the ground will be getting too dry to-morrow; will you come with me?' she said gently.

The younger woman made a movement with her hand, as though she said 'What is the use?' and redropped her hand on the table.

'It may go on for long, our burghers must have food,' the old woman said gently.

The younger woman looked into her face, then she rose slowly and taking one of the brown kappies from her hand, put it on, and hung one of the bags over her left arm; the old woman did the same and together they passed out of the door. As the older woman stepped down the younger caught her and saved her from falling.

'Take my arm, mother,' she said.

But the old woman drew her shoulders up. 'I only stumbled a little!' she said quickly. 'That step has been always too high;' but before she reached the plank over the sloot the shoulders had dropped again, and the neck fallen forward.

The mould in the lands was black and soft; it lay in long ridges, as it had been ploughed up a week before, but the last night's rain had softened it and made it moist and ready for putting in the seed.

The bags which the women carried on their arms were full of the seed of pumpkins and mealies. They began to walk up the lands, keeping parallel with the low hedge of dried bushes that ran up along the side of the sloot almost up to the top of the ridge. At every few paces they stopped and bent down to press into the earth, now one and then the other kind of seed from their bags. Slowly they walked up and down till they reached the top of the land almost on the horizon line; and then they turned, and walked down, sowing as they went. When they had reached the bottom of the land before the farm-house it was almost sunset, and their bags were nearly empty; but they turned to go up once more. The light of the setting sun cast long, gaunt shadows from their figures across the ploughed land, over the low hedge and the sloot, into the bare veld beyond; shadows that grew longer and longer as they passed slowly on pressing in the seeds ... The seeds! ... that were to lie in the dank, dark, earth, and rot there, seemingly, to die, till their outer

covering had split and fallen from them ... and then, when the rains had
fallen, and the sun had shone, to come up above the earth again, and high
in the clear air to lift their feathery plumes and hang out their pointed
leaves and silken tassels! To cover the ground with a mantle of green and
gold through which sunlight quivered, over which the insects hung by
thousands, carrying yellow pollen on their legs and wings and making
the air alive with their hum and stir, while grain and fruit ripened surely
... for the next season's harvest!

When the sun had set, the two women with their empty bags turned
and walked silently home in the dark to the farmhouse.

NINETEEN HUNDRED AND ONE

Near one of the camps in the Northern Transvaal are the graves of two
women. The older one died first, on the twenty-third of the month, from
hunger and want; the younger woman tended her with ceaseless care and
devotion till the end. A week later when the British Superintendent came
round to inspect the tents, she was found lying on her blanket on the
mud-floor dead, with the rations of bread and meat she had got four days
before untouched on a box beside her. Whether she died of disease, or
from inability to eat the food, no one could say. Some who had seen her
said she hardly seemed to care to live after the old woman died; they
buried them side by side.

There is no stone and no name upon either grave to say who lies there
... our unknown ... our unnamed ... our forgotten dead.

IN THE YEAR NINETEEN HUNDRED AND FOUR

If you look for the little farm-house among the ridges you will not find it
there today.

The English soldiers burnt it down. You can only see where the farmhouse once stood, because the stramonia and weeds grow high and very
strong there; and where the ploughed lands were you can only tell, because the veld never grows quite the same on land that has once been
ploughed. Only a brown patch among the long grass on the ridge shows
where the kraals and huts once were.

In a country house in the north of England the owner has upon his
wall an old flint-lock gun. He takes it down to show his friends. It is a
small thing he picked up in the war in South Africa, he says. It must be at
least eighty years old and is very valuable. He shows how curiously it is
constructed; he says it must have been kept in such perfect repair by continual polishing for the steel shines as if it were silver. He does not tell
that he took it from the wall of the little mud house before he burnt it
down.

It was the grandfather's gun, which the women had kept polished on the wall.

In a London drawing-room the descendant of a long line of titled forefathers entertains her guests. It is a fair room, and all that money can buy to make life soft and beautiful is there.

On the carpet stands a little dark wooden stoof. When one of her guests notices it, she says it is a small curiosity which her son brought home to her from South Africa when he was out in the war there; and how good it was of him to think of her when he was away in the back country. And when they ask what it is, she says it is a thing Boer women have as a foot-stool and to keep their feet warm; and she shows the hole at the side where they put the coals in, and the little holes at the top where the heat comes out.

And the other woman puts her foot out and rests it on the stoof just to try how it feels, and drawls 'How f-u-n-n-y!'

It is grandmother's stoof, that the child used to sit on.

The wagon chest was found and broken open just before the thatch caught fire, by three private soldiers, and they divided the money between them; one spent his share in drink, another had his stolen from him, but the third sent his home to England to a girl in the East End of London. With part of it she bought a gold brooch and ear-rings, and the rest she saved to buy a silk wedding-dress when he came home.

A syndicate of Jews in Johannesburg and London have bought the farm. They purchased it from the English Government, because they think to find gold on it. They have purchased it and paid for it ... but they do not possess it.

Only the men who lie in their quiet graves upon the hill-side, who lived on it, and loved it, possess it; and the piles of stones above them, from among the long waving grasses, keep watch over the land.

Perceval Gibbon

Like Unto Like

from *The Vrouw Grobelaar's Leading Cases* (1918)

For the most part the Vrouw Grobelaar's nephews and nieces were punc-
tually obedient. Doubtless this was policy; for the old lady founded her
authority on a generous complement of this world's goods. However,
man is as the grass of the field (as she would constantly aver); and it fell
that Frikkie Viljoen, otherwise a lad of promise, became enamoured of a
girl of lower caste than the Grobelaars and Viljoens, and this, mark you,
with a serious eye to marriage. Even this, after a proper and orthodox
reluctance on the part of his elders and betters, might have been con-
doned; for the Viljoens had multiplied exceedingly in the land, and the
older sons were not yet married. But, as though to aggravate the business, Frikkie took a sort of glory in it, and openly belauded his lowly
sweetheart.

'Mark you,' said the Vrouw Grobelaar with tremendous solemnity,
'this choice is your own. Take care you do not find a Leah in your
Rachel.'

Frikkie replied openly that he was sure enough about the girl.

The Vrouw Grobelaar shook a doubtful head. 'Her grandfather was a
bijwohner,' she said. 'Pas op! or she will one day go back to her own
people and shame you.'

The misguided Frikkie saw fit to laugh at this.

'Oh, you may laugh! You may laugh, and laugh, until your time
comes for weeping. I tell you, she will one day return to her own people,
bijwohners and rascals all of them, as Stoffel Mostert's wife did.'

The old lady paused, and Frikkie defiantly demanded further particu-
lars.

'Yes,' continued the Vrouw Grobelaar, 'I remember all the disgrace
and shame of it to this day, and how poor Stoffel went about with his
head bowed and looked no one in the face.

'He had a farm under the Hangklip, and a very nice farm it was, with two wells and a big dam right up above the lands, so that he had no need for a windmill to carry his water. If he had stuck to the farm Stoffel might have been a rich man; and perhaps, when he was old enough to be listened to, the Burghers might have made him a feldkornet.

'But no! He must needs cast his eyes about him till they fell on one Katrina Ruiter, the daughter, so please you, of a dirty *takhaar bijwohner* on his own farm. He went mad about the girl, and thought her quite different from all other girls, though she had a troop of untidy sisters like herself galloping wild about the place. I will own she was a well-grown slip of a lass, tall and straight, and all that; but she had a winding, bending way with her that struck me like something shameless. For the rest, she had a lot of coal-black hair that bunched round her face like the frame round a picture; but there was something in the colour of her skin and the shaping of her lips and nostrils that made me say to myself, "Ah, somewhere and somewhen your people have been meddling with the Kaffirs."

'Black? No, of course she wasn't black. Nor yet yellow; but I tell you, the black blood showed through her white skin so clearly that I wonder Stoffel Mostert did not see it and drive her from his door with a sjambok.

'But the man was clean mad, and, spite of all we could do – spite of his uncle, the Predikant; spite of the ugly dirty family of the girl herself – he rode her to the dorp and married her there; for the Predikant, godly man, would not turn a hand in the business.

'Now, just how they lived together I cannot tell you for sure; for you may be very certain I drank no coffee in the house of the *bijwohner's* daughter. But, by all hearings, they bore with one another very well; and I have even been told that Stoffel was much given to caressing the woman, and she would make out to love him very much indeed.

'Perhaps she really did? What nonsense! How can a *bijwohner's* baggage love a well-to-do Burgher? You are talking foolishness. But anyhow, if there was any trouble between them, they kept it to themselves for close upon a year.

'Then (this is how it has been told to me) one night Stoffel woke up in the dark, and his wife was not beside him.

' "Is it morning already?" he said, and looked through the window. But the stars were high and bright, and he saw it was scarcely midnight.

'He lay for a while, and then got up and drew on his clothes – doing everything slowly, hoping she would return. But when he was done she was not yet come, and he went out in the dark to the kitchen, and there he found the outer door unlocked and heard the dog whining in the yard.

'He took his gun from the beam where it hung and went forth. The dog barked and sprang to him, and together they went out to the veld, seeking Katrina Ruiter.

'The dog seemed to know what was wanted, and led Stoffel straight out towards the Kaffir stad by the Blesbok Spruit. They did not go fast, and on the way Stoffel knelt down and prayed to God, and drew the cartridges from the gun. Then they went on.

'When they got to the spruit they could see there was a big fire in the stad and hear the Kaffirs crying out and beating the drums. The dog ran straight to the edge of the water, and then turned and whined, for there was no more scent. But Stoffel walked straight in, over his knees and up to his waist, and climbed the bank to the wall of the stad.

'Inside, the Kaffirs were dancing. Some were tricked out with ornaments and skins and feathers; some were mother-naked and painted all over their bodies. And there was one, a gaunt figure of horror, with his face streaked to the likeness of a skull, and bones hanging clattering all about him. They capered and danced round the fire like devils in hell, and behind them the men with the drums kept up their noise and seemed to drive the dancers to madness.

'And suddenly the figures round the fire gave way, save the one with the painted face and the bones; for from the shadow of a hut at the back of the fire came another, who rushed into the light and swayed wildly to the barbarous music. The newcomer was naked as a babe new born; wild as a beast of the field; lithe as a serpent; and crazy to savageness with the fire and the drums.

'Madly she danced, bending forwards and backwards, casting her bare arms above her, while the horror who danced with her writhed and screamed like a soul in pain.

'Stoffel, behind the wall, stood stunned and bound – for here he saw his wife. He thought nothing, said nothing; but without an effort his hand ran a cartridge into the gun, and levelled it across the wall. He fired, and the lissom body dropped limp across the fire.'

Frikkie Viljoen rose in great wrath.

'This is how you talk of my sweetheart, is it?' he cried. 'Well, I will hear no more of your lies.' And he forthwith walked out of the house.

'Look at that!' said the Vrouw Grobelaar. 'I never said a word about his sweetheart.'

Arthur Shearly Cripps

The Black Death

from *Cinderella in the South: South African Tales* (1918)

This is a story of a voyage home. The boat was one of the finest on the line and we were not overcrowded. We had wonderful weather that trip, brilliant sunshine relieved by a fresh little breeze that kept its place, doing its duty without taking too much upon itself, or making itself obnoxious. In the third-class we were quiet on the whole, and what is called well-behaved, though neither with millennial serenity nor millennial sobriety.

A red-cheeked gentleman took a red-cheeked married lady and her child under his vigilant protection. Two or three Rhodesians and Joburgers enriched the bar with faithful fondness. Cards and sweeps on the run of the boat and the selling of sweep-tickets – these all stimulated the circulation of savings. Hues of language vied with hues of sunset not seldom of an eventide.

Life was not so very thrilling on that voyage, the treading of 'borderland dim 'twixt vice and virtue' is apt to be rather a dull business.

There was no such incident as that which stirred us on another voyage – the taking of a carving knife to the purser by a drunkard. On the other hand there was no unusual battle-noise of spiritual combat such as may have quickened the pulses of one or two of the boats the year of the English Mission.

We were middling, and dull at that, on the *Sluys Castle*, till we reached Madeira. Then the description I have given of our voyage ceases to apply. The two or three days after that were exciting enough to one or two passengers at any rate.

James Carraway had come down from Kimberly, he told me. He was a spare, slight man, with a red moustache. He sought me occasionally of an eventide, and confided to me views of life in general, and of some of his fellow-passengers in particular. I remember one night especially, when the Southern Cross was in full view and the water about the keel splotched with phosphorescence. Carraway had a big grievance that night. He commented acridly on a coloured woman that I had espied on board. She was not very easily visible herself, but one or two faintly coloured children played often about the deck, and she herself might now and then be seen nursing a baby. I had seen her on a bench sometimes when I had gone to the library to change a book. I had seen her more rarely in the sunshine on deck, nursing the aforesaid baby.

'One man's brought a Kaffir wife on board,' growled Carraway.

I said, 'I thought she might be a nurse.'

'No, she's his wife,' contended Carraway. 'It's cheek of him bringing her on board with the third-class passengers.'

I said, 'Which is her husband?'

'He's been pointed out to me,' he said. 'The other white men seem rather to avoid him. I don't know what your opinion on this point may be,' he said. 'I consider that a man who marries a Kaffir sinks to her status.'

I said nothing. He did not like my silence much, I gathered. He was not so very cordial afterwards. He was a man with many grievances – Carraway.

When we were drawing close to Madeira, two nights before, on the Sunday – Carraway touched the subject again.

The parson had preached incidentally on the advisability of being white – white all round. I thought he played to his gallery a bit, in what he said.

'An excellent sermon,' said Carraway. 'Did you hear how he got at that josser with the Kaffir wife? That parson's a white man.'

I said nothing.

'What God hath divided let no man unite,' said Carraway, improving the occasion. 'I don't uphold Kaffirs. The white man must always be top dog,' etc., etc.

Carraway grew greasily fluent on rather well-worn lines. I smoked my pipe and made no comment. By-and-by he tired of his monologue.

He gave me no further confidences till the night after we left Madeira.

Then he came to me suddenly about eleven o'clock as I stood on the well-deck, smoking a pipe before turning in.

'Come and have a walk,' he said, in a breathless sort of way.

We climbed some steps and paced the upper deck towards the wheelhouse. There were few electric lights burning now. After a turn or two he drew up under one of them and looked round to see whether anyone listened.

'Don't give me away for God's sake,' he said. He held up a hand towards the light pathetically.

'It's showing,' he said. 'God knows why. God knows what I've done to bring it.'

I said nothing, but looked at him and considered him carefully. He certainly did not seem to be drunk.

Then I examined the hand he gave me.

'I don't see anything particular,' I said. 'What's wrong?'

'Good Lord! The nails.'

But the nails looked to me pink and healthy.

'Tell me,' I said, 'what you think's wrong.'

Yet he could not tell me that night. He tried to tell me. He was just like a little boy in most awful trepidation, trying to confess some big transgression. He gasped and spluttered, but he nevber got it out that night. I couldn't make head nor tail of what he said. After he was gone to bed it is true I put two and two together and guessed something. But I was fairly puzzled at the time.

'You're a bit upset to-night,' I said. 'You're not quite yourself, it's the sea I suppose, or something. Come to bed and get a good night.' His teeth chattered as he came down the ladder. I got him down to his cabin.

'Thanks!' he said. 'Good-night! I may come all right in the morning. Anyhow I'll have a bath and try.'

He said it so naïvely that I could not help laughing.

'Yes, have a sea-water bath, a jolly good idea,' I said. 'You'll have to be up early. There's only one and there's a run on it before breakfast. Good night!'

I saw him again in the morning outside the bath-room. He came out in his pink-and-white pyjamas; the pink was aggressive and fought with the tint of his moustache. He looked very blue and wretched.

'Well,' I asked, 'Have you slept it off whatever it was?'

'No,' he said, 'let me tell you about it.' He began to gasp and splutter. Just then another postulant came up, making for the bath-room door.

'Afterwards!' I said, 'After breakfast.' And I vanished into the bath-room. It was probably Carraway, I thought, that had left a little collection of soaps in that bath-room. He had brought a bucket of fresh water with him apparently to give them a fair trial. There was yellow soap, a pumice stone, and carbolic soap, and scented soap. 'I'll keep them for him,' I thought. 'Somebody may jump them if I leave them here. I wonder why in the world he's so distrait.' I had my suspicions as to the reason, and I laughed softly to myself.

After breakfast he invited me back to the bath-room; there was no run on it then.

'It's quiet,' he said. Then after many gasps and splutters he enlightened me. His nails were turning colour, he told me.

'Anyone would think I had Kaffir blood in me,' he said.

Also his skin was giving him grave cause for solicitude. I did not resist the temptation to take him rather seriously. I administered philosophic consolation. I reminded him of Dumas and other serviceable coloured people. I rather enjoyed his misery; poetic justice seemed to me to need some satisfaction. He, the negrophobe, who was so ultra-keen on drawing the line was now enjoying imaginative experiences on the far side of it.

'It seems then,' I remarked, 'That you are now a person of colour.'

He nearly fainted. He did not swear. He seemed to have lost all his old truculence. He began to whimper like a child.

'After all, I never shared your prejudices.' I said. 'Cheer up, old man, I won't drop you like a hot potato even if you have a touch of the tar brush.'

He cried as if his heart would break. I saw I had gone too far. It was like dancing on a trodden worm.

'Carraway,' I said, 'It's a pure delusion. Your nails are all right, and so's your skin. You're dreaming, man. You've got nerves or indigestion, or something. It's something inside you that's wrong. There's nothing outside for anyone to see.'

His eyes gleamed. He shook my hand feebly. Then he held up his own hand to the light.

'It's there,' he said wearily, after a while. 'You want to be kind, but you can't make black white. That's what I've always said. It's the Will of God, and there's nothing to gain by fighting it. Black will be black, and white will be white till crack of doom.'

I told him sternly that I was going to fetch the doctor to him. He sprang at me and gripped my arm.

'I trusted you,' he said. 'I needn't have told you. You promised.'

So I had like a simpleton.

'Only give me two days,' he said, 'then I'll go to the doctor myself, if nothing works in all that time.'

So I said I would respect my promise loyally for those two days.

'I only told *you*', he said 'because my head was splitting with keeping it in. It's awful to me. I thought you were a negrophil and wouldn't think so much of it as other fellows. But for God's sake don't give me away to them. There's lots of things to try yet. By the way, ask that parson to pray for one afflicted and distressed in mind, body, and estate.'

He did try many sorts of things, poor fellow. He was in and out of that bath-room a good share of both days. He also tried drugs and patent medicines. I saw his cabin littered with them. He would sneak into meals those two days when people had almost finished, and gobble his food furtively.

I caught him once or twice smoking his pipe in the bath-room or the bath-room passage. He would not venture amid the crowd on deck. Only when many of the passengers were in bed would he come up with me, and take my arm and walk up and down. That was on the Wednesday night.

Wednesday night came, then Thursday morning. Thursday forenoon was long, and Thursday afternoon longer.

At last the sun was low, and I began to count the hours to the time when I might consult the doctor.

I secured an interview with Carraway in the bath-room soon after sunset.

'Any better?' I asked for about the twentieth time.

He shook his head dejectedly.

'All right. We must go to the doctor to-morrow morning. But, O Carraway, do go to him to-night, don't be afraid. It's only imagination. Do go.'

I'll see,' he said in a dazed, dreary sort of way, I'll see, but I want to play the last card I have in my hand before I go. It's a trump card perhaps.'

'On my honour,' I said, 'You're tormenting yourself for nothing. You're as white as ever you were.'

Then I said 'Good-night.' I stopped for a moment outside the door, and heard him begin splashing and scrubbing. The thing was getting on my own nerves.

I went off up on deck, and smoked hard, then I read, and wrote letters, and smoked again, and went to bed very late. I had steered clear of the bath-room and all Carraway's haunts so far as I could. Yes, and I had gone over to the second class, and I had asked the parson to do as he wanted. I had asked him the day before. Now I asked him over again.

The steward handed me a letter when he brought me my coffee in the morning. I opened it and read:

'Dear Sir,
Perhaps my negrophoby is wrong. Anyhow, it's real to me. I had and have it, and see no way to get rid of it properly here on earth. Now God has touched me, me the negrophobe, and coloured me. And to me the thing seems very hard to bear. Therefore I am trying the sea to-night.

'In the bath-room there never seemed to be enough water. I want to try a bath with plenty of water. But I am afriad it may be with me as it would have been with Macbeth or Lady Macbeth. Those red hands of murder could not be washed white by the ocean, they could only 'the multitudinous seas incarnadine, making the green one red'. What if I cannot be decolorized by any sea? What if my flesh only pollutes the sea, when I plunge, and makes all black? God help me!!! You are a negrophil and don't half understand.

'Yours truly,

'J. Carraway.'

I questioned the steward. He had found the letter in my place at table.

Sure enough there was a third-class passenger missing. I suppose Carraway had slipped off quietly in the moonlight to try his desperate experiment. It was a cruel business – his monomania.

If I had broken my promise and called the doctor earlier, could he have been cured? Or would he have lingered in an asylum – shuddering over the fictitious glooming of his nails and skin, shaking in a long ague of negrophoby.

Anyhow, I'm sorry I didn't do more for him, didn't walk him round the deck the last night at least, and try my best to cheer him. Yes, I blame myself badly for not doing that.

May God who allowed his delusion pardon that last manoeuvre of his! I do not think Carraway had any clear wish to take his own life.

I can imagine the scene so convincingly – Carraway pausing, hesitating, then plunging into the moon-blanched water from the dizzy height above, eager to find which the multitudinous seas would do – would they change his imagined colour, or would they suddenly darken, matching in their tints his own discoloration?

Pauline Smith

Desolation

from *The Little Karoo* (1925)

Alie van Staden was close on seventy-two years old when she went with her son, Stephan, and her motherless little grandson, Stephan's Koos, to Mijnheer Bezedenhout's farm of Koelkuil in the Verlatenheid. She was a short squarely-built woman, slow in thought and slow in movement, with dark brown eyes set deep in a long, somewhat heavy and expressionless face. In her youth her eyes had been beautiful, but there was none who now remembered her youth and in old age she looked out upon the world with a patient endurance which had in it something of the strength and something of the melancholy of the labouring ox.

All her life, save for six months in her girlhood, Alie had lived in the Verlatenheid – that dreary stretch of the Great Karoo which lies immediately to the north of the Zwartkops Mountains and takes its name from the desolation which nature displays here in the grey volcanic harshness of its kopjes and the scanty vegetation of its veld. This grey and desolate region was her world. Here, as the child of poor whites and as the mother of poor whites she had drifted for seventy years from farm to farm in the shiftless, thriftless labour of her class. Here in a bitter poverty she had married her man, borne her children, and accepted dumbly whatever ills her God had inflicted upon her. With her God she had no communion save in the patient uncomplaining fulfilment of His will as the daily circumstances of her life revealed it to her. Prayer was never wrung from her. That cry of 'Our Father! Our Father!' which comes so naturally to the heart and from the lips of her race never came from hers. Sorrow had been her portion, but this was life as she conceived it, and tearless she had borne it. And now of all her sons Stephan alone was left to her, and already Stephan was suffering from that disease of the chest which had killed first his father and then his three brothers, Koos, Hendrick and Piet.

In her son, the bijwoner Stephan van Staden, there was none of old Alie's quiet endurance of life. The bijwoner could not without protest accept the ills which his God so persistently visited upon him. He was a weak and obstinate man who saw in his God a power actively engaged in direct opposition to himself, and at each fresh blow dealt him by his God he lifted up his voice and cried aloud his injury. At Koelkuil his voice was often thus raised, for here his illness rapidly increased, and here he found in his new master a harsh man made harsher by a drought which had brought him close to ruin.

The drought was in fact the worst that any middle-aged man of the Verlatenheid remembered. When Stephan went as bijwoner to Koelkuil the farm had had no rain for over two years and through all his eighteen months of service with Mijnheer only three light showers fell. Day after day men rose to a cloudless sky and hot shimmering air, or to a dry and burning wind that scorched and withered as it blew. Slowly, steadily, the grey earth became greyer, the bare kopjes barer, the veld itself empty of familiar life. The herds of spring-buck seeking water at the dried-up fountains grew smaller and smaller. The field mice, the tortoises, the meer-kats – all the humbler creatures of the veld – died out of ken. The starving jackal played havoc among the starving sheep. The new-born lamb was killed to save the starving ewe. The cattle, the sheep, the ostriches and the donkeys were drawn in their extremity closer to the abodes of men in their vain search for food. Their lowing and bleating drifted mournfully across the stricken land as slowly, steadily, their famished bodies were gathered into the receiving earth and turned again to the dust from which they had sprung.

In the strain of these months there was constant friction between Stephan van Staden and his master. Nothing done by the one was right in the eyes of the other. Stephan, ill and irritable, was loud in his criticism of Mijnheer. Mijnheer, a ruined man, was unjust in the demands he made of his bijwoner. They came at last to an active open warfare into which all on the farm save old Alie were drawn. From their conflict she alone remained quietly aloof. Sitting on the high stone step in front of the bijwoner's house, gazing in melancholy across the Verlatenheid, she would listen in silence to the arguments of both master and man alike. Stephan's vehemence made him indifferent to her silence. Mijnheer resented and feared it. He read in it judgement of himself, and who was this Alie, the poor white, that she should judge him? Why did she never speak that he might answer? Of what did she think as she sat there, immovable as God, on the high stone step in front of the door? He did not know, and would never know, but he came in the end to hate this old woman, so strong, it seemed to him, in her silence, so powerful in her patience. And when, in a spell of bitter cold, the bijwoner suddenly died, he thought with relief that now old Alie must go.

It was in the early winter of the fourth year of the drought that Stephan van Staden died, and on the day that he was buried Mijnheer, standing by the graveside, told Alie van Staden that his bijwoner's house would be needed at once for the man who was coming in her son's place. He was, he said, but naturally sorry for herself and the child, but doubtless they had relatives to whom they might go, and she must see for herself that it was impossible for him, a man well-nigh ruined by the drought, to do anything whatever to help her. She must know, also, that her son's illness had made him a poor bijwoner and added much to his losses among his sheep. In fact the more he thought of it the more convinced he was that no other farmer in the Verlatenheid would have borne with Stephan so long as he, Godlieb Bezedenhout, had done. And on this note of righteousness he ended.

To all that Mijnheer had to say Alie listened, as always, in silence. What, indeed, was there for her to answer? Mijnheer spoke of relatives to whom she might turn for help for herself and Stephan's child but in fact she had none. She was the last of her generation as Stephan had been the last of his. The poor white is poor also in physique, and of all her consumptive stock only Stephan's Koos remained. Stephan's wife had died when her son was born, and her people had long since drifted out of sight, she could not say where. The child, therefore, had none but herself to stand between him and destitution. All that was to be done for him she herself must do. All that was to be planned for him she herself must plan.

Slowly, while her master spoke, these thoughts passed through her mind. But by no word did she betray them or the desolation of her heart. When he ceased she parted from him with a quiet 'Good-day' and went back to the bijwoner's house with Stephan's Koos.

For her six-year-old grandson Alie had a deep but inarticulate tenderness. All the little warmth that life still held for her came to her through Stephan's Koos. It was she who had saved him when Anna died. It was she who had stood between him and the fury of his father when Stephan, in his illness, turned against his own son. All that Stephan's son had known of love had come to him through her, yet for that love she had found no words and to it she could give no expression beyond a rare and awkward gesture, too harsh or too restrained to be called a caress. Yet the boy – a slim small child with eyes as dark as her own, and long thin fingers like the claws of a bird – was conscious of no shortcomings in his grandmother. His father had always been strange to him, and death had but added another mystery to the many which had surrounded him in life. But with his grandmother nothing was strange or mysterious. With his grandmother he knew where he was going, he knew what he was doing. She was his tower of strength, his shadow of a great rock in a dry and thirsty land. By her side he was safe. Wherever she went, whatever she did, by her side he was safe ...

When they reached the house Alie sat down, as was her custom, upon the high stone step in front of the door, and the boy, pressing close to her side to deepen his sense of security there, sat down beside her. For a time they were silent, the child content, his grandmother brooding on the past. She was a woman of little imagination. Her mind, moving slowly among familiar things, was heavy always with the melancholy of the Verlatenheid, and from it she had but one escape – to the village of Hermansdorp where once as a girl she had lived with her mother's cousin, Tan' Betje, and worked with her at mattress-making at one of the stores. Beyond this her thoughts never ventured. And it was to Hermansdorp that her thoughts travelled slowly now with their dawning hope.

Before them, as they sat on the step, there stretched for mile after mile the grey and barren veld, the wild and broken kopjes of the Verlatenheid. But it was not these that old Alie saw. Her vision travelled slowly, painfully through the years to the long low line of hills to the north, in a fold of which lay the village, with near it, in the shade of a clump of thorn-trees, a dam where men and women journeying to the dorp for Sacrament, outspanned their carts and wagons. She saw again the white-washed church, and the graveyard, with its tall dark cypress-trees among the whitewashed tombs, where she and Tan' Betje had walked together on Sunday afternoons spelling out the names of those who lay buried there. She saw again the long wide straight Kerk Straat, with its running furrows of clear water and its double row of pear-trees in blossom. Behind the pear-trees were whitewashed dwelling-houses set back in gardens or green lands, and stores with *stoeps* built out on to the street under the trees. At the head of the street, across it, stood the square whitewashed gaol – and she remembered how, when first she had seen it, not knowing it to be the gaol, there had come into her mind that saying of our Lord: 'In my Father's house are many mansions' – so big and gracious had this building seemed to her.

Tan' Betje's little house, she remembered, had been up a narrow lane. Three rooms it had had, with green wooden shutters, and a pear-tree in the yard. Under the pear-tree they had sat together cleaning the coir for mattresses – dipping it first into buckets of hot water, then teasing it and spreading it out in the sun to dry. For the poor they had made mattresses of mealie-leaves, stripping the dried leaves into shreds with a fork and packing them into sacks ... It had been pleasant in the yard, and Tan'

Betje's talk pleasant to hear. And in the little house there had always been food. She could not remember a day when there had not been food. Good food. Tan' Betje had been kind to her, and at the store too they had been kind. Her master's son had himself come several times to speak to her when she went for the coir. The old master would be dead now, perhaps. But the young master would be there. And he would remember. He would give her work . . .

As if following her thoughts her fingers, stiff with labour and old age, fell awkwardly into the once familiar movements of teasing the coir in the sunlit yard. The boy, wearied at last of her long silence, pressed closer to her side. She looked down upon him sombrely and drew his thin, clawlike hand into hers. Slowly, halting often in her speech, she began to talk to him of Hermansdorp where together they would go. And into the child's sense of security there came a new sense of romance and adventure, deepening his confidence in the wisdom and rightness of all that his grandmother said and did.

That night, while her grandson slept, old Alie bundled together their few possessions. Mijnheer had given her three days in which to make her plans and preparations, but she needed in her poverty less time than that for these. Stephan had come to Koelkuil a poor man and he had died a poorer, and in the meagre plenishing of the bijwoner's house there was little that could not be piled on to the rough unpainted cart by which, eighteen months earlier, they had journeyed to the farm. At dawn she roused the boy and with his help loaded the cart and inspanned the two donkeys. The donkeys were poor and starved, as were also the pitiful handful of sheep and goats which were all that remained of Stephan's flock. These, when all was ready, Koos drove out of the kraal towards her. And slowly, as the sun rose, they set off.

As they left the farm – the boy on foot herding the little flock, his grandmother perched high on the cart peering out upon the world from the depths of her black calico sunbonnet – there was little to mark their exodus as differing from any other than one might meet at any time in the Verlatenheid. The poor white here, though he belongs to the soil, has no roots in the soil. He is by nature a wanderer, with none of that conservative love of place which makes to many men one spot on earth beloved above all others. Yet the range of his wanderings is limited, and the Verlatenheid man remains as a rule in the Verlatenheid, dwelling in no part of it long, and coming, it may be, again and again for short spells at a time to the farms which lie, for no clear reason, within the narrow course he sets himself.

For old Alie there was no longer any such course by which she might steer the rough unpainted cart across the wide stretches of the Verlatenheid. The graves of her sons were now the only claims she held there, and to the vision of old age these graves were become but dwindling mounds of earth in a grey and desolate veld which treasured no memories. The bitter freedom of the poor and the bereft was hers. But it was without bitterness that she accepted it and, uncomplaining, took the road to Hermansdorp.

Throughout the first day it was in the Verlatenheid, with frequent outspans, that they journeyed. And here, from sun-up to sun-down they met no human being and saw in the distance only one whitewashed and deserted farmhouse, bare and treeless in the drought-stricken veld. Every *kuil* or water-hole they passed was dry, and near every *kuil* were the skeletons of donkeys and sheep which had come there but to perish of their thirst. Of living things they saw only, now and then, a couple of *koorhan* rising suddenly in flight, or a lizard basking lazily in the sun. And once, bright as a jewel in that desert of sand and stone, they came upon a small green bush poisonous to sheep and cattle alike.

On the following day they struck the Malgas-Hermansdorp road and, turning north, left the Verlatenheid behind them. The country ahead of them now was flat as a calm grey sea, its veld unbroken by any kopje until the long low line of the Hermansdorp hills was reached. Yet in the shimmering heat of noon this sea became a strange fantastic world that slipped into being, vanished, and slipped into being again as they gazed upon it. Around them now were ridges of hills where no hill could be, banks of trees where no trees grew, and water that was not water lying in sheets and lakes out of which rose strange dark islands and cliffs. For these phenomena old Alie had neither explanation nor name. They were indeed less clear to her than they were to the boy. But to him their very mystery brought an added sense of his own personal security. Whatever amazing and inexplicable things the distance, like the future, might hold, here, on the Hermansdorp road with his grandmother in the cart by his side, he was safe.

Yet already, as his grandmother well knew, their margin of safety on the Hermansdorp road was narrowing. Though on that second day they reached a water-hole in which, surrounded by deep slime, there still remained a small pool at which she could water her flock and her donkeys, by nightfall three of her sheep had died by the roadside and she knew that she must lose more. The veld here, though less bare than that of the Verlatenheid, yielded no grazing for them, and the longer the journey the less could she save. Yet in their weakness she dare not press them, and their progress was broken now by more and more frequent outspans which meant no food as well as no water for her donkeys and sheep, no food as well as no coffee for herself and Koos. The water in the water-cask which hung below the cart must be dealt out sparingly if it were to carry them to the end of their journey, and there had been little to pack into the tin canister of food when they set out. This she explained to Koos when, after lighting a fire of dried-up bushes, she put on no kettle to boil for coffee. The boy accepted her ruling as she herself accepted the ruling of God. All, he felt, would be right when they reached Hermansdorp.

It was on the morning of the third day that they came within sight of the township, lying, as old Alie remembered it, in a fold of the hills. In the cold bright winter air its whitewashed buildings stood our clearly against their dark background, and the boy forgot for a moment his increasing hunger and burst into eager questioning. His grandmother answered him slowly, patiently, her thoughts on the dam outside the village where she would water her donkeys and sheep.

This day, however, was the hardest and most tedious of their journey. Many hours passed before they reached the dam and in these hours more of the sheep died and the going of the donkeys became a painful somnambulistic crawl. To ease their burden of her weight old Alie left her seat in the cart and walked by the side of the patient suffering beasts, calling them quietly by name. From time to time they turned towards her seeking with their tongues such moisture as her clothes might hold. And always when they did so she would speak to them quietly, as if speaking to children, of the Hermansdorp dam.

The dam lay about three miles to the south of the township, and for over fifty years men journeying to the village for market or the Sacrament had watered their flocks and spans here, and made it their last outspan on entering the dorp, their first upon leaving it. It had been, too, the general picnic place of the village, and all old Alie's memories of it were stirring and gay. But as at last they neared it in the fading light of that winter afternoon there crept into her heart a sombre foreboding. The thorn-trees around it were not, as she had remembered them, laden with the scented golden balls of spring, for this was winter, and in winter they must be bare. But she knew before she reached them that they were bare not because winter had made them so but because drought had killed them. And she needed no telling, though a small dark girl broke away from an inspanned wagon, standing solitary beneath the trees, to cry the news aloud, that the dam was dry.

In the bitter wind of winter drought, which all day long had blown across the veld, these barren trees, this empty sunbaked hollow gaping to the indifferent heavens, this eager child triumphant with disaster, brought desolation to old Alie as it had never been brought to her in the familiar world of the Verlatenheid. Yet she gave no sign that her strength of mind and of body were well-nigh spent, but, wheeling the donkeys off the road began patiently to outspan. As she did so there came towards her from the wagon a tall dark man smoking a pipe, and a cheeful round-faced woman carrying a child in her arms.

These strangers gave her greeting, and the man, beginning at once to help her, fell into easy friendly talk. It was true, he said, that there was no water in the dam, and never before had any man seen it so. If Mevrouw needed water and food for her donkeys and sheep there was none to be had until one reached the coffee-house in Hermansdorp. But it was clear that Mevrouw could take her sheep and donkeys no farther now. Let her rest then at the fire he had made for his wife, and which they were just leaving, and he would see what he could do for her.

Old Alie thanked him, and asked his name. He was, he said, Jan Nortje, bijwoner to Mijnheer Ludovic Westhuisen of Leeukuil, and this was Marta his wife. He had been to the dorp on business for his master and was now on his way back to the farm. Had Mevrouw come from far, and had she far to go? It looked to him as if she had made a hard journey.

From Koelkuil in the Verlatenheid, answered old Alie, where but three days ago she had buried her son, the father of her little Koos here. And to Hermansdorp they were now going.

Then surely, said Jan Nortje, Mevrouw had journeyed in sorrow. But let her go now and sit with his wife by the fire and drink coffee and he would see to her donkeys and sheep.

With the numbed docility of utter weariness Alie obeyed him and, holding Koos by the hand, followed Marta to the fire. Here, handing the baby over to the child who had first run out to greet them, Jan Nortje's wife busied herself about her guests, putting coffee and food before them. She was a plump motherly young woman, many years her husband's junior, and in her pleasant soothing voice there was a persuasive kindliness which made old Alie think of her mother's cousin Tan' Betje. Just in the same gentle and pitying way had Tan' Betje mourned over the sorrows of others. Was it but three days ago, asked Jan Nortje's wife, that Ouma had buried her son? Our Father! And this was his only child! And an orphan? Then surely the hand of the Lord had been heavy upon her! But upon whom was His hand not heavy in this bitter time of drought? Throughout all the land was ruin and desolation such as no man living remembered. Turn where one would there was sorrow. Men that had been rich were now poor, and those that had been poor were now starving, taking their children like sheep to be fed at the orphan-house in Hermansdorp. It was to the orphan-house that they had been that day with gifts from Mijnheer and Mevrouw at Leeukuil. The pastor had asked that all who could do so should send food and clothing to the orphan-house for those in need, and several times now Mijnheer had sent Jan Nortje in with the wagon. Was it perhaps to the orphan-house that Ouma was taking the child?

To the orphan-house? repeated old Alie vaguely. No, it was not to the orphan-house she was going. It was to Canter's store. To work there at mattress-making.

Was Ouma then a mattress-maker? asked Jan Nortje's wife in wonder. And where was this Canter's store?

At the head of the Kerk Straat, answered old Alie. Close by the gaol.

Was Ouma sure?

Sure? asked old Alie sombrely. How could she be but sure? Had she not worked there with her mother's cousin Tan' Betje?

In her answers, as in her silence, there was that quiet aloofness which had so baffled Mijnheer Bezedenhout, and Jan Nortje's wife said no more. There was no such store as Canter's in the Kerk Straat, nor had there ever been within her memory. But who was she that she should disturb the faith of old age? In Hermandsdorp Ouma must surely have friends, or why should she go there? And they would see how it was with her ... She turned smiling, to the boy. His little eager face was pinched with hunger and cold, but his eyes were bright, his spirit still adventurous, his safety still assured. For him, she knew, Canter's store was where his grandmother said it was – at the head of the Kerk Straat, close to the gaol. And who was she that she should disturb the faith of childhood?

She had turned to more practical matters and was packing some food into a canister for Ouma and the boy when Jan Nortje rejoined them. He had, he said reloaded Mevrouw's cart so that its weight should be more evenly balanced, and he had done what he could for her sheep, but it was doubtful if more than four of them could reach the dorp. As things were Mevrouw had better spend the night here and set off again at dawn. He wished much that he could have done more for her, but doubtless in Hermansdorp she had friends who would help her. And now, as it was already late, he himself must be moving ...

When Jan Nortje and his wife had left them and the sound of their wagon wheels had died away into the swiftly gathering darkness old Alie settled down with the boy before the fire. Warmed and comforted he soon fell asleep, but for her there was no sleep, no escape from her weariness, no relief to her melancholy. Throughout the long night pain crept through her body with the quiet gentle insistence of a slowly rising tide. By no effort of will and no physical means within her power could she stem it. In her discomfort her mind fell into confusion of thought for the future and memory of the past. It was now Tan' Betje's voice that she heard, speaking of work to do for Canter's store. It was now Jan Nortje's wife who spoke, telling of the orphan-house in Hermansdorp. Out of the darkness beyond the firelight the orphan-house and the store took shape in her thoughts, vanished and took shape again as the mirages in the veld had done in the heat of the previous noon. When dawn came it was in weariness of body and with mind unrested that she roused herself to the labours of a new day and set off for the coffee-house.

The coffee-house in Hermansdorp, one of the oldest houses in the village, was a long, gabled, yellow-washed building at the lower end of the Kerk Straat. Its yard stood open to the street, and here, as in the market-square, carts and wagons were outspanned by those who came to the dorp for the quarterly Sacrament or the weekly market. In good seasons Andries Geldenhuis and his wife did brisk trade with their coffee and cakes, but in this time of drought there were few with money to spend, and those who outspanned at the coffee-house now were those who had been driven in distress from their lands to seek help from their church, or relief from the government. Among these, when she reached the village at noon, old Alie with her grandson, her rough, unpainted cart, her exhausted donkeys and famished sheep, took her place almost un-noticed. Only with Andries himself did she have speech. And to him, when her sheep and donkeys had been watered and fed, she said briefly that she had business at the head of the Kerk Straat: that tomorrow she would be selling her sheep and her donkeys at the morning market: and that after the sale she would pay him what was due.

In spring, when the pear-trees which lined it were in blossom against the dark background of the enfolding hills, the wide straight Kerk Straat in Hermansdorp had an enchanting beauty, and it was in spring that, as a young girl, old Alie had first seen it. Today, like the thorn-trees at the dam, the trees were bare, and the furrows at their roots all waterless. In the open roadway the dust lay deep in ruts, and here, as in the veld, the wind which raised the dust in stinging blinding clouds had the bitter cold of winter drought. Against the wind and the flying dust old Alie's progress was slow. There was, it seemed to her now, no part of her body which was not in pain. As she leant on his shoulder for a moment her hand felt hot to Koos through his jacket and shirt. She spoke little, but the boy who had never seen the Kerk Straat in spring and to whom the bare trees, the stir of life, the shops, the houses, the very dust brought an enchantment of their own, was unconscious of her silence. This was not perhaps the Hermansdorp his grandmother had described – but that, as yet, he had hardly realized. Here was romance. Here was adventure. And here still, at his grandmother's side, was safety.

They came presently to a high, long, whitewashed wall and here his grandmother halted. Over the top of the wall the boy could see row upon row of straight slender trees, all a dull rusty brown – cypress-trees killed by the drought. Between the trees, out of his sight, were the whitewashed tombs among which in her youth old Alie had wandered. But what had been a garden to her then was now a wilderness in the drought and she turned heavily away.

Beyond the graveyard came the church and the parsonage, and dwelling-houses set back in deep gardens or built close on the street with *stoeps* slightly raised above the side-walk. Fifty years had brought little change to these, but at the upper end of the street where the business of the dorp was carried on, only the old whitewashed gaol was as she remembered it. And here, when at last they reached the grey stone buildings which now surrounded the gaol, she searched for Canter's store in vain. That it still existed she could not bring herself to doubt. And as the signs above the doorways meant nothing to her – for without Tan' Betje's help she could not spell them out – she entered the building which stood, as far as she could judge, where Canter's once had stood and asked to see the master.

A young man was appealed to and came forward pleasantly to ask what he could do for her. She said again that she wished to see the master, and was told that he himself was the master.

Was his name Canter? she asked. And was answered that it was Isaacs.

Was not this then Canter's store?

The young man repeated that it was Isaacs's. There was, he said, no Canter's store in Hermansdorp nor any family of that name, though there might well have been before his time. But what was it that she had wished to buy at Canter's store? No doubt, whatever it was, he himself, Isaacs, would be able to supply it.

Old Alie answered that she had not come to buy but to seek for work. Many years ago she had worked here, at Canter's store, at mattress-making, and it was such work she sought now. Could Mijnheer perhaps employ her?

That, said the young man, was impossible. Mattresses were sent to him ready-made from wholesale stores in Cape Town, and no stores in Hermansdorp now made their own. But was she sure that there was nothing he could sell her? Prints? ... Calicoes? A warm shawl, let down in price because of the drought? A coat for the boy?

There was nothing. Aloof, patient, giving no sign of the blow that had fallen upon her, old Aie waited for the young man to cease, then bade him a quiet good-day and left the store.

Out in the wind-swept street she paused, and the boy, conscious for the first time of some hesitation in her movements, looked up at her anxiously. In the store he had heard nothing of the young man's talk with his grandmother, for his mind had been held by the strange and wonderful things displayed around him there. But now suddenly, in his grandmother's hesitation, came his first hint of insecurity, and with it romance died out of the long bare Kerk Straat in which they stood forlorn. Quickly his hand slipped again into hers. She looked down upon him vaguely, strangely, and saying no word moved heavily down the street.

Against the wind, on their way to the store, their progress had been slow, but it was slower than ever now. What now must she do for the child? Where now must she turn for work? Andries Geldenhuis had said that in the morning market donkeys were sold for a shilling and less, for who in this drought could afford to feed donkeys? And sheep, he had said, in such poor condition as hers, could bring her but little more. When these and the cart were sold she would have money perhaps for a few day's shelter and food at the coffee-house – but afterwards? . . .

She could not see what was to come afterwards . . . Yet the boy must have food. At Tan' Betje's little house there had always been food. Good food. If she could find Tan' Betje's house now there might still be people there who remembered her – Betje Ferreira, the mattress-maker. And they, perhaps, might help her . . .

In their slow progress they had come now to the opening of a lane which ran from the Kerk Straat to the upper street, and it was up such a lane that Tan' Betje had lived. Right at the head of the lane the house had stood . . . and to the head of the lane she would go.

To the head of the lane they went in silence – and came not to the whitewashed green-shuttered house of Betje Ferreira, the mattress-maker, but to a plain double-storeyed building in a bare wide playground. Here boys and girls together, some Koos's age, some older and some younger, were playing at ball. In a corner of the playground, against a sunny wall, sat a young girl of twenty, sewing. From time to time the children appealed to her in their play, or were joined by her in their laughter. In the cookhouse, close to the main building, the midday meal was being prepared, and from the house itself come the clatter of plates being set out on a long trestle table by a coloured girl who sang at her work.

Slowly, as she halted with Koos in front of the fence, these sights and sounds impressed themselves upon old Alie's mind. The talk of Jan Nortje's wife came back to her. This, then, was the orphan-house. This, then, was where the children of the poor were taken to be fed . . . At first her mind grasped nothing but this . . . Then slowly she began to reason. If she could not find work how could she feed Koos? And where was she to find work in a place where mattresses were no longer made? How was she now to plan for the child? He, too, like these others, must have food. And here, for the asking – had not Jan Nortje's wife said it? – was food.

For herself old Alie had at that moment no thought. What she herself would do if she left the boy here, and where she herself would turn for food were questions which simply did not arise in her mind. Nor, in her ignorance of the ways of the world, did it occur to her that certain formalities might have to precede a child's acceptance at the orphan-house. With no note from the pastor, no order from any of those who supported the orphan-house, but with Koos's hand held close in her own, she pushed open the gate and entered the yard.

From the seat against the wall the young girl came forward quickly to greet her. Had Mevrouw come to leave the child with them? she asked. The pity then was that Juffrouw Volkwijn was not here to receive him. Only she herself, Justine de Jager, was here – in charge for the day. But if it was all in order that the child was to come to them, would Mevrouw leave him and come again herself in the evening to see Juffrouw Volkwijn? Would it suit Mevrouw to do so?

She spoke at a rush, giving no pause for answer. That old Alie had come with the necessary note of admission she never doubted and did not stop to question. Her eager nature had little time for formality of any kind. Let Koos – Koos was his name? Koos van Staden? – let Koos take his place as the children lined up for the midday meal – the bell was just about to ring – and let Mevrouw come again in the evening...

As she spoke the bell rang. Instantly the children ceased their play and formed into line, the girls in one row, the boys in another. Taking him quickly but not unkindly by the shoulder Justine pushed Koos into place at the end of the row of boys. At a sharp word of command from her the girls filed into the house, the boys followed. At the doorway Koos lagged, looking back in bewilderment and appeal to his grandmother. Again Justine seized him by the shoulder and pushed him into the room before her. The door closed, but through the open windows old Alie could hear the tramp of feet on the bare carpetless floor: then silence: then the raising of sweet clear shrill voices in the children's grace – 'Thanks to our Father now we give' ... She turned and made her way with slow heavy steps to the gate.

It was long past the dinner hour when old Alie at last reached the coffee-house and crossed the yard to her outspanned cart. As she passed them two women seated near a wagon gave her greeting. She made no answer. The women exchanged glances. Who was she then, this old woman who was too proud to return their greeting? For a moment or two they watched her curiously, resenting, as Mijnheer Bezedenhout had resented, her aloofness – then fell again to their talk.

Unaware of their glances as she had been of their greeting old Alie sat down on her low folding-stool. The pain which had racked her limbs throughout the previous night and throughout the morning had given way now to a numbness which made it difficult for her to control her movements, and she sat awkwardly on the stool, seeking such support as she could get from the wheel at her back. Her hands lay idle on her lap, and from the depths of her black calico sunbonnet her dark eyes looked out upon a world that was growing each moment more strange and unreal to her. It was not the coffee-house yard that she saw. It was the Verlatenheid: it was the orphan-house: it was Canter's store: it was Tan' Betje's little house with the pear-tree in the yard. But always, whatever it was, it was Koos's face turned towards her in bewilderment and appeal – adding sorrow to her sorrow ... The young girl, Justine, ought not to have parted them so, closing the door between them. But surely she had meant no harm. And presently, when it came towards evening, she, Alie, would go back to the orphan-house and explain to him that she must leave him there until she found work ... Just a little while she would leave him, and then, when she had found work, she would come for him again and they would go together to Tan' Betje's little house. Up some other lane it must be, but she would find it. A little house with green shutters and a pear-tree in the yard ... buckets under the pear-tree ... and coir spread out in the sun ...

Once again the bent fingers began to play in her lap – teasing the coir as once long ago she had teased it: dipping it into the bucket at her side: shaking it: teasing it: spreading it out in the sun to dry ...

One of the women seated by the wagon, chancing to look up, saw this strange play, watched it for a moment, then rose and ran towards the cart. She shook old Alie's shoulder gently and spoke to her.

'Ouma, are you ill? Are you ill then, Ouma?'

Old Alie did not hear. A little while longer she played with the coir – teasing it, plucking it – then at last her fingers grew still.

Sarah Gertrude Millin

A Sack for Ninepence

from *London Mercury* 17 (101) 1928

The tall native, with his dirty shirt and trousers, the colour of mud, with his greenish-brown coat and dusty peppercorn hair and bare feet, stood in the dock, and his eyes were concentrated on the interpreter. The interpreter was translating to him the judge's concluding remarks to the jury:

'... On the other hand, gentlemen, you must bear in mind, as the learned counsel for the defence has pointed out, that when a native says he will kill a man, he is not necessarily threatening to take his life. He may only mean that he will hurt him. The expression, "You shall not see the sun tomorrow" is another such exclamation of rage which may have no real significance. Moreover, it must be remembered that the principal testimony against the prisoner is that of his wife, Masangape, who has lost her child, and who has been badly treated by him. The matter of the stone has not been satisfactorily explained, yet there is no evidence that the prisoner placed it where it was found, nor did anyone see the burning of the hut. The child is dead. The man who wore the sack is dead. All the inhabitants of the hut are dead. Only Masangape, the wife, is here to tell the story of that day and night. It is for you to say whether you believe Masangape, and whether in the light of the other evidence I have outlined to you, you think the prisoner committed this crime. If you find the evidence insufficient to establish his guilt beyond reasonable doubt, it is your duty to find him not guilty. Consider your verdict ...'

Pepetwayo listened to the interpreter, but he could discover no meaning in the judge's words. The jurymen scrambled to their feet. The judge gathered together his red robes and stood up, and, as he did so, the people in court – mostly natives – rose. The policeman touched the prisoner's arm. The prisoner gave a start, looked round with rolling eyes and, on the policeman's word, began hurriedly to descend the steps that led from the dock to the cells below.

He was still thinking about the sack.

2

This was the story of the sack:

Pepetwayo had married his wife when she was a widow with a year-old child. And it was now seven years since their marriage, and this child she had borne by another man was still the only child in their hut. Pepetwayo spoke to her about it often, and sometimes he beat her. He consulted a witch-doctor and he fought men who made jokes, but the days passed and the days passed and forever he had to father only this child of the dead man.

He grew to hate the child with a terrible deep hatred. He could not bear to see the small white teeth crunching the bread for which he had to break his back hauling up stones on the Transvaal diamond diggings. In summer Gule ran naked, but this winter he had been bought a thick cotton singlet, and Pepetwayo could not rest his eyes on it without wanting to tear it from the boy's back. He could not keep his voice from scolding him or his hands from striking him. He said to Masangape in their speech: 'Send Gule away, or there will be great trouble.'

She decided finally to bestow Gule on some friends in a neighbouring hut. It was, like all the other huts, a circular construction of rags and reeds and mud, a dozen feet in diameter, with no opening for entrance or exit but a flap of sacking. It stood, surrounded by a reed fence, on the side of a low, stony hill, a little apart from the rest of the location where Masangape lived with her husband. In the whole of that location there was no tree or flower or blade of grass. There was no well for water. Little girls, with tin cans on their heads, walked three miles to fetch the muddy water of the Vaal River. Only on the top of the hill there grew, near the half-hearted and abandoned beginnings of a stone wall, a few prickly pears, and, when the sun went down in a flare of scarlet scribbled with fire, these bold and fleshy weeds leaned against the sky in black relief, and the huts themselves clung together like the hives of gigantic wasps.

In this hut there were already five people maintained on the sixteen shillings a week earned by the head of the household. But no native ever questions the right of a fellow-tribesman to share with him, and Gule was accepted without bargain or comment.

Yet only for a few days was there peace in Pepetwayo's home. It happened that he returned from his work on the diggings and Masangape was not there. Where she was he knew, of course. But he particularly resented her absence this evening because he was happy, because he wanted her to exult with him over a bargain. He had bought a grain-sack from the shop for ninepence when everyone knew that the price of one so large as this was always a shilling. But he had said to the store-keeper: 'Look, Baas, how poor I am, and how the weather is cold. I want this sack to wear on my body to keep the wind out. But it is Monday today and I have just this ninepence, and why shall such a great person as the Baas wait till next Saturday for only a little threepence? Let the Baas give me the sack for ninepence.'

And, actually, the Baas had done it, and Pepetwayo loved the sack as if it were a trophy in a game he had won.

Now he wanted his wife to open the sides for him and cut a hole for his head so that he might wear it against the cold. He could work better with his hands than she could – he had in his day sewn together the skins of jackals with sinew to make those great rugs which are called karosses – but it simply was his desire that she should do this thing for him.

And the hut was empty. There was no fat-soaked mealie-meal cooking in the tripod pot. His belly was fainting against his backbone, for he had eaten nothing all day except, at twelve o'clock, a piece of bread. There was no one to share his triumph about the sack.

He flung it down in a corner of the hut, and rushed over to the neighbours who housed Gule.

There his wife sat chattering with other women. There his wife's child ran about playing with other children. The air was leaping with gaiety. The terrific smell of sheep's head and trotters cooking in a tripod pot attacked his nostrils ...

He thought of his quiet hut, of his unused pot, of the absence of small, rotund, black bodies and rushing noises and high laughter in his yard, of his bargain of a sack lying rumpled, unhailed, in a corner, and he ran up to his wife and jerked her up by the shoulder and shouted awful words at her and dragged her home.

He beat her when they got home, and would not eat, and would not let her make in the hut the smoky fire of dung and sticks with which they kept themselves warm in the winter nights. And throughout the black hours, wearing still the clothes they used by day, they lay side by side on the goatskins which separated them from the naked earth, covered with two cotton blankets, bitter, hostile, and yet drawn together by the cold.

In the morning Pepetwayo went to work as usual, a white scurf of frost in his face and hands. And when he was gone, his wife packed her belongings into the sack she found lying in the corner and left him, to go and live in the hut that sheltered also her child.

3

Pepetwayo was hungry and tired and cold all day long. And for this he blamed his wife and her child. If his wife had not neglected him the night before to go to see her child, he would have had something in his belly, he thought, he would have slept in the night, he would have been able to wear the sack today against the whipping wind. He could not forget the animation in the other people's yard.

In the evening he walked towards the location, picking up here and there as he went along a stick for the fire. But again, as he reached home, no smoke rose to greet him, and he saw soon enough that Masangape was gone, and her belongings. He stood in the hut looking at he knew not what, and suddenly he remembered his sack. Where was his sack? Had she had the effrontery to take his sack, to steal his sack for which only the day before he had paid ninepence ... not a shilling, as was usual, but – a bargain, a diplomatic achievement – ninepence?

Once more he ran along to the other hut. This time there were no visitors in the yard, only the inhabitants of the hut were present, and his wife was sitting, silent, in their midst. She was frightened. She could not live with her husband any more, and she did not know what he would now do to her.

But he entered in among them shouting the word 'sack'.

'Give me my sack. What have you done with my sack?'

He pulled his wife up by the stuff of her dress between her shoulders. 'You –'

His eyes fell on the child.

'He shall not see the sun tomorrow!' he cried. 'There will not be cause for you to leave me again. Where is my sack?'

His wife looked at him dumbly.

He let her go, for his eyes had seen something. There was a man barely visible in the smoke-filled hut and he was wearing a baggy garment over his shoulders. Pepetwayo sprang at the man, and they struggled towards the yard. He could see now, in the last light of the day, that the man was the brother of Gule's protector, and that here was his very sack.

He attempted to pull it from the man as they fought. 'You shall not,' he panted, '– none of you – see the sun tomorrow.'

The sack was torn. His own clothes were torn. People flung themselves forward and separated them. He threatened to kill his wife if she did not come back with him. She walked beside him, weeping.

And, as on the night before they lay down together on the ground in the small, dark hut.

But this time, in the middle of the night, Pepetwayo got up, and began fumbling about the hut.

His wife lay still, listening to his movements. Then she felt that – something – was happening. Terror filled her.

'Pepetwayo! What are you doing?'

'Nothing,' he said, in a voice unexpectedly peaceable.

She heard the rattle of matches as in the dark he put his hand on the box.

Now he went outside. She sat up.

'Pepetwayo! Where are you going? Pepetwayo!'

He came back to the hut.

'Lie still. I will be here again in a minute.'

She began to moan.

'Are you mad?' he said. 'Be quiet. I am not going to leave you for long. Wait for me. Don't make this noise. If I do not find you here when I come in I will kill you.'

She drew the blankets over her head, and lay waiting and shivering.

He was gone for minutes – for an hour.

When he returned he put his arms round her.

'I am happy again. Let us sleep,' he said.

4

In the morning the hut that contained Gule and the man who had worn Pepetwayo's sack and four other people was found burnt down, and everyone in it was dead. A stone was lying against the flap that was the only opening to the hut, and the inhabitants had thus been fastened in while the old sacks and reeds of which the hut was made burnt round them and over them.

Masangape was led, screaming, to the police-station to tell her story. Pepetwayo was arrested. 'I know nothing,' he said. The police did not question him, and when, towards the end of the six months that intervened before his trial his young counsel came to talk with him he maintained firmly: 'I know nothing.'

At the trial he was not put in the box. And when he gathered dimly that the defending advocate was explaining to the jury how ridiculous it was that a man should kill six people for the sake of an empty sack, he nodded his head slightly. Yes, that was wise tale. 'I need not inform you, gentlemen,' the advocate continued, 'how often native huts are burnt down, or how often sleeping natives are suffocated because the fire made for warmth has not been removed ...'

The judge addressed the jury. Pepetwayo was led back to his cell. The jury went away to deliberate.

They returned presently. The prisoner was once more prodded up the steps to the dock. The judge, who had retired, resumed his seat on the bench. The people in court duly stood up and sat down.

The registrar addressed the foreman of the jury.

'Have you considered your verdict?'

'We have.'

'Are you all agreed?'

'We are.'

'What is your verdict?'

'Not guilty.'

The judge addressed Pepetwayo. He put the facts as he saw them before the jury, though it was reasonably clear to him that Pepetwayo had committed the crime. However, they had apparently considered the evidence insufficient.

He sat up and looked at Pepetwayo from under his heavy brow. 'The jury have found you not guilty. You may go.'

'You may go,' the interpreter translated.

The policeman tapped his shoulder.

'You may go.'

Pepetwayo looked from one to the other. What had happened? Was he free? He could not believe it.

'Hurry up,' said the policeman.

The native did not move.

The policeman pushed him. The man began to scramble down as if an hypnotic influence were directing him.

Outside the court other natives surrounded Pepetwayo, giving him tobacco to chew, and cigarettes.

He was free. He was a hero. The justice of the white man was a miracle.

He blew out a mouthful of smoke, and in a voice hushed by six months of waiting in gaol, he began to tell his worshipful audience about this sack, worth a shilling, which he had bought for ninepence, and which had been given by his wife to the brother of the man who had sheltered Gule.

R. R. R. Dhlomo

Murder on the Mine Dumps

from *The Sjambok* (1930)

Those who slept in room thirteen seemed worried and anxious as though something was at the back of their minds. Their eyes were fixed on the compound gate; they kept looking at it and now and then uttered profane oaths.

What worried them at that gate was the presence of the compound manager. He was standing there waiting for the shift to come off, before he went to his own house. These people knew this; he did this every day. To-night, however, their hearts were very bad. It was the night of their meeting on the mine dump.

Presently the shift was declared off and the compound manager went home. Just as he turned round the corner of the compound, these men left room thirteen one by one. The first made as if he were going to the Jew stores to buy; the second walked slowly in the direction of the dump with his carbide lamp, as though to clean it with sand. The third went on picking bits of dry wood for the good purpose of making a fire in the room.

When eight o'clock struck they had all assembled on the dump. They then followed one another down a deep, dark, narrow tunnel which became wide and gloomy at the bottom, though it was wet and somewhat muddy. They sat down in a semi-circle.

'Men,' began their leader, 'we have come here this night for two things. The first thing is this: the dump on which we now are is our hiding place. It is full of small holes which would help us when we were in trouble with the police. They would not follow us here, even in the day. We can stay here for many months even without passes. We can also put all our stolen things here. No one would think of looking for them here. We can here form all our plans for sending to hell our exploiters.

'Remember, men, that this dump was piled here by our blood. You hear that, fools? By our blood! Keep that in your minds so that on the great day you will know that you are fighting for your rights as all civilised men have had to fight.'

'We hear you well, Sipepo.'

Sipepo glared at them and then spat angrily on the ground. They listened silently. Fear did not allow them to speak. They were mine workers these boys. But from some foolish meetings which they had attended they had been impressed by the idea that they should rise as one man and make the white people feel the pinch, too, as they felt it. They now hated white people.

So every evening they made it their African duty to meet on the mine dump and talk of what they would do to 'down the rich people who exploited them'. They had appointed Sipepo as their leader because it was he who went to those meetings and knew what was meant by 'exploitation' and 'revolutions'.

In these meetings Sipepo was always impressed by the words: 'Passive resistance', 'Down with tools', or 'to hell with our exploiters – the capitalists!'

So he had formed this gang for his own purposes.

'Now open your ears,' began Sipepo. 'There is a great thing I want you to see tonight. You know that in these past days our compound manager nearly sacked me for going to the meetings on Sunday? You know, too, that the induna knows that we have joined the meetings in town and that we also want to spread the spirit of burning passes here in the compound on the day of Dingane. Who tells these people all these things? Eh, You don't know. I know and I'll make you know to-night, true – follow me!'

They followed him along a narrow, muddy tunnel, their hearts beating with fear and wonder.

'Blow out your candles!'

They did so.

'We are now out of our hole,' said Sipepo. 'Do you see that small white spot there which looks like water?'

'We see it, Sipepo,' they said in answer.

Sipepo their leader, laughed a funny, bad laugh. Into his eyes came a wild light.

'You have not seen it. You are about to see it well. Sit down here. Yes, speak as much as you like, policemen never come up here.'

They sat down, their lungs lifted, as the Zulu tongue expressed it.

Sipepo eyed them strangely for five minutes and then said: 'You, July, go straight to that spot and stand on it.'

July, a tall, broadchested Msutu, rose and stood. His brow became a little wet, and his big chest began to move quicker. He tried to smile but the smile died foolishly on his face, for it was he who had told the compound manager that they went to town meetings on Sundays and came back with evil talks about burning passes and refusing to work. This had led to some of the boys losing their work and to others being given blows down in the mine.

Foolishly, July had also divulged to the induna their secret meeting place on the mine dumps. But he had done this under the influence of skokiaan. He was not to blame for that, was he? All these thoughts and others ran swiftly across his mind as he stood trembling before the members of the gang.

There was nothing strange in being told to go and stand on a certain spot upon the dump and yet there was something fearful in the way Sipepo spoke and in the way he looked at him with his blood-shot eyes.

'He is afraid, the Msutu,' said Sipepo quietly. 'What is the use of your fear, July? You are going to stand on that spot to-night – you hear? To-night and now! Go and stand there, do you hear what I say – this dog!'

As July obeyed he thought of his mother, and what she said when he left his father's kraal for the mines:

'July, my child,' she had said, with tears in her eyes, 'where are you going? To Johannesburg? You are my only child. You leave me for the mines – Your death, where you'll come back a man of nothing: full of sickness – ho!'

He had laughed then at his mother's tears. And now? He went slowly towards the patch of mud and stood on it.

'Now,' Sipepo's voice had changed. It was hard and cold like the hissing of a puff adder. 'Look at that bloody Msutu well,' he said.

The others were now greatly excited. They felt that something bad was going to take place. They felt this by looking at Sipepo's face.

Now they looked at July, and their lungs again rose and stood close to their mouths.

'Do you see him?' asked Sipepo laughing.

'Hau, we see him, Sipepo. But he seems to be sinking down. What is it, Sipepo? Isimangaliso Impela.'

'Look at him! Look at him!'

Again they looked at July; and heard his pitiful cry. For July was slipping down the slimy hole. Desperately he tried to jump over to a firmer place, but his feet stuck fast in the mud. When he stretched out his hands to clutch seemingly strong ground, it caved in. Something seemed to be dragging him down ...

Down, down, down, down he sank!

He lifted up his voice and shrieked in terror and bitterness of heart.

'Help me, my fellowmen!' he choked. 'Help me, my kind and good brothers. Help me, please, I am dying!'

Now he was waist deep in the slimes.

Impulsively one of the weak-hearted of the gang rose to his feet, only to be struck on the face by Sipepo's cycle chain. 'Sit down, dog!'

Bleeding and frightened the man fell down beside his trembling fellows.

'Save me, my own brother'!' wept the poor Msutu. 'Help me ... help me ...'

But the slimy mud covered him entirely and he choked to death before the eyes of the gang.

Sipepo laughed and drew strongly on his dagga-filled pipe.

'Now you have seen him die who told all our secrets to the white people. A dog of dogs ... Suka!'

And he spat on the ground.

William Plomer

The Child of Queen Victoria

from *The Child of Queen Victoria and other Stories* (1933)

'Coelum non animum ...

I

A Ford car, rattling its way up a rough road in Lembuland in the most brilliant sunshine, carried two very different people – a hard-bitten colonial of Scotch descent, a trader, MacGavin by name, nearer thirty than forty, with a sour red face, and a young Englishman called Frant who had just left school. It was really very awkward. They did not know what to say to each other. MacGavin thought his passenger was despising him simply for being what he was, and Frant, feeling foolish and useless in contrast with this sunburnt, capable man, made a painful effort to be hearty, and looked inquiringly at the country. The road wound in and out, climbing through grassy hills, with patches of virgin forest here and there, especially in the hollows. There were outcrops of rock, and small tilled fields of red earth, and any number of beehive-shaped huts perched here and there in twos and threes. And there were always natives in sight, with herds of bony cattle and ragged goats. It did not need a specially acute eye to see that the landscape, though picturesque, was overcrowded, and that the whites, coveting the lowlands for sugar-cane, had gradually squeezed the natives up into these heights which were poor in soil, coarse in pasturage, and too full of ups and downs to afford space for any proper attempts at cultivation. Frant looked at the natives, naturally, with some curiosity. He wondered what they were like when you got to know them, and then he wondered if he couldn't say something suitable to MacGavin about them. At last he said:

'It seems a pity the natives haven't got a higher standard of living, then there would be so much more money to be made out of them.'

MacGavin looked at him with the savage expression sometimes to be seen on the faces of the ignorant when confronted with what seems to them a new and difficult and rather mad idea.

'The black bastards!' he exclaimed. 'There's bloody little to be made out of *them*, as you'll pretty soon find out.'

And he violently changed gear. As the car began to strain its way up a steep hill, Frant, vibrating by his side, was glad that the noise of the engine destroyed what would have been a painful silence.

Sons of the 'new poor', young wasters, retrenched civil servants or Indian Army officers, and other mostly misguided wretches, they went to settle overseas – one even heard of suicides, because not everybody is tough enough to stand an absolute change of environment, or frightful isolation in some magnificent landscape. And Frant, lured by advertisements, driven by enterprise, encouraged by supposedly responsible persons, went out like them, only fresh from a public school.

His incipient relationship with MacGavin was not made easier by the practical basis on which it rested, for Frant came to him neither as a partner, nor as a servant, nor as a guest, nor had he paid one penny by way of premium. A committee in London had picked out MacGavin's name as that of a person who had declared himself willing to give a young Englishman free board and lodging and two or three years' training in the art of trading with the Lembus in exchange for nothing but that young stranger's 'services'. MacGavin was in some ways a practical man, and the chance of obtaining a responsible white servant who need be paid no wages seemed to him a good one. Frant had been brought up to be eager to oblige. And that was how they started.

Frant was young – so young that, bumping adventurously along into the heart of Lembuland, he could not help thinking of his former schoolfellows and of how they would have envied him if they could have seen him at that moment. A fatal eagerness possessed him. He was flying in the face of the world, as the young are apt to do, with the finest of ambitions. For some of us when young it does not seem so important that we should be successful in a worldly sense and at once enjoy money and comfort, so that we should try and become our true selves. We want to blossom out and fulfil our real natures. The process is complex, and is obviously conditioned by our approaches to the work we mean to do or have to do in life, by the way our heredity and upbringing make us react to our environment, and especially by our relations with other people. In the long run this affair of becoming a grown-up person, a real person (for that is what it amounts to) is, for most of us, an affair of the heart. We hear a great deal about sex nowadays; it is possible to overestimate its importance, because there are always people who pay it little attention or who apparently manage, like Sir Isaac Newton, to get along, without giving it a thought. But Frant came of a susceptible family. He arrived in Lembuland with a pretty appetite for life, and little knew what he was letting himself in for.

2

The trading station at Madumbi occupied the top of a slope a little back from the road, or track rather, and consisted of two main buildings, the store and the house, about fifty yards apart, and a number of ramshackle outhouses. In front, there had been some attempt at a garden – not much of an attempt, for cows and chickens always roamed about in it, and it was now and then invaded by monkeys. At the back, there was some rough grazing land and a patch of forest that went with the place. The buildings themselves were made of corrugated iron, painted khaki and lined with deal boards, looking out, curiously hideous, on the land which sloped away from them on all sides with streams, and clumps of trees, and grassy spaces like a well-planned park. But Mr and Mrs MacGavin, in settling at Madumbi, had been little influenced by the scenery.

The store itself was lighted only by two small windows and the open door, and as you came in from the strong sunlight it was at first difficult to get your bearings. The place was so crowded with goods that it looked like a cave crowded with all sorts of plunder. Your head bumping against a suspended trek-chain or storm-lantern, you looked up and saw that the ceiling was almost entirely hidden in festoons of kettles and baskets, hanks of Berlin wool, enormous bouquets of handkerchiefs of all sizes and colours, bunches of tunics and trousers interspersed with camisoles, frying-pans, wreaths of artificial forget-me-nots, hatchets and matchets, necklaces and ploughshares. As for the shelves, they were entirely crammed with different kinds of goods, for the production of which a hundred factories had smoked and roared in four continents. All kinds of shoddy clothing and showy piece-goods, brittle ironmongery and china-ware, the most worthless patent medicines, the gaudiest cheap jewellery, the coarsest groceries, bibles, needles, pipes, celluloid collars, soup tureens, hair-oil, notebooks, biscuits and lace curtains rose in tiers and patterns on every side. Certain shelves were full of refuse left over from the war – grey cotton socks made in Chicago for American recruits who had never enlisted, khaki tunics and breeches, puttees, Balaclava helmets and so forth, all ugly and serviceable, made and carried by machinery to contribute to a scene of universal murder, produced in too great quantities, by contract instead of by necessity or impulse, and at last deposited here, so that a profit might be made out of the pleasure these things, by their novelty, gave to the blacks. The whole world seemed to have conspired to make a profit on this lonely Lembu hilltop.

Two doors at the back of the store itself gave access to two other rooms. One was large, and was used for storing reserves of bulky goods – sacks of salt, sugar and grain; ironware; boxes of sweets and soap; besides a profusion of bunches of Swazi tobacco leaves, at least two feet long, their fragrance preserved by an occasional sprinkling with water. It was the custom to give away a leaf or two of tobacco to each adult shopper, and to the young a handful of the cheapest sweets, their virulent pinks and greens and acid chemical flavours promising a quick decay to strong white teeth. The other and smaller room was used as an office, and contained a table, a chair, a safe, and a great accumulation of MacGavin's papers. The window, which received the afternoon sun, would not open, and was always buzzing with flies and hornets in various stages of fatigue. A flea-bitten dog was usually asleep on a pile of unpaid bills in the corner, while the ink, from standing so much in the sun, was always evaporating, so that when one had occasion to write one had to use a pencil.

But all that was only the background. The space before the counter was often thronged with Lembus of all ages and both sexes. The noise was overpowering. They would all be talking at once, some laughing, some arguing, some gossiping, some bargaining, while all the time a peculiarly strident gramophone was playing records of Caruso and Clara Butt. Sometimes an old black woman, nearly blind and nearly naked, her last peppercorns of hair grizzled to a pepper-and-salt colour, and her dry old dugs so long that she could comfortably tuck the ends of them into her belt, might be seen listening to it, with her head on one side, for the first time, uttering occasional exclamations of incredulity (*'Abantu! Inkosi yami! Maye babo!'*) and slapping her scrawny thighs, as she demanded whether the voice was the voice of a spirit.

In another part of the room the only vacant space on the wall was occupied by a pier-glass, before which a group of very fat girls were fond of comparing their charms, to the accompaniment of shrieks of delight. Their main wish was to observe the reflection of their bottoms, partly out of pure curiosity and partly with a view to interesting the men present. Standing among the older customers there were always some children, patiently awaiting their turn to be served with threepennyworths of this and that. Some brought eggs or wild fruit to trade, which they carried in small bowl-shaped baskets on their heads. One might have a fowl under her arm, and a little boy of seven would perhaps bring an enormous scarlet lily, complete with leaves and root.

To say that all this was strange to Frant would be an understatement. It was a new world. Into this exotic atmosphere he was plunged; this was where he had to work; this was what he had to learn. What is called adaptability is little more than freshness and keenness and readiness to learn, and Frant, who had been brought up to obey, made himself completely and at first willingly subservient to MacGavin's instructions. He didn't like MacGavin, and it was plain that he never would do so, but it was also plain that MacGavin knew his business, and Frant's presence at Madumbi was, in theory, a business matter. So he rose early and retired late, working hours that no trade union would approve at a job that needed endless patience and good humour, with diligence and imagination as well. He struggled with a strange language, did accounts, avoided cheating or being cheated (he had been brought up to be honest) and toiled morning, noon and night, without haste, without rest, never for a moment questioning what he conceived to be his duty. And Mac-Gavin, finding that he had to do with an honest and docile and responsible person, confided to his wife that the plan was succeeding beyond his hopes. Very soon, he felt, he would be able to leave Frant in entire charge of the proceedings, while he himself attended to other money-making operations out of doors. Mrs MacGavin was pleased too, because she found she was less often required to help in the store, and could spend more time in the house. Though God knows the store was the pleasanter building of the two.

On his very first afternoon Frant had been given tea on the veranda of the house, in order to afford Mrs MacGavin an early chance of sizing him up, but after that his tea was always sent over to the store. Apart from that he had meals in the house, and he slept in it, and spent part of his Sunday leisure in it as well. There were only four rooms. Frant's own room, nine feet by seven, was oppressively hot, was never properly cleaned, and had a disagreeable smell. The living-room, not large in itself, was so crammed with furniture that one person could with difficulty turn round in it, whereas three people were supposed to eat and sleep and rest in it, quite in addition to the fact that, the house lacking either hall or passage, it had to serve as both. Thus the pattern on the linoleum was in places quite worn away, and behind the front door was a rack bulging with hats, coats and mackintoshes, which gave off a greenish odour of stale sweat, cheap rubber and mildew. The middle of the room was occupied by a large table covered with a khaki mohair table-cloth with bobbles round the edges, and in the middle of that stood a large oil-lamp with a shade of crinkly pink paper. A sideboard held a load of worthless ornaments, and on the walls faded wedding-groups in bamboo Oxford frames alternated with dusty paper fans, cuckoo clocks and fretwork brackets supporting electro-plated vases containing dusty everlasting flowers in process of perishing from dry-rot. With difficulty it was possible to make one's way to a small bookcase which stood beneath a reproduction of a problem picture, showing a woman in evening dress in the fashion of 1907 kneeling on the floor before a man in a dinner-jacket, the whole suffused in a red glow from a very hot-looking fire in the background, and called 'The Confession'. Among the books were several by Marie Corelli, a brochure on the diseases of cattle, and a girlish album of Mrs MacGavin's, in which her friends had written or attempted to draw personal tributes and pleasantries. Had this album been a little more vulgar, it might have been almost a curiosity, but the commonness of colonial schoolgirls in the second decade of this century has scarcely even a period interest. It must be admitted, however, that one contributor had written the following very appropriate wisecrack:

> *Roses are red and violets blue,*
> *Pickles are sour and so are you.*

'Fond of reading?' MacGavin, in an expansive moment, once asked Frant. 'No time myself.'

'Yes and no,' said Frant, who was trying to make up for his education and had a copy of *The Brothers Karamazov* in his bedroom. 'It depends.'

On the table in that front room there was nearly always a fly-haunted still-life consisting of a teapot and some dirty cups, for Mrs MacGavin drank very strong tea seven times daily, a habit which no doubt accounted partly for the state of her complexion. But all day long and most evenings the double doors on to the veranda were open, and there was the view. As the trading station was on the top of a hill and partly surrounded with groves of mimosa trees, the outlook was very fine. Beyond the trees, it could be seen that every depression in the landscape had its rivulet and patch of forest, and that in every sheltered and elevated place there was a kraal of beehive-shaped huts with small fields of grain and roots; cattle were grazing here and there; and in the distance rose range upon range of blue mountains. At first sight it seemed, like so many African landscapes, a happy mixture of the pastoral and the magnificent, but those who lived under its influence came to feel gradually a mingled sense of uneasiness and sorrow, so that what at first seemed grand became indifferent or menacing, what at first seemed peaceful was felt to be brooding, and stillness and quietness seemed to be an accumulation of repressed and troubled forces, like the thunderclouds that often hung over the horizon of an afternoon. Those sunny hills seemed to be possessed by a spirit that nursed a grievance.

3

Frant's approach to the natives was complicated by his character and education, which in some ways helped and in some ways hindered him. As a polite person, he treated them with a good-humoured consideration which they were quite unused to receiving from the whites, but then the whites in Lembuland are an unusually discouraging lot – the way they behave to one another is proof of that. A natural quick sympathy and warmth in his character immediately attracted the natives, who are uncannily quick at character, but at the same time they found a certain reserve in him. It was not that he stood on his dignity with them, but simply that he was a little too conscientious. There were certain vague ideas about the white man's prestige and so on which made him rather careful in his behaviour. He imagined that if he let himself go at all he might in some way damage MacGavin's standing and do harm to the trade, and of course MacGavin, in teaching him the trade, was careful to try and instil various principles about treating the natives firmly. And to MacGavin's credit it may be added that he insisted on the natives being treated as fairly as possible, though this was a matter of business rather than principle with him. And after all, there was no need to tell Frant to be fair – it was clear that though a trifle priggish, he was no swindler. This priggishness of his was easy to account for. It was partly in his nature, but also he had been brought up with certain rigid English ideas about being a gentleman, playing the game, and all that sort of thing, and until now he had had no reason to doubt that they were right. The effect of being abruptly transferred to a completely new environment; of being cut off from those familiar companions and surroundings which had enabled his principles to be taken for granted; and of associating with Mr and Mrs MacGavin, was not to make him doubt those principles but to convince him that they were right. And to be all by oneself and to think oneself right is really rather fatal, especially if one naturally tends to be both straightforward and severe. Already he would receive some of the opinions of MacGavin and his wife in a silence that was even stronger in its effect than the quiet and smiling 'Oh, I'm afraid I can't quite agree with you' which he often had to use in conversation with them.

'He always thinks he's right,' MacGavin remarked to his wife, 'but it doesn't matter about that. What's more important is that the niggers like him. There's a slight improvement in the takings this month, and I shouldn't be surprised if it's partly due to him. He does what he's told for the most part, and I shouldn't be surprised if he turns out a good salesman when he knows the lingo a bit better.'

The Lembu language presents no great difficulties, and it is surprising what good use one can make of a language as soon as one has a small working vocabulary and a few colloquial turns of phrase. Frant enjoyed speaking it, because it is one of those Bantu languages which, to be spoken well, have to be spoken with gusto, and it can be both sonorous and elegant. His progress in the language naturally made his work more easy and pleasant, but it had other effects – it drew him closer into sympathy with the Lembus, and showed him how little they liked the whites. In fact, he began to realize that the remains of the white man's prestige, in Lembuland at least, rested mainly on fear – fear of the white man's money, his mechanical genius and his ruthless and largely joyless energy – and not on love or respect. And since he himself had very little money, no mechanical genius and a certain joyful vitality, he felt that there must be something rather 'un-white' about himself. This discovery acted directly upon his pride – it made him resolve to treat the natives with as much kindness and dignity as were consonant with his odd position (the ruling race behind the counter!), as if to show that there were still white men who knew how to behave humanely. This made him think himself better than MacGavin and the few other whites with whom he came in touch, and shut him up in a small cell of his own (as it were) closely barred with high principles.

He did not pretend to himself that the Lembus were paragons of virtue. The very fact that as customers in a shop they had a certain right to order the shopkeepers about, added to the fact that these shopkeepers were nominally their 'superiors', was a temptation to some of the natives to be tiresome, cheeky or even insolent, and that was one reason why a great deal of persevering good temper was needed in dealing with them. By the time they had convinced themselves that Frant was both patient and cheerful he had already begun to get a good name amongst them. They were used to MacGavin, whom they thought of as a beast, but a just beast, and finding Frant just without being a beast, and youthful and personable as well, they undoubtedly began to come to Madumbi in greater numbers.

At first he had been much struck by the extreme suspiciousness and diffidence of the customers. They never entered the place with that air of cheerful confidence which, in the dreams of good shopkeepers, is found on every customer's face. On the contrary, they always seemed to come in expecting the worst. Many an old, wild woman, skirted in skins, smeared with fat and ochre, hung with charms, a bladder or an antelope's horn suspended at her neck, her hair dressed high and stuck with bone ornaments, a snuff-box at her waist, perhaps having about her too a couple of pounds, every penny of which she meant to spend, would pause in the doorway with a roving eye and an expression of extreme disillu-

sionment and contempt, as though she found herself there unwillingly
and by chance. After some time she would perhaps help herself to a
cupful of water from a tank that stood at the door, and would then sit
down in the shade and take a lot of snuff with immense deliberation, the
expression on her face seeming to say, 'Well, here I am, and I don't give a
damn for anybody. I haven't lived all these years for nothing. Experience
has taught me to expect the worst of every situation and every person,
particularly if he or she happens to be white. If I condescend to do any
shopping here, I mean to see everything, and to have exactly what I want
or nothing at all. Don't think you can swindle me, because you can't.
However, I shall proceed on the assumption that you mean to try, that
all your goods are damaged, that you're a cunning profiteer, and that
you think I'm a fool.' And when at last she deigned to enter the store,
she would proceed accordingly.

But it was not only old women who were so much on their guard.
Many and many a customer would show the same symptoms of a deep
and cynical mistrust, walking in as if they were threading their way
among mantraps all carefully set for them. Even children would show
plainly how they had been forewarned, repeating innocently the last par-
ental injunctions, and carefully counting their change from sixpence.
And all this was not due to MacGavin but to the reputation which the
white overlords of Lembuland had managed, in the course of two or three
decades, to build up for themselves.

If for Frant this unpleasant relationship between the two races was one
of his earliest and most enduring impressions, even stronger was that of
the immediate physical presence of the Lembus. So many more or less
naked bodies of men and women, coloured a warm brown, smooth-
skinned and mostly graceful, with white teeth, straight backs and easy
manners, do not leave one, when one is young and susceptible and unfamiliar with them, exactly indifferent.

'Don't worry about the stink,' MacGavin had said. 'You'll get used to
it.'

Stink? The whites always say that the blacks have a bad smell. Well,
there at Madumbi was a confined space usually tightly packed with natives, but although the weather was hot and the air sometimes scarcely
moving, it could not have been said that the smell was much more than
strange, though to Frant it was heady, like the very smell of life itself,
and excited him with a promise of joys not yet tasted. The wholesome
smell of an out-of-door race cannot in any case seem unpleasant, except
to diseased nerves, and the lightly clad or unclad bodies of the Lembus
are continually exposed to sun, air and water, while they are almost as
vegetarian as their flocks and herds. If some of the old women were a

little inclined to accumulate several layers of ochre and fat all over them by way of skin treatment, they were quite amusing enough in their manners and conversation, and had quite enough natural style, to make up for it. At Madumbi there was a far more oppressive smell than that of the natives, and that was the combined aroma of the dressing that stiffened the calicoes of Osaka and Manchester into a dishonest stoutness, and, to speak figuratively, of the sand in the sugar.

4

In places like Madumbi, time seems more of a thief and enemy than in crowded cities or even in circles where the months are frittered away in useless leisure. In that part of Lembuland the changing of the seasons is less marked than in the highlands, and at Madumbi life was a packed routine; work began at half-past five or six in the morning; fatigue often precluded thought; and the tired eyes, turning towards clock or calendar, would close in sleep. Sometimes all sense of chronological sequence was lost; sometimes it seemed almost as if time were going backwards; and now and again Frant would realize with a shock how many weeks or months had slipped by since this or that trifling break in his existence. But he was not discontented, for he was interested in his work, not so much for its own sake as for the close contact with some of the realities of human nature into which it brought him.

There were certain things which he could never sell without a smile. Now and then a young Lembu would come in and say rather furtively, '*Amafuta wemvubu akona na?* That is to say, 'Have you got any hippopotamus fat?' Whereupon Frant used to go to the small showcase in which the medicines were kept, and produce a small bottle with a label bearing a Lembu inscription, and underneath, in very small letters, PEDERSEN'S GENUINE HIPPO FAT. This commodity looked like ordinary lard, probably was ordinary lard, was put up by a Norwegian chemist in Dunnsport, and sold for a shilling a bottle. It was used for a love philtre, and helped the manufacturer to maintain his son at a theological seminary in Oslo. But other 'lines' were more lucrative than hippo fat. Love philtres, after all, were usually only required by the young and romantically inclined, whereas PEDERSEN'S BLUE WONDERS, as another Lembu inscription testified, were indispensable to both young and old. Certainly they were always in demand. Pills as large as peas and the colour of gun-metal, they were not merely an infallible, but a powerful aphrodisiac. When MacGavin happened to be asked for either of these medicines, he would never sell them without a clumsy pleasantry, a habit which had resulted in a falling-off of the sales of the hippo fat, for the younger natives, though their morals, according to some standards, were not above reproach, had their finer feelings. However, his misplaced humour did not much affect the demand for Blue Wonders, which were usually bought by customers of a coarser fibre. Mrs MacGavin herself came to lend a hand in the store when business was brisk, and it would sometimes happen that she would be called upon to serve a customer with these things, which she would do with the grimmest face in the world – her expression might well have suggested a subject for an allegorical picture, 'Avarice overcoming Chastity'. But still, out of all the hotchpotch that the store contained, there was one kind of goods which she would neither buy nor sell. The male natives of those parts were in the habit of using a peculiar kind of *cache-sexe* made of the leaves of the wild banana. At Madumbi these were made, in assorted sizes, by an old vagabond of a native who sold them to MacGavin at wholesale prices. When he came to the store it was always at some odd time, when there was nobody else about, either on a very hot afternoon or just after the store had been locked up, or at dawn, or when the moon was rising. If he saw MacGavin, the business was soon settled. If he encountered Mrs MacGavin, he would wave his bundle of unmentionables right under her nose, saluting her with his free hand and uttering all sorts of highflown and wholly ironical compliments before crying the virtues of his wares. Nothing annoyed her more, as he very well knew. She always told him rudely to wait for her husband. If it was Frant he chanced to find, he would say with real politeness, '*Sa' ubona, umtwana ka Kwini Victoli!*' Greetings, child of Queen Victoria! This became shortened later to 'Child of the Queen' and at last simply to 'Child'. The very first time he had seen Frant he had said, 'Ah, I can see you're a real Englishman from *over there*,' and since England suggested Queen Victoria to him more than anything else it was not hard to account for the complimentary title. The old man, to whom Frant always gave an extra-large leaf or two of tobacco, was also fond of saying that the *amaBhunu*, the Boers, were 'no good', which was partly his real opinion and meant partly as a piece of indirect flattery, though as Frant had not had anything to do with any Dutch people it was not particularly effectual.

'How can you allow that dirty old swine to call you "child"!' exclaimed MacGavin.

'Why, he's old enough to be my grandfather!' Frant retorted.

Frant's point of view seemed so fantastic to MacGavin that he laughed a short, harsh laugh.

'My advice is, don't stand any cheek from any nigger,' he said.

'He isn't cheeky to *me*,' said Frant. 'Only friendly.'

And with an irritable grunt from MacGavin the conversation was closed. It seemed extraordinary how full of prejudice the trader was. He was fond of generalizations about the natives which were not even remotely true, such as that they were incapable of gratitude (as if they had such a lot to be grateful for!) and he seemed to have a fixed idea that every black is determined to try and score off every white, under any conditions whatsoever. And when, as occasionally happened, a native addressed him politely in English, it made him so furious that he was no longer master of himself – it seemed to him a suggested assumption of equality between the races!

The MacGavins were amazed at Frant's continued progress, and if they welcomed his popularity with the natives as being good for trade, they resented a little that a stranger and a rooinek should be able to beat them at their own game. As to what went on in his mind, they knew and cared nothing. They neither knew nor cared that neither work nor fatigue could prevent him from feeling at times an overwhelming loneliness and an intolerable hunger for experiences which his youth, the climate and the glorious suggestiveness of his surroundings did everything to sharpen, while its satisfaction was firmly forbidden by circumstances – or so it seemed to Frant. Already esteemed by the natives, he valued their good opinion of him too much to take chances with it, and in the background of his thoughts, in spite of the MacGavins, or perhaps because of them, there still presided that tyrannical spectre, the 'white man's prestige'. What it is to be an ex-prefect of an English public school!

5

It was bound to happen that sooner or later his attention would become centred in some individual out of the hundreds he had to do with in the course of a week. One drowsy afternoon, when he was alone behind the counter and there was nobody in the store but a couple of gossips and a child, a young woman came in rather shyly and stood near the door, hesitating to speak. He couldn't see her very well because of the bright sunshine behind her, but he asked her what she wanted and she made a small purchase.

'Do you remember me?' she asked suddenly in a very quiet voice, looking at him gravely while she spoke.

He was surprised. He didn't remember ever having seen her before, but not wishing to offend her, he said in a slightly ironical tone of voice:

'Oh, when I've once seen people, *just once*, I never forget them.'

'Well!' she exclaimed, and uttered a little peal of laughter, partly because she was surprised at his ready answer and amused at his white man's accent; partly because, as a Lembu, she could appreciate irony; and partly because it made her happy that he should talk to her. But as soon as she had uttered that little laugh she grew shamefaced and cast down her eyes with the incomparable grace of a young woman with whom modesty is natural, and not a mere device of coquetry. There was more sadness than usual in her expression, because she had at once understood that he did not remember her, and no woman likes to be forgotten by any young man. She had moved now, and the diffused radiance reflected from the sunburnt hilltop outside shone full upon her through the open door. Her hair was dressed in a cylinder on the crown of her head, stained with red ochre, and stuck with a long bone pin at the broad end of which was a minute incised design; she wore no ornament but a flat necklace of very small blue beads and a few thin bangles and anklets of silver and copper wire. She was dressed in a single piece of dark red stuff which was supported by her pointed young breasts and fastened under the arms – it fell in straight, classical folds almost to her feet, and at the sides it did not quite join but revealed a little her soft flanks. From bearing weights on her head from early childhood she carried herself very erect; she was slender, and an awareness of her graceful nubility gave every movement the value of nature perfectly controlled by art. The fineness of her appearance may have been due to some remote Arab strain in her blood, for though unmistakably negroid, her features were in no sense exaggerated. Her nose, for example, though the nostrils were broad, was very slightly aquiline; her skin was unusually light in tone; and the modelling of her cheeks and temples could only be described as delicate. Her mouth was good-humoured, her eyes were lustrous, and though one side of her face was marked with a long scar, this only drew closer attention to its beauty.

'You don't come here very often, do you?' said Frant, leaning on the counter, partly because he did not want their conversation to be overheard by anybody else, and partly because he felt somehow weak in the legs. He was in the grip of an unaccustomed shyness, he felt unsure of himself, and so excited that his heart was beating very quickly.

'No,' she said, avoiding his eyes. 'I don't live very near.'

'Where do you live?'

'Down there – down in the valley,' she said, extending an exquisite arm and looking out through the open doorway with a vague and dreamy air. He noticed the light colour of the insides of her hands. 'Near the river,' she said.

'That's not very far away,' he said.

'You've been there, then?' she said. 'You know the place?'

'No, but I don't think it's very far.'

'The hill is long and steep,' she said

Frant suddenly remembered two lines of verse –

Does the road wind uphill all the way?
Yes, to the very end.

'I don't know your name,' he said.

She looked at him quickly and uttered an exclamation of surprise.

'What's the matter?' he said.

'Why do you want to know my name?' she asked anxiously, for the use of names is important in witchcraft.

'I'm just asking. I just want to know it.'

'My name is Seraphina,' she said, with a mixture of modesty and seductiveness.

'*What?*'

'Seraphina.'

'How on earth did you get a name like that? It's not a Lembu name! You're not a Christian, are you?'

She laughed, as though the idea of her being a Christian was absolutely ridiculous – which indeed it was.

'No!' she said. 'A missionary gave it to me when I was a child. He made magic water on my head and said that Christ wanted me to be called Seraphina.'

This time Frant laughed.

'Christ chose well,' he said. 'But none of your family are Christians, are they?

'No, it just happened like that.'

He laughed again.

'You don't know my name,' he said.

'Yes, I do,' she said, and pronounced it 'Front', and they both laughed.

Just then some noisy customers arrived, and he had to leave her. Suddenly bold, he said:

'Goodbye, go in peace. Please come again. I like talking with you.'

He couldn't possibly have dared to speak so directly of his feelings in English, but somehow in Lembu it was easier. Besides, he was stirred as he had never been stirred before.

'Goodbye', she said, smiling. 'Stay in peace.'

She turned to go, and looked like some virgin in an archaic frieze saying farewell to the world. As for Frant, his hands were trembling, and there was a wild gladness in his heart.

6

His tortures now began in earnest. His dreams and waking thoughts were haunted by the image of the black girl, tantalising and yet infinitely remote. As his desire for her increased, so did its fulfilment seem to recede. He knew little or nothing of her; he knew little enough of her language and nothing at all of her situation in life. He had been so busy learning to make a profit out of the natives that he had had little chance of learning much about their customs, the way they lived and thought. Supposing, he said to himself, for the sake of argument, this girl were to become my mistress? First of all, is it possible? I am certain that to some extent she reciprocates my feelings, but to what extent? What would she expect of me? What would her family think of her? How would the affair be possible in any case? How am I to communicate with her? And then the MacGavins – presumably his success in his trading depends to some extent on the fact that he is not one of these white men who get mixed up with the natives; and if I were to become the lover of Seraphina, should I not damage his livelihood, besides ruining my own? Whatever happened, everybody would know about it, of course. And how could we live together? Are we to meet furtively in the forest? And have I the right to take this black girl? How can I pretend to myself that I love her? Is it not simply that I want to sleep with her, to touch, kiss, embrace and caress her? He found no answers to his questions, but the very fact that he could ask them was significant. His loneliness and his difficulties had taught him one of the very things that his education had been evolved to prevent – the habit of introspection. He was being Hamletized by circumstances.

Of the numerous forms of anguish which Providence has designed for her creatures few can be more intense than the state of mind and body of a man who is young, sensual by nature and sexually repressed; and who, instead of yielding to the voluptuous provocations of his surroundings, tries to exorcize them with the public-school spirit. When he might well have acted with boldness, he found himself filled with doubts, scruples and equivocations, in addition to the ordinary fears of a lover. And he had nobody to turn to, there was nobody who would say to him what so much needed to be said, 'Well, go ahead and have the woman. You will have your pleasure and she will have hers, and you will both be a bit the wiser and possibly the happier for the experience. You will treat her with consideration, because it is your nature to be considerate. You are in no danger of 'going native', because you aren't the sort of person who goes native. And as for worrying about the MacGavins, do you imagine they worry at all about you, or are likely to do so as long as you rake in the bawbees for them? Be a man! *Carpe diem*, etc.' Lacking such an adviser, Frant continued to torment himself.

Each day he got up with Seraphina in his thoughts. Day followed day, and Seraphina did not appear. Round the trading station, meanwhile, Africa unrolled her splendours and her cruelties. The seasons did not assert themselves overmuch. One waited for the rains to stop, or one suddenly noticed buds among thorns. One was aware, all too aware, of the spring, the season of trouble, when more people die, in all countries, than at any other time of the year. The sap was troubled, and the heart with it. All the mimosa trees at Madumbi broke into pollenous clouds of blossom, creaming in a light wind against the cobalt morning sky. Glossy toucans with scarlet bills nested in them, swooping among the boughs, and uttering the most touching mating-cries. Fireflies went through their luminous rites under a coral-tree; crested hoopoes, the colour of cinnamon, pursued their fitful flight across the clear green of dawn; on long, sultry afternoons a group of turkey-bustards, as grave as senators, would plod grumbling across some grassy plateau, looking carefully for the snakes which they could kill at a blow; raindrops pattered down on leaves as large as tables, magenta-veined; and on dry, tranquil afternoons, when the days were still short and some solitary voice was singing far away, an aromatic smell of burning sweet-grass sometimes drifted through the air, the clear light, and the music, and the odour all playing together on the nerves, and inducing an emotion inexpressibly painful and delicious.

When he was free, Frant could not bear to stay near the house: but in roaming about, which became his habit, he was none the less a prisoner. Fettered by scruples and afflicted with a kind of moral impotence, he wandered in a lovely world from which he was barred almost as effectually as if he were literally in a steel cage on wheels. His troubled eyes turned to the natural scenes around him but found no rest in them, and his repression might just have gone on increasing in morbidity had not a number of unexpected things happened.

Now the arrival of Frant at Madumbi had put a check on certain of MacGavin's habits. At one time, when the Scotchman was alone in the store, in the afternoons for instance, when the weather was hot or wet and business slack, or when his wife was busy in the house, he had not been disinclined for a little amusement at the expense of some of the coarser Lembu girls who came to deal with him. Joking with them in order to try and convert their apprehensive titters into abandoned fits of giggling, he had sometimes gone so far as to pinch their breasts and slap their behinds in order to win their confidence. The bolder ones had quickly taken advantage of his susceptibilities in order to try and get something for nothing, and pointing to this or that, had copied the horse-leech's daughters and cried, 'Give, give!' When MacGavin so far overcame his sense of commercial fitness as to give them a string of beads or a damaged jew's harp, they immediately asked for more, determined to lose nothing for the want of asking. He would then refuse, but they would not go away, leaning on the counter and repeating their requests over and over again in a whining voice until he began to fear that his wife might come in. Whereupon he would suddenly fly into a raging temper. Purple in the face and trembling with anger, he would hammer on the counter with his fists and utter violent threats and abuse, and if that did not frighten the young women away he would hustle them out. One or two in particular loved to provoke him to the utmost, and then fly screaming with laughter down the road, their large naked breasts wobbling and flapping and tears running out of their eyes. But he had grown tired of these scenes, and even before Frant's arrival had abstained from inducing them. With the arrival of Frant he determined to behave himself, at least in Frant's presence, as he wanted the young man to concentrate on business and not begin his stay by getting obsessed with black women. But now that he had found Frant what he could have called 'steady', he was about to revert to his old habits, and it cannot be said that his wife, that freckled virago, with her ever-increasing indigestion and her less and less amiable moods, acted exactly as a strong deterrent.

But the first time Frant saw MacGavin behaving familiarly with a gross fat girl it gave him a shock – not because he was prudish by nature, but because it was something he was not used to, and the discovery that MacGavin did not always practise what he preached seemed likely to modify his own behaviour. The thought immediately occurred to him that MacGavin might abuse the modesty of Seraphina, and the idea that the trader's bloodshot and slightly protuberant eye might focus itself upon her natural elegance produced in him a most violent reaction. He said nothing. After MacGavin's wench had departed he came up to Frant and said:

'You'll excuse my saying so, Frant, but don't you feel you want a woman sometimes?'

The effect of this remark upon the young man was extraordinary.

'I do,' he answered at once in a quiet voice, 'but not a black one.'

And he launched into a flood of abuse! He said that he would rather do anything than touch a black woman; he said that they were dirty, that they stank, that they were not better than animals; he said that the blacks and whites were in his opinion races apart, and that on no account should they mix in any way; he said that white men ought to be respected by black ones, and that that could only be possible if they treated them as inferiors, absolute inferiors. He grew white with passion and the heat of his denunciation. His words almost choked him.

MacGavin was astonished beyond measure. He did not know whether to take it all as an attack on himself, or whether Frant had not gone a little out of his mind.

'Well, you do surprise me,' he said, in what was meant to be a sarcastic tone of voice. 'You've always given me the impression of being a bit too fond of the niggers, and treating them a bit too much as if they were really human beings.'

'I get a bit sick of the sight of them at times,' said Frant in a much quieter voice, not in the least meaning and indeed hardly knowing what he said. Then he turned away, and the incident was closed, except that MacGavin confided to his wife that he thought Frant was getting a bit restless, and perhaps needed a change or a holiday.

'He can surely wait till Christmas,' she said in an aggrieved whisper, for the walls of the house were thin. 'We could take him away with us then for a couple of days. But if you ask me, he's unsociable and disagreeable by nature.'

'Don't forget that the takings showed another increase last month,' said MacGavin.

'That's just why I don't want him to go away now,' she said.

It was a brilliant moonlight night, as quiet as the grave, and in his little room Frant was asking himself what on earth could have made him say a whole lot of things he did not mean, what on earth had made him lose control of himself. He felt he had come to the end of everything, that he could not bear this impossible kind of life any longer, and would have to go away. His head was hot, he could not sleep, and he rolled uneasily on his bed. Suddenly, somewhere in a tree, a galago began to scream. Its screams filled the naked air and the heavy silence, the African silence; scream after scream, like prophecies of endless and unthinkable supernatural horrors, uttered by a furred and furtive little creature, hidden large-eyed among moon-drenched branches. Frant got up from his bed and drew back the curtains on a world chalk-white like the face of a clown or pierrot, silent and heartless, and with a sense of terror, of madness almost, let them fall back again.

And the next day Seraphina appeared.

7

There she stood, balancing on her head a light bundle tied with grass. Her arms hung by her side, and when she turned her head authority and resignation, patience and sensibility were in the movement.

Nowhere but here did ever meet
Sweetness so sad, sadness so sweet.

Before the coming of the white man the Lembus lived under a system of strict discipline and formality, which did not, however, fail to allow various channels for the various passions of the Lembu heart. It was a system which recognised that some of life's best rewards are best appreciated by those who have not been able to win them too easily. In those days they were all warriors under a mad military autocrat, who believed that too easy an access to heterosexual pleasures might impair the morale and efficiency of his regiments; he trammelled them with a hundred taboos and would not allow them to marry young, while adultery was punished by pushing the guilty parties over separate cliffs of no small height. As for the girls and women, they had a most clearly prescribed course of life, and each stage in their development was made to conform to strict rules. The later relaxation of tribal ethics, for which the white man offered little substitute but calico drawers and hymns A. and M., rapidly weakened the fibre of the race. But it still happened that there were members of it who managed to live lives not wholly devoid of order and dignity, there were still families 'of the old school' who from the force of heredity or a kind of good breeding managed to do homage to the ghosts of the beliefs of their forefathers. And such a family was Seraphina's. Both its ancient pride and its present obscurity had gone to the making of her features, and its vigour and vitality as well.

They were alone together in the space before the counter.

'Greeting, Seraphina.'

'Greeting, my white-man.'

Frant could hardly speak, he was so agitated. His heart seemed to fill the whole of his breast with its leaping, and he could scarcely recognize the sound of his own voice as he asked:

'Why have you been so long returning?'

'Do I know?' she said. 'Perhaps I was afraid.'

She had reason to be afraid – of gossip, of her family, of herself, of Frant, of consequences. With an unhurried movement she took down the bundle from her head and laid it on the floor without bending her knees. Then she untied the grass ropes that held it together and began to open it.

'A snakeskin!' said Frant.

It was a broad snakeskin, and crackled stiffly as it was unrolled. She put her foot on the tail to hold it down while Frant unrolled it. Fully opened, it was at least fifteen feet long, and a great part of it was quite two feet in width. It was the skin of a python, and there were two large rents in the middle of the back as if a spear had killed it. It was not often that the natives traded such things.

'How much are you asking for it?' said Frant in a caressing voice most unsuitable for a commercial transaction.

'I am not selling it,' said Seraphina without looking at him. 'I am giving it.'

'Giving it! To me?'

'To you.'

'I thank you very much indeed,' he said. In Lembu the same word means to thank and to praise.

There was a pause, then he said:

'Where did it come from? Who killed it?'

'I was hoeing in a maize-field near the river, and it disturbed me. Besides, two of the children were with me. So I killed it.'

'You killed it! What with?'

'With my hoe.'

When he had got over his astonishment he said, his face shining with admiration:

'But you mustn't give it to me. I must give you some money for it.'

'I don't want money,' she said, and looked at him with troubled, almost angry eyes.

'I thank you very much,' he said again, with the humility and the pride of a lover, and hardly knowing what he was doing he caught hold of her and kissed her on the mouth.

She uttered a cry of surprise and sprang away from him. She simply did not understand him, and was afraid. Natives do not make love as we do. She laughed, just a trifle hysterically.

'What are you doing?' she said.

'What's the matter?' said Frant, approaching again. 'I won't hurt you.'

'How do I know?' she said.

And he would have answered 'Because I love you' (which would have been so hard to say in English and was so easy in Lembu) had they not just at that moment been interrupted.

'Come again soon,' Frant said hurriedly. 'I want to see you.'

And he stooped down and rolled up his snakeskin. When he had finished she was gone.

In the evening he nailed up the skin on the walls of his bedroom. It was so long that it took up the whole of two sides. And very late, before putting out the light, he lay in bed looking at it. Like a banner it hung there to celebrate the intensity of his happiness; it hung like a trophy –

the skin of the dragon of his misery, killed by Seraphina as she hoed her father's field of maize.

The next day at noon Mrs MacGavin said:

'Oh, Mr Frant, that skin in your room – it gave me such a nasty turn when I went in there this morning!'

'Isn't it a beauty? You don't mind my putting it up, I suppose?'

'Oh, *I* don't mind,' she said, 'though I couldn't bear to have such a thing over *my* bed. If there's one thing I can't stand it's snakes, alive or dead.'

It was nearly Christmas time and the MacGavins told Frant they thought a holiday would do him good, and that they would take him with them to the nearest town. The trading station would be closed for three days, and would be quite safe in the care of the servants. They were extremely surprised when he refused – not because he wanted to help to guard their property, but because the nearest town, of which he had had a few glimpses, did not attract him, and because he had other plans in mind. He felt no inclination to attend the gymkhana or the dance at which, in an atmosphere of false bonhomie and commonplace revelry, the white inhabitants tried annually to forget for a time all about the white man's burden. The MacGavins thought him almost mad for refusing.

'Whatever will you do with yourself?' they said.

'I shall be quite happy,' he said.

They felt that something was amiss.

'What, are you "going native" or something?' cried MacGavin. 'You need a change, you know.'

He always did his work well, and on account of his natural air of independence they both respected and feared him a little. They gave up trying to argue with him and murmured to each other instead. Then on Christmas Eve the Ford car, newly washed, went rattling away, leaving behind it a cloud of blue smoke and a stink, both of which soon vanished. After the MacGavins had gone Frant felt greatly relieved. It was such a blessing to be free to see and hear what was going on round him instead of being haunted by those harsh stupid voices, that sour red face and that pasty drab one, which had already got on his nerves. Unlike most white men alone in native territories, he had neither a gun nor alcohol in his possession. He did not feel the want of them. For the first time in his life he was to spend Christmas by himself. There would be no exchange of presents; no heavy meals; no forced gaiety; no stuck-up relations. His time, for once, was his own.

8

On Christmas morning he stood on the veranda and stretched his arms, filled with a delicious sense of anticipation. Then he felt in his pocket for a cigarette, and failing to find one took a key and went to fetch a packet from the store. The atmosphere in that building, so closely shuttered at holiday times, was more than oppressive. It was a brilliant morning, and the heat of the sun on the corrugated-iron roof made the interior like an oven. He found some cigarettes, and paused a moment in the doorway to look round at the place where his days were spent. He shuddered slightly, then went out, locking the door behind him. Enjoying his cigarette, and the sun, and the shade, and the peacefulness of not having to look at *those* faces, of not having to listen to *those* voices, he took a path which led through a deserted garden, on the site of the first set-tlement at Madumbi, towards the forest. In the old garden the founda-tions of the earlier house remained, but the whole place was now a tangle of vegetation. The hardier growths had survived, and some still with-stood the wildings that struggled to oust them. Thickets of ragged junipers and berberis made a forbidding fence which few ever sought to penetrate, and indeed the natives thought the place haunted. Snake apples, those cruel trees, with every bud a barb, and every fruit an ugly bulb filled with dry and poisonous powder, extended their angry foliage over crumbling brickwork. Rankly growing mimosas split with their coarse-grained roots what had once been a path, and month by month in the summer raised their smooth bark and feathery foliage perceptibly higher into the air. A solitary yucca, survivor of several, had produced a single spire thickly hung with white bells, which the mountain wind shook together as if they were made of paper. Tendrils of Christ-thorn put out here and there a few sticky scarlet flowers, and passion flowers hung in unexpected places, in the grass or high up among the junipers, together with the oval, dented granadillas into which they too would change.

Leaving the garden, Frant followed the path to the forest. Then, forcing his way through the undergrowth, parting lianas and monkey-ropes, breaking cobwebs so thick that their breaking was audible, being scratched by thorns, sinking up to the ankles in leaf-mould, he reached a glade he had been to before in times of unhappiness. In the middle of the glade there was a shallow stream of very clear water gliding over sand, and it was sheltered by the vast indigenous trees from the heat of the day.

Here, as he had done before, he threw himself on the breast of earth, surrendering himself to the trees, the water and the quietness. He lay on his back and looked up through half-closed eyes at the topmost branches, watching the fall of a leaf, hearing the call of a bird, the lapse of water, and the thin cries of insects. Under his hand lay a skeleton leaf, over his head a few epiphytic orchids lolled their greenish mouths open over the ancient, rotting bough that gave them life, and at times the wind brought a hint of the perfume of a hidden syringa or laurustinus. A clump of clivia lilies were blooming in a deep shadow – they were living and dying in secret, without argument, and untroubled by eyes and voices. A humming-bird appeared from nowhere, and poising itself on the wing before every open flower, whirred there like a moth, gleamed like a jewel, darting its thin curved beak, as sharp as a needle, into each for honey. Nature is inevitable – this stone lies on that one, because it must; fronds uncurl from the hairy trunk of a tree-fern; each new growth and decay seems spontaneous and impersonal; there is a kind of harmony of conflict, and it may have been some sense of that harmony that brought Frant to a decision he might, had he not been so solitary, have taken long before. He was roused. He would act boldly. He would give up caution, discretion, doubt, hesitation, he would forget all about the MacGavins, the trade, the future, he would break through the bars of his prison. He would go that very day down into the valley and visit the home of Seraphina. He would behave with candour, he would be open in his dealings. He had proved in commerce that he was 'a white man'; he would now be bold, and prove it in love.

Such was his resolution, but the enterprise was not entirely successful. He set out early in the afternoon, carrying a camera, and a stick in case he should meet snakes. He walked as fast as if he were in a more temperate climate, and felt the heat. The first part of the journey took him across an undulating plateau, through country much like that immediately round Madumbi. But after about an hour he came to the top of a hill which marked the end of an escarpment ('The hill is long and steep,' Seraphina had said) and he began to follow a downward path winding among rocks and thorn trees. This brought him out on to a platform or small tableland and before him lay suddenly open an immense view. Directly below lay the valley of the Umgazi river, where Seraphina lived, and he sat down under a bean tree to rest and to gaze at the scene.

Somebody was coming up the hill. It was a young man. He was a typical Lembu, naked except for a fur codpiece and some bead ornaments, upright, slender and vigorous. He came striding along, singing joyfully as he went, glistening with oil and sweat, his movements full of natural pride. He was holding a tiny shield, a stick and a knobkerrie in one hand, and in the other a large black cotton Brummagem umbrella, to shelter himself from the sun. When he saw Frant he looked surprised and then saluted him with a large and cheerful gesture. Frant knew him by sight and responded cordially.

'What are you doing here?' said the young man. 'Are you out on holiday?'

'Yes,' said Frant. 'I am just out on holiday.'

'Why aren't you riding?'

'I have no horse.'

'But white men don't walk!'

'I like walking.'

The native expressed surprise.

'Is that a camera?' he said.

'Yes, it's a camera.'

'Will you take my picture?'

'All right. Go and stand over there. But you must close your umbrella.'

'What, must I close my umbrella?'

So Frant stood under the bean tree with his feet among the open pods and little black-and-scarlet beans that had fallen from it, and took a photograph of the native, who stood smiling and glistening in the sun.

'Do you know me?' said the young man.

'Yes,' said Frant.

'Do you know Seraphina?'

Frant was startled.

'Yes,' he said, unable to conceal his surprise.

'She is my sister.'

'What! You're her brother?'

'Yes.'

'Fancy that!'

'Seraphina likes you,' said her brother. But, thought Frant, is he really her brother? The natives used such terms somewhat loosely. Was this perhaps a rival trying to warn him off? He put the thought out of his mind, for the native was so friendly. 'Seraphina likes you,' he said. But in Lembu the same word means to like and to love, so perhaps he meant 'Seraphina loves you'.

'I like Seraphina,' said Frant.

'It is not good', said the native, 'when a white man likes a black girl.'

There was no condemnation in his tone, no threat, no high moral purpose. He smiled as he spoke what he no doubt regarded as a self-obvious truism.

'Why?' said Frant.

'Do I know? It is so.'

Frant wanted to say 'Would you be angry if your sister married a white man?' But he had no wish to suggest any such thing. And it seemed too crude to say 'Would you be angry if your sister slept with a white man?' So he said:

'We are all people.'

'Yes, we are all people, but we are different.'

'I like natives,' said Frant.

'I know you do. But you live in Lembuland, and there are no white people near here for you to like.'

This was really unanswerable.

'There are Mr MacGavin and his wife,' said Frant.

Seraphina's brother (if he was Seraphina's brother) laughed.

'Nobody likes *them*!' he said.

'What is your name?' said Frant.

'Me? Umlilwana.'

'And where do you live?'

'Down there,' said Umlilwana, pointing to the valley.

The river Umgazi, which seemed to consist mostly of a broad bed of stones, with only a small stream of water in the middle, curved in a gigantic S-shaped bend just below where they stood. And on some slightly raised ground in one of the curves of the S were a group of grass domes, which were huts, and a cattle kraal made of thorn trees and brushwood, and a few patches of maize and millet and sweet potatoes. And that was the home of Seraphina. It looked the most peaceful place in the world.

'Will you take me there?' said Frant.

'Take you there! What would you do there?'

'I want to see your home. I want to see Seraphina.'

'Seraphina is not there.'

'Not there! Where is she?'

'She has gone on a journey to the mountains for several days with our mother and father to see our cousins. There's nobody down there but an old woman and some children.'

'Oh,' said Frant, and was silent a moment. 'I am sorry,' he said then. 'I wanted to see Seraphina.'

And suddenly everything seemed utterly remote. The view was like a view in a dream. Seraphina (*could* that be her name?) seemed only an idea and her cousins like characters in a myth. And even the friendly smiling Umlilwana seemed utterly strange and unapproachable.

'Yes, I am sorry,' Frant repeated in a dull voice. 'But I should like some day to visit your home and take photographs of Seraphina – and of all your family.'

Umlilwana was a little suspicious of this, but he said Frant would be welcome.

'Will you do something for me?' said Frant. 'Will you come and tell me when Seraphina returns? Tell Seraphina I want to see her. Tell her I want to see her again.'

'All right,' said Umlilwana in English and with great affability. It was about all the English he knew.

'Umlilwana, you are my friend.'

'All right, will you give me some cigarettes?'

Frant smiled, and gave him all he had. Umlilwana was loud in thanks.

Some children could be seen playing near Seraphina's kraal. They looked as small as ants. The distant mountains looked infinitely blue and remote, with the shadows of a few light clouds patterning their peaks. There was nothing to do but to return to Madumbi.

9

Frant returned to Madumbi. So, a couple of days later, did the MacGavins, both with a touch of righteous indignation at Frant's oddness in not having gone with them, and Mrs MacGavin with more than a touch of dyspepsia. Life then resumed its usual course. But things were not quite the same. First of all, Frant was in a far more cheerful frame of mind. Not only had he begun to act with some initiative, not only had he seen Seraphina's home and made friends with her brother, but he had told somebody of his love for her. As soon as she returned he meant to bring matters to a head, even though he and she were 'different'. And if her continued absence was a great trial to his patience, he got up every morning in hopes of a visit and news from Umlilwana in the course of the day. But day followed day, and Umlilwana did not appear. Frant played with the idea of sending him a message, but as it would have to be a verbal one, he thought it more prudent not to do so. And when he once ventured to inquire about Umlilwana, and to ask if he were really Seraphina's brother, the people he spoke to said they had never heard of either of them. And at night he lay naked and sweating on his bed, tortured continually with the image of Seraphina, remembering her gestures, her 'sadness so sweet', and the touch of her flesh.

'Frant should have gone away with us,' MacGavin remarked to his wife. 'He's quite liverish now at times.'

'This weather's enough to make anybody liverish,' said she. 'I always did say that January was the worst month of the year. It's bilious weather. But it's not his liver, if you ask me, it's his nerves.'

January was certainly a bad month at Madumbi, and that year it was more trying than ever. There had been no rain for weeks, and things were beginning to look parched. The heat was dry and intense. And then, day after day, clouds would collect in the morning and accumulate in the afternoon, thunder was occasionally heard and once even a few drops of rain fell in the dust, as if a few devils had spat from a great height. Every morning seemed to promise a thunderstorm, and one began to imagine how the earth would smell after rain, and how cool the air would be, and how the flying ants would come out in the twilight, but every evening the clouds dispersed and left a hot moon to glare down on the veld, or the glittering arrogance of the stars. And every morning Frant said to himself, 'Umlilwana will come, or Seraphina herself,' but every evening he found himself alone again, exhausted and restless. Even the natives, in their anxiety about their crops, were beginning to get on one another's nerves. The air seemed charged with electricity, it seemed to brace one's very muscles against a shock which was not forthcoming, and to leave them at once taut and tired. Even MacGavin took to glancing often at the sky, at the great cumulus clouds that hung in it all the afternoon, and he would say, 'It'll be serious if something doesn't happen soon.'

It was like waiting for an earthquake, a revolution, the day of judgement almost. There was an awful mixture of certainty that something was going to happen, and of uncertainty as to when it would happen. 'We only want a storm to clear the air,' Mrs MacGavin repeated every day until Frant almost felt that he could murder her. The sweat ran down inside his shirt, his overheated blood inflamed his overstrained imagination, he found it more and more difficult to sleep and eat. Trade grew slack, because few could endure to climb up the slopes to Madumbi, and when the store was empty it was far less tolerable than when it was full. The morning sun beat down on the corrugated iron and the interior grew so hot that it failed to cool down during the night. Strange stories came in — that some grass had caught fire simply from the heat of the sun shining through an empty bottle, and several huts had been burnt in consequence; that a young crocodile had come right up one of the little tributaries of the Umgazi and had been found less than a mile from Madumbi itself, an occurrence never before known; and that a native woman had been arrested for killing a newborn baby with six fingers on one hand, in the belief that this deformity was keeping the rain away. Where was Umlilwana? Where was Seraphina? 'I will wait till next Sunday,' said Frant to himself, 'and if neither of them has come by then I shall go down to the kraal itself on the pretext of wanting to take photographs.' But he did not have to wait till Sunday, for the weather broke.

The worst day of all was the fourteenth of the month.

'Well, this is the worst we've had yet,' said Mrs MacGavin at supper time.

'You've said that for the last four days,' observed her husband.

All the doors and windows were wide open. The sky was completely overcast and nothing was stirring but the moths and other insects which flew in from the garden and bumped against the paper lampshade, or against the glass which covered 'The Confession', or fell into the soup, the powder from their wings mingling with the film of grease which already covered that liquid. The rays of lamplight lay on the creepers of the veranda itself and on the path, but beyond them was utter silence and hot, heavy darkness.

'Hark! Was that thunder?' said Mrs MacGavin.

'You always say that at supper time,' remarked her husband.

'It *was* thunder,' she said, her head on one side, as she pushed a stray wisp of hair out of her eye.

Yes, it *was* thunder. They all heard it. Low, continuous thunder.

'That's up in the mountains,' said MacGavin. 'It's a bad sign if it begins up there. If there is a storm, it'll probably miss us altogether ... Ah, did you see the lightning? Yes, that's where it is. I bet it's pouring up there already. And I don't like a dry storm. It's much more dangerous. More likely to strike the trees.'

Frant's heart was beating loud and fast as if in anticipation of some personal, not a meteorological event. He walked alone to the bottom of the garden, and stood there watching the play of lightning in the distance, but it did not seem much more than on previous nights. He came in and tried to read a paper, lighted several cigarettes in succession, throwing one or two away half-smoked, paced up and down in the garden, glancing up at the darkness, and then retired to his room where he lay on his bed without undressing. His hands were clenched, the nails dug into the palms, and he was conscious of little but the beating of his heart. He couldn't hear the MacGavins talking anywhere, or any natives, and had lost all sense of the time. He put out his light, and like a convict without a crime, in a prison that was not locked, for a sentence of indeterminate duration, he just lay there sweating.

At last he got up and went to the window. The moon was out again. It was almost full, and stood high in the sky, flooding the landscape with light. To the south, vast banks of cloud were ranged above the forest, and among them, now and then, a worm of lightning played, followed by a distant roll of thunder. Not a leaf seemed to be stirring, when he noticed that a light breeze was rising and feathering the tops of the distant trees. Very soon the tops of the mimosas near the house bowed, lightly swaying towards the moon, and a tremor ran through the grass as if an invisible hand had stroked it. The wind rose, the clouds towered and toppled upwards, the moon was caught in a web of flying mist, the thunder grew louder, and the flashes of lightning more frequent. A greenish light seemed to emanate from the moon, and as the sky grew more heavily loaded, the forest, by contrast, appeared more ethereal, the heavy boscage and the trunks of the huge indigenous trees appearing in great detail, all dry and luminous and lurid, the foliage beginning to churn and writhe slowly on the topmost boughs. The tenseness of the atmosphere, the expectancy of nature, and the way in which the whole landscape, the very buildings and their shadows, seemed to take part in the great symphony of the impending storm, combined to produce an effect so dramatic as to seem almost supernatural.

The rolling of the thunder was now continuous. All the mountain country was overhung with incessant play of sheet-lightning, as if a curtain of fire, continually agitated by unseen forces, hung over half the world. The wind began to howl round the house, leaves and twigs to fly from the trees, a pile of timber was blown over, and the moon was half hidden in a swirl of clouds. Chains and forks of lightning, steely-blue and sulphurous red, larger and brighter and more frequent than Frant had ever seen, lighted everything with a continuous, shaken glare. Thunder pealed almost overhead, phalanxes of cloud advanced like avenging armies, the house shook, the windows rattled, and he put his hand to his burning and throbbing head. His pulses raced, sweat poured down his face and body, and he felt as if his veins would burst. Suddenly he caught sight of a white horse, which had broken loose from heaven knows where, and was careering madly, its mane and tail flying, its halter trailing, along the slope of the nearest hill. It seemed a creature of fire as it tossed its head, swerved at sudden obstacles, and galloped up to the ridge. There for a moment it stood, quivering with fear and exertion in the quivering glare of the lightning, and then, made splendid by freedom, disappeared from view.

'I can't stay in the house an instant longer!' Frant said aloud to himself, and taking up an electric torch, he stepped out into the garden. A strong refreshing breeze was blowing, but not a drop of rain had fallen. 'It looks as though MacGavin was right – the storm seems to have missed us altogether ...' He wondered what on earth he had brought the torch for, since the lightning was quivering incessantly, like a network of luminous nerves.

'Is that you, Frant?'

It was MacGavin calling from the house.

'Yes. I can't sleep. I'm going for a walk. It's much fresher out now.'

'A walk. At this time! Don't go far. It's risky. And if it should come on to rain ...'

'I'll be all right, thanks. Good night.'

He disappeared from view, and instinctively found himself taking the path he had taken on Christmas Day. He was frightened of the night, of losing his way, of the storm. He had at first no thought of going far, but when he paused to try and calculate how far he had already come he was almost as afraid to turn back as to go on, so he went on. He had got an idea that he must get to the bean tree, and he kept telling himself that it was not really very far. The wind was behind him now, and its freshness gave him energy. The glare and racket of the storm grew no less – it now seemed to be everywhere except immediately overhead. He hurried on, stumbling now and again, for the path was in places rough and narrow. He saw lights once or twice but did not meet a soul. And back at Madumbi MacGavin had grown anxious about him.

Before he came to the escarpment there was a loud detonation just overhead, and it began to rain. He had come too far now to turn back, so he hurried on, vaguely imagining that he would ask for shelter at Seraphina's. Near the top of the hill he realised that the worst of the weather was in front of him. The lightning revealed a thick grey veil of rain beyond the valley, and he could hear a tremendous steady downpour in the distance. The nearer he got to the top the louder the tumult grew, and he thought, 'the river must be a lot fuller by now than when I last saw it.' He was going downhill at last, but not so fast as he wanted, for it was raining pretty hard now and the paths were getting slippery. A feeling of terror seized him. He felt that he would never get down to the valley, that the storm would beat him, that it was no good thinking of turning back.

There was no doubt as to what he could hear now. The river must be in flood. And he suddenly thought, would the kraal be safe? Hardly ... He was running now, to reach the bean tree. He was soaked to the skin, and his feet kept slipping. He missed the way twice and found it again, and then, waiting for the lightning to show him where he was, he found he was only a few yards from the tree.

And just at that moment, exactly as before, he saw a man coming towards him. Only this time the man was running. And this time it was not Umlilwana he saw. And this time he was terrified.

The man didn't see Frant until he almost ran into him, and he was too frightened.

'*Au!*' cried a familiar voice. '*Umtwana ka Kwini!* Child of the Queen! What are you doing here? Where are you going? Child! My child! Have you *seen*? Look, look!'

He dragged Frant over the slippery rocks to the very edge of the table-land.

'Look!' he cried.

A prolonged flash of lightning lit up the whole valley with a tremulous, pale violet glare like the light of some hellish arc-lamp, and in a few seconds Frant had understood. Gone was the S-shaped bend, gone were the grassy domes, kraal and little fields! There was nothing where they had been but a gigantic swirl of greyish water, in which trunks of trees could be seen travelling, spinning and half raising themselves above the surface like animate things.

'Seraphina!' cried Frant. 'Do you know Seraphina?'

He had caught hold of the little old man, who was shivering with fear and cold and seemed the only reality left in the world.

'Seraphina'!' cried Frant. 'Do you know her? Did she come back? Was she at home?'

'She was at home for two weeks, *umtwana*,' said the old man, shaking like a leaf. 'The cattle are drowned!' he cried in the voice of Job and of Lear. 'The houses, the people – all are drowned!'

'Drowned?' cried Frant, shining his torch full in the old man's face. 'Why? Why are they drowned?'

'The water came like a wall, my child,' said the old man, and the torchlight made the raindrops running down his face look as if it was covered with tears. He was shivering violently from top to toe, and his old tunic clung to his skin.

'Umlilwana,' said Frant. 'Was Umlilwana her brother?'

'Umlilwana?' said the old man. 'Umlilwana wasn't her brother! She was going to marry Umlilwana.'

In the lightning glare he saw Frant's face.

'All is finished!' he cried, putting out a black and bony claw, as if to defend himself from some unknown danger. In Lembu the same word means to be finished or to be destroyed. 'Are you bewitched?'

Yes, all was finished, all was destroyed. Already the rolling of the thunder was increasing in volume, but the roar of the flood seemed to grow louder, and the rain was coming down like whips of ice and steel. It was like the coming of the deluge itself. It was like the end of the world.

Something in Frant urged him to leave the old man and run down the hill and plunge into those maddened waters and lose himself, but something stronger told him that he must return to Madumbi, to the store, to the MacGavins, to the making of a livelihood, to the fashioning of a way of life, to a roll of undeveloped negatives, and to a python skin nailed to a wall like a banner, with two large holes in it cut by a girl with a hoe.

'I must go back!' he said to the old man, and gripped his shoulder for an instant. Then he made off in the direction of Madumbi, flashing the torch on the path. The old man called after him to take care, but he was at once out of earshot in the downpour. After he had stumbled a short way one spasmodic sob escaped from him, and he began to run.

Frank Brownlee

The Cannibal's Bird

from *Lion and Jackal* ... (1938)

The girls of a certain village went one day to fetch red clay for colouring their clothing and bodies.

The day being warm, the suggestion of one of the girls that they should bathe in a pool in the neighbouring river was readily agreed to.

The girls sported for a while in the water, then dressed themselves and made for home, each carrying her lumps of red clay. When they had gone some distance a girl who was daughter of the chief of their village, found that she had left one of her ornaments at the pool where she and her companions had bathed. She asked one girl, then another, and another to accompany her back to the pool, but each refused; so the chief's daughter had to return alone.

As she approached the water a cannibal sprang out from the reeds, caught her, and put her in his bag. The girl was very frightened and lay still in the bag. The cannibal carried her off and took her to a village. When he got there the people asked what he had in his bag. He said it was a bird, and if he were given meat he would make his bird sing. These people gave him meat and he caused the girl to sing. So the cannibal went from village to village, and on being given meat he caused the girl, who he always said was a bird, to sing.

Meantime the chief missed his daughter, and the girls who had gone with her to fetch red clay, being questioned, said that the daughter of the chief, having reached womanhood, had, as custom required, 'gone into seclusion'.

With this explanation the chief was satisfied, and in celebration of his daughter's coming of age killed a fat ox. The ox was cut up, and the meat apportioned among people who had gathered at the chief's kraal.

The boys, not being permitted to eat with the men, took their portion of meat to the bush, where they lit a fire and began to grill it. As the meat was grilling, the cannibal, who had the girl in his bag, came up. The boys asked what he had in his bag. As before, he said he had a bird in his bag and if he were given meat he would make the bird sing.

The boys gave the cannibal some meat, and when the girl sang, one of the boys who was the son of the chief, thought he recognised the voice as that of his sister, but being afraid to ask the cannibal to let him see what was in the bag, he advised him to go to the place of the chief where, he said, there was plenty of meat.

The cannibal went to the chief's village, and when he got there, without asking for meat he made his bird sing. The chief was very anxious to see the bird but the cannibal would not open his bag. The chief offered him an ox, then two oxen, if he would open his bag, but the cannibal refused.

Then one of the councillors, speaking to the chief in whispers, arranged a plan. The cannibal was asked to go and fetch water on the promise that on his return he would be given plenty of meat. The cannibal said he would fetch water if everyone promised not to touch his bag till his return. The people agreed to this.

The cannibal was given a leaky pot with which to fetch the water. While he was away the chief opened the bag and released the girl. He did not at first recognise her as his daughter, the other girls having told him that she was in the hut of seclusion but when he found out who she was and how he had been deceived by the other girls, he gave orders that they be killed. After that he put scorpions and snakes in the bag.

When the cannibal came back with water, he complained of the leaky pot and said it had taken him a long time to patch up the cracks with clay. He was given plenty of meat and when he had eaten it he picked up his bag and went on his way.

When he got to his home he bade his wife make a fire and call his friends to a feast he would make ready for them.

Expecting a great feast, his friends came in numbers. When the bag was opened and only snakes and scorpions were found in it, the other cannibals were so angry that they killed their host and ate him.

Peter Abrahams

One of the Three

from *Dark Testament* (1942)

The three of us had always stuck together after we had met. Tommy, Johnny and myself. We had been in the same class and had gone through school together. These two, Tommy and Johnny, were the only fast friends I had throughout those years at school.

Tommy was not very ambitious. He just wanted to overcome the dreaded thing: Poverty. All he wanted of life was a chance to earn enough money, so that his mother would stop having to carry big bundles of washing on her grey head. He loved her very much. He was an only son, and both his mother and father lived only for him. They used to say their day was past, and now they wanted to see the day of their son. So part of his one ambition was to get them out of the one room that was too small and stuffy for the three of them, and to make the old people rest from their labours. The other part of his ambition, completing it, was to have a fairly secure job, with enough money to marry a good-looking Coloured girl; to have enough to eat in their home, go to shows and dances as often as they could, and live as comfortably as possible. He used to say that he wanted, at any rate, a good run out of life. He worked very hard. His aim was to obtain a teacher's certificate. Both Johnny and I criticised him for his narrow ambition, but secretly we envied him. But that did not worry Tommy. He laughingly told us that he would love to do bigger and greater things, but that his life had been starved too long, and that he just had not the strength to go on starving for something that he might never achieve. He was always reminding us that this was South Africa, and that everything worthwhile here was reserved for Europeans only.

Both Johnny and I wished that we could adopt the same attitude. We knew it was the safest; then at least there would be some sort of certainty about things. But we could not look at the future as Tommy did.

Tommy was in love with a girl who worked on the Hill. She was simple and beautiful. He was happy with her. He enjoyed talking about simple nothings with her. She could not discuss any of the things that were so important to the three of us. Books meant nothing to her, if they were not of the *Peg's Paper* variety. The only music she knew was the music to which she danced. To Tommy serious books and music, and, above all, the discussion of these, were very important. She knew nothing about these things. She just tried to sink her identity in Tommy's.

Johnny and I could not understand it. The girl was sweet and simple, and we loved her as a little sister. This may sound highbrow, but it is not. Even Tommy admitted that he could not turn to her for serious companionship. But he said it was impossible to find the type of girl who would suit him in this country, with conditions as they were, so he was making the best of a bad job. And he was happy with the girl.

Johnny and I tried to do the same, but we failed completely. Johnny was very different from Tommy. The three of us were so utterly different from one another that we sometimes wondered what kept us together.

Johnny was very jovial and noisy. Always doing the wrong thing. Always playing pranks on somebody. Always getting into trouble, out of which Tommy and I had to help him. To those who did not know him he appeared an entirely superficial person with no sense of values whatever. But deep down he was very sensitive. His devil-may-care attitude was a mask which hid the true Johnny.

His mother had died of starvation. He had been at school, and he knew about it only when it was too late. She had starved to keep him at school, and he had not known. For a long time afterwards he was alone and quiet. Even Tommy and I could not get to him. He had built a wall round himself. His strongest weapon of defence was mockery. But after a while the three of us were together again. To us he was the same Johnny, only very unhappy. To everyone else he had changed. He had taken up a queer mocking attitude to everything. They all said that his brilliant brain was useless. Johnny did not shrink from hurting people, and he had a brilliantly biting tongue and brain with which to do it. But for all the old and poor he had a motherly tenderness. Very few people understood him. Most condemned him.

My life was pretty much the same. Poverty, want of a woman's companionship, and the other things which the non-European South African of education knows so well. There were the three of us. Tommy, Johnny and myself.

When we had finished our schooling we broke up, and each went his own way. Tommy tried to persuade us to teach. He said: 'What's the use of passing anything if you are not going to make money out of it?' But

Johnny said he wanted to see the world. He did not know for sure what he wanted out of the world, but he would find out. I said I was going to wander about the country and learn to know my people, and try to earn my living as a writer. They were both worried because of my poor physical condition, but I was insistent.

So we agreed to keep in touch with one another, and broke up. Johnny was going to a coastal town, where he would try to get away in a boat; I was going inland among the natives; Tommy was going to take up a teacher's post after the holidays.

For three years I wandered about. Now and then I received a letter from Tommy, when he saw something of mine in the African papers, and traced my whereabouts through that. Then one day he wrote to me to tell me that Johnny was coming back, and that I must be there for the reunion. Somehow I managed to scrape my fare together and went back.

I arrived a day before Johnny was expected, and I spent it with Tommy. He was married to the girl with whom he had been in love. They were not happy. There were continual fights in the house. I asked him about his mother. She had died. His father had gone off, and there was no trace of him. Tommy had changed. His quiet acceptance of things had hurt him more than he had expected. He could not live the superficial life of the average Coloured teacher. He wanted to break away and do something worthwhile for his people. He had read revolutionary literature, and wanted to do something about conditions, but he was terribly afraid of losing his job. Afraid of insecurity. So he chafed against his chains, but could not break them.

The next day we went to the station to meet Johnny.

The fine sensitive Johnny was no more. There were only glimpses of him. They appeared only when we spoke of old times. Life had beaten Johnny. All the fire and force had gone out of him. His fine brown eyes, that used to sparkle with defiance when things were black, were dull and lifeless. He had come home, he said, to try and see himself as he used to be ...

For a few months he drifted about. Tommy and I did everything we could to bring the old life back, but we failed. Then one night Johnny took lysol ...

One out of the three had gone.

Things were black with Tommy. He was afraid of insecurity, but the keeping up of appearances was getting him down. And always when we were together Johnny came and weighed heavily upon us. Tommy and I agreed not to see each other again. We both felt it would be better that way. Fighting ourselves was bad enough; if we had to fight Johnny too it might be too much for us.

It is one of the saddest things I remember.

Herman Charles Bosman

Birth Certificate

from *The Forum* (1950)

It was when At Naudé told us what he had read in the newspaper about a man who had thought all his life that he was White, and had then discovered that he was Coloured, that the story of Flippus Biljon was called to mind. I mean, we all knew the story of Flippus Biljon. But because it was still early afternoon we did not immediately make mention of Flippus. Instead, we discussed, at considerable length, other instances that were within our knowledge of people who had grown up as one sort of person and had discovered in later life that they were in actual fact quite a different sort of person.

Many of these stories that we recalled in Jurie Steyn's voorkamer as the shadows of the thorn-trees lengthened were based only on hearsay. It was the kind of story that you had heard, as a child, at your grandmother's knee. But your grandmother would never admit, of course, that she had heard that story at *her* grandmother's knee. Oh, no. She could remember very clearly how it all happened, just like it was yesterday. And she could tell you the name of the farm. And the name of the landdrost who was summoned to take note of the extraordinary occurrence, when it had to do with a more unusual sort of changeling, that is. And she would recall the solemn manner in which the landdrost took off his hat when he said that there were many things that were beyond human understanding.

Similarly now, in the voorkamer, when we recalled stories of white children that had been carried off by a Bushman or a baboon or a werewolf, even, and had been brought up in the wilds and without any proper religious instruction, then we also did not think it necessary to explain where we had first heard those stories. We spoke as though we had been actually present at some stage of the affair – more usually at the last scene, where the child, now grown to manhood and needing trousers and a pair of braces and a hat, gets restored to his parents and the magistrate after studying the birth certificate says that there are things in this world that baffle the human mind.

And while the shadows under the thorn-trees grew longer the stories we told in Jurie Steyn's voorkamer grew, if not longer, then, at least, taller.

'But this isn't the point of what I have been trying to explain,' At Naudé interrupted a story of Gysbert van Tonder's that was getting a bit confused in parts, through Gysbert van Tonder not being quite clear as to what a werewolf was. 'When I read that bit in the newspaper I started wondering how must a man *feel*, after he has grown up with adopted parents and he discovers, quite late in life, through seeing his birth certificate for the first time, that he isn't White, after all. That is what I am trying to get at. Supposing Gysbert were to find out suddenly –'

At Naudé pulled himself up short. Maybe there were one or two things about a werewolf that Gysbert van Tonder wasn't too sure about, and he would allow himself to be corrected by Oupa Bekker on such points. But there were certain things he wouldn't stand for.

'All right,' At Naudé said hastily, 'I don't mean Gysbert van Tonder, specially. What I am trying to get at is, how would any one of us feel? How would any White man feel, if he has passed as White all his life, and he sees for the first time, from his birth certificate, that his grandfather was Coloured? I mean, how would he *feel*? Think of that awful moment when he looks in the palm of his hands and he sees ...'

'He can have that awful moment,' Gysbert van Tonder said. 'I've looked at the palm of my hand. It's a White man's palm. And my fingernails have also got proper half-moons.'

At Naudé said he had never doubted that. No, there was no need for Gysbert van Tonder to come any closer and show him. He could see quite well enough just from where he was sitting. After Chris Welman had pulled Gysbert van Tonder back on to the rusbank by his jacket, counselling him not to do anything foolish, since At Naudé did not mean *him*, Oupa Bekker started talking about a White child in Schweizer-Reneke that had been stolen out of its cradle by a family of baboons.

'I haven't seen that cradle myself,' Oupa Bekker acknowledged, modestly. 'But I met many people who have. After the child had been stolen, neighbours from as far as the Orange River came to look at that cradle. And when they looked at it they admired the particular way that Heilart Nortjé – that was the child's father – had set about making his household furniture, with glued klinkpenne in the joints, and all. But the real in-

terest about the cradle was that it was empty, proving that the child had
been stolen by baboons. I remember how one neighbour, who was not
on very good terms with Heilart Nortjé, went about the district saying
that it could only have *been* baboons.

'But it was many years before Heilart Nortjé and his wife saw their
child again. By *saw*, I mean getting near enough to be able to talk to him
and ask him how he was getting on. For he was always too quick, from
the way the baboons had brought him up. At intervals Heilart Nortjé
and his wife would see the tribe of baboons sitting on a rant, and their
son, young Heilart, would be in the company of the baboons. And once,
through his field-glasses, Heilart had been able to observe his son for
quite a few moments. His son was then engaged in picking up a stone
and laying hold of a scorpion that was underneath it. The speed with
which his son pulled off the scorpion's sting and proceeded to eat up the
rest of the scorpion whole filled the father's heart of Heilart Nortjé with
a deep sense of pride.

'I remember how Heilart talked about it. "Real intelligence," Heilart
announced with his chest stuck out. ' "A real baboon couldn't have done
it quicker or better. I called my wife, but she was a bit too late. All she
could see was him looking as pleased as anything and scratching himself.
And my wife and I held hands and we smiled at each other and we asked
each other, where does he get it all from?" '

'But then there were times again when that tribe of baboons would
leave the Schweizer-Reineke area and go deep into the Kalahari, and
Heilart Nortjé and his wife would know nothing about what was happening to their son, except through reports from farmers near whose
homesteads the baboons had passed. Those farmers had a lot to say about
what happened to some of their sheep, not to talk of their mealies and
watermelons. And Heilart would be very bitter about those farmers.
Begrudging his son a few prickly-pears, he said.

'And it wasn't as though he hadn't made every effort to get his son
back, Heilart said, so that he could go to catechism classes, since he was
almost of age to be confirmed. He had set all sorts of traps for his son,
Heilart said, and he had also thought of shooting the baboons, so that it
would be easier, after that, to get his son back. But there was always the
danger, firing into a pack like that, of shooting his own son.'

'The neighbour that I have spoken of before,' Oupa Bekker continued,
'who was not very well disposed towards Heilart Nortjé, said that the
real reason Heilart didn't shoot was because he didn't always know – actually *know* – which was his son and which was one of the more flat-
headed kees-baboons.'

It seemed that this was going to be a very long story. Several of us started getting restive … So Johnny Coen asked Oupa Bekker, in a polite sort of way, to tell us how it all ended.

'Well, Heilart Nortjé caught his son, afterwards, ' Oupa Bekker said. 'But I am not sure if Heilart was altogether pleased about it. His son was so hard to tame. And then the way he caught him. It was with the simplest sort of baboon trap of all … Yes, *that* one. A calabash with a hole in it just big enough for you to put you hand in, empty, but that you can't get your hand out of again when you're clutching a fistful of mealies that was put at the bottom of the calabash. Heilart Nortjé never got over that, really. He felt it was a very shameful thing that had happened to him. The thought that his son, in whom he had taken so much pride, should have allowed himself to be caught in the simplest form of monkey-trap.'

When Oupa Bekker paused, Jurie Steyn said that it was indeed a sad story, and it was no doubt, perfectly true. There was just a certain tone in Jurie Steyn's voice that made Oupa Bekker continue.

'True in every particular,' Oupa Bekker declared, nodding his head a good number of times. 'The landdrost came over to see about it, too. They sent for the landdrost so that he could make a report about it. I was there, that afternoon, in Heilart Nortjé's voorkamer, when the landdrost came. And there were a good number of other people, also. And Heilart Nortjé's son, half-tamed in some ways but still baboon-wild in others, was there also. The landdrost studied the birth certificate very carefully. Then the landdrost said that what he had just been present at surpassed ordinary human understanding. And the landdrost took off his hat in a very solemn fashion.

'We all felt very embarrassed when Heilart Nortjé's son grabbed the hat out of the landdrost's hand and started biting pieces out of the crown.'

When Oupa Bekker said those words it seemed to us like the end of a story. Consequently, we were disappointed when At Naudé started making further mention of that piece of news he had read in the daily paper. So there was nothing else for it but that we had to talk about Flippus Biljon. For Flippus Biljon's case was just the opposite of the case of the man that At Naudé's newspaper wrote about.

Because he had been adopted by a Coloured family, Flippus Biljon had always regarded himself as a Coloured man. And then one day, quite by accident, Flippus Biljon saw his birth certificate. And from that birth certificate it was clear that Flippus Biljon was as White as you or I. You can imagine how Flippus Biljon must have felt about it. Especially after he had gone to see the magistrate at Bekkersdal, and the magistrate, after studying the birth certificate, confirmed the fact that Flippus Biljon was a White man.

'Thank you, baas,' Flippus Biljon said. 'Thank you very much, my basie.'

Uys Krige

Death of the Zulu

from *The Dream and the Desert* (1953)

It was about two hours after our capture. We were marching from Figtree towards Tobruk port. It was midsummer, the sun well up, but, thank God, not too hot yet – though I knew by the brittle cobalt look of the sky that it would not be long before the heat would become unbearable, beating down upon that bone-dry earth in shimmering, scorching waves ... We weren't doing anything, not even thinking, just trudging along, dragging our heavy feet through the sand, raising the dust in yellowish-grey clouds in the dips and in little lingering puffs round our boots on the straight.

I appeared to have two minds: the one stunned, the other perfectly conscious, taking in coolly and dispassionately our surroundings. Only one sight was clear-cut, vivid: that silent mob of men streaming towards Tobruk. And only one sound audible: the click or scrunch of desert boots when we struck a rock vein or a loose surface of grit across our path.

Those boots, that everlasting dragging, clogged tramp, tramp tramp ... Like a drum ... Like the slow, dull, monotonous beat of a drum. And with a single monotonous refrain: out of nothing, through nothing, towards nothing ... Out of nothing: the thunderous vacuum of the battle. Through nothing: this strange, unreal scene, as if flickering in a film. Towards nothing: the huge inconceivable emptiness of our life of captivity and exile to come ...

It would be more accurate to say I seemed to have, not two minds, but three, the third listening to a monologue by the conscious mind. 'Yes, before it often seemed to you,' it was saying, 'that you were living only in the past or the future, never in the present. The present was always escaping you, slipping like sand through your fingers. Now you have your present, my boy, and a fine present it is too! Very present, very real ... And you can't barricade yourself against it by drawing on your

memories. They've been washed out. Nor can you throw up a rampart
against it with hopes, plans for the future. For your future, too, has gone
down the drain. there is no past. There is no future. There's only the
present...'

There were bodies lying beside the road, some singly, some in batches.
Dead or wounded, I didn't look, I wasn't interested. My eyes slid over
them as if they were so many pieces of old motor junk scattered about a
disused yard somewhere. 'They're dead and they've a wife like you ...' I
heard a faint voice whisper somewhere far off. 'They're dead and they've
a mother like you ...' The voice was taking shape, getting stronger.
'They're dead and they've a child like you ...' The voice, now, was quite
loud. It was my unconscious mind awaking; and the monologue had
become a dialogue.

'I don't care a damn ...' I heard the calm mind say, but it was fast
losing its imperturbability. 'Let them all go to hell ... Let them all go
straight to hell! I don't care a damn!'

Below the escarpment the track we were following made a curve. I was
on the left-hand side of the curve when I heard a shout. Mechanically I
looked up. To the right, in the curve's bulge, about fifty metres away, a
German officer was standing over someone stretched out on the ground.
He shouted again, beckoned with his arm. Though there must have been
at least a dozen men in our group, numbly, apathetically, I thought: 'It's
me he wants, he's looking straight at me, I can see the blue of his eyes ...'

Automatically I stepped off the track. There were two other South Africans beside me also walking towards the German. I did not know who
they were, I had never seen them before. They must have been beside
me – or just behind me – during that long, weary trek from Figtree, but I
hadn't noticed them. It was only now as, one on each side of me, they too
moved forward towards the officer and the figure at his feet, that their
presence began impinging upon my consciousness. And though I was to
spend at least a quarter of an hour in their company I cannot, to this day,
recollect a single feature or physical characteristic of either of them.

The next minute I was standing beside the man lying on the ground. It
was one of our native soldiers, and I could tell by his build and features
that he was a Zulu. As a Government official in Natal for some years, I
had got to know this Bantu race, their language and customs well. A shell
must have burst near him. His left arm was off at the elbow. A large
splinter must have snapped it off as one snaps crisply and cleanly between one's fingers a dried mealie stalk. His shirt, I noticed, was full of
little craters, stiff with caked blood.

Then I saw his eyes. They were a luminous jet black, stricken with
pain; yet they seemed, somehow, detached. Although the man was

looking straight at me he appeared unaware of my presence.

'*Kiyini umfana* (What is it, young Zulu?)' I asked, bending over him and hearing my voice go trailing over the sand with a gruff undertone as if this were yet another imbecility for which I wasn't in the least responsible and I resented being implicated in it; as if what that droning voice really wanted to say was: 'I'm out of it, do you hear? Out of it ... Leave me alone! Why drag me back? Why –'

Hearing his own language, the young Zulu raised his head slightly. His eyes seemed brighter, but their expression had changed; it was no longer remote, had become intimate. Then his head fell back, his eyes, however, never leaving my face. '*Hau ... umlungu ...*' he groaned. '*Kuhi ... Insimbi ing-shayili ...* (O ... white man ... It is not a good thing ... The iron has hit me ...).'

Suddenly I realised I was normal again, with my mind no longer split into segments, but an integrated whole with perfectly logical perceptions and reactions.

I had come erect, was looking around. The German officer had gone. About four hundred metres away I saw him, driving away in his truck. I turned to the Zulu again. He was in a half-sitting position with one of the two men who had stepped out of our lines with me, crouched down behind him, holding him up.

'How do you feel, *umfana*?' I asked going down on my right knee. A hard glitter came into his eyes, then he said slowly, clearly: '*Umlungu, ngidubule ...* (White man, shoot me ...)' There was no doubting it, he was pleading with me – apparently unaware that I, like him, was now a prisoner no longer carrying a weapon and therefore as powerless as he against his fate.

'Don't talk like that, *umfana*,' I said peremptorily, more to get a grip on myself than to rebuke him. 'You've only lost an arm. Many men have lost an arm, and they're walking about now, laughing, with their heads in the sun.'

'*ca ... ca ...* (No ... no ..),' he muttered, almost angrily.

'Yes, yes ...' I continued, speaking fast. 'We'll get a doctor for you and we'll take you to the hospital' – we, we, who the hell's we, I thought, we're nothing, less than nothing – 'and they'll be good to you there, soon you'll be a whole man again and it won't be many moons before you'll be going about your work, watching the pumpkins fill out, the maize swell in the cob, and the cattle grow fat in the fields back in Zululand ...'

I do not know what made me say this. I knew it wasn't true. My own words, with a hollow false sound, echoed back on my ears.

'*Ca, umlungu ... Ngidubule! Ngidubule!* (No, white man ... Shoot me! Shoot me!).' How strong his voice is, I thought, out of all proportion to his strength.

'Soon,' I repeated, 'you'll be a whole man again.'

'No, no, white man ...' He was shaking his head in exactly the way I had so often seen old Zulu indunas shake their heads, when in tribal councils they would, by their whole expression and attitude, gently but firmly convey to the European that the sum of all his knowledge was as nothing compared with their ancient African wisdom. '*Ngipelile* ... (I am finished...).'

A little desert car drew up twenty metres away. A tall, thin German officer with sharp features jumped out and was beside us in a few quick darting steps. Another German officer, short and squat, had followed him – and the next moment the tall officer was bending over the native, feeling his chest beneath the blood-stiffened shirt. Noticing his stars and the snake of Aesculapius in his badge, I felt at once greatly relieved.

I looked at the Zulu's arm again. Most of the stump's end was caked over with dry, hardened blood. It still bled, but very little, only a trickle oozing through the shattered flesh.

'*Ngidubule!*' His voice was no longer supplicating but had a fierce, ringing quality as if raised in protest that this was no extravagant demand but a fitting and just claim upon me. My gaze travelled over his magnificent body. The broad torso bulged beneath the army shirt. The thighs, curving into sight under the dirty bloodstained shorts, were of a classic symmetry, the calves and legs as harmoniously proportionate.

Then the thought struck me that the Zulus, physically, are one of the most beautiful races in the world; that Zulu males have an extraordinary pride in their physique; that they consider any deformity of the body – and particularly disfigurement – as something unnatural, even monstrous; and that formerly they killed all children unfortunate enough to be born cripples. Naturally this young Zulu, descended from generations of warriors, wanted to die now, clamoured for death; for this cracked useless body, this stump of an arm, were they not a shame and a disgrace, a crying offence against both man and the gods?

My eyes slipped over his chest again, met his. I knew they had never left my face even though the German doctor was still bending over him examining him, feeling tentatively for his wounds. Now, quite simply, as if he had read my thought and was confident that his wish would be granted, he said slowly: '*Ngidubule, umlungu* ...'

'No, you speak foolish things.'

'*Ngidubule!*' The short spell of calm had broken, the voice was again urgent. Did it contain a note of reproach?

'*Ngidubule, umlungu, ngidubule!*' Yes, it was reproachful. God, would that eternal cry of '*Ngidubule ...*' never stop?

The doctor had pulled out his hand, turned and was looking at me.

'What does he say?' he asked me in German.

'It is his request that we shoot him ...' I answered, realising at once that I was giving a stiff literal German translation not of what the Zulu had said but of what his headman would have said in slow solemn tone to the other assembled members of the tribe were they here now, squatting in a half circle round the dying man, deliberating his case.

Whether the Zulu finally understood that I could not, would not do it, or whether he recognised the German doctor as his enemy who, according to his subconscious reasoning, would be less averse to such an action, I do not know; but as soon as he had heard this new, foreign voice intruding upon our dialogue, he was no longer looking at me but at the German.

Leaning up against the South African supporting him from behind, he had had until now his right hand on the ground. But now, in a great effort, his lips twitching in pain – there were foam flecks on them, spotted with blood – he brought his hand to his shirt front and slowly, gropingly, uncovered his chest. Next, straining himself forward, he said in a deep resonant voice to the German captain: '*Wena aungiduble!* (You shoot me!)' Strange, but at that moment it sounded almost like a command.

'He wants you to shoot him ...' I told the doctor. Standing stiffly beside me, the German made no reply.

'What chance has he of living?' I asked.

'None,' came the incisive answer. 'He must have been wounded yesterday afternoon, has lain here all night. He's lost so much blood, he can't have much more to lose. Had he been a European he would have been dead long ago ...' His voice was as jerky as his movements. Though speaking German, we had instinctively moved a few paces away as if afraid the wounded man would understand.

'And he still speaks,' the voice staccatoed on, 'with all that shrapnel inside him! He'll probably die when we move him. Then again, he's so strong he might live for hours.'

I turned to the native. 'The doctor says you are badly hurt, but that you have great strength and must not worry. We're going to carry you to that truck, take you to the hospital.'

'No, no ... I am finished ... Shoot me ... I cannot live any more. The pain is too deep ... *umlungu* ...' He was groaning again, his voice getting weaker, and for the first time he closed his eyes for longer than a second. His hand, too, had fallen back on the ground, black against the pale yellow earth.

The doctor touched me on the arm. 'Perhaps it would be the easiest way out,' he said, and motioned to the young lieutenant standing a few paces away. An order from the captain, and the lieutenant had pulled out his pistol and handed it to me. I stood there, as if petrified, with the pistol in my right hand.

'Umlungu ... umlungu ...' were the only two words now uttered by the Zulu lying at my feet with closed eyes and quivering lips. He kept on muttering them, his voice never rising above a whisper. Yet the repeated 'umlungu ... umlungu ...' seemed to contain a note of awe, almost of reverence – not, I felt, because I was an officer and he a private, but because at the moment I must have appeared to his bewildered mind, half crazed with pain, the great benefactor bearing in my hands the supreme gift of peace and the healing oblivion of death.

I looked from the pistol to the captain, from the captain back to the pistol, then at the Zulu. He, in the meanwhile, had opened his eyes.

'Ngidubule!' his voice rang in my ears, as strong as ever.

I shook my head. 'No,' I said to the captain handing him the pistol, 'I do not shoot my friends.'

It was at least two seconds before I realised I had addressed the German in Zulu.

The Zulu's gaze had followed the motion of the pistol; he now stared at the captain. The German stood, irresolute, as if embarrassed by the pistol. He seemed to be debating a point. Then turning to me, he said:

'My business is to preserve life not to destroy it.'

'And not to lessen pain?'

'Yes, to lessen pain.' He was speaking much more slowly; the bark had gone out of his voice. 'But that would be contrary to Red Cross regulations. I'm not even allowed to carry firearms ...' This typical German respect for rules and regulations, I thought, how incongruous!

The next moment the captain had handed the pistol back to its owner. 'Herr Oberleutnant Muller,' he rapped out in military tone: 'Shoot this man!'

Then I noticed the Zulu's hand come creeping up his chest again and I forgot everything, watching it, fascinated. It was a broad compact hand with a fair-sized wart on the index finger and at that moment it seemed to pulse with life, to be one of the most living things I had ever seen. The big strong fingers felt for the edge of the shirt-front where the V-opening ended, closed over it in a firm grip, there was the quick, sharp rip of khaki drill tearing, and the shirt fell apart, revealing the entire chest. The right side had hardly been touched but the left, until now concealed by the shirt, was a mass of torn flesh.

I looked away. The lieutenant had stepped forward, was standing a few paces from the Zulu. He had a set look on his face, holding the weapon stiffly in front of him, pointing it at the dying man.

The Zulu's hand was buried deep in the sand, gripping the earth, supporting his body. To me, at that moment, it seemed that in a last superhuman effort he wanted to lift himself, rise and with both feet planted firmly on the ground, meet his death face to face. He had squared his shoulders, throwing them back and was straining his chest out and up, as if to present a better target to the enemy, or to thrust it against the very muzzle of the pistol.

Now his eyes were ablaze as if all the fierce passionate life that remained to him were concentrated in their jet-black depths.

'Ngidubule! Ngidubule!' broke from his dry, cracked lips in a crescendo, like a shout of joy, a triumphant roar; and I was reminded of the Zulu battle cry I had so often heard, sonorous and barbaric, bursting from a thousand throats when the war dance reaches its frenzied, crashing climax.

'Ngidubule! Ngidubule!'

Yes, he was roaring at his body, roaring at his pain, roaring at death.

Rooted to the spot, I stood looking down at him. I wanted to tear myself away. I couldn't.

Carefully, methodically, the lieutenant took aim along the pistol barrel.

I felt a hand clutch my shoulder. For a second it lay there lax. Then it tightened over my collarbone. I half turned. It was the captain. Slowly he turned me completely round. He took a step forward. I followed. I was waiting, I felt, for yet another *'Ngidubule!'* rather than the pistol's report; and when a snail-shell (one of those countless bone-white shells scattered like tiny skulls about the desert) popped under my feet, I shuddered.

We were about five metres away when the pistol cracked. It did not go off again.

I have a very hazy recollection of what happened after that.

I remember the German captain saying, *'Auf Wiedersehen'*; the two officers driving off in the small car; and that for a long time I sat on a flat stone beside the road.

Legs, many legs, milled past, kept slipping in and out of my vision. But they made no impression on me; in a dull, disconnected way I was more interested in the little wisps of sand that kept spiraling, circling about my boots and then settling in a thin, pale yellow dust on the broad square toecaps.

How long I sat there, staring at my boots, I don't know. Someone shouted in Afrikaans: 'Come along, Du Toit! Come along!' and when I found myself again, I was once more among that crowd of prisoners tramping slowly, wearily towards Tobruk.

Bertha Goudvis

Thanks to Mrs Parsons

from *The Mistress of Mooiplaas and Other Stories* (1956)

It all began with the shooting of the little pigs. Mrs Parsons, the storekeeper's wife, believed in pig breeding as a side line. Not in a large way, of course, for she had not the time. She helped Parsons in the store, for he wasn't much of a salesman, and the women usually waited about until she could attend to them. Her sister looked after the house and the cooking, so she was able to do a little maternity work as well. You must know that in her maiden days Mrs Parsons had trained at Queen Charlotte's Hospital, and the women of our little dorp, which is nearly forty miles from a railway station, had infinite faith in her.

When the government eventually appointed a district surgeon he found that there was no call for his services when the stork flew. Dr Drysdale was hardworking and capable, but the jolly little woman who looked so well after her charges was an established favourite. She was very good natured, always ready, as she put it, to do a hand's turn for anybody, but when it came to her professional work the fixed fee had to be paid. On this point she was firm.

With all these duties Mrs Parsons found time to raise a few pigs, and the pigsty was kept in admirable order. She loved to display a newly arrived litter to a favoured customer. 'Come and see my darlings,' she would say, and take you across the yard to the pigsty, where the sow wallowed amongst her pink podgy offspring. I went with her only once, for I thought the sight an ugly one, and when she told me one day of the loss of a whole litter through the voracious appetite of the unnatural mother I refused to look upon that particular sow again, a decision which caused Mrs Parsons to regard me as the victim of a foolish squeamishness. It was her custom to sell the pigs when they were quite small, but for some reason or another she kept one lot till they were old enough to be troublesome to the neighbours, and one day they contrived to wriggle through the fence and find their way to Simon van Rooyen's sweet potato patch, where they did much damage.

Simon was furious and he was only deterred from a violent attack on the despoilers by the pleadings of his wife, who was much attached to Mrs Parsons and feared to lose her friendship. Simon spoke to Parsons and warned him as to what would happen if the pigs trespassed again. Parsons promised his wife that he would render the fence impassable without further delay, but there came a heavy mail that morning and, as he kept the post office in his shop, he was busy and forgot all about the pigs. But the pigs had not forgotten the sweetness of that potato patch, and when Van Rooyen found them in his garden that afternoon he saw red. Before his wife could intervene he fetched his gun and killed the lot. Then he made his natives pick up the carcasses and toss them over the fence of Parsons's garden.

The brutality of this last procedure capped his iniquity in the eyes of Mrs Parsons. When her own servants called her to view the bleeding corpses she broke down and cried. Then she said hard things about Simon van Rooyen. Half the village sided with her, but the other half sympathised with the owner of the ruined garden.

Although Mrs Parsons was a Cockney by birth, you would have suspected an Irish strain if you had heard her lament the little pigs. They were the dearest and most innocent of pets that she had reared from birth, and how anyone could have had the heart to butcher them in cold blood was more than she could ever understand.

She brought an action against Van Rooyen, and the case was tried by Mr Curtis, who was Acting Magistrate during Mr Fellowes's absence on holiday. He was a bachelor of some sardonic humour, who said afterwards that he had found it hard to maintain the dignity of the Bench during Mrs Parsons's impassioned declaration of the innocent lovableness of her slaughtered piglets.

But it was with the utmost gravity that he delivered judgment. He said that the pig's first trespass had been forgiven and their owner duly warned. When their offence was repeated the defendant was justified in taking action. The decision must, therefore, be one of justifiable homicide.

Mrs Parsons burst into tears. Afterwards she transferred some of her anger to the man who had delivered this heartless judgment, saying that he seemed to be actually enjoying himself, but what could one expect of a stony-hearted bachelor who had never reared chick or child. If Mr Fellowes had been on the Bench she knew the result would have been a different one. But while she railed against the magistrate her anger with the Van Rooyens showed no signs of abatement. She vowed that she would have no more truck with them and Anna could look elsewhere for a midwife when her next baby was due.

This was a cruel blow to Anna for she was already expecting her third infant and was convinced that no one could deliver her with the skill of Mrs Parsons, who had brought her two previous babes into the world. Although she was such a busy woman the little midwife usually found time to visit mothers-to-be before their time came, and her bright looks and cheerful rallying were as good as a tonic, or so they said.

She fretted the more because Mrs Parsons met her one morning returning from the opposition store where Simon had transferred his custom and cut her dead.

'I wanted to stop her and tell her that I begged you not to shoot the pigs,' Anna wept to her husband, 'but she never gave me the chance. She didn't even look at little Julie who was with me, and she used to be so fond of her.'

'She was fonder of her pigs,' growled Van Rooyen. He tried to comfort his wife by telling her that she could engage Dr Drysdale for her confinement and also Mrs Steenkamp who had had ten children of her own and should, therefore, know as much about maternity cases as Mrs Parsons.

The months passed quickly, and now the time drew near not only for Anna's confinement but for a vastly more important event in the eyes of the villagers. This was the annual gymkhana and sports meeting, which owed its origin to the sporting proclivities of Dr Drysdale, Jan Vermaak the stock inspector, and Donelly who recruited native labour for the Rand mines.

The programme was so varied and attractive that the attendance increased yearly. Nearly all the neighbouring farmers came in with their families, and even visitors from Meyersdorp would drive over for the meeting and the dance in the schoolroom which wound up the festivities. For days beforehand we would watch the skies for weather signals, but so far the gods had not disappointed and this year was no exception. A sky deeply blue, drifting clouds to mask the sun when it burned too fiercely, a faint cool breeze: the day was perfect.

Early in the morning carts and wagons began to arrive and line up on either side of the racecourse. Women and children who had not met since the last Nachtmaal in Meyersdorp talked and laughed together, while the men inspected the horseflesh. Derby runners were never scanned more closely than the entries for the day's events. No bookmaker would think it worth his while to attend our gymkhanas, but there were many private bets.

The doctor's grey horse, Charlie, was mostly fancied for the big event, a hurdle race with a purse of £25, but many thought that Jan Vermaak's Swartbooi stood a better chance. There were other entries but the experts foretold that the race would be between these two. After some pony races and sports competitions the bell rang for the big event. The spectators hastened to find places on carts and wagons and you could feel the excitement that possessed the crowd.

Bester's roan mare, Maanlicht, with Tom Bester up, led at the start, but she was soon overtaken by Charlie and Swartbooi. Both owners were riding and as they approached the last hurdle there was much shouting. 'Come on Doc.' 'Jan will do it.' 'No, the Doctor!' They leaped the hurdle almost simultaneously, and then a cry of horror rang out, for Charlie had stumbled and thrown his rider.

Jan dismounted as soon as he could and many others ran forward, but before they reached him the doctor was on his feet. 'I am all right, only a broken arm,' he shouted.

He directed their operations, and his arm was soon in a sling. Vermaak offered to drive him to the doctor in Meyersdorp and they set off almost immediately. Drysdale said to Simon van Rooyen before he left: 'Tell your wife not to worry. I'll be all right long before she will want me.'

That night there was a great gathering in the schoolroom. A surprising number of dress suits were to be seen and the ladies looked so elegant that many ventured the opinion that you could not see finer dresses in a Johannesburg ballroom. The hall was gay with bunting and paper streamers; the platform banked with hydrangeas and the blue agapanthus lilies, which grew so plentifully in the spruit beyond. A pianist and a violinist had come from Meyersdorp to supply the music.

Mrs Parsons looked the happiest of all in her new black evening frock with a cluster of red flowers that vied with the flush of excitement on her cheeks. She was a noticeable figure. Her black eyes were shining and her hair had been brushed and brilliantined to a jet-like glisten. Her feet could hardly keep still while the musicians tuned up. She squeezed my arm as she went by with her partner. 'Oh, isn't it wonderful?' she whispered. 'To think that we're going to have real music to dance to.'

I knew how passionately she loved dancing. Whenever she could find an opportunity she would promote a 'social' in the schoolroom, and of all who danced to the strains of Prinsloo's concertina none were more energetic than Mrs Parsons. Her vital little body swayed to music with the rhythm of a born dancer. Given the training and opportunity in her younger days she might have been the leader of a London *corps de ballet*.

The dancing began and I went with Mrs Fellowes, the magistrate's wife into the marquee to have a look at the supper tables. We were there only a few minutes before a flap lifted and Simon van Rooyen came towards us. He looked as if he were dazed, and I would have suspected a too long sojourn in the hotel bar if I had not known him to be a temperate man.

'My wife's been taken bad,' he said.

'But I thought . . .,' began Mrs Fellowes. Then she stopped.

'Yes. Not for another three weeks but she started to worry when she heard about the doctor. Now she's took bad and she's crying for Mrs Parsons.'

Mrs Fellowes looked at me and I looked at Mrs Fellowes. We knew the story of the feud and there was Mrs Parsons just beginning to enjoy the dance she had worked for and looked forward to for such a long time.

'Can't you get someone else? asked the magistrate's wife. 'It may be only a false alarm.'

Simon shook his head. 'No, it isn't a false alarm. She knows. I've left Mrs Steenkamp with her but she doesn't want her. She says she knows she's going to die if she can't have Mrs Parsons.'

'Then you will have to ask her.'

'I can't. She wouldn't listen to me.' There was anguish in his eyes. Simon was very fond of Anna.

'I'll bring her here,' said Mrs Fellowes. The dance was over; we could hear the clapping. Mrs Fellowes returned followed by a tight-lipped little woman.

'What is this I hear about Anna?' asked Mrs Parsons.

Simon told her and continued, for despair lent him courage: 'She says she won't have Mrs Steenkamp now the doctor's gone and that she doesn't care if she has to die. She sits there rocking herself and crying for you.'

'That Steenkamp woman is nothing but an old fool. I suppose I'll have to go.'

She fetched her cloak and came back to us.

'Come,' she said to Van Rooyen, 'we must go first to the house to get my things.'

We knew that the little black bag would soon be on its way to Anaa.

The next day the village heard that another sturdy boy had been added to the population, and all was well with the mother.

When Dr Drysdale came back he took the news as a good joke against himself, but Mrs Parsons was not quite happy about it.

'Queer that he shouldn't be able to take his first confinement case here,' she remarked. 'But goodness knows it wasn't my fault.'

A fortnight later I was in the shop when Simon van Rooyen came in and asked to speak to Mrs Parsons. He began to urge something in a low voice but she obstinately shook her head.

'No, not this time,' came her penetrating accents, 'I always stand up for what's due to me as a rule, but this case is different. I'll not have the doctor thinking I wanted to pinch his fee.'

Simon went on urging but she proved obdurate saying as she walked back to the counter where I stood: 'No, not a penny. I mean it.'

He went towards the door shamefaced and unhappy. Coals of fire are such uncomfortable wear.

Suddenly her hard look vanished, and a laugh broke over her face. 'Simon,' she called out. He paused in the doorway. 'You can send me a couple of pigs, if you like.'

And he did.

Dan Jacobson

Stop Thief!

from *A Long Way from London* (1958)

A black-browed angry-looking man he was, and the games he played with his children were always angry games; he was chasing them, he was growling at them, he was snapping his teeth at them, while they shrieked with delight and fear, going pale and tense with fear, but coming back for more, and hanging on to his hands when he declared that he had had enough. There was a boy and a girl, both dark-haired and thin, the boy a little older than his sister and protective towards her with servants and strangers, with everyone but his father: he did not dare to protect her when his father sprang at her from behind a bush, and carried her shrieking, upside down, to his lair that was, he told them, littered with the bones of other children that he had already eaten.

The mother sat aside from these games – she sat at the tea table at the head of the small sweep of lawn towards the swimming bath, beyond which were the trees where her husband and children played, or she lay in the sun on the side of the swimming bath, with a towel about her head, and it was only rarely that she called to them or warned them of their father's stealthy, mock approaches. She sun-bathed or she read in the sun; they were all sun-tanned in that family, from spending so much time at their swimming bath, and from their annual six-weeks' holiday at the Cape, where they lived the life simple in a seaside cottage with only one servant. The big house in Johannesburg seemed to have innumerable servants, all black men in gleaming white jackets and aprons and little white caps like those of an Indian political movement, but in fact only another sign of their servitude, and these black men kept the house like a house on show: the house shone, unmarked by the pressures, the stains and splashes, the disorder of living. Not that the children were the least bit tidy – they dropped things about them as they went, and left the toys and the sticks and the items of clothing lying where they had been dropped, but the servants followed picking up things and putting them in drawers, as though that was all that they had been born for, this dance of attendance on the two nervous, dark-haired children. And the mother, who had been poorly brought up, loved it in the children that they had, so without question or wonder, the insolence of wealth. Once when he had hardly been more than a baby she had asked the boy: 'Would you like to be a little black boy?'

The child had been puzzled that his mother should have asked this. 'No,' he said, frowning, bringing his dark eyebrows together, and looking up in puzzled distaste.

'Why not?'

The puzzlement had left the boy's face, and there had been only distaste as he replied, 'They have nasty clothes.' And for this he had been given a kiss, which he accepted demurely. The children accepted their mother's affection as a matter of course; it was for their father's mock-anger that they lived. The mother knew this and did not resent it: she believed that the insolence she loved in them had come from their father, and for her her husband's violence was profoundly confused with his wealth.

But sometimes, watching the children at their perilous play with their father, even the mother would be afraid. She would lift her eyes from her book, or unwrap the towel which had been muffling the sun's rays to a yellow blur on her eyes, and her heart would sink with fear to see them run and stand breathing behind some tree while their father prowled on tiptoe towards them. So frail they seemed, with their bony elbows poking out from their short-sleeved blouses, and their knees large and round below the dress or khaki shorts that each wore. And he seemed so determined, so muscular in the casual clothing he wore in the evenings, after he had come from work, so large above the children. But she accepted his violence and his strength, and she never protested against the games. She would sometimes watch them play, but her eyes would go back to the book, or she would again carefully wrap the towel about her eyes and her ears, and sink back into her drowse. She seemed sunken under her husband, under his wealth, under his strength; they had come down upon her as the sun did where she lay at the side of the swimming bath, and she questioned them no more than she could have questioned the sun. She had submitted to them.

The father laughed, showing his white teeth, when the children ran yelling from him. In the shadows of the trees they waited for him to come again. He moved slowly towards them, and a lift of his arm made them scamper. He was king of his castle – and castle enough the house was too, in its several acres of ground, and its trees that cut it off from sight of the road.

Then one night the burglar came to their house. It was not for nothing that their house, like every other house in Johannesburg, had every window barred with steel burglar-proofing, that every door had a double lock, that two large dogs were let loose in the grounds at night. It was not for nothing that the father had a revolver in his wardrobe, always loaded and on a high shelf out of reach from the children. For the burglars in Johannesburg can be an ugly lot – gangsters, marauders, hard black men who seem to have nothing to lose, who carry with them knives and knuckledusters and guns.

But this one was not one of these. This one was a boy, a fool, a beginner, come by himself to the wrong house, barked at by the dogs where he stood in the darkness of a corner of the garage between the large painted mudguard of a car and a workbench behind him. He did not even reach for one of the chisels on the bench behind him, but stood squeezing the fingers of one hand in the grasp of the other, as though by that alone he might be able to stop the shivering which shook his shoulders in quick, awful spasms.

But the house did not know what he was and what he might do. The whole house was wild with lights and shouts and the banging of doors. Men, women, they had tumbled out pell-mell from the rooms in which they slept; one of the servants had been roused by the barking of dogs and had seen the burglar slipping into the garage. The house had all been in darkness, and still, so still that not even the trees had moved under the brilliance of the stars in the early morning sky, when the shouts of the servant had first come calamitously upon it. Wild, hoarse, archaic, the shouts had sounded, like the shouts a dreamer might dream he is making, in his deep terror of the darkness around him. Then there had been the other shouts, the house in uproar.

And the father in his pyjamas and dressing gown, with the revolver thrust unsteadily before him, was advancing across the back yard. The servants fell in behind him, even the one who had been guarding the window of the garage. 'Get to the window, you fool!' the father shouted. 'Guard the window!' Unwillingly, one or two went to the window, while the father came closer to the garage door.

He did not know what might be behind the door; he found that he could not push the garage door open, for fear the burglar might spring at him. He was a stranger to himself, roused out of bed by hoarse shouts, hurried downstairs by danger, chilled by the early morning air: to him it seemed that he had never before seen the place he was in; never before felt the lock under his hand; and when he looked back, the house, with the light falling on the paved yard from the open kitchen door, was the house of a stranger, not his at all. The servants were simply people, a throng, some carrying improvised clubs in their hands, all half-dressed, none of them known.

He could not push the door open. The dread of opening himself to whatever might be there was too great. The servants pushed a little closer; and he felt his fear growing tighter and closer within him. They pressed so closely upon him his fear had no room to move, and when he did at last lift up the revolver it was in desperation to drive away the people, who were constricting his fear and pressing it upon him. He lifted the revolver and shouted. 'Leave me!' He tilted it towards the stars and fired. The clamour of the shot was more loud and gross in his ears than he could have imagined, and with it there sprang from the muzzle a gout of flame, vivid in the darkness. When the servants shrank back he felt a momentary sense of release and relaxation, as though he had done the thing for which he had been dragged out of bed, and could be left now to go in peace. Then he felt the door behind him budge.

He leaped away from the door so violently that he stumbled and fell, and he was on his knees with the revolver scratching uselessly against the paving when the burglar came out of the garage. The servants too had staggered back when their master had leaped towards them, so the burglar stood alone in the doorway, with his hands still squeezed together, but lifted now to his chest, like someone beseeching mercy. From where he sprawled on the ground the master could only gasp: 'Catch him. Get round him!' And one or two of the men-servants came forward. They hesitated, and then they saw the spasms shaking the burglar, so they came to him and took him roughly, pinioning him. Their master was struggling to his feet.

'Bring him into the kitchen,' he said. There was a sigh from the group of servants, and a babble, then eagerly they began jostling the burglar towards the kitchen, and he went unresistingly.

To the father the kitchen too looked harsh and strange, a place of urgency, and there seemed to be too many people in it: all the servants, and his wife, and the two children, and the burglar, and the servants' friends, those who had been sleeping illegally but without harmful intent in the rooms in the back yard. These shrank back now, as if only now realising that the events of the night might have consequences for themselves too, and not only for the burglar they had helped to catch.

'You've phoned the police?' the father asked.

'Yes,' the mother said. 'The flying squad's coming.'

The father sat down at the kitchen table, blowing his cheeks out with exhaustion, feeling the tension beginning to ebb from the pit of his stomach. He could not look at the burglar. The mother too, for different reasons, avoided looking at the burglar, but the two children, in their neat white pyjama suits, had eyes for nothing else. They knew all about burglars: they had grown up in Johannesburg, and they knew why the steel bars lay across their bedroom windows, and why they were not allowed outside the house after nightfall, and why the dogs roamed loose at night. But this was the first burglar they had seen. Even the revolver loose in their father's hand could not draw their eyes from the burglar.

He stood in the middle of the kitchen, and his dark eyes were dazed, unseeing. He was a young African – he looked no more than seventeen – an undersized, townbred seventeen years of age. He was wearing a soiled grey sports coat and a pair of ragged trousers that reached only about half-way down his shins, and when the spasms came he shook from his shoes upwards, even his strained brown ankles shaking, his knees, his loins, his shoulders, his head, all shaking. Then the fit would pass and he would simply stand, supported on each side by the household servants.

He seemed to see nothing, to look at nothing, to hear nothing: there seemed to be within him a secret war between his will and the spasms of shaking that came upon him, like a fit. The colour of his face was terrible: he was grey, an ash-grey, a grey like that of the first thinning of the darkness after a rain-sodden night. Sometimes when every other part of his body was free of the spasm, his mouth would still be shaking; his lips were closed, but they shook , as if there were a turbulence in his mouth that he had to void. Then that too would pass.

The little boy at last looked away from the burglar to his father, and saw him sitting weakly in the chair, exhausted. The hand that held the revolver lay laxly on the kitchen table, and from it there rose a faint acrid scent, but the gun looked in his hand like a toy. The father could not move and he could not speak, he sat collapsed, until even the servants looked curiously at him, as the little boy had done, from the burglar to him, and then back to the burglar again. They murmured a little, uncertainly; the two who were holding the burglar loosened their grip on him and shuffled their feet. They waited for direction from their master, but no direction came. The little boy waited for action from his father, but no action came. The son was the first to see that his father could make no action, could give no word.

So he gave the word himself. In a voice that was barely recognisable as his own, his face with its little point of a nose contorted, he screamed in rage and disappointment: 'Hit the burglar! Hit the burglar!' He danced on his bare feet, waving his small fists in the air. 'Why don't you hit the burglar? You must hit the burglar.' He danced like a little demon in his light pyjamas. 'Hit!' he screamed. 'Hit!' His little sister joined in because she heard her brother shouting, and she added her high yell to his: 'Hit the burglar!'

'Get the children out of here!' the father shouted. The children had raised their voices for a moment only, but it had seemed endless, their little voices shrilling for blood. 'What are they doing here?' the father shouted in a fury at the mother, pulling himself up at last. 'Get them out of here!' But he made no move to help the mother, though he saw that she could not manage both dancing, capering children. And when the little boy saw that his father did not move towards him, again he screamed, 'Hit the burglar!'

'Jerry,' the mother gasped to one of the servants, 'help me. Don't stand there!' She was grappling at arm's length with the flailing hands of the little girl.

The dark body of the servant bent over the boy. Then he sprang back waving his hand. The boy had bitten him. So he too being near-distraught with excitement and this last unexpected little assault, reached out and hit the little boy across the back of the head. The boy staggered; he fell down and lay on the sparkling kitchen floor. But it was only for a moment. He came up growling, with hands lifted, curled inwards, and fell upon the burglar. It took two servants to prise him off, and when he was finally carried away over the black powerful shoulder of the one, he had left two deep scratches on the face of the burglar, both from the forehead down, broken by the shelf of bone over the eyes, and continued down the cheeks. The burglar had made no effort to defend himself, knowing what would happen to him if he did anything to hurt the child.

Then the police came and took the burglar away. By that time the children were safe and quiet in the nursery; and later the mother too fell asleep after taking a sedative.

But the servant who had hit the boy was dismissed the very next day, by the mother, who could not bear it that a servant should have struck a child of hers. Least of all the son to whom she now submitted, the son who after the night the burglar had come to the house was not afraid to protect his sister, when her father fell upon her in their games in the garden, and who fought, when he himself was picked up and carried away, as an adult might fight, with his fists and his feet and his knees, to hurt. His will was stronger than his father's, and soon they were facing each other like two men, and the wild games and the shrieking among the trees grew rarer. For the father was afraid of the games he sometimes still had to play with his son, and there was none among them who did not know it, neither the son, nor the daughter, nor the mother, nor the father from whose hands in one night the violence in the family had passed.

Jack Cope

The Flight

from *The Tame Ox and other Stories* (1960)

'Don't touch me, don't touch me. You'll regret it.'

He took her by the jaw with one hand and his fingers pressed into the soft flesh of her cheek and throat. Seeing her so close under the light, he turned paler. The wild bitter fury, the unquenched hate in her look gave him a start of physical fear.

'Are you mad?' he said in his old private voice. And then in the voice and manner which had slowly taken possession of him he began to shout in her face. His colour came back. He was the public man, the estate agent and country auctioneer, forceful, brash.

'What can you do, threatening me?'

'Leave me alone,' she said, and she repeated in a way that chilled him: 'You will regret it, when you are sober.'

'What have I to regret, what more, tell me that. Hell ... you! When are you going to admit the child you are carrying is not mine?'

She shook off his hand and panting for breath in a way that sounded like a succession of little sighs she said, looking him in the eyes: 'Danie, before my Holy Maker I have never dishonoured you, all the time you have left me here alone – never. Ah, but what you have done to me ...'

'Take that back. It's a lie!'

'I will not take back one word, and I have not ...'

He struck her in the face and she stumbled against the table. She turned and he struck her again, shouting in her face.

'Ah, ah,' she panted. She went through to the bedroom. While he poured himself a drink he heard her moving about. Going out on the stoep he was aware at first of the feeling of total darkness and isolation and he listened to the trickle of rain in the downpipes. A fine winter rain but the night was luminous with a moon somewhere behind the clouds, and after a minute he could make out the big bulk of trees standing quite motionless and dripping. The town was two miles off and the nearest house was the forest station beyond the road on the hilltop, a long way even by the footpath. From the bedroom window a soft light shone across the garden and on the white trunk of a tree. Her shadow moved across the light once, twice. A sharp uneasiness came back to him again, remembering her expression, the terrifying concentration that told him as nothing else could the utter truth in her heart. She, small and alone, had the unbearable power to make him afraid.

He heard her footstep on the threshold and she came out on to the stoep. She had put on a raincoat and on one arm was their two-and-a-half-year-old Grieta wrapped in a blanket and a black shawl. In her free hand she carried a small suitcase.

'So!' he put down his glass on the stoep wall.

'Goodbye, you will never see me again if I can help it.'

'So you want to shame me.'

She merely fixed on him her dark large eyes.

'You are running away, you are a coward, Johanna.'

'I am no coward.' She shuddered and her lips trembled so violently that he suddenly laughed.

'Go on – go on then! And where are you heading?'

'I should tell you.'

'All right – you will be back in half an hour. There's nothing out there but the darkness and the forest. And between here and the town no one at all, only the bush Kaffirs and the Kaffirs in the cutters' camp. A nice lot. How will you get past them?'

She went down the steps terribly afraid he would stop her. Her one thought was to get past him and she dared not say anything in case his mood changed and he came down after her. Grieta was asleep with her head resting on her shoulder.

She walked quickly and came out of the open gate on the road. It was all quiet and muffled under the fine cold drizzle; no sound save the drip from the trees, a rustle going like a whisper through the leaves and the faint hum of the overhead telephone wires. In her anxiety to get free from the house she had broken into a run, pausing in moments to listen for her husband's footsteps, and then hurrying on. She did not notice the weight of Grieta or of the case. Being six months with her second baby she did not have her old strength and was easily tired. He had called her mad. Perhaps she was mad. She did not feel things as she used to – she was not fine and balanced and sensitive to all things at once as a girl was and her mind swung about clumsily like a heavy weather-vane. At one moment she was full of a raging self-pity. And then fear took her, fear of all sorts of unknown things, fear for Grieta and herself and the unborn baby, nightmares of fear. And another mood that shut out all other feelings was remorse, bitter regret for the past, for her failings, her love of Danie that she could not keep alive.

They were building two houses on speculation down the road from her entrance and she could smell the wet pine timber and cement. Nobody would be there, not even a watchman. She stood in the road, thinking. Towards the town was the cutters' camp. She was frightened of the hard fierce men living there, black men who were part of the night, wandering the road in twos and threes. The twin thoughts of night on the endless veld and of its possessor the black man were, in her generations, deep blood-anxiety. Sometimes looking at the dark window-panes when her husband was away for the country auctions she would see gleaming eyes in a black face. It might be her own face in the glass or a wild fancy, but it made her heart stop.

Then she thought if her husband followed her in the car he would overtake her on the road to the town. That decided her. She turned the other way thinking to spend the night at the forest station. Geldenhuys, the sub-forester, was an uncouth man, often drunk, but his wife would take in any soul, out of pity. They had twelve children.

She had to keep on the alert for the forest road, a mere gap in the dark wall of trees, and once she went back a little way, thinking she had passed it by. But she found it and heard the water gurgling under the cross-culvert. It was from now on a mere track through the wood and plantations, two paths beaten by truck tyres and grown between with grass and a weed that gave up a strong wild scent when trodden on. Above was the faint ribbon of the sky, and sometimes she passed clearings dotted with pale stumps and timber piles.

Now her whole mind swung on the thought of reaching the Geldenhuys cottage. She was not afraid or anxious, but over her limbs and muscles and joints was settling a lead blanket of weariness. She thought how far she had come and how much farther she had to go. She must be half-way – no, not nearly that. The weight of Grieta was drawing fiery bands of fatigue under her shoulder-blades and she set down the case more frequently to change the child from one arm to the other. If only she could sling her on her back like a black woman. But that was a custom of theirs and she would not be seen doing it. Who would see her, there, at dead of night? All the while the road was climbing but dipped here and there into a gully and the water of a stream talked to her quietly among the stones. The rain was slowly soaking the shawl and blanket round Grieta – how the child slept! Heart against heart, and the little one fearing nothing.

She stopped to change Grieta again. The forest was thick and close on all sides and the tree tops almost touching above. So dark she could hardly see anything, arranging the folds of the blanket. The child woke and began whimpering.

'Shhh darling, Mammie is holding you,' she crooned. She rocked the big bundle and her heart was low; she wanted to sit on the ground and cry. Could she ever get to the cottage? And what if she had taken a wrong turning of the service track. It wound here and there and she could not remember if there were forks or crossings.

At last the child fell asleep again. She settled its weight on her hip and bent to pick up the case. Away off in the darkness she heard the sound of plucked strings. She listened acutely for it to be repeated, and it came on the night like an echo – five or six falling notes ending on a low distinct beat. The hair seemed to rise on the back of her neck and a feeling of numb cold entered her hands and around her lips. The notes came again, varied, soft and faint guitar notes always ending on the same beat – toom – toom! From the first moment she knew what it was beyond doubt – the way a black man played a guitar keeping pace with his steps and perhaps his thoughts. What dark thoughts? He walked through the night playing, it was his private music played to himself, his private night. A man playing music might not be dangerous, yet how could one trust? It was his way of proclaiming himself, his contempt of everything, his possession of the darkness. Toom – toom, the low note repeating.

She wanted to turn and run, but which way? The sound of the guitar came out of the night as if it were a ripple on the forest's slow steady breath. It was everywhere, now a clear note and now an echo among the dripping trees. She stood so deathly still that Grieta woke again and began talking in a sleepy, milk-warm voice.

'Why is it so dark? Where are we, Mammie?'

'Sshh, my baby-lamb. Go to sleep again. We are going to visit Oom Frik and them.'

'Why are you whispering, Mammie?'

'Sshh, lamb.' They both listened to the guitar.

'Who is that playing, is it Oom Frik?'

The mother kissed her. 'It might be. Are you quite warm, my love?'

'I'm so warm! But your face is wet. Mammie, are you crying? Look! there's a light.'

There was a flare of a match being lit off to the left and for a moment it shone like a spark at the end of a long tunnel. It went out. The guitar had stopped and now she heard voices, liquid voices of the black people, and one laughed. They were ahead of her and coming down the track. If she ran now she could escape them; tired as she was she could run for home.

But she did not move. Her heart and stomach were going in painful flutters and the ground heaved dizzily.

She let the case slip to the ground and sank down on it, folding Grieta in both her arms. 'Lord save me, Lord save this child of mine.' She felt firmer and her head cleared and she was busy for a minute making Grieta comfortable on her lap. It was no use running. She had no strength and nowhere to go. Not back to her husband.

The men's footsteps were quite plain to hear now. She could see nothing but imagined them, one on each wheel-track swinging easily along and at home in the forest and the darkness. The night was theirs and she was in their hands. The guitar started again and Grieta, who had caught her terror, gripped her, crying.

The guitar stopped. They came up cautiously, there were two men looking huge looming shapes in their greatcoats, and one struck a match.

'Hai! Hai!' he said intensely, 'It's a white *nooi* and a child.'

The other who was taller almost by a head, laughed in a strange, almost childlike manner as if such an event was beyond his experience.

'Where is the *nooi* going?' the smaller man asked. She had seen by the flare of his match a glistening savage face, the skin roughly pitted and eyes almost lost between high cheekbones and a bony brow. And yet the voice was milk; it could hardly be the same man.

The mother tried to answer but no sound came from her. Grieta said: 'We are going to Oom Frik.'

'Ha!' they both murmured together.

'It is a long way,' the first man said. 'We will take you.'

'No,' the mother said, 'I will go by myself. I was only resting, I will go now.'

She stood up although her knees trembled. Her supreme moment, she knew, had come. She picked up the case and with all the authority and firmness left in her she said: 'Now leave me.'

'Give me the case,' the smaller man said.

She relaxed her fingers and let it fall. 'Take it and leave me. Leave me and my child. Let me go, will you.'

He took the case and handed it to his companion. She began walking. Grieta clung to her, quiet and tense and her eyes round like a little bushbaby. The men followed. She knew they were behind her and she did not know how long she could go without screaming. No one would hear, and a scream might rouse them. They whispered to each other. She went on and on, she could not stop now. Grieta's head sank against her breast and she fell asleep. It was a miracle, she thought, that the child could sleep. 'Lord save her. Lord save us,' she repeated under her breath. The track dipped fairly steeply to cross a gully and there was an opening in the trees to the right, the sky lifting and full of suffused moonlight. The weight of the child made a burning stripe over her shoulders and it was impossible, going downhill, to keep her knees and ankles from wobbling. She turned her shoe on a loose stone and stumbled but still kept Grieta in her arms. In a moment the black man caught up with her. 'Give me the child, *nooi*,' he said. He took the sleeping baby in her bundle, opened one side of his greatcoat and made a big pouch for her. She disappeared into the coat. He had an acrid smell of wood-smoke and tobacco and sweat. The child went on sleeping in the warm shelter against the smell and the movement of his iron-hard body.

He went ahead and the mother followed, and behind them came the taller man carrying the bag. The guitar was slung by a string on the leader's back and it was a silent procession until he began to sing. She did not understand the words but the song was sad and gentle. It had the melancholy of the guitar music yet it was more complicated, falling in slow rhythms. The man behind added his deeper voice in a natural harmonic and the two seemed to share a feeling between them that shut out and excluded her utterly. Still she was carried along between them and her limbs were like machines and the dead weight of fatigue slipped off her. In her heart was a small flame of gladness and a sense of safety. Grieta was safe. In the strong bitter-smelling folds of the man's coat she was secure. She could not have come all this way without them, she would have fallen and lain there and maybe miscarried. How terrified she had been.

At the forest station a dog barked at them, a small white dog that darted among their legs and almost choked in the fierceness of its alarm. The taller man went on the stoep and banged at the door. 'Baas, baas, baas Frik!'

They banged again and called. Suddenly the door was wrenched open and a tall white man stood on the threshold with a rifle in one hand and carrying a storm lantern, 'Ja?'

He was in a crumpled shirt and khaki trousers and locks of unkempt grey hair strayed down to his beard.

'Baas, we found the *nooi* in the forest and we brought her to you.'

He looked at them in turn, holding up the light. 'Mevrou, what is the meaning of this, Mevrou?' he said, astounded.

'Let me rest,' she said. She took Grieta from the man. 'Thank you,' she said.

'Now clear off,' the forester shouted. 'Ag, you vagabonds, Don't let me catch you in these forests.'

'Baas Frik, what have we done, then?'

'Don't ask me, but you are up to no good. That I know.'

They grinned and touched their hats and together they faded back into the darkness. The forester went in to drag his wife from her bed and the mother could hear her sleepy voice somewhere inside the dim, close-smelling house. With all those children sleeping two and three in a bed she knew there would be no place for her, but she sat on a box on the stoep too tired to care. The rain had stopped and somewhere down in the forest the guitar began its endless little private tune coming always to the deep beat, toom – toom! It did not disturb her. Grieta was sleeping and the bundle in which she was wrapped had the smoky acrid smell of the man. Listening and half drowsing she felt mysteriously safe.

Alan Paton

A Drink in the Passage

from *Debbie Go Home* (1961)

In the year 1960 the Union of South Africa celebrated its Golden Jubilee, and there was a nation-wide sensation when the one-thousand-pound prize for the finest piece of sculpture was won by a black man, Edward Simelane. His work, 'African Mother and Child', not only excited the admiration, but touched the conscience or heart or whatever it is, of white South Africa, and was likely to make him famous in other countries.

It was by an oversight that his work was accepted, for it was the policy of the Government that all the celebrations and competitions should be strictly segregated. The committee of the sculpture section received a private reprimand for having been so careless as to omit the words 'for whites only' from the conditions, but was told, by a very high personage it is said, that if Simelane's work was indisputably the best, it should receive the award. The committee then decided that this prize must be given along with the others, at the public ceremony which would bring this particular part of the celebrations to a close.

For this decision it received a surprising amount of support from the white public, but in certain powerful quarters there was an outcry against any departure from the 'traditional policies' of the country, and a threat that many white prize-winners would renounce their prizes. However, a crisis was averted, because the sculptor was 'unfortunately unable to attend the ceremony'.

'I wasn't feeling up to it,' Simelane said mischievously to me. 'My parents, and my wife's parents, and our priest, decided that I wasn't feeling up to it. And finally I decided so too. Of course Majosi and Sola and the others wanted me to go and get my prize personally, but I said, "Boys, I'm a sculptor, not a demonstrator." '

'This cognac is wonderful,' he said, 'especially in these big glasses. It's the first time I've had such a glass. It's also the first time I've drunk a brandy so slowly. In Orlando you develop a throat of iron, and you just put back your head and pour it down, in case the police should arrive.'

He said to me, 'This is the second cognac I've had in my life. Would you like to hear the story of how I had my first?'

You know the Alabaster Bookshop in Von Brandis Street? Well, after the competition they asked me if they could exhibit my 'African Mother and Child'. They gave a whole window to it, with a white velvet backdrop, if there is anything called white velvet, and some complimentary words, *'Black man conquers white world.'*

Well somehow I could never go and look in that window. On my way from the station to the Herald office, I sometimes went past there, and I felt good when I saw all the people standing there, but I would only squint at it out of the corner of my eye.

Then one night I was working late at the Herald, and when I came out there was hardly anyone in the streets, so I thought I'd go and see the window, and indulge certain pleasurable human feelings. I must have got a little lost in the contemplation of my own genius, because suddenly there was a young white man standing next to me.

He said to me, 'What do you think of that, mate?' And you know, one doesn't get called 'mate' every day.

'I'm looking at it,' I said.

'I live near here,' he said, 'and I come and look at it nearly every night. You know it's by one of your own boys, don't you? See, Edward Simelane.'

'Yes, I know.'

'It's beautiful,' he said. 'Look at that mother's head. She's loving that child, but she's somehow watching too. Do you see that? Like someone guarding. She knows it won't be an easy life.'

He cocked his head on one side, to see the thing better.

'He got a thousand pounds for it,' he said.

'That's a lot of money for one of your boys. But good luck to him. You don't get much luck, do you?'

Then he said confidentially, 'Mate, would you like a drink?'

Well honestly I didn't feel like a drink at that time of night, with a white stranger and all, and me still with a train to catch to Orlando.

'You know we black people must be out of the city by eleven,' I said.

'It won't take long. My flat's just round the corner. Do you speak Afrikaans?'

'Since I was a child,' I said in Afrikaans.

'We'll speak Afrikaans then. My English isn't too wonderful. I'm van Rensburg. And you?'

I couldn't have told him my name. I said I was Vakalisa, living in Orlando.

'Vakalisa, eh? I haven't heard that name before.'

By this time he had started off, and I was following, but not willingly. That's my trouble, as you'll soon see. I can't break off an encounter. We didn't exactly walk abreast, but he didn't exactly walk in front of me. He didn't look constrained. He wasn't looking round to see if anyone might be watching.

He said to me, 'Do you know what I wanted to do?'

'No,' I said.

'I wanted a bookshop, like that one there. I always wanted that, ever since I can remember. When I was small, I had a little shop of my own.' He laughed at himself. 'Some were real books, of course, but some of them I wrote myself. But I had bad luck. My parents died before I could finish school.'

Then he said to me, 'Are you educated?'

I said unwillingly, 'Yes.' Then I thought to myself how stupid, for leaving the question open.

And sure enough he asked, 'Far?'

And again unwillingly, I said, 'Far.'

He took a big leap and said, 'Degree?'

'Yes.'

'Literature?'

'Yes.'

He expelled his breath, and gave a long 'Ah'. We had reached his building, Majorca Mansions, not one of those luxurious places. I was glad to see that the entrance lobby was deserted. I wasn't at my ease. I don't feel at my ease in such places, not unless I am protected by friends, and this man was a stranger. The lift was at ground level, marked 'Whites only. Slegs vir Blankes'. Van Rensburg opened the door and waved me in. Was he constrained? To this day I don't know. While I was waiting for him to press the button, so that we could get moving and away from that ground floor, he stood with his finger suspended over it, and looked at me with a kind of honest, unselfish envy.

'You were lucky,' he said. 'Literature, that's what I wanted to do.'

He shook his head and pressed the button, and he didn't speak again until we stopped high up. But before we got out he said suddenly, 'If I had had a bookshop, I'd have given that boy a window too.'

We got out and walked along one of those polished concrete passageways, I suppose you could call it a stoep if it weren't so high up; let's call it a passage. On the one side was a wall, and plenty of fresh air, and far down below, Von Brandis Street. On the other side were the doors, impersonal doors; you could hear radios and people talking, but there wasn't a soul in sight. I wouldn't like living so high; we Africans like being close to the earth. Van Rensburg stopped at one of the doors, and said to me, 'I won't be a minute.' Then he went in, leaving the door open, and inside I could hear voices. I thought to myself, he's telling them who's here. Then after a minute or so, he came back to the door, holding two glasses of red wine. He was warm and smiling.

'Sorry there's no brandy,' he said. 'Only wine. Here's happiness.'

Now I certainly had not expected that I would have my drink in the passage. I wasn't only feeling what you may be thinking. I was thinking that one of the impersonal doors might open at any moment, and someone might see me in a 'white' building, and see me and van Rensburg breaking the liquor laws of the country. Anger could have saved me from the whole embarrassing situation, but you know I can't easily be angry. Even if I could have been, I might have found it hard to be angry with this particular man. But I wanted to get away from there, and I couldn't. My mother used to say to me, when I had said something anti-white, 'Son, don't talk like that, talk as you are.' She would have understood at once why I took a drink from a man who gave it to me in the passage.

Van Rensburg said to me, 'Don't you know this fellow Simelane?'

'I've heard of him,' I said.

'I'd like to meet him,' he said. 'I'd like to talk to him.' He added in explanation, 'You know, talk out my heart to him.'

A woman of about fifty years of age came from the room beyond, bringing a plate of biscuits. She smiled and bowed to me. I took one of the biscuits, but not for all the money in the world could I have said to her 'Dankie, my nooi,' or that disgusting 'Dankie, missus,' nor did I want to speak to her in English because her language was Afrikaans, so I took the risk of it and used the word *'mevrou'* for the politeness of which some Afrikaners would knock a black man down, and I said, in high Afrikaans, with a smile and a bow too, 'Ek is u dankbaar, mevrou.'

But nobody knocked me down. The woman smiled and bowed, and van Rensburg, in a strained voice that suddenly came out of nowhere, said, 'Our land is beautiful. But it breaks my heart.'

The woman put her hand on his arm, and said, 'Jannie, Jannie.'

Then another woman and a man, all about the same age, came up and stood behind van Rensburg.

'He's a B.A.,' van Rensburg told them. 'What do you think of that?'

The first woman smiled and bowed to me again, and van Rensburg said, as though it were a matter for grief, 'I wanted to give him brandy, but there's only wine.'

The second woman said, 'I remember, Jannie. Come with me.'

She went back into the room, and he followed her. The first woman said to me, 'Jannie's a good man. Strange, but good.'

And I thought the whole thing was mad, and getting beyond me, with me a black stranger being shown a testimonial for the son of the house, with these white strangers standing and looking at me in the passage, as though they wanted for God's sake to touch me somewhere and didn't know how, but I saw the earnestness of the woman who had smiled and bowed to me, and I said to her, 'I can see that, mevrou.'

'He goes down every night to look at the statue,' she said. 'He says only God could make something so beautiful, therefore God must be in the man who made it, and he wants to meet him and talk out his heart to him.'

She looked back at the room, and then she dropped her voice a little, and said to me, 'Can't you see, it's somehow because it's a black woman and a black child?'

And I said to her, 'I can see that, mevrou.'

She turned to the man and said of me, 'He's a good boy.'

Then the other woman returned with van Rensburg, and van Rensburg had a bottle of brandy. He was smiling and pleased, and he said to me, 'This isn't ordinary brandy, it's French.'

He showed me the bottle, and I, wanting to get the hell out of that place, looked at it and saw it was cognac. He turned to the man and said, 'Uncle, you remember? When you were ill? The doctor said you must have good brandy. And the man at the bottle-store said this was the best brandy in the world.'

'I must go,' I said. 'I must catch that train.'

'I'll take you to the station,' he said. 'Don't you worry about that.'

He poured me a drink and one for himself.

'Uncle,' he said, 'what about one for yourself?'

The older man said, 'I don't mind if I do,' and he went inside to get himself a glass.

Van Rensburg said, 'Happiness,' and lifted his glass to me. It was good brandy, the best I've ever tasted. But I wanted to get the hell out of there. I stood in the passage and drank van Rensburg's brandy. Then Uncle came back with his glass, and van Rensburg poured him a brandy, and Uncle raised his glass to me too. All of us were full of goodwill, but I was waiting for the opening of one of the impersonal doors. Perhaps they were too, I don't know. Perhaps when you want so badly to touch someone you don't care. I was drinking my brandy almost as fast as I would have drunk it in Orlando.

'I must go,' I said.

Van Rensburg said, 'I'll take you to the station.' He finished his brandy, and I finished mine too. We handed the glasses to Uncle, who said to me, 'Good night, my boy.' The first woman said, 'May God bless you,' and the other woman bowed and smiled. Then van Rensburg and I went down in the lift to the basement, and got into his car.

'I told you I'd take you to the station,' he said. 'I'd take you home, but I'm frightened of Orlando at night.'

We drove up Eloff Street, and he said, 'Did you know what I meant?' I knew that he wanted an answer to something, and I wanted to answer him, but I couldn't, because I didn't know what that something was. He couldn't be talking about being frightened of Orlando at night, because what more could one mean than just that?

'By what?' I asked.

'You know,' he said, 'about our land being beautiful?'

Yes, I knew what he meant, and I knew that for God's sake he wanted to touch me too and he couldn't; for his eyes had been blinded by years in the dark. And I thought it was a pity, for if men never touch each other, they'll hurt each other one day. And it was a pity he was blind, and couldn't touch me, for black men don't touch white men any more; only by accident, when they make something like 'Mother and Child'.

He said to me, 'What are you thinking?'

I said, 'Many things,' and my inarticulateness distressed me, for I knew he wanted something from me. I felt him fall back, angry, hurt, despairing, I didn't know. He stopped at the main entrance to the station, but I didn't tell him I couldn't go in there. I got out and said to him, 'Thank you for the sociable evening.'

'They liked having you,' he said. 'Did you see that they did?'

I said, 'Yes, I saw that they did.'

He sat slumped in his seat, like a man with a burden of incomprehensible, insoluble grief. I wanted to touch him, but I was thinking about the train. He said good night, and I said it too. We each saluted the other. What he was thinking, God knows, but I was thinking he was like a man trying to run a race in iron shoes, and not understanding why he cannot move.

When I got back to Orlando, I told my wife the story, and she wept.

James Matthews

The Park

from *Présence Africaine* 16 (44) 1962

He looked longingly at the children on the other side of the railings; the children sliding down the chute, landing with feet astride on the bouncy lawn; screaming as they almost touched the sky with each upward curve of their swings; their joyful demented shrieks at each dip of the merry-go-round. He looked at them and his body trembled and ached to share their joy; buttocks to fit board, and hands and feet to touch steel. Next to him, on the ground, was a bundle of clothing, washed and ironed, wrapped in a sheet.

Five small boys, pursued by two bigger ones, ran past, ignoring him. One of the bigger boys stopped. 'What are you looking at, you brown ape?' the boy said, stooping to pick up a lump of clay. He recognised him. The boy had been present the day he was put out of the park. The boy pitched the lump, shattering it on the rail above his head, and the fragments fell on his face.

He spat out the particles of clay clinging to the lining of his lips, eyes searching for an object to throw at the boys separated from him by the railing. More boys joined the one in front of him and he was frightened by their number.

Without a word he shook his bundle free of clay, raised it to his head and walked away.

As he walked he recalled his visit to the park. Without hesitation he had gone through the gates and got onto the nearest swing. Even now he could feel that pleasurable thrill that travelled the length of his body as he rocketed himself higher, higher, until he felt that the swing would up-end him when it reached its peak. Almost leisurely he had allowed it to come to a halt like a pendulum shortening its stroke and then ran towards the see-saw. A white boy, about his own age, was seated opposite him. Accordion-like their legs folded to send the see-saw jerking from the indentation it pounded in the grass. A hand pressed on his shoulder stopping a jerk. He turned around to look into the face of the attendant.

'Get off!'

The skin tightened between his eyes. Why must I get off? What have I done? He held on, hands clamped onto the iron attached to the wooden see-saw. The white boy jumped off from the other end and stood a detached spectator.

'You must get off!' The attendant spoke in a low voice so that it would not carry to the people who were gathering. 'The council say,' he continued, 'that us blacks don't use the same swings as the whites. You must use the swings where you stay,' his voice apologizing for the uniform he wore that gave him the right to watch that little white boys and girls were not hurt while playing.

'There's no park where I stay.' He waved a hand in the direction of a block of flats. 'Park on the other side of town but I don't know where.' He walked past them. The mothers with their babies, pink and belching, cradled in their arms, the children lolling on the grass, his companion from the see-saw, the nurse girls – their uniforms their badge of indemnity – pushing prams. Beside him walked the attendant.

The attendant pointed an accusing finger at a notice board at the entrance. 'There. You can read for youself.' Absolving him of all blame.

He struggled with the red letters on the white background. 'Blankes Alleen. Whites Only.' He walked through the gates and behind him the swings screeched, the see-saw rattled, and the merry-go-round rumbled.

He walked past the park each occasion he delivered the washing, eyes wistfully taking in the scene.

He shifted the bundle to a more comfortable position, easing the pain biting into his shoulder muscles. What harm would I be doing if I were to use the swings? Would it stop the swings from swinging? Would the chute collapse? The bundle pressed deeper and the pain became an even line across his shoulders and he had no answer to his reasoning.

The park itself, with its wide lawns and flower beds and rockeries and dwarf trees, meant nothing to him. It was the gaily painted red-and-green tubing, the silver chains and brown boards, transport to never-never land, which gripped him.

Only once, long ago, and then almost as if by mistake, had he been on something to beat it. He had been taken by his father, one of the rare times he was taken anywhere, to a fairground. He had stood captivated by the wooden horses with their gilded reins and scarlet saddles dipping in time to the music as they whirled by.

For a brief moment he was astride one, and he prayed it would last forever, but the moment lasted only the time it took him to whisper the prayer. Then he was standing clutching his father's trousers, watching the others astride the dipping horses.

Another shifting of the bundle and he was at the house where he delivered the clothing his mother had washed in a round tub filled with boiling water, the steam covering her face with a film of sweat. Her voice, when she spoke, was as soft and clinging as the steam enveloping her.

He pushed the gate open and walked around the back watching for the aged lap-dog, which at his entry would rush out to wheeze asthmatically around his feet and nip with blunt teeth at his ankles.

A round-faced African girl, her blackness heightened by the white starched uniform she wore, opened the kitchen door to let him in. She cleared the table and he placed the bundle on it.

'I call madam,' she said, the words spaced and highly pitched as if she had some difficulty in uttering the syllables in English. Her buttocks bounced beneath the tight uniform and the backs of her calves shone with fat.

'Are you sure you've brought everything?' was the greeting he received each time he brought the bundle, and each time she checked every item and as usual nothing was missing. He looked at her and lowered his voice as he said, 'Everything there, merrum.'

What followed had become a rountine between the three of them.

'Have you had anything to eat?' she asked him.

He shook his head.

'Well, we can't let you go off like that.' Turning to the African woman in the white, starched uniform. 'What have we got?'

The maid swung open the refrigerator door and took out a plate of food. She placed it on the table and set a glass of milk next to it.

The white woman left the kitchen when he was seated and he was alone with the maid.

His nervousness left him and he could concentrate on what was on the plate.

A handful of peas, a dab of mashed potatoes, a tomato sliced into bleeding circles, a sprinkling of grated carrot, and no rice.

White people are funny, he told himself. How can anyone fill himself with this? It doesn't form a lump like the food my mama makes.

He washed it down with milk.

'Thank you, Annie,' he said as he pushed the glass aside.

Her teeth gleamed porcelain-white as she smiled.

He sat fidgeting, impatient to be outside away from the kitchen with its glossy, tiled floor and steel cupboards ducoed a clinical white to match the food-stacked refrigerator.

'I see you've finished.' The voice startled him. She held out an envelope containing the rand note – payment for his mother's weekly struggle over the washtub. 'This is for you.' A five-cent piece was dropped into his hand, a long fingernail raking his palm.

'Thank you, merrum.' His voice was hardly audible.

'Tell you mother I'm going away on holiday for about a month and I'll let her know when I'm back.'

Then he was dismissed and her high heels tapped out of the kitchen.

He nodded his head at the African maid who took an apple from a bowl bursting with fruit and handed it to him.

He grinned his thanks and her responding smile bathed her face in light.

He walked down the path finishing the apple with big bites.

The dog was after him before he reached the gate, its hot breath warming his heels. He turned and poked his toes on its face. It barked hoarsely in protest, a look of outrage on its face.

He laughed delightedly at the expression which changed the dog's features into those of an old man.

'See you do that again.' He waved his feet in front of the pug's nose. The nose retreated and made an about-turn, waddling away with its dignity deflated by his affront.

As he walked, he mentally spent his sixpence.

I'll buy a penny drops, the sour ones that taste like limes, a penny bull's-eyes, a packet of sherbet with the licorice tube at the end of the packet, and a penny star toffees, red ones that turn your spit into blood.

His glands were titillated and his mouth filled with saliva. He stopped at the first shop and walked in.

Trays were filled with expensive chocolates and sweets of a type never seen in the jars on the shelves of the Indian shop on the corner where he stayed. He walked out not buying a thing.

His footsteps lagged as he reached the park.

The nurse girls with their babies and prams were gone, their places occupied by old men, who, with their hands holding up their stomachs, were casting disapproving eyes over the confusion and clatter confronting them.

A ball was kicked perilously close to an old man, and the boy who ran after it stopped short as the old man raised his stick, daring him to come closer.

The rest of them called to the boy to get the ball. He edged closer and made a grab at it as the old man swung his cane. The cane missed the boy by more than a foot and he swaggered back, the ball held under his arm. Their game was resumed.

He watched them from the other side of the railings – the boys kicking the ball, the children cavorting on the grass, even the old men, senile on the seats; but most of all, the children enjoying themselves with what was denied him, and his whole body yearned to be part of them.

'Shit it!' He looked over his shoulder to see if anyone had heard him. 'Shit it!' he said louder. 'Shit on them! Their park, the grass, the swings, the see-saw, everything! Shit it! Shit it!'

His small hands impotently shook the tall railings towering above his head.

It struck him that he would not be seeing the park for a whole month, that there would be no reason for him to pass it.

Despair filled him. He had to do something to ease his anger.

A bag filled with fruit peelings was on top of the rubbish stacked in a waste basket fitted to a pole. He reached for it and frantically threw it over the railings. He ran without waiting to see the result.

Out of breath three streets further, he slowed down pain stabbing beneath his heart. The act had brought no relief, only intensified the longing.

He was oblivious of the people passing, the hoots of the vehicles whose paths he crossed without thinking. And once, when he was roughly pushed aside, he did not even bother to look and see who had done it.

The familiar shrieks and smells told him that he was home.

The Indian shop could not draw him out of his melancholy mood and he walked past it, his five-cent piece unspent in his pocket.

A group of boys were playing with tyres on the pavement.

Some of them called him but he ignored them and turned into a short side-street.

He mounted the flat stoep of a two-storeyed house with a façade that must once have been painted but had now turned a nondescript grey with the red brick underneath showing.

Beyond the threshold the room was dim. He walked past the scattered furniture with a familiarity that did not need guidance.

His mother was in the kitchen hovering over a pot perched on a pressure stove.

He placed the envelope on the table. She put aside the spoon and stuck a finger under the flap of the envelope, tearing it into half. She placed the rand note in a spoutless teapot on the shelf.

'You hungry?'

He nodded his head.

She poured him a cup of soup and added a thick slice of brown bread.

Between bites of bread and sips of soup which scalded his throat, he told his mother that there would not be any washing coming during the week.

'Why? What the matter? What I do?'

'Nothing. Merrum say she go away for month. She let mama know she back.'

'What I do now?' Her voice took on a whine and her eyes strayed to the teapot containing the money. The whine hardened to reproach as she continued. 'Why don't she let me know she going away then I look for another merrum?' She paused. 'I slave away and the pain never leave my back but it too much for her to let me know she go away. The money I get from her keeps us nice and steady. How I go cover the hole?'

He wondered how the rand notes he had brought helped to keep them nicely steady. There was no change in their meals. It was, as usual, not enough, and the only time they received new clothes was at Christmas.

'I must pay the burial, and I was going to tell Mr Lemonsky to bring lino for the front room. I'm sick looking at the lino full of holes but I can forget now. With no money you got as much hope as getting wine on Sunday.'

He hurried his eating to get away from the words wafted towards him, before it could soak into him, trapping him in the chair to witness his mother's miseries.

Outside, they were still playing with their tyres. He joined them half-heartedly. As he rolled the tyre his spirit was still in the park on the swings. There was no barrier to his coming and he could do as he pleased. He was away from the narrow streets and squawking children and speeding cars. He was in a place of green grass and red tubing and silver steel. The tyre rolled past him. He made no effort to grab it.

'Get the tyre.' 'You sleep?' 'Don't you want to play anymore?'

He walked away ignoring their cries.

Rage boiled up inside him. Rage against the houses with their streaked walls and smashed panes filled by too many people; against the over-flowing garbage pails outside doors; the alleys and streets; and against a law he could not understand – a law that shut him out of the park.

He burst into tears. He swept his arms across his cheeks to check his weeping.

He lowered his hands to peer at the boy confronting him.

'I think you cry!'

'Who say I cry? Something in my eye and I rub it.'

He pushed past and continued towards the shop. 'Cry-baby!' the boy's taunt rang after him.

The shop's sole iron-barred window was crowded. Oranges were mixed with writing paper and dried figs were strewn on school slates.

Clothing and crockery gathered dust. Across the window a cockroach made its leisurely way, antennae on the alert.

Inside the shop was as crowded as the window. Bags covered the floor leaving a narrow path to the counter.

The shopkeeper, an ancient Indian with a face tanned like cracked leather, leaned across the counter. 'Yes, boy?' He showed teeth scarlet with betel. 'Come'n, boy. What you want? No stand here all day.' His jaws worked at the betel nut held captive by his stained teeth.

He ordered penny portions of his selection.

He transferred the sweets to his pockets and threw the torn containers on the floor and walked out. Behind him the Indian murmured grimly, jaws working faster.

One side of the street was in shadow. Her sat with his back against the wall, savouring the last of the sun.

Bull's-eye, peppermint, a piece of licorice – all lumped together in his cheek. For a moment the park was forgotten.

He watched without interest the girl advancing.

'Mama say you must come'n eat.' She stared at his bulging cheek, one hand rubbing the side of her nose. 'Gimme.' He gave her a bull's-eye which she dropped into her mouth between dabs at her nose.

'Wipe your snot!' he ordered her, showing his superiority. He walked past. She followed sucking and sniffing.

Their father was already seated at the table when they entered the kitchen.

'Must I always send somebody after you?' his mother asked.

He slipped into his seat and then hurriedly got up to wash his hands before his mother could find fault with yet another point.

Supper was a silent affair except for the scraping of spoon across a plate and an occasional sniff from his sister.

A thought came to his mind almost at the end of the meal. He sat spoon poised in the air shaken by its magnitude. Why not go to the park after dark? After it had closed its gates on the old men, the children, and nurses with their prams! There would be no one to stop him.

He could think no further. He was light-headed with the thought of it. His mother's voice, as she related her day to his father, was not the steam that stung, but a soft breeze wafting past him, leaving him undisturbed. Then qualms troubled him. He had never been in that part of town at night. A band of fear tightened across his chest, contracting his insides, making it hard for him to swallow his food. He gripped his spoon tightly, stretching his skin across his knuckles.

I'll do it! I'll go to the park as soon as we're finished eating. He controlled himself with difficulty. He swallowed what was left on his plate

and furtively watched to see how the others were faring. Hurry up!
Hurry up!

He hastily cleared the table when his father pushed the last plate aside
and began washing up.

Each piece of crockery washed was passed to his sister whose sniffing
kept pace with their combined operation.

The dishes done, he swept the kitchen and carried out the garbage bin.

'Can I go play, mama?'

'Don't let me have to send for you again.'

His father remained silent, buried behind the newspaper.

'Before you go,' his mother stopped him, 'light the lamp and hang it in
the passage.'

He filled the lamp with paraffin, turned up the wick and lit it. The light
glimmered weakly through the streaked glass.

The moon, to him, was a fluorescent ball: light without warmth – and
the stars, fragments chipped off it. Beneath street lights, card games
were in session. He sniffed the nostril-prickling smell of dagga as he
walked past. Dim doorways could not conceal couples clutching at each
other.

Once clear of the district, he broke into a trot. He did not slacken his
pace as he passed through the downtown area with its wonderland shop
windows. His elation seeped out as he neared the park and his footsteps
dragged.

In front of him was the park with its gate and iron railings. Behind the
railings, impaled, the notice board. He could see the swings beyond. The
sight strengthened him.

He walked over, his breath coming faster. There was no one in sight.
A car turned a corner and came towards him and he started at the sound
of its engine. The car swept past, the tyres softly licking the asphalt.

The railings were icy-cold to his touch and the shock sent him into
action. He extended his arms and with monkey-like movements pulled
himself up to perch on top of the railings then dropped onto the newly
turned earth.

The grass was damp with dew and he swept his feet across it. Then he
ran and the wet grass bowed beneath his bare feet.

He ran towards the swings, the merry-go-round, see-saw to chute,
hands covering the metal.

Up the steps to the top of the chute. He stood outlined against the sky.
He was a bird; an eagle. He flung himself down on his stomach, sliding
swiftly. Wheeeeee! He rolled over when he slammed onto the grass. He
looked at the moon for an instant then propelled himself to his feet and
ran for the steps of the chute to recapture that feeling of flight. Each time

he swept down the chute, he wanted the trip never to end, to go on sliding, sliding, sliding.

He walked reluctantly past the see-saw, consoling himself with pushing at one end to send it whacking on the grass.

'Shit it!' he grunted as he strained to set the merry-go-round into action. Thigh tensed, leg stretched, he pushed. The merry-go-round moved. He increased his exertions and jumped on, one leg trailing at the ready to shove if it should slow down. The merry-go-round dipped and swayed. To keep it moving, he had to push more than he rode. Not wanting to spoil his pleasure, he jumped off and raced for the swings.

Feet astride, hands clutching silver chains, he jerked his body to gain momentum. He crouched like a runner then violently straightened. The swing widened its arc. It swept higher, higher, higher. It reached the sky. He could touch the moon. He plucked a star to pin to his breast. The earth was far below. No bird could fly as high as he. Upwards and onwards he went.

A light switched on in the hut at the far side of the park. It was a small patch of yellow on a dark square. The door opened and he saw a figure in the doorway. Then the door was shut and the figure strode towards him. He knew it was the attendant. A torch glinted brightly as it swung at his side.

He continued swinging.

The attendant came to a halt in front of him, out of reach of the swing's arc, and flashed his torch. The light caught him in mid-air.

'God dammit!' the attendant swore. 'I told you before you can't get on the swings.'

The rattle of the chains when the boy shifted his feet was the only answer he received.

'Why you come back?'

'The swings. I come back for the swings.'

The attendant catalogued the things denied them because of their colour. Even his job depended on their goodwill.

'Blerry whites! They get everything!'

All his feelings urged him to leave the boy alone, to let him continue to enjoy himself but the fear that someone might see them hardened him.

'Get off! Go home!' he screamed, his voice harsh, his anger directed at the system that drove him against his own. 'If you don't get off, I go for the police. You know what they do to you.'

The swing raced back and forth.

The attendant turned and hurried towards the gate.

'Mama, Mama.' His lips trembled, wishing himself safe in his mother's kitchen, sitting next to the still-burning stove with a comic spread across his knees. 'Mama. Mama.' His voice mounted, wrenched from this throat, keeping pace with the soaring swing as it climbed the sky. Voice and swing. Swing and voice. Higher. Higher. Higher. Until they were one.

At the entrance of the park the notice board stood tall, its shadow elongated, pointing towards him.

Can Themba

The Will to Die

from *The Will to Die* (1972, written c. 1964)

I have heard much, have read much more, of the Will to Live; stories of fantastic retreats from the brink of death at moments when all hope was lost. To the aid of certain personalities in the bleakest crises, spiritual resources seem to come forward from what? Character? Spirit? Soul? Or the Great Reprieve of a Spiritual Clemency – hoisting them back from the muddy slough of the Valley of the Shadow.

But the Will to Die has intrigued me more . . .

I have also heard that certain snakes can hypnotise their victim, a rat, a frog or a rabbit, not only so that it cannot flee to safety in the over-whelming urge for survival, but so that it is even attracted towards its destroyer, and appears to enjoy dancing towards its doom. I have often wondered if there is not some mesmeric power that Fate employs to engage some men deliberately, with macabre relishment, to seek their destruction and to plunge into it.

Take Foxy . . .

His real name was Philip Matauoane, but for some reason, I think from the excesses of his college days, everybody called him Foxy. He was a teacher in a small school in Barberton, South Africa. He had been to Fort Hare University College in the Cape Province, and had majored in English (with distinction) and Native Administration. Then he took the University Education Diploma (teaching) with Rhodes University, Grahamstown.

He used to say, 'I'm the living exemplar of the modern, educated African's dilemma. I read English and trained to be a teacher – the standard profession for my class those days; but you never know which government department is going to expel you and pitchfork you into which other government department. So I also took Native Administration as a safety device.'

You would think that that labels the cautious, providential kind of human.

Foxy was a short fellow, the type that seems in youth to rush forward towards old age, but somewhere, around the eve of middle-age, stops dead and ages no further almost forever. He had wide, owlish eyes and a trick with his mouth that suggested withering contempt for all creation. He invariably wore clothes that swallowed him: the coat overflowed and drowned his arms, the trousers sat on his chest in front and billowed obscenely behind. He was a runt of a man.

But in that unlikely body resided a live, restless brain.

When Foxy first left college, he went to teach English at Barberton High School. He was twenty-five then, and those were the days when high school pupils were just ripe to provoke or prejudice a young man of indifferent morals. He fell in love with a young girl, Betty Kumalo, his own pupil.

I must explain this spurious phenomenon of 'falling in love'. Neither Foxy nor Betty had the remotest sense of commitment to the irrelevance of marrying some day. The society of the times was such that affairs of this nature occurred easily. Parents did not mind much. Often they would invite a young teacher to the home, and as soon as he arrived, would eclipse themselves, leaving the daughter with stern but unmistakable injunctions to 'be hospitable to the teacher'.

We tried to tell Foxy, we his fellow-teachers, that this arrangement was too nice to be safe, but these things had been written in the stars.

Foxy could not keep away from Betty's home. He could not be discreet. He went there every day, every unblessed day. He took her out during weekends and they vanished into the countryside in his ancient Chevrolet.

On Mondays he would often say to me, 'I don't know what's wrong with me. I know this game is dangerous. I know Betty will destroy me, but that seems to give tang to the adventure. Hopeless. Hopeless,' and he would throw his arms out.

I had it out with him once.

'Foxy,' I said, 'you must stop this nonsense. It'll ruin you.'

There came a glint of pleasure, real ecstasy it seemed to me, into his eyes. It was as if the prospect of ruin was hallelujah.

He said to me, 'My intelligence tells me that it'll ruin me, but there's a magnetic force that draws me to that girl, and another part of me, much stronger than intelligence, just simply exults.'

'Marry her, then, and get done with it.'

'No!' He said it so vehemently that I was quite alarmed. 'Something in me wants that girl pregnant but not a wife.'

I thought it was a hysterical utterance.

You cannot go flinging wild oats all over a fertile field, not even wild weeds. It had to happen.

If you are a school-teacher, you can only get out of a situation like that if you marry the girl, that is if you value your job. Foxy promptly married – another girl! But he was smart enough to give Betty's parents £50. That, in the hideous system of *lobola*, the system of bride-price, made Betty his second wife. And no authority on earth could accuse him of seduction.

But when his wife found out about it, she battered him, as the Americans would say, 'To hell and back.'

Foxy started drinking heavily.

Then another thing began to happen; Foxy got drunk during working hours. Hitherto, he had been meticulous about not cultivating one's iniquities in the teeth of one's job, but now he seemed to be splashing in the gutter with a will.

I will never forget the morning another teacher and I found him stinkingly drunk about half-an-hour before school was to start. We forced him into a shebeen and asked the queen to let him sleep it off. We promised to make the appropriate excuses to the headmaster on his behalf. Imagine our consternation when he came reeling into the assembly hall where we were saying morning prayers with all the staff and pupils. How I prayed that morning!

These things happen. Everybody noticed Foxy's condition, except, for some reason, the headmaster. We hid him in the Biology Laboratory for the better part of the day, but that did not make the whole business any more edifying. Happily, he made his appearance before we could perjure ourselves to the headmaster. Later, however, we learned that he had told the shebeen-queen that he would go to school perforce because we other teachers were trying to get him into trouble for absence from work and that we wished to 'outshine' him. Were we livid?

Every one of his colleagues gave him a dressing down. We told him that no more was he alone in this: it involved the dignity of us all. The whole location was beginning to talk nastily about us. Moreover, there was a violent, alcoholic concoction brewed in the location called Barberton. People just linked 'Barberton', 'High' and 'School' to make puns about us.

Superficially, it hurt him to cause us so much trouble, but something deep down in him did not allow him really to care. He went on drinking hard. His health was beginning to crack under it. Now, he met every problem with the gurgling answer of the bottle.

One night, I heard that he was very ill, so I went to see him at home.

His wife had long since given him up for lost; they no more even shared a bedroom. I found him in his room. The scene was ghastly. He was lying in his underwear in bed linen which was stained with the blotches of murdered bugs. There was a plate of uneaten food that must have come the day before yesterday. He was breathing heavily. Now and then he tried to retch, but nothing came up. His bloodshot eyes rolled this way and that, and whenever some respite graciously came, he reached out for a bottle of gin and gulped at it until the fierce liquid poured over his stubbled chin.

He gibbered so that I thought he was going mad. Then he would retch violently again, that jolting, vomitless quake of a retch.

He needed a doctor but he would not have one. His wife carped, 'Leave the pig to perish.'

I went to fetch the doctor, nevertheless. We took quite a while, and when we returned, his wife sneered at us, 'You wouldn't like to see him now.' We went into his room and found him lost in oblivion. A strange girl was lying by his side.

In his own house!

I did not see him for weeks, but I heard enough. They said that he was frequenting dangerous haunts. One drunken night he was beaten up and robbed. Another night he returned home stark naked, without a clue as to who had stripped him.

Liquor should have killed him, but some compulsive urge chose differently. After a binge one night, he wandered hopelessly about the darksome location streets, seeking his home. At last, he decided on a gate, a house, a door. He was sure that that was his home. He banged his way in, ignored the four or five men singing hymns in the sitting-room, and staggered into the bedroom. He flung himself on to the bed and hollered, 'Woman, it's time that I sleep in your bed. I'm sick and tired of being a widower with a live wife.'

The men took up sticks and battered Foxy to a pulp. They got it into their heads that the woman of the house had been in the business all the time; that only now had her lover gone and got drunk enough to let the cat out of the bag. They beat the woman, too, within millimetres of her life. All of them landed in jail for long stretches.

But I keep having a stupid feeling that somehow, Philip 'Foxy' Matauoane would have felt: 'This is as it should be.'

Some folks live the obsession of death.

Dugmore Boetie

Three Cons

from *The Classic* (1968, written c. 1964)

My friend Tiny and I were walking through the streets of Johannesburg back to Sophiatown, determined to steal nothing on the way. To ensure this, we rammed our hands in our pockets and kept our eyes glued on to the pavement before us. As we crossed Main Street, someone in a khaki dust coat with a duster rag in his hand paused from cleaning a shoe shop window and greeted Tiny. After walking on for a few yards, Tiny said to me, 'Will you believe it, Duggie, if I tell you that the man we just saw cleaning the window back there doesn't work at that shop?' I nearly stopped in my tracks. Tiny said, 'Don't stop, man, walk on ... He works all the blocks in town dressed as he is: dust coat and red duster. His name is Victor. He's what the Americans call a confederate trickster.'

'Confidence trickster,' I corrected.

'When he sees a likely victim admiring what's in a window, he'll move and start cleaning that window. After a few strokes with the duster he'll move in and say, ' If you like that, I can get it for you. You see, I work here. If you want it I can get it for your Back Door at half price.' It never fails, Duggie. Victor goes to the back of the shop. When he comes back, he'll be carrying a neatly-wrapped shoe box. The victim won't open the box for fear of getting Victor into trouble with his employers. Money will exchange hands. His victims are mostly domestic servants. When they reach wherever they're going, they find that they've just bought themselves something like a pair of old useless shoes. I don't care for such a profession, Duggie, it's too slimy for my liking. I prefer the open game. Like the gangster, the shop-lifter, the smash-and-grabber. A life with no strings attached, no conscience pricker. Something that needs no brains, you know what I mean, something like jazz that goes in the one ear and out the other. No regrets, no nothing. Like food you ate the previous day.

'But Victor's game, it's too classic. It has to be because it lives with you forever. It sticks to the subconscious mind like meat in pie. A future of "Brother, look over your shoulder!" The danger in this game Duggie, lies in injured ego. Not the deed, but the principle will get you in the end. What greater provocation is there on earth than when you enter a human being's mind and start misplacing things? No living soul wants to be made a fool of.

'The success of every confe ... I mean confidence trickster depends upon cleverness. Cleverness that oozes from a brain that gets its stimulants from the vitamins of an empty stomach. It's like a game of snakes and ladders; the victim usually prefers the rungs of the ladders instead of the long and safe way around. Only to be swallowed by the snakes, and emerging from its bowels with nothing to show but grief and misery.

'The seekers of manna from heaven are responsible for the con-man's bulging waist-line, Duggie. If they ignore the shortcuts of life, they won't be touched. They should let the perspiration of their brows tighten their purse strings. Be deaf, and he'll never reach you, let alone touch you. Remember, his life depends upon explaining.'

'Tiny,' I said with awe, 'I didn't know you got education!'

After listening to Tiny, I started thinking deeply. I was mauling over what Tiny told me. Like Tiny, I didn't care much for such a game. In spite of that, that confidence trickster gave me an idea. An idea that could be made to work. All it needed was guts and brains. And I think I had them both.

The following day I went to the Indian Market alone. I didn't want to tell Tiny my idea, in case it back-fired. At the Market I bought a second-hand khaki overall. I took it to an Indian tailor shop. I instructed the Indian to sew the letters 'O.K' on the shoulder-blades. The letters should be red. This is the uniform of the African staff at the O.K. Bazaar, a department store.

This Bazaar is big. It boasts three storeys and a basement and about two to three hundred African workers. It's always packed with customers of all races, so it's only natural to see African labourers carrying goods about the place.

I spent one whole week studying the place from the inside. When I was sure of all the angles, I donned my overalls and went to work. I wasn't a registered employee, but that did not worry me because only I knew it.

I took advantage of two facts. One: to all whites, a black man's features don't count. Only his colour does. To them, we are all alike. When you're black, you're just another black man. It's all contempt. They don't even bother about your real name. To them, you're just John, Jim, or Boy. Your daddy spends nine months thumbing through a dictionary for a fancy name to bestow on you and then some white trash comes and calls you what he feels like without even bothering to think or look at you. If that isn't contempt, then what is?

The second fact – and I like it best – is that they have a total disregard for our mental efficiency. That's why they couldn't dream that anyone, especially a black man, could be capable of doing what I did in this big Bazaar.

If I took from the third floor, the staff there thought I was from the second floor. If I looted the basement they thought I was from the ground floor. A white assistant actually said to me in the basement department, 'Boy, leave that and help me here.'

If I carried the goods across town to Black Mischark's shop, the police thought I was a delivery boy. I was the only one who didn't think. It wasn't worth it. Not while everyone else did the thinking for me.

As time went on things became even easier for me. I was getting accustomed to the place. I learned where to take and where not to take. Best of all, the staff, both black and white, took a liking to me. Hell, it looked as if I was going to get promotion. A few white sales ladies would send me out for sandwiches and cigarettes for them. I was a John-do-this and a John-do-that. The only place I kept well away from was the pay-master's office. Hell, I'm not greedy. Fridays, when the boys queued for their pay, I was gone.

Good things never last, and they always seem to stop lasting on a Saturday.

'Stop thief!'

I froze. At last, I thought. When I looked back, I saw one of our European female workers frantically pointing at an African who was hurrying away with four boxes under his armpits.

'Stop thief! Stop him, John!' She was looking directly at me. When I hesitated, she said, 'Hurry, he's getting away!' I cursed the thief under my breath and made after him with every intention of letting him get away. Just as I was about to veer off at one of the entrances, two interfering white men caught him just as he was about to sprint through the street door.

'Here Boy, we got him for you.' I was going to ignore them when I became conscious of someone breathing down my neck. Looking back, I saw the floor manager breathing flames like a dragon. With him were two African workers. There was nothing I could do. So I did the next best thing. I grabbed the thief.

There was fear in the man's eyes; he was shaking badly. I was shaking just as badly, but they must have thought that it was because I was holding him.

As we led the thief back to the manager's office, I sought for a way out of this awkward situation. I felt certain that once I entered that office my doom would be sealed. Desperately I reviewed my position, but everything looked hopeless. I stole a quick glance at the floor manager and saw him angrily grinding his teeth as he led the procession toward his office. Clearly this was no time for me to ask one of the African workers to hold the thief for me. Spectators made way for us and as we moved on our number swelled with officials and curious onlookers. You'd have thought we'd just caught a dangerous maniac. I saw my chances of getting away slip with every step we took. As he opened the office door, the manager looked at me and growled, 'Don't lose him, or you lose your job.' I didn't mind. You can't lose what you haven't got. I pushed the thief roughly in, meaning to retreat, but someone pushed me from behind and heeled the door shut. It was the second white man.

Putting up a bold front, I went to the closed door. My hand was closing around the knob when the floor manager paused, phone in hand and said to the second white man, 'Don't think we didn't know.'

'Oh God!' I groaned. So all the time he knew. Turning to me he said, 'You stay right here and guard this kaffir.' The kettle and the pot are on the same stove, I thought. All sizzling equally. After that I was completely disregarded. It was as if I didn't exist.

There's nothing so gnawing and nerve-wracking as uncertainty, especially if you're guilty. It's like hanging in mid-air with nothing holding you up. You know you're going to fall and break your neck. That's all right, you've half expected it. But what produces mental agony to a point of madness is this unseen thing that's holding you up. I was fast becoming a total nervous wreck.

There was a light tap on the door. Me and the thief both stiffened visibly. Instead of the expected police, the lady who served at the counter where the goods were stolen came in. She gave me a dazzling smile and the thief a dirty look.

'You want me, *mynheer*?' she asked, addressing herself to the floor manager.

'No, Miss Smith, you go back to your counter, I'll send for you when the time comes.' She turned and left the office, but not before flashing me another smile.

I was changing my weight to the other foot when my jaw itched violently. Before I could guess again, they came in. I don't know whether it's imagination, but every time I see a policeman, my jaw begins to itch violently. They didn't even knock, and I didn't have to guess their size. They were there. I felt my skin crawl.

'Boy!' The floor manager had to call me twice before I could swallow my fear.

'Boy, will you go and tell Miss Smith that the police are here.'

'Heh? Yes *Baas*.'

'Then come back here with her.'

I walked out of that office stiff-legged, as if I was leading a funeral procession. I just couldn't believe such luck.

'Then come back here,' the man had said. What kind of fool did he take me to be? In pirate stories, once they make you walk the plank, you don't walk it twice.

Once through that door, they never saw me again.

* * *

Durban stank of one problem. All the domestic servants were men. In Johannesburg we have women. You can always make love to one of them and live with her in her room at the back of the master's house. No rent, free food and one or two of the master's shirts while he imagines that they are in the wash.

In Durban there was no such thing. Otherwise I wouldn't have bothered with sleeping accommodation. I would have done what I used to do back in Johannesburg. Made love to one of the working girls and lived with her. Even if living in the backyards of white men's houses is not without its ups and downs.

I'm reminded of one night when I went to my girl's room at the back of a white man's house. It was late when I got there and my girl must have long been through with her duties. What I really remember about that night, is that it was so cold that my nose wouldn't stop running. When I got to the room I knocked. But there was no reply. I tried again. Still no result. I made for the spot where she always kept the key for me to find when she was on her day off, but I drew a blank.

Again I repeated the knock and still nothing happened. I was afraid to knock loud for fear of waking up the house. That time of night they have a dangerous tendency to shoot first and ask questions after. After repeated knocks, I gave up. I decided to think.

One thing stood out like the sharp point of a Zulu warrior's spear, and that was if I tried reaching Sophiatown at that time of the night, I would end up in gaol for having no night special. I looked around for a place to spend the night, but could see none. Then I became conscious that I was leaning against one of those giant trees that are so frequently found in white suburbs. Without a moment's hesitation, I climbed the tree, meaning to spend the remainder of the night there. Better a human bird than a gaol bird.

I must have dozed off because something startled me. I would have fallen headfirst to the ground if I hadn't taken the precaution of tying my belt to a branch and then around my arm. I peered into the night hoping to see what it was. Then I heard a noise coming from my girl's room. Someone unfamiliar with the mechanism of the lock was fumbling with it from inside.

Hurriedly I undid my belt from the branch. My fingers were numb with cold and my descent was not without hazards. Finally, I made the ground without much damage except bruised hands and torn pants. I was in time to see a stark naked figure emerging from the door and making his way to the toilet which was situated on the other side of the garden. Like lightning I went into the dark room and locked the door behind me. I groped toward the bed where the bitch was deep in sleep. Undressing quickly, I crawled into bed. As my icy body came into contact with hers, she moaned and said, 'Why so cold dear?'

'Shut up you bitch.' I felt her shiver, and knew it was not from cold.

I waited. Then it came. First softly, then loud, then louder, then frantic. It was the naked bum outside. Unlike him, I raised my voice triumphantly and said, 'Climb the tree pal, climb the tree.'

As usual, I'm not the brainiest of men. There are people with far more. The bastard pushed the mouth of the garden-hose through the small window, and before I knew what was happening, the water tap was turned on full force, soaking me, bitch, blankets and all . . .

* * *

'How do you like the town, Duggie, after three whole weeks at home?'

'I don't.'

It was Tiny talking to me. We were walking down Bree Street in the direction of Doornfontein. There was a bitter feeling in me. I don't know whether it was caused by failure to prove myself, or just plain fear. I had just recovered after getting my jaw broken in a mix-up with the police.

Tiny was penniless. I had a shilling piece somewhere in one of my pockets.

He interrupted my troubled thoughts by saying, 'Give me one of your cigarettes, Duggie.' Shaking my head, I said, 'I wish I had some, Tiny.'

The tips of my fingers went into the top small pocket of my jacket where I kept stubs. They came out empty. I went through all my pockets with the same results. Then my fingers met with the shilling piece.

I looked around and spied a tea-room. Holding the shilling exposed in the palm of my hand I said to Tiny, 'What do I get with this? Lotus or Rhodian?'

'Get Lotus Duggie, I want to smoke, not brag. When one is broke, it's always wise to stick to necessities.' I went into the shop.

In the shop, lined next to the counter, stood five Africans all dressed in blue overalls. In their hands were empty jam tins for tea-buying purposes. Daily customers I thought. Just behind, sat European customers having their lunch.

I took a place next to the first African, I didn't want to waste time. I rapped the shilling piece on the glass counter to draw the owner's attention. If you irritate them that way, they quickly get rid of you by serving you first.

'Packet of ten Lotus please.' He gave me the packet I handed over the shilling. He was about to give me my four pennies change and there the matter would have ended. But fate took a hand. Just before he gave me my change, he was urgently beckoned by one of his servants. Instead of giving me my change he answered the summons.

Then I saw it. I didn't see it before because his body had been screening it. A roll of pounds as thick as my wrist lay just within arm's reach. It was tied with a rubber band.

I must be a born thief. A real stranger to hesitation with impulses that work overtime. Without thinking or looking around, my hand shot out like the tongue of a deadly cobra. At the same time I sensed rather than saw Tiny inspecting the window display just outside the shop entrance.

It was fast. Too damn fast, especially for the naked eye. One minute the roll was in my hand, the next it was sailing through the air towards Tiny who caught it expertly and without thinking. Then he slowly made his way to the opposite pavement.

I was about to bolt through the door after Tiny, but when I looked at the African next to me, I saw to my amazement that he wasn't a bit concerned with me. Instead, he was grumbling to his fellow worker about the slowness of the shopkeeper. It was unbelievable, yet it happened. NO ONE SAW ME!

I decided to wait for my change.

When the shopkeeper came back, the first thing he noticed was that the money was missing. Next, he looked at me. The look he gave me made me curse myself for still being where I was. What kept me rooted to the spot still disturbs me right up to this day.

Without a word he went around the counter and bolted the door, surprising everyone in the cafe. Then he told the Africans to point out the one who took the money. They all denied having seen the money, let alone having stolen it.

After carefully searching each one of them, he told them to go. Then he turned to me. Before touching me he told me to give back the money. For the first time in my life I became truthful. I told him I didn't have any money. As always, people just never believe.

'Look,' he said as he released a long-held breath. His body bent sideways and he leaned with his elbow on the glass counter. 'I know you have the money even if I didn't see you take it. Now let's be sensible; if you give me the money of your own free will I promise to let you go and there the matter will end. But if I search you and find it on you, I'll make you suffer.'

'Go to hell! I haven't got your money, but you got mine, you got my four penny change.'

'Listen, for the last time, give me the money.' I stood my ground.

Then he searched me. He didn't find anything of course. How could he when the money was on the other side of the street?

'Now you give me my change.' I said, full of confidence.

'You stay right there,' he said meaningfully.

He was picking on me because those other Africans were his daily customers, also I was nicely dressed in a way. My clothes alone made me suspect number one, also the fact that it was my first time in his bloody shop. He was bright, but in a dull way.

Again he searched me. This time he was more careful. When he didn't find anything, he went to the phone and rang for the police. While we waited, he kept pestering me about his money, promising to let me go if I showed him where it was.

I told him I didn't know anything about any money. That the only money I know of was my four pennies change. And that still had to come to me.

I was more sure of myself. My only prayer was that they wouldn't send the same policeman who broke my jaws the month before. The shopkeeper could go to hell. He wasn't going to get any money from me even if he borrowed.

There was a sharp rap on the door and in they came. I mean the police. It wasn't the same one as before. This one was even bigger. With him was another one with a young pink face.

'Where is the Kaffir?' he asked. The shopkeeper indicated with his head towards where I stood.

He turned to me and bellowed, 'Where is the money Kaffir?' I told him I don't know anything about any money except my four pennies change. The child policeman came nearer me and started jabbing me in the ribs with his baton. I kept facing the burly one who kept repeating the question. I was about to repeat that I didn't know anything about any money when they started working on me.

Suddenly, I heard a female voice scream, 'Stop! Stop! Can't you see you're killing him?'

The burly policeman said, 'Keep out of this lady, it's none of your business.'

'Where's the money Kaffir?'

'No money Baas, only my change.'

'You'll talk yet, you black bastard.'

My face was so numb, it didn't seem to hurt anymore. It lost all sense of feeling.

He was throttling me with the front of my shirt by screwing it into my adam's apple. The veins on my forehead stood out like ropes.

His right knee turned my face into putty while his right fist kneaded different images into it.

I heard the lovely voice again, now more furious, 'Of course it's my business. I was sitting right here when this whole filthy business started!'

'Lady, for Godsake,' said the policeman impatiently, 'Will you for Godsake keep out of this?'

Squinting, I saw a white woman glaring at my tormentors with bared teeth, hair drooping over eyelids and arms resting plam-down on the table. She was spitting out words faster than a green snake could spit poison. And the words were just as venomous. The way she went on, it was as if she was suffering more than I was. A lovely bundle of fury.

'The fact that I was sitting right here when this whole thing started makes it my business.'

'Lady, for the last time mind your own business.' I began to wonder if those were the only words he knew.

'To begin with, that boy didn't take the blasted money.'

'How do you know?' scowled the policeman.

'Because it's a logical, if not a physical impossibility for him to have taken the money.'

'Lady, you're not telling me anything.'

'If,' continued my guardian angel, 'God did not use some of your brains to give you extra buttocks, you would have arrived at the same conclusion. Stop behaving like a third rate bully and start using that machinery in your head! Leaving it to rust won't get the money back!'

'Madam, one more word out of you and I'll run you in for obstructing the police in the course of their duty.'

'Since when does duty mean beating up a man who hasn't been formally charged, and on private premises for that matter? In fact you are so brainless that I believe you would make a fool of yourself in front of your superiors by locking me up for trying to help you!'

As the man straightened up from beating me, I saw that his trouser at the knee was soggy with my blood.

'All right, lady,' he said harshly, 'You tell us what happened to the money.'

'I can give you a hundred reasons why it is absurd to think that this poor boy could have taken the money. But three should be enough for a brain like yours!'

Then she went into detail. It was like a school teacher explaining a simple subject to a sixteen-year-old pupil who had no business in the third grade.

'That boy was searched twice by that insolent shopkeeper, yet the money was not found. If, as you say, he took the money, then where in heaven's name could he have hidden it? Because,' said my lady with great emphasis and spacing every word, 'he never once left the shop, nor did he move from where you found him! Tell me now,' she was almost begging, 'do you for one minute think that if anyone could steal a roll of pounds he would be so stupid as to stand and wait for a measly fourpence change when the door was wide open and he had every chance of running away? I', she spat, 'would give everything I possess, and I can assure you it's considerable,' (Chancer, I thought) 'if that boy is guilty of theft.' I stole a glance at the other customers and saw most of them shaking their heads in agreement.

The burly policeman said, 'Then who the hell has stolen the money?'

'That's the first sensible question you've asked since coming through that door! Now kindly direct that same question to the man who phoned for you. For all we know, he might not have lost a penny, it's just his word against this poor boy's.'

The law turned his eyes from the lady to the shopkeeper and there was fury in them.

The shopkeeper said to the lady, 'Do you think I would have gone to all the trouble of searching the Natives and calling the police all for nothing?'

'There! You have done it!' said my lady triumphantly.

'Did you really lose money?' asked the policeman facing the shopkeeper.

'Of course!' sputtered the man indignantly.

'Show me the spot where the money was.' The man pointed at the spot behind the counter. The policeman released his hold on me for the first time, leaving me to sway with the tide. Examining the spot the policeman asked, 'Was he the only Kaffir that was standing next to the counter at the time?' Worriedly the shopkeeper shook his head.

'There were four or five others,' he added hastily, 'But those were my daily customers. They would not steal from me.'

'What!' barked the policeman, throwing his hands into the air in a hopeless show of disgust. 'Are you standing there telling me that Kaffirs don't steal when they were born for nothing else? Why did you let the rest of them go?'

There was a note of anger in the shopkeeper's voice as he said, 'I tell you those other natives are my daily customers, and this boy, well, you can see for yourself how he's dressed, he's a skellum.'

'Now you're judging the man by his clothes!' came the voice of my guardian angel. 'If I remember right, those boys that were here were in a much better position to have made off with the money! They were all dressed in overalls – right! And in their hands they carried jam tins – right! Jam tins full of tea bought from this shop! It's my guess that the roll of pounds – if he did lose a roll of pounds – is safely reposing at the bottom of a jam tin of tea!'

The big policeman started to say something, when an eager voice from the cradle said, 'Should I lock up this Kaffir?'

'No, better let him go. What will we charge him with? We've already messed up his face.'

Turning to me, the policeman said, 'Scoot Kaffir.' I slowly shook my head and stood my ground. Glaring at me he said, 'Well, what the hell are you waiting for?' Through bloody, swollen lips I said, 'My four-penny change.'

Turning to the shopkeeper he asked, 'Has he got change coming?'

'Yes, he gave me a shilling for an eight-penny packet of cigarettes.'

From his pocket he selected four pennies and threw them at me. I picked up the pennies and counted them carefully before pocketing them.

Nadine Gordimer

A Chip of Glass Ruby

from *Not for Publication* (1965)

When the duplicating machine was brought into the house, Bamjee said, 'Isn't it enough that you've got the Indians' troubles on your back?' Mrs Bamjee said, with a smile that showed the gap of a missing tooth but was confident all the same, 'What's the difference, Yusuf? We've all got the same troubles.'

'Don't tell me that. We don't have to carry passes; let the natives protest against passes on their own, there are millions of them. Let them go ahead with it.'

The nine Bamjee and Pahad children were present at this exchange as they were always; in the small house that held them all there was no room for privacy for the discussion of matters they were too young to hear, and so they had never been too young to hear anything. Only their sister and half-sister, Girlie, was missing; she was the eldest, and married. The children looked expectantly, unalarmed and interested, at Bamjee, who had neither left the dining-room nor settled down again to the task of rolling his own cigarettes which had been interrupted by the arrival of the duplicator. He looked at the thing that had come hidden in a wash-basket and conveyed in a black man's taxi, and the children turned on it too, their black eyes surrounded by thick lashes like those still, open flowers with hairy tentacles that close on whatever touches them.

'A fine thing to have on the dining-room table,' was all he said at last. They smelled the machine among them; a smell of cold black grease. He went out, heavily on tiptoe, in his troubled way.

'It's going to go nicely on the sideboard!' Mrs Bamjee was busy making a place by removing the two pink glass vases filled with plastic carnations and the hand-painted velvet runner with the picture of the Taj Mahal.

After supper she began to run off leaflets on the machine. The family lived in the dining-room – the three other rooms in the house were full of beds – and they were all there. The older children shared a bottle of ink while they did their homework, and the two little ones pushed a couple of empty milk bottles in and out the chair legs. The three-year-old fell asleep and was carted away by one of the girls. They all drifted off to bed eventually; Bamjee himself went before the older children – he was a fruit and vegetable hawker and was up at half-past four every morning to get to the market by five. 'Not long now,' said Mrs Bamjee. The older children looked up and smiled at him. He turned his back on her. She still wore the traditional clothing of a Moslem woman, and her body, which was scraggy and unimportant as a dress on a peg when it was not host to a child, was wrapped in the trailing rags of a cheap sari, and her thin black plait was greased. When she was a girl, in the Transvaal town where they lived still, her mother fixed a chip of glass ruby in her nostril; but she had abandoned that adornment as too old-style, even for her, long ago.

She was up until long after midnight, turning out leaflets. She did it as if she might have been pounding chillies.

Bamjee did not have to ask what the leaflets were. He had read the papers. All the past week Africans had been destroying their passes and then presenting themselves for arrest. Their leaders were jailed on charges of incitement, campaign offices were raided – someone must be helping the few minor leaders who were left to keep the campaign going without offices or equipment. What was it the leaflets would say – 'Don't go to work tomorrow', 'Day of Protest', 'Burn Your Pass for Freedom'? He didn't want to see.

He was used to coming home and finding his wife sitting at the dining-room table deep in discussion with strangers or people whose names were familiar by repute. Some were prominent Indians, like the lawyer, Dr Abdul Mohammed Khan, or the big businessman, Mr Moonsamy Patel, and he was flattered, in a suspicious way, to meet them in his house. As he came home from work next day he met Dr Khan coming out of the house, and Dr Khan – a highly educated man – said to him, 'A wonderful woman.' But Bamjee had never caught his wife out in any presumption; she behaved properly, as any Moslem woman should, and once her business with such gentlemen was over would never, for instance, have sat down to eat with them. He found her now back in the kitchen, setting about the preparation of dinner and carrying on a conversation on several different wave lengths with the children. 'It's really a shame if you're tired of lentils, Jimmy, because that's what you're getting – Amina, hurry up, get a pot of water going – don't worry, I'll mend that in a minute, just bring the yellow cotton, and there's a needle in the cigarette box on the sideboard.'

'Was that Dr Khan leaving?' said Bamjee.

'Yes, there's going to be a stay-at-home on Monday. Desai's ill, and he's got to get the word around by himself. Bob Jali was up all last night printing leaflets, but he's gone to have a tooth out.' She had always treated Bamjee as if it were only a mannerism that made him appear uninterested in politics, the way some woman will persist in interpreting her husband's bad temper as an endearing gruffness hiding boundless goodwill, and she talked to him of these things just as she passed on to him neighbours' or family gossip.

'What for do you want to get mixed up with these killings and stonings and I don't know what? Congress should keep out of it. Isn't it enough with the Group Areas?'

She laughed. 'Now, Yusuf, you know you don't believe that. Look how you said the same thing when the Group Areas started in Natal. You said we should begin to worry when we get moved out of our own houses here in the Transvaal. And then your own mother lost her house in Noorddorp, and there you are; you saw that nobody's safe. Oh, Girlie was here this afternoon, she says Ismail's brother's engaged – that's nice, isn't it? His mother will be pleased; she was worried.'

'Why was she worried?' asked Jimmy, who was fifteen, and old enough to patronize his mother.

'Well, she wanted to see him settled. There's a party on Sunday week at Ismail's place – you'd better give me your suit to give to the cleaners tomorrow, Yusuf.'

One of the girls presented herself at once. 'I'll have nothing to wear, Ma.'

Mrs Bamjee scratched her sallow face. 'Perhaps Girlie will lend you her pink, eh? Run over to Girlie's place now and say I say will she lend it to you.'

The sound of commonplaces often does service as security, and Bamjee, going to sit in the armchair with the shiny armrests that was wedged between the dining-room table and the sideboard, lapsed into an unthinking doze that, like all times of dreamlike ordinariness during those weeks, was filled with uneasy jerks and starts back into reality. The next morning, as soon as he got to market, he heard that Dr Khan had been arrested. But that night Mrs Bamjee sat up making a new dress for her daughter; the sight disarmed Bamjee, reassured him again, against his will, so that the resentment he had been making ready all day faded into a morose and accusing silence. Heaven knew, of course, who came and went in the house during the day. Twice in that week of riots, raids, and arrests, he found black women in the house when he came home; plain ordinary native women in doeks, drinking tea. This was not a thing other Indian women would have in their homes, he thought bitterly; but then his wife was not like other people, in a way he could not put his finger on, except to say what it was not: not scandalous, not punishable, not rebellious. It was, like the attraction that had led him to marry her, Pahad's widow with five children, something he could not see clearly.

When the Special Branch knocked steadily on the door in the small hours of Thursday morning, he did not wake up, for his return to consciousness was always set in his mind to half-past four, and that was more than an hour away. Mrs Bamjee got up herself, struggled into Jimmy's raincoat, which was hanging over a chair, and went to the front door. The clock on the wall – a wedding present when she married Pahad – showed three o'clock when she snapped on the light, and she knew at once who it was on the other side of the door. Although she was not surprised, her hands shook like a very old person's as she undid the locks and the complicated catch on the wire burglar-proofing. And then she opened the door and they were there – two coloured policemen in plain clothes. 'Zanip Bamjee?'
  'Yes.'
  As they talked, Bamjee woke up in the sudden terror of having overslept. Then he became conscious of men's voices. He heaved himself out of bed in the dark and went to the window, which, like the front door, was covered with a heavy mesh of thick wire against intruders from the dingy lane it looked upon. Bewildered, he appeared in the dining-room, where the policemen were searching through a soapbox of papers beside the duplicating machine. 'Yusuf, it's for me,' Mrs Bamjee said.
  At once, the snap of a trap, realisation came. He stood there in an old shirt before the two policemen, and the woman was going off to prison because of the natives. 'There you are!' he shouted standing away from her. 'That's what you've got for it. Didn't I tell you? Didn't I? That's the end of it now. That's the finish. That's what it's come to.' She listened with her head at the slightest tilt to one side, as if to ward off a blow, or in compassion.
  Jimmy, Pahad's son, appeared at the door with a suitcase; two or three of the girls were behind him. 'Here, Ma, you take my green jersey.' 'I've found your clean blouse.' Bamjee had to keep moving out of their way as they helped their mother to make ready. It was like the preparation for one of the family festivals his wife made such a fuss over; wherever he put himself, they bumped into him. Even the two policemen mumbled,

'Excuse me,' and pushed past into the rest of the house to continue their search. They took with them a tome that Nehru had written in prison; it had been bought from a persevering travelling salesman and kept, for years, on the mantelpiece. 'Oh, don't take that, please,' Mrs Bamjee said suddenly, clinging to the arm of the man who had picked it up.

The man held it away from her.

'What does it matter, Ma?'

It was true that no one in the house had ever read it; but she said, 'It's for my children.'

'Ma, leave it.' Jimmy, who was squat and plump, looked like a merchant advising a client against a roll of silk she had set her heart on. She went into the bedroom and got dressed. When she came out in her old yellow sari with a brown coat over it, the faces of the children were behind her like faces on the platform at a railway station. They kissed her goodbye. The policemen did not hurry her, but she seemed to be in a hurry just the same.

'What am I going to do?' Bamjee accused them all.

The policemen looked away patiently.

'It'll be all right. Girlie will help. The big children can manage. And Yusuf —' The children crowded in around her; two of the younger ones had awakened and appeared, asking shrill questions.

'Come on', said the policemen.

'I want to speak to my husband.' She broke away and came back to him, and the movement of her sari hid them from the rest of the room for a moment. His face hardened in suspicious anticipation against the request to give some message to the next fool who would take up her pamphleteering until he, too, was arrested. 'On Sunday,' she said. 'Take them on Sunday.' He did not know what she was talking about. 'The engagement party,' she whispered, low and urgent. 'They shouldn't miss it. Ismail will be offended.'

They listened to the car drive away. Jimmy bolted and barred the front door, and then at once opened it again; he put on the raincoat that his mother had taken off. 'Going to tell Girlie,' he said. The children went back to bed. Their father did not say a word to any of them; their talk, the crying of the younger ones and the argumentative voices of the older, went on in the bedrooms. He found himself alone; he felt the night all around him. And then he happened to meet the clock face and saw with a terrible sense of unfamiliarity that this was not the secret night but an hour he should have recognised: the time he always got up. He pulled on his trousers and his dirty white hawker's coat and wound his grey muffler up to the stubble on his chin and went to work.

The duplicating machine was gone from the sideboard. The policemen had taken it with them, along with the pamphlets and the conference reports and the stack of old newspapers that had collected on top of the wardrobe in the bedroom – not the thick dailies of the white men, but the thin, impermanent-looking papers that spoke up, sometimes interrupted by suppression or lack of money, for the rest. It was all gone. When he had married her and moved in with her and her five children, into what had been the Pahad and became the Bamjee house, he had not recognised the humble, harmless, and apparently useless routine tasks – the minutes of meetings being written up on the dining-room table at night, the government blue books that were read while the latest baby was suckled, the employment of the fingers of the older children in the fashioning of crinkle-paper Congress rosettes – as activity intended to move mountains. For years and years he had not noticed it, and now it was gone.

The house was quiet. The children kept to their lairs, crowded on the beds with the doors shut. He sat and looked at the sideboard, where the plastic carnations and the mat with the picture of the Taj Mahal were in place. For the first few weeks he never spoke of her. There was the feeling, in the house, that he had wept and raged at her, that boulders of reproach had thundered down upon her absence, and yet he had said not one word. He had not been to inquire where she was; Jimmy and Girlie had gone to Mohammed Ebrahim, the lawyer, and when he found out that their mother had been taken – when she was arrested, at least – to a prison in the next town, they had stood about outside the big prison door for hours while they waited to be told where she had been moved from there. At last they had discovered that she was fifty miles away in Pretoria. Jimmy asked Bamjee for five shillings to help Girlie pay the train fare to Pretoria, once she had been interviewed by the police and had been given a permit to visit her mother; he put three two-shilling pieces on the table for Jimmy to pick up, and the boy, looking at him keenly, did not know whether the extra shilling meant anything, or whether it was merely that Bamjee had no change.

It was only when relations and neighbours came to the house that Bamjee would suddenly begin to talk. He had never been so expansive in his life as he was in the company of these visitors, many of them come on a polite call rather in the nature of a visit of condolence. 'Ah, yes, yes, you can see how I am – you see what has been done to me. Nine children, and I am on the cart all day. I get home at seven or eight. What are you to do? What can people like us do?'

'Poor Mrs Bamjee. Such a kind lady.'

'Well, you see for yourself. They walk in here in the middle of the night and leave a houseful of children. I'm out on the cart all day, I've got a living to earn.' Standing about in his shirt sleeves, he became quite animated; he would call for the girls to bring fruit drinks for the visitors. When they were gone, it was as if he, who was orthodox if not devout and never drank liquor, had been drunk and abruptly sobered up; he looked dazed and could not have gone over in his mind what he had been saying. And as he cooled, the lump of resentment and wrongedness stopped his throat again.

Bamjee found one of the little boys the centre of a self-important group of championing brothers and sisters in the dining-room one evening. 'They've been cruel to Ahmed.'

'What has he done?' said the father.

'Nothing! Nothing!' The little girl stood twisting her handkerchief excitedly.

An older one, thin as her mother, took over, silencing the others with a gesture of her skinny hand. 'They did it at school today. They made an example of him.'

'What is an example?' said Bamjee impatiently.

'The teacher made him come up and stand in front of the whole class, and he told them, "You see this boy? His mother's in jail because she likes the natives so much. She wants the Indians to be the same as natives." '

'It's terrible,' he said. His hands fell to his sides. 'Did she ever think of this?'

'That's why Ma's *there*,' said Jimmy, putting aside his comic and emptying out his schoolbooks upon the table. 'That's all the kids need to know. Ma's there because things like this happen. Petersen's a coloured teacher, and it's his black blood that's brought him trouble all his life, I suppose. He hates anyone who says everybody's the same, because that takes away from him his bit of whiteness that's all he's got. What d'you expect? It's nothing to make too much fuss about.'

'Of course, you are fifteen and you know everything,' Bamjee mumbled at him.

'I don't say that. But I know Ma, anyway.' The boy laughed.

There was a hunger strike among the political prisoners, and Bamjee could not bring himself to ask Girlie if her mother was starving herself too. He would not ask; and yet he saw in the young woman's face the gradual weakening of her mother. When the strike had gone on for nearly a week one of the elder children burst into tears at the table and could not eat. Bamjee pushed his own plate away in rage.

Sometimes he spoke out loud to himself while he was driving the vegetable lorry. 'What for?' Again and again: 'What for?' She was not a modern woman who cut her hair and wore short skirts. He had married a good plain Moslem woman who bore children and stamped her own chillies. He had a sudden vision of her at the duplicating machine, that night just before she was taken away, and he felt himself maddened, baffled, and hopeless. He had become the ghost of a victim, hanging about the scene of a crime whose motive he could not understand and had not had time to learn.

The hunger strike at the prison went into the second week. Alone in the rattling cab of his lorry, he said things that he heard as if spoken by someone else, and his heart burned in fierce agreement with them. 'For a crowd of natives who'll smash our shops and kill us in our houses when their time comes.' 'She will starve herself to death there.' 'She will die there.' 'Devils who will burn and kill us.' He fell into bed each night like a stone, and dragged himself up in the mornings as a beast of burden is beaten to its feet.

One of these mornings, Girlie appeared very early, while he was wolfing bread and strong tea – alternate sensations of dry solidity and stinging heat – at the kitchen table. Her real name was Fatima, of course, but she had adopted the silly modern name along with the clothes of the young factory girls among whom she worked. She was expecting her first baby in a week or two, and her small face, her cut and curled hair, and the sooty arches drawn over her eyebrows did not seem to belong to her thrust-out body under a clean smock. She wore mauve lipstick and was smiling her cocky little white girl's smile, foolish and bold, not like an Indian girl's at all.

'What's the matter?' he said.

She smiled again. 'Don't you know? I told Bobby he must get me up in time this morning. I wanted to be sure I wouldn't miss you today.'

'I don't know what you're talking about.'

She came over and put her arm up around his unwilling neck and kissed the grey bristles at the side of his mouth. 'Many happy returns! Don't you know it's your birthday?'

'No,' he said. 'I didn't know, didn't think –' He broke the pause by swiftly picking up the bread and giving his attention desperately to eating and drinking. His mouth was busy, but his eyes looked at her, intensely black. She said nothing, but stood there with him. She would not speak, and at last he said, swallowing a piece of bread that tore at his throat as it went down, 'I don't remember these things.'

The girl nodded, the Woolworth baubles in her ears swinging. 'That's the first thing she told me when I saw her yesterday – don't forget it's Bajie's birthday tomorrow.'

He shrugged over it. 'It means a lot to children. But that's how she is. Whether it's one of the old cousins or the neighbour's grandmother, she always knows when the birthday is. What importance is my birthday, while she's sitting there in a prison? I don't understand how she can do the things she does when her mind is always full of woman's nonsense at the same time – that's what I don't understand with her.'

'Oh, but don't you see?' the girl said. 'It's because she doesn't want anybody to be left out. It's because she always remembers; remembers everything – people without somewhere to live, hungry kids, boys who can't get educated – remembers all the time. That's how Ma is.'

'Nobody else is like that.' It was half a complaint.

'No, nobody else', said his stepdaughter.

She sat herself down at the table, resting her belly. He put his head in his hands. 'I'm getting old' – but he was overcome by something much more curious, by an answer. He knew why he had desired her, the ugly widow with five children; he knew what way it was in which she was not like the others; it was there, like the fact of the belly that lay between him and her daughter.

Ezekiel Mphahlele

Mrs Plum

from *In Corner B* (1967)

My madam's name was Mrs Plum. She loved dogs and Africans and said
that everyone must follow the law even if it hurt. These were three big
things in Madam's life.

I came to work for Mrs Plum in Greenside, not very far from the
centre of Johannesburg, after leaving two white families. The first white
people I worked for as a cook and laundry woman were a man and his
wife in Parktown North. They drank too much and always forgot to pay
me. After five months I said to myself No. I am going to leave these
drunks. So that was it. That day I was as angry as a red-hot iron when it
meets water. The second house I cooked and washed for had five children
who were badly brought up. This was in Belgravia. Many times they
called me You Black Girl and I kept quiet. Because their mother heard
them and said nothing. Also I was only new from Phokeng my home, far
away near Rustenburg, I wanted to learn and know the white people
before I knew how far to go with the others I would work for afterwards.
The thing that drove me mad and made me pack and go was a man who
came to visit them often. They said he was a cousin or something like
that. He came to the kitchen many times and tried to make me laugh. He
patted me on the buttocks. I told the master. The man did it again and I
asked the madam that very day to give me my money and let me go.

These were the first nine months after I had left Phokeng to work in
Johannesburg. There were many of us girls and young women from
Phokeng, from Zeerust, from Shuping, from Kosten, and many other
places who came to work in the cities. So the suburbs were full of black-
ness. Most of us had already passed Standard Six and so we learned more
English where we worked. None of us likes to work for white farmers,
because we know too much about them on the farms near our homes.
They do not pay well and they are cruel people.

At Easter time so many of us went home for a long weekend to see our people and to eat chicken and sour milk and *morogo* – wild spinach. We also took home sugar and condensed milk and tea and coffee and sweets and custard powder and tinned foods.

It was a home-girl of mine, Chimane, who called me to take a job in Mrs Plum's house, just next door to where she worked. This is the third year now. I have been quite happy with Mrs Plum and her daughter Kate. By this I mean that my place as a servant in Greenside is not as bad as that of many others. Chimane too does not complain much. We are paid six pounds a month with free food and free servant's room. No one can ever say that they are well paid, so we go on complaining somehow. Whenever we meet on Thursday afternoons, which is time-off for all of us black women in the suburbs, we talk and talk and talk: about our people at home and their letters; about their illnesses; about bad crops; about a sister who wanted a school uniform and books and school fees; about some of our madams and masters who are good, or stingy with money or food, or stupid or full of nonsense, or who kill themselves and each other, or who are dirty – and so many things I cannot count them all.

Thursday afternoons we go to town to look at the shops, to attend a women's club, to see our boy-friends, to go to bioscope some of us. We turn up smart, to show others the clothes we bought from the black men who sell soft goods to servants in the suburbs. We take a number of things and they come round every month for a bit of money until we finish paying. Then we dress the way of many white madams and girls. I think we look really smart. Sometimes we catch the eyes of a white woman looking at us and we laugh and laugh and laugh until we nearly drop on the ground because we feel good inside ourselves.

II

What did the girl next door call you? Mrs Plum asked me the first day I came to her. Jane, I replied. Was there not an African name? I said yes, Karabo. All right, Madam said. We'll call you Karabo, she said. She spoke as if she knew a name is a big thing. I knew so many whites who did not care what they called black people as long as it was all right for their tongue. This pleased me, I mean Mrs Plum's use of *Karabo*; because the only time I heard the name was when I was at home or when my friends spoke to me. Then she showed me what to do: meals, meal times, washing, and where all the things were that I was going to use.

My daughter will be here in the evening, Madam said. She is at school. When the daughter came, she added, she would tell me some of the things she wanted me to do for her every day.

Chimane, my friend next door, had told me about the daughter Kate, how wild she seemed to be, and about Mr Plum who had killed himself with a gun in a house down the street. They had left the house and come to this one.

Madam is a tall woman. Not slender, not fat. She moves slowly, and speaks slowly. Her face looks very wise, her forehead seems to tell me she has a strong liver: she is not afraid of anything. Her eyes are always swollen at the lower eyelids like a white person who has not slept for many many nights or like a large frog. Perhaps it is because she smokes too much, like wet wood that will not know whether to go up in flames or stop burning. She looks me straight in the eyes when she talks to me, and I know she does this with other people too. At first this made me fear her, now I am used to her. She is not a lazy woman, and she does many things outside, in the city and in the suburbs.

This was the first thing her daughter Kate told me when she came and we met. Don't mind mother, Kate told me. She said, She is sometimes mad with people for very small things. She will soon be all right and speak nicely to you again.

Kate, I like her very much, and she likes me too. She tells me many things a white woman does not tell a black servant. I mean things about what she likes and does not like, what her mother does or does not do, all these. At first I was unhappy and wanted to stop her, but now I do not mind.

Kate looks very much like her mother in the face. I think her shoulders will be just as round and strong-looking. She moves faster than Madam. I asked her why she was still at school when she was so big. She laughed. Then she tried to tell me that the school where she was was for big people, who had finished with lower school. She was learning big things about cooking and food. She can explain better, me I cannot. She came home on weekends.

Since I came to work for Mrs Plum Kate has been teaching me plenty of cooking. I first learned from her and Madam the word *recipes*. When Kate was at the big school, Madam taught me how to read cookery books. I went on very slowly at first, slower than an ox-wagon. Now I know more. When Kate came home, she found I had read the recipe she left me. So we just cooked straightaway. Kate thinks I am fit to cook in a hotel. Madam thinks so too. Never never! I thought. Cooking in a hotel is like feeding oxen. No one can say thank you to you. After a few months I could cook the Sunday lunch and later I could cook specials for Madam's or Kate's guests.

Madam did not only teach me cooking. She taught me how to look after guests. She praised me when I did very very well; not like the white people I had worked for before. I do not know what runs crooked in the heads of other people. Madam also had classes in the evenings for servants to teach them how to read and write. She and two other women in Greenside taught in a church hall.

As I say, Kate tells me plenty of things about Madam. She says to me she says, My mother goes to meetings many times. I ask her I say, What for? She says to me she says, For your people. I ask her I say, My people are in Phokeng far away. They have got mouths, I say. Why does she want to say something for them? Does she know what my mother and what my father want to say? They can speak when they want to. Kate raises her shoulders and drops them and says, How can I tell you Karabo? I don't say your people – your family only. I mean all the black people in this country. I say Oh! What do the black people want to say? Again she raises her shoulders and drops them, taking a deep breath.

I ask her I say, With whom is she in the meeting?

She says, With other people who think like her.

I ask her I say, Do you say there are people in the world who think the same things?

She nods her head.

I ask, What things?

So that a few of your people should one day be among those who rule this country, get more money for what they do for the white man, and – what did Kate say again? Yes, that Madam and those who think like her also wanted my people who have been to school to choose those who must speak for them in the – I think she said it looks like a *Kgotla* at home who rule the villages.

I say to Kate I say, Oh I see now. I say, Tell me Kate why is Madam always writing on the machine, all the time everyday nearly?

She replies she says, Oh my mother is writing books.

I ask, You mean a book like those? – pointing at the books on the shelves.

Yes, Kate says.

And she told me how Madam wrote books and other things for newspapers and she wrote for the newspapers and magazines to say things for the black people who should be treated well, be paid more money, for the black people who can read and write many things to choose those who want to speak for them.

Kate also told me she said, My mother and other women who think like her put on black belts over their shoulders when they are sad and they want to show the white government they do not like the things being done by whites to blacks. My mother and the others go and stand where the people in government are going to enter or go out of a building.

I ask her I say, Does the government and the white people listen and stop their sins? She says. No. But my mother is in another group of white people.

I ask, Do the people of the government give the women tea and cakes? Kate says, Karabo! How stupid; oh!

I say to her I say, Among my people if someone comes and stands in front of my house I tell him to come in and I give him food. You white people are wonderful. But they keep standing there and the government people do not give them anything.

She replies, You mean strange. How many times have I taught you not to say *wonderful* when you mean *strange!* Well, Kate says with a short heart and looking cross and she shouts, Well they do not stand there the whole day to ask for tea and cakes stupid. Oh dear!

Always when Madam finished to read her newspapers she gave them to me to read to help me speak and write better English. When I had read she asked me to tell her some of the things in it. In this way, I did better and better and my mind was opening and opening and I was learning and learning many things about the black people inside and outside the towns which I did not know in the least. When I found words that were too difficult or I did not understand some of the things I asked Madam. She always told me You see this, you see that, eh? with a heart that can carry on a long way. Yes, Madam writes many letters to the papers. She is always sore about the way the white police beat up black people; about the way black people who work for whites are made to sit at the Zoo Lake with their hearts hanging, because the white people say our people are making noise on Sunday afternoon when they want to rest in their houses and gardens; about many ugly things that happen when some white people meet black man on the pavement or street. So Madam writes to the papers to let others know, to ask the government to be kind to us.

In the first year Mrs Plum wanted me to eat at table with her. It was very hard, one because I was not used to eating at table with a fork and knife, two because I heard of no other kitchen worker who was handled like this. I was afraid. Afraid of everybody, of Madam's guests if they found me doing this. Madam said I must not be silly. I must show that African servants can also eat at table. Number three, I could not eat some of the things I loved very much: mealie-meal porridge with sour milk or *morogo*, stamped mealies mixed with butter beans: sour porridge for breakfast and other things. Also, except for morning porridge, our food is nice when you eat with the hand. So nice that it does not stop in the mouth or the throat to greet anyone before it passes smoothly down.

We often had lunch together with Chimane next door and our garden boy – Ha! I must remember never to say boy again when I talk about a man. This makes me think of a day during the first few weeks in Mrs Plum's house. I was talking about Dick her garden man and I said 'garden boy'. And she says to me she says Stop talking about a 'boy', Karabo. Now listen here, she says, You Africans must learn to speak properly about each other. And she says White people won't talk kindly about you if you look down upon each other.

I say to her I say Madam, I learned the word from the white people I worked for, and all the kitchen maids say 'boy'.

She replies she says to me, Those are white people who know nothing, just low-class whites. I say to her I say I thought white people know everything.

She said, You'll learn my girl and you must start in this house, hear? She left me there thinking, my mind mixed up.

I learned. I grew up.

III

If any woman or girl does not know the Black Crow Club in Bree Street, she does not know anything. I think nearly everything takes place inside and outside that house. It is just where the dirty part of the City begins, with factories and the market. After the market is the place where Indians and Coloured people live. It is also at the Black Crow that the buses turn round and go back to the black townships. Noise, noise, noise all the time. There are women who sell hot sweet potatoes and fruit and monkey nuts and boiled eggs in the winter, boiled mealies and the other things in the summer, all these on the pavements. The streets are always full of potato and fruit skins and monkey nut shells. There is always a strong smell of roast pork. I think it is because of Piel's cold storage down Bree Street.

Madam said she knew the black people who work in the Black Crow. She was happy that I was spending my afternoon on Thursdays in such a club. You will learn sewing, knitting, she said, and other things that you like. Do you like to dance? I told her I said, Yes, I want to learn. She paid the two shillings fee for me each month.

We waited on the first floor, we the ones who were learning sewing; waiting for the teacher. We talked and laughed about madams and masters, and their children and their dogs and birds and whispered about our boy-friends.

Sies! My Madam you do not know – *mojuta oa' nete* – a real miser . . .

Jo – jo – jo! you should see our new dog. A big thing like this. People! Big in a foolish way . . .

What! Me, I take a master's bitch by the leg, me, and throw it away so that it keeps howling, *tjwe – tjwe! ngo – wu ngo – wu!* I don't play about with them, me . . .

Shame, poor thing! God sees you, true . . . !

They wanted me to take their dog out for a walk every afternoon and I told them I said It is not my work in other houses the garden man does it. I just said to myself I said they can go to the chickens. Let them bite their elbow before I take out a dog, I am not so mad yet . . .

Hei! It is not like the child of my white people who keeps a big white rat and you know what? He puts it on his bed when he goes to school. And let the blankets just begin to smell of urine and all the nonsense and they tell me to wash them. *Hei*, people, ! . . .

Did you hear about Rebone, people? Her Madam put her out, because her master was always tapping her buttocks with his fingers. And yesterday the madam saw the master press Rebone against himself . . .

Jo – jo – jo! people . . . !

Dirty white man!

No, not dirty. The madam smells too old for him.

Hei! Go and wash your mouth with soap, this girl's mouth is dirty . . .

Jo, Rebone, daughter of the people! We must help her to find a job before she thinks of going back home.

The teacher came. A woman with strong legs, a strong face, and kind eyes. She had short hair and dressed in a simple but lovely floral frock. She stood well on her legs and hips. She had a black mark between the two top front teeth. She smiled as if we were her children. Our group began with games, and then Lilian Ngoyi took us for sewing. After this she gave a brief talk to all of us from the different classes.

I can never forget the things this woman said and how she put them to us. She told us that the time has passed for black girls and women in the suburbs to be satisfied with working, sending money to our people and going to see them once a year. We were to learn, she said, that the world would never be safe for black people until they were in the government with the power to make laws. The power should be given by the Africans who were more than the whites.

We asked her questions and she answered them with wisdom. I shall put some of them down in my own words as I remember them.

Shall we take the place of the white people in the government?

Some yes. But we shall be more than they as we are more in the country. But also the people of all colours will come together and there

are good white men we can choose and there are Africans some white
people will choose to be in the government.

There are good madams and masters and bad ones. Should we take the
good ones for friends?

A master and a servant can never be friends. Never, so put that out of
your head, will you! You are not even sure if the ones you say are good
are not like that because they cannot breathe or live without the work of
your hands. As long as you need their money, face them with respect.
But you must know that many sad things are happening in our country
and you, all of you, must always be learning, adding to what you already
know, and obey us when we ask you to help us.

At other times Lilian Ngoyi told us she said, Remember your poor
people at home and the way in which the whites are moving them from
place to place like sheep and cattle. And at other times again she told us
she said, Remember that a hand cannot wash itself, it needs another to
do it.

I always thought of Madam when Lilian Ngoyi spoke. I asked myself,
What would she say if she knew that I was listening to such words.
Words Like: A white man is looked after by his black nanny and his
mother when he is a baby. When he grows up the white government
looks after him, sends him to school, makes it impossible for him to
suffer from the great hunger, keeps a job ready and open for him as soon
as he wants to leave school. Now Lilian Ngoyi asked she said, How many
white people can be born in a white hospital, grow up in white streets be
clothed in lovely cotton, lie on white cushions; how many whites can
live all their lives in a fenced place away from people of other colours and
then, as men and women learn quickly the correct ways of thinking,
learn quickly to ask questions in their minds, big questions that will
throw over all the nice things of a white man's life? How many? Very
very few! For those whites who have not begun to ask, it is too late. For
those who have begun and are joining us with both feet in our house, we
can only say Welcome!

I was learning. I was growing up. Every time I thought of Madam, she
became more and more like a dark forest which one fears to enter, and
which one will never know. But there were several times when I
thought, This woman is easy to understand, she is like all other white
women.

What else are they teaching you at the Black Crow, Karabo?

I tell her I say, nothing, Madam. I ask her I say Why does Madam ask?

You are changing.

What does Madam mean?

Well, you are changing.

But we are always changing Madam.

And she left me standing in the kitchen. This was a few days after I had told her that I did not want to read more than one white paper a day. The only magazines I wanted to read, I said to her, were those from over-seas, if she had them. I told her that white papers had pictures of white people most of the time. They talked mostly about white people and their gardens, dogs, weddings and parties. I asked her if she could buy me a Sunday paper that spoke about my people. Madam bought it for me. I did not think she would do it.

There were mornings when, after hanging the white people's washing on the line Chimane and I stole a little time to stand at the fence and talk. We always stood where we could be hidden by our rooms.

Hei, Karabo, you know what? That was Chimane.

No – what? Before you start, tell me, has Timi come back to you?

Ach, I do not care. He is still angry. But boys are fools they always come back dragging themselves on their empty bellies. *Hei* you know what?

Yes?

The Thursday past I saw Moruti K.K. I laughed until I dropped on the ground. He is standing in front of the Black Crow. I believe his big stomach was crying from hunger. Now he has a small dog in his armpit, and is standing before a woman selling boiled eggs and – *hei* home-girl! – tripe and intestines are boiling in a pot – oh, – the smell! you could fill a hungry belly with it, the way it was good. I think Moruti K.K. is waiting for the woman to buy a boiled egg. I do not know what the woman was still doing. I am standing nearby. The dog keeps wriggling and pushing out its nose, looking at the boiling tripe. Moruti keeps patting it with his free hand, not so? Again the dogs wants to spill out of Moruti's hand and it gives a few sounds through the nose. *Hei* man, home-girl! One two three the dog spills out to catch some of the good meat! It misses falling into the hot gravy in which the tripe is swimming I do not know how. Moruti K.K. tries to chase it. It has tumbled on to the woman's eggs and potatoes and all are in the dust. She stands up and goes after K.K. She is shouting to him to pay, not so? Where am I at that time? I am nearly dead with laughter the tears are coming down so far.

I was myself holding tight on the fence so as not to fall through laughing. I help my stomach to keep back a pain in the side.

I ask her I say, Did Moruti K.K. come back to pay for the wasted food?

Yes, he paid.

The dog?

He caught it. That is a good African dog. A dog must look for its own food when it is not time for meals. Not these stupid spoiled angels the whites keep giving tea and biscuits.

Hmm.

Dick our garden man joined us, as he often did. When the story was repeated to him the man nearly rolled on the ground laughing.

He asks who is Reverend K.K.?

I say he is the owner of the Black Crow.

Oh!

We reminded each other, Chimane and I, of the round minister. He would come into the club, look at us with a smooth smile on his smooth round face. He would look at each one of us, with that smile on all the time, as if he had forgotten that it was there. Perhaps he had, because as he looked at us, almost stripping us naked with his watery shining eyes – funny – he could have been a farmer looking at his ripe corn, thinking many things.

K.K. often spoke without shame about what he called ripe girls –*matjitjana* – with good firm breasts. He said such girls were pure without any nonsense in their heads and bodies. Everybody talked a great deal about him and what they thought he must be doing in his office whenever he called in so-and-so.

The Reverend K.K. did not belong to any church. He baptised, married, and buried people for a fee, who had no church to do such things for them. They said he had been driven out of the Presbyterian Church. He had formed his own, but it did not go far. Then he later came and opened the Black Crow. He knew just how far to go with Lilian Ngoyi. She said although she used his club to teach us things that would help us in life, she could not go on if he was doing any wicked things with the girls in his office. Moruti K.K. feared her, and kept his place.

IV

When I began to tell my story I thought I was going to tell you mostly about Mrs Plum's two dogs. But I have been talking about people. I think Dick is right when he says What is a dog! And there are so many dogs cats and parrots in Greenside and other places that Mrs Plum's dogs do not look special. But there was something special in the dog business in Madam's house. The way in which she loved them, maybe.

Monty is a tiny animal with long hair and small black eyes and a face nearly like that of an old woman. The other, Malan, is a bit bigger, with brown and white colours. It has small hair and looks naked by the side of the friend. They sleep in two separate baskets which stay in Madam's bedroom. They are to be washed often and brushed and sprayed and they sleep on pink linen. Monty has a pink ribbon which stays on his neck most of the time. They both carry a cover on their backs. They make me fed up when I see them in their baskets, looking fat, and as if they knew all that was going on everywhere.

It was Dick's work to look after Monty and Malan, to feed them, and to do everything for them. He did this together with garden work and cleaning of the house. He came at the beginning of this year. He just came, as if from nowhere, and Madam gave him the job as she had chased away two before him, she told me. In both those cases, she said that they could not look after Monty and Malan.

Dick had a long heart, even although he told me and Chimane that European dogs were stupid, spoiled. He said One day those white people will put ear-rings and toe-rings and bangles on their dogs. That would be the day he would leave Mrs Plum. For, he said, he was sure that she would want him to polish the rings and bangles with Brasso.

Although he had a long heart, Madam was still not sure of him. She often went to the dogs after a meal or after a cleaning and said to them Did Dick give you food sweethearts? Or, Did Dick wash you sweethearts? Let me see. And I could see that Dick was blowing up like a balloon with anger. These things called white people! he siad to me. Talking to dogs!

I say to him I say, People talk to oxen at home do I not say so?

Yes, he says, but at home do you not know that a man speaks to an ox because he wants to make it pull the plough or the wagon or to stop or to stand still for a person to inspan it. No one simply goes to an ox looking at him with eyes far apart and speaks to it. Let me ask you, do you ever see a person where we come from take a cow and press it to his stomach or his cheek? Tell me!

And I say to Dick I say, We were talking about an ox, not a cow.

He laughed with his broad mouth until tears came out of his eyes. At a certain point I laughed aloud too.

One day when you have time, Dick says to me, he says, you should look into Madam's bedroom when she has put a notice outside her door.

Dick, what are you saying? I ask.

I do not talk, me. I know deep inside me.

Dick was about our age, I and Chimane. So we always said *moshi-man'o* when we spoke about his tricks. Because he was not too big to be a boy to us. He also said to us *Hei, lona banyana kelona* – Hey you girls, you! His large mouth always seemed to be making ready to laugh. I think Madam did not like this. Many times she would say What is there to make you laugh here? Or in the garden she would say This is a flower and when it wants water that is not funny! Or again, If you did more work and stopped trying to water my plants with your smile you would be more useful. Even when Dick did not mean to smile. What Madam did not get tired of saying was, If I left you to look after my dogs without anyone to look after you at the same time you would drown the poor things.

Dick smiled at Mrs Plum. Dick hurt Mrs Plum's dogs? Then cows can fly. He was really – really afraid of white people, Dick. I think he tried very hard not to feel afraid. For he was always showing me and Chimane in private how Mrs Plum walked, and spoke. He took two bowls and pressed them to his chest, speaking softly to them as Madam speaks to Monty and Malan. Or he sat at Madam's table and acted the way she sits when writing. Now and again he looked back over his shoulder, pulled his face long like a horse's making as if he were looking over his glasses while telling me something to do. Then he would sit on one of the armchairs, cross his legs and act the way Madam drank her tea; he held the cup he was thinking about between his thumb and the pointing finger, only letting their nails meet. And he laughed after every act. He did these things, of course, when Madam was not home. And where was I at such times? Almost flat on my stomach, laughing.

But oh how Dick trembled when Mrs Plum scolded him! He did his house-cleaning very well. Whatever mistake he made, it was mostly with the dogs; their linen, their food. One white man came into the house one afternoon to tell Madam that Dick had been very careless when taking the dogs out for a walk. His own dog was waiting on Madam's stoep. He repeated that he had been driving down our street; and Dick had let loose Monty and Malan to cross the street. The white man made plenty of noise about this and I think wanted to let Madam know how useful he had been. He kept on saying Just one inch, just one inch. It was lucky I put on my brakes quick enough ... But your boy kept on smiling – Why? Strange. My boy would only do it twice and only twice and then ...! His pass. The man moved his hand like one writing, to mean he would sign his servant's pass for him to go and never come back. When he left, the white man said Come on Rusty, the boy is waiting to clean you. Dogs with names, men without, I thought.

Madam climbed on top of Dick for this, as we say.

Once one of the dogs, I don't know which – Malan or Monty – took my stocking – brand new, you hear – and tore it with its teeth and paws. When I told Madam about it, my anger as high as my throat, she gave me money to buy another pair. It happened again. This time she said she was not going to give me money because I must also keep my stockings where the two gentlemen would not reach them. Mrs Plum did not want us ever to say *Voetsek* when we wanted the dogs to go away. Me I said this when they came sniffing at my legs or fingers. I hate it.

In my third year in Mrs Plum's house, many things happened, most of them all bad for her. There was trouble with Kate; Chimane had big trouble; my heart was twisted by two loves; and Monty and Malan became real dogs for a few days.

Madam had a number of suppers and parties. She invited Africans to some of them. Kate told me the reasons for some of the parties. Like her mother's books when finished, a visitor from across the seas and so on. I did not like the black people who came here to drink and eat. They spoke such difficult English like people who were full of all the books in the world. They looked at me as if I were right down there whom they thought little of – me a black person like them.

One day I heard Kate speak to her mother. She says I don't know why you ask so many Africans to the house. A few will do at a time. She said something about the government which I could not hear well. Madam replies she say to her You know some of them do not meet white people often, so far away in their dark houses. And she says to Kate that they do not come because they want her as a friend but they just want a drink for nothing.

I simply felt that I could not be the servant of white people and of blacks at the same time. At my home or in my room I could serve them without a feeling of shame. And now, if they were only coming to drink!

But one of the black men and his sister always came to the kitchen to talk to me. I must have looked unfriendly the first time, for Kate talked to me about it afterwards as she was in the kitchen when they came. I know that at that time I was not easy at all. I was ashamed and I felt that a white person's house was not the place for me to look happy in front of other black people while the white man looked on.

Another time it was easier. The man was alone. I shall never forget that night, as long as I live. He spoke kind words and I felt my heart grow big inside me. It caused me to tremble. There were several other visits. I knew that I loved him, I could never know what he really thought of me, I mean as a woman and he as a man. But I loved him, and I still think of him with a sore heart. Slowly I came to know the pain of it. Because he was a doctor and so full of knowledge and English I could not reach him. So I knew he could not stoop down to see me as someone who wanted him to love me.

Kate turned very wild. Mrs. Plum was very much worried. Suddenly it looked as if she were a new person, with new ways and new everything. I do not know what was wrong or right. She began to play the big gramophone aloud, as if the music were for the whole of Greenside. The music was wild and she twisted her waist all the time, with her mouth half-open. She did the same things in her room. She left the big school and every Saturday night now she went out. When I looked at her face, there was something deep and wild there on it, and when I thought she looked young she looked old, and when I thought she looked old she was young. We were both 22 years of age. I think that I could see the reason why her mother was so worried, why she was suffering.

Worse was to come.

They were now openly screaming at each other. They began in the sitting-room and went upstairs together, speaking fast hot biting words, some of which I did not grasp. One day Madam comes to me and says You know Kate loves an African, you know the doctor who comes to supper here often. She says he loves her too and they will leave the country and marry outside. Tell me, Karabo, what do your people think of this kind of thing between a white woman and a black man? It *cannot* be right is it?

I reply and I say to her. We have never seen it happen before where I come from.

That's right, Karabo, it is just madness.

Madam left. She looked like a hunted person.

These white women, I say to myself I say these white women, why do not they love their own men and leave us to love ours!

From that minute I knew that I would never want to speak to Kate. She appeared to me as a thief, as a fox that falls upon a flock of sheep at night. I hated her. To make it worse, he would never be allowed to come to the house again.

Whenever she was home there was silence between us. I no longer wanted to know anything about what she was doing, where or how.

I lay awake for hours on my bed. Lying like that, I seemed to feel parts of my body beat and throb inside me, the way I have seen big machines doing, pounding and pounding and pushing and pulling and pouring some water into one hole which came out at another end. I stretched myself so many times so as to feel tired and sleepy.

When I did sleep, my dreams were full of painful things.

One evening I made up my mind, after putting it off many times. I told my boy-friend that I did not want him any longer. He looked hurt, and that hurt me too. He left.

The thought of the African doctor was still with me and it pained me to know that I should never see him again; unless I met him in the street on a Thursday afternoon. But he had a car. Even if I did meet him by luck, how could I make him see that I loved him? Ach, I do not believe he would even stop to think what kind of woman I am. Part of that winter was a time of longing and burning for me. I say part because there are

always things to keep servants busy whose white people go to the sea for
the winter.

To tell the truth, winter was the time for servants; not nannies, because they went with their madams so as to look after the children. Those
like me stayed behind to look after the house and dogs. In winter so
many families went away that the dogs remained the masters and
madams. You could see them walk like white people in the streets. Silent
but with plenty of power. And when you saw them you knew that they
were full of more nonsense and fancies in the house.

There was so little work to do.

One week word was whispered round that a home-boy of ours was
going to hold a party in his room on Saturday. I think we all took it for a
joke. How could the man be so bold and stupid? The police were always
driving about at night looking for black people; and if the whites next
door heard the party noise – *oho*! But still, we were full of joy and wanted
to go. As for Dick, he opened his big mouth and nearly fainted when he
heard of it and that I was really going.

During the day on the big Saturday Kate came.

She seemed a little less wild. But I was not ready to talk to her. I was
surprised to hear myself answer her when she said to me Mother says
you do not like a marriage between a white girl and a black man, Karabo.

Then she was silent.

She says But I want to help him, Karabo.

I ask her I say You want to help him to do what?

To go higher and higher, to the top.

I knew I wanted to say so much that was boiling in my chest. I could
not say it. I thought of Lilian Ngoyi at the Black Crow, what she said to
us. But I was mixed up in my head and in my blood.

You still agree with my mother?

All I could say was I said to your mother I had never seen a black man
and a white woman marrying, you hear me? What I think about it is my
business.

I remembered that I wanted to iron my party dress and so I left her.
My mind was full of the party again and I was glad because Kate and the
doctor would not worry my peace that day. And the next day the sun
would shine for all of us, Kate or no Kate, doctor or no doctor.

The house where our home-boy worked was hidden from the main
road by a number of trees. But although we asked a number of questions
and counted many fingers of bad luck until we had no more hands or
fingers, we put on our best pay-while-you-wear dresses and suits and
clothes bought from boys who had stolen them, and went to our home-
boy's party. We whispered all the way while we climbed up to the house.

Someone who knew told us that the white people next door were away
for the winter. Oh, so that is the thing! we said.

We poured into the garden through the back and stood in front of his
room laughing quietly. He came from the big house behind us, and were
we not struck dumb when he told us to go into the white people's house!
Was he mad? We walked in with slow footsteps that seemed to be
sniffing at the floor, not sure of anything. Soon we were standing and
sitting all over the nice warm cushions and the heaters were on. Our
home-boy turned the lights low. I counted fifteen people inside. We saw
how we loved one another's evening dress. The boys were smart too.

Our home-boy's girl-friend Naomi was busy in the kitchen preparing
food. He took out glasses and cold drinks – fruit juice, tomato juice,
ginger beers, and so many other kinds of soft drink. It was just too nice.
The tarts, the biscuits, the snacks, the cakes, *woo*, that was a party, I tell
you. I think I ate more ginger cake than I had ever done in my life.
Naomi had baked some of the things. Our home-boy came to me and
said I do not want the police to come here and have reason to arrest us, so
I am not serving hot drinks, not even beer. There is no law that we cannot
have parties, is there? So we can feel free. Our use of this house is the
master's business. If I had asked him he would have thought me mad.

I say to him I say, You have a strong liver to do such a thing.

He laughed.

He played pennywhistle music on gramophone records – Miriam
Makeba, Dorothy Masuka and other African singers and players. We
danced and the party became more and more noisy and more happy. *Hai*,
those girls Miriam and Dorothy, they can sing, I tell you! We ate more
and laughed more and told more stories. In the middle of the party, our
home-boy called us to listen to what he was going to say. Then he told us
how he and a friend of his in Orlando collected money to bet on a horse
for the July Handicap in Durban. They did this each year but lost. Now
they had won two hundred pounds. We all clapped hands and cheered.
Two hundred pounds *woo*!

You should go and sit at home and just eat time, I say to him. He
laughs and says You have no understanding not one little bit.

To all of us he says Now my brothers and sisters enjoy yourselves. At
home I should slaughter a goat for us to feast and thank our ancestors.
But this is town life and we must thank them with tea and cake and all
those sweet things. I know some people think I must be so bold that I
could be midwife to a lion that is giving birth, but enjoy yourselves and
have no fear.

Madam came back looking strong and fresh.

The very week she arrived the police had begun again to search servants' rooms. They were looking for what they called loafers and men without passes who they said were living with friends in the suburbs against the law. Our dog's meat boys became scarce because of the police. A boy who had a girl-friend in the kitchens, as we say, always told his friends that he was coming for dog's meat when he meant he was visiting his girl. This was because we gave our boy-friends part of the meat the white people bought for the dogs and us.

One night a white and a black policeman entered Mrs Plum's yard. They said they had come to search. She says, no they cannot. They say Yes, they must do it. She answers No. They forced their way to the back, to Dick's room and mine. Mrs Plum took the hose that was running in the front garden and quickly went round to the back. I cut across the floor to see what she was going to say to the men. They were talking to Dick, using dirty words. Mrs Plum did not wait, she just pointed the hose at the two policemen. This seemed to surprise them. They turned round and she pointed it into their faces. Without their seeing me I went to the tap at the corner of the house and opened it more. I could see Dick, like me, was trying to keep down his laughter. They shouted and tried to wave the water away, but she kept the hose pointing at them, now moving it up and down. They turned and ran through the back gate, swearing the while.

That fixes them, Mrs Plum said.

The next day the morning paper reported it.

They arrived in the afternoon – the two policemen – with another. They pointed out Mrs Plum and she was led to the police station. They took her away to answer for stopping the police while they were doing their work.

She came back and said she had paid bail.

At the magistrate's court, Madam was told that she had done a bad thing. She would have to pay a fine or else go to prison for fourteen days. She said she would go to jail to show that she felt she was not in the wrong.

Kate came and tried to tell her that she was doing something silly going to jail for a small thing like that. She tells Madam she says this is not even a thing to take to the high court. Pay the money. What is £5?

Madam went to jail.

She looked very sad when she came out. I thought of what Lilian Ngoyi often said to us: You must be ready to go to jail for the things you believe are true and for which you are taken by the police. What did Mrs Plum really believe about me, Chimane, Dick and all the other black people? I asked myself. I did not know. But from all those things she was writing for the papers and all those meetings she was going to where white people talked about black people and the way they are treated by the government, from what those white women with black bands over their shoulders were doing standing where a white government man was going to pass, I said to myself I said This woman, *hai*, I do not know she seems to think very much of us black people. But why was she so sad?

Kate came back home to stay after this. She still played the big gramophone loud-loud-loud and twisted her body at her waist until I thought it was going to break. Then I saw a young white man come often to see her. I watched them through the opening near the hinges of the door between the kitchen and the sitting-room where they sat. I saw them kiss each other for a long long time. I saw him lift up Kate's dress and her white-white legs begin to tremble, and – oh I am afraid to say more, my heart was beating hard. She called him Jim. I thought it was funny because white people in the shops call black men Jim.

Kate had begun to play with Jim when I met a boy who loved me and I loved. He was much stronger than the one I sent away and I loved him more, much more. The face of the doctor came to my mind often, but it did not hurt me so any more. I stopped looking at Kate and her Jim through openings. We spoke to each other, Kate and I, almost as freely as before but not quite. She and her mother were friends again.

Hallo, Karabo, I heard Chimane call me one morning as I was starching my apron. I answered. I went to the line to hang it. I saw she was standing at the fence, so I knew she had something to tell me. I went to her.

Hallo!

Hallo, Chimane!

O kae?

Ke teng. Wena?

At that moment a woman came out through the back door of the house where Chimane was working.

I have not seen that one before, I say, pointing with my head.

Chimane looked back. Oh, that one. *Hei*, daughter-of-the-people, *Hei*, you have not seen miracles. You know this is Madam's mother-in-law as you see her there. Did I never tell you about her?

No, never.

White people, nonsense. You know what? That poor woman is here now for two days. She has to cook for herself and I cook for the family.

On the same stove?

Yes, She comes after me when I have finished.

She has her own food to cook?

Yes, Karabo. White people have no heart no sense.

What will eat them up if they share their food?

Ask me, just ask me. God! She clapped her hands to show that only God knew, and it was His business, not ours.

Chimane asks me she says, Have you heard from home?

I tell her I say, Oh daughter-of-the-people, more and more deaths. Something is finishing the people at home. My mother has written. She says they are all right, my father too and my sisters, except for the people who have died. Malebo, the one who lived alone in the house I showed you last year, a white house, he is gone. The teacher Sedimo. He was very thin and looked sick all the time. He taught my sisters not me. His mother-in-law you remember I told you died last year – no, the year before. Mother says also there is a woman she does not think I remember because I last saw her when I was a small girl she passed away in Zeerust she was my mother's greatest friend when they were girls. She would have gone to her burial if it was not because she has swollen feet.

How are the feet?

She says they are still giving her trouble. I ask Chimane, How are your people at Nokaneng? They have not written?

She shook her head.

I could see from her eyes that her mind was on another thing and not her people at that moment.

Wait for me Chimane eh, forgive me, I have scones in the oven, eh! I will just take them out and come back, eh!

When I came back to her Chimane was wiping her eyes. They were wet.

Karabo, you know what?

E–e. I shook my head.

I am heavy with child.

Hau!

There was a moment of silence.

Who is it, Chimane?

Timi. He came back only to give me this.

But he loves you. What does he say have you told him?

I told him yesterday. We met in town.

I remembered I had not seen her at the Black Crow.

Are you sure, Chimane? You have missed a month?

She nodded her head.

Timi himself – he did not use the thing?

I only saw after he finished, that he had not.

Why? What does he say?

He tells me he says I should not worry I can be his wife.

Timi is a good boy, Chimane. How many of these boys with town ways who know too much will even say Yes it is my child?

Hai, Karabo, you are telling me other things now. Do you not see that I have not worked long enough for my people? If I marry now who will look after them when I am the only child?

Hm. I hear your words. It is true. I tried to think of something soothing to say.

Then I say You can talk it over with Timi. You can go home and when the child is born you look after it for three months and when you are married you come to town to work and can put your money together to help the old people while they are looking after the child.

What shall we be eating all the time I am at home? It is not like those days gone past when we had land and our mother could go to the fields until the child was ready to arrive.

The light goes out in my mind and I cannot think of the right answer. How many times have I feared the same thing! Luck and the mercy of the gods that is all I live by. That is all we live by – all of us.

Listen, Karabo. I must be going to make tea for Madam. It will soon strike half-past ten.

I went back to the house. As Madam was not in yet, I threw myself on the divan in the sitting-room. Malan came sniffing at my legs. I put my foot under its fat belly and shoved it up and away from me so that it cried *tjunk – tjunk – tjunk* as it went out. I say to it I say Go and tell your brother what I have done to you and tell him to try it and see what I will do. Tell your grandmother when she comes home too.

When I lifted my eyes he was standing in the kitchen door, Dick. He says to me he says *Hau*! now you have also begun to speak to dogs!

I did not reply. I just looked at him, his mouth ever stretched out like the mouth of a bag, and I passed to my room.

I sat on my bed and looked at my face in the mirror. Since the morning I had been feeling as if a black cloud were hanging over me, pressing on my head and shoulders. I do not know how long I sat there. Then I smelled Madam. What was it? Where was she? After a few moments I knew what it was. My perfume and scent. I used the same cosmetics as Mrs Plum's. I should have been used to it by now. But this morning – why did I smell Mrs Plum like this? Then, without knowing why, I asked myself I said, Why have I been using the same cosmetics as Madam? I wanted to throw them all out. I stopped. And then I took all the things and threw them into the dustbin. I was going to buy other kinds on Thursday; finished!

I could not sit down. I went out and into the white people's house. I walked through and the smell of the house made me sick and seemed to fill up my throat. I went to the bathroom without knowing why. It was full of the smell of Madam. Dick was cleaning the bath. I stood at the door and looked at him cleaning the dirt out of the bath, dirt from Madam's body. *Sies*! I said aloud. To myself I said, Why cannot people wash the dirt of their own bodies out of the bath? Before Dick knew I was near I went out. Ach, I said again to myself, why should I think about it now when I have been doing their washing for so long and cleaned the bath many times when Dick was ill. I had held worse things from her body times without number ...

I went out and stood midway between the house and my room, looking into the next yard. The three-legged grey cat next door came to the fence and our eyes met. I do not know how long we stood like that looking at each other. I was thinking, Why don't you go and look at your grandmother like that? when it turned away and mewed hopping on the three legs. Just like someone who feels pity for you.

In my room I looked into the mirror on the chest of drawers. I thought Is this Karabo this?

Thursday came, and the afternoon off. At the Black Crow I did not see Chimane. I wondered about her. In the evening I found a note under my door. It told me if Chimane was not back that evening I should know that she was at 660 3rd Avenue, Alexandra Township. I was not to tell the white people.

I asked Dick if he could not go to Alexandra with me after I had washed the dishes. At first he was unwilling. But I said to him I said, Chimane will not believe that you refused to come with me when she sees me alone. He agreed.

On the bus Dick told me much about his younger sister whome he was helping with money to stay at school until she finished; so that she could become a nurse and a midwife. He was very fond of her, as far as I could find out. He said he prayed always that he should not lose his job, as he had done many times before, after staying a few weeks only at each job; because of this he had to borrow monies from people to pay his sister's school fees, to buy her clothes and books. He spoke of her as if she were his sweetheart. She was clever at school, pretty (she was this in the photo Dick had shown me before). She was in Orlando Township. She looked after his old people, although she was only thirteen years of age. He said to me he said Today I still owe many people because I keep losing my job. You must try to stay with Mrs Plum, I said.

I cannot say that I had all my mind on what Dick was telling me. I was thinking of Chimane: what could she be doing? Why that note?

We found her in bed. In that terrible township where night and day are full of knives and bicycle chains and guns and the barking of hungry dogs and of people in trouble. I held my heart in my hands. She was in pain and her face, even in the candle-light, was grey. She turned her eyes at me. A fat woman was sitting in a chair. One arm rested on the other and held her chin in its palm. She had hardly opened the door for us after we had shouted our names when she was on her bench again as if there were nothing else to do.

She snorted, as if to let us know that she was going to speak. She said There is your friend. There she is my own-own niece who comes from the womb of my own sister, my sister who was make to spit out my mother's breast to give way for me. Why does she go and do such an evil thing. *Ao*! you young girls of today you do not know children die so fast these days that you have to thank God for sowing a seed in your womb to grow into a child. If she had let the child be born I should have looked after it or my sister would have been so happy to hold a grandchild on her lap, but what does it help? She has allowed a worm to cut the roots, I don't know.

Then I saw that Chimane's aunt was crying. Not once did she mention her niece by her name, so sore her heart must have been. Chimane only moaned.

Her aunt continued to talk, as if she was never going to stop for breath, until her voice seemed to move behind me, not one of the things I was thinking: trying to remember signs, however small, that could tell me more about this moment in a dim little room in a cruel township without street lights, near Chimane. Then I remembered the three-legged cat, its grey-green eyes, its *miau*. What was this shadow that seemed to walk about us but was not coming right in front of us?

I thanked the gods when Chimane came to work at the end of the week. She still looked weak, but that shadow was no longer there. I wondered Chimane had never told me about her aunt before. Even now I did not ask her.

I told her I told her white people that she was ill and had been fetched to Nokaneng by a brother. They would never try to find out. They seldom did, these people. Give them any lie, and it will do. For they seldom believe you whatever you say. And how can a black person work for white people and be afraid to tell them lies. They are always asking the questions, you are always the one to give the answers.

Chimane told me all about it. She had gone to a woman who did these things. Her way was to hold a sharp needle cover the point with the finger, and guide it into the womb. She then fumbled in the womb until she found the egg and then pierced it. She gave you something to ease the bleeding. But the pain, spirits of our forefathers!

Mrs Plum and Kate were talking about dogs one evening at dinner. Every time I brought something to table I tried to catch their words. Kate seemed to find it funny, because she laughed aloud. There was a word I could not hear well which began with *sem–*: whatever it was, it was to be for dogs. This I understood by putting a few words together. Mrs Plum said it was something that was common in the big cities of America, like New York. It was also something Mrs Plum wanted and Kate laughed at the thought. Then later I was to hear that Monty and Malan could be sure of a nice burial.

Chimane's voice came up to me in my room the next morning, across the fence. When I come out she tells me she says *Hei* child-of-my-father, here is something to tickle your ears. You know what? What? I say. She says, These white people can do things that make the gods angry. More godless people I have not seen. The madam of our house says the people of Greenside want to buy ground where they can bury their dogs. I heard them talk about it in the sitting-room when I was giving them coffee last night. *Hei*, people let our forefathers come and save us!

Yes, I say, I also heard the madam of our house talk about it with her daughter. I just heard it in pieces. By my mother one day these dogs will sit at table and use knife and fork. These things are to be treated like people now, like children who are never going to grow up.

Chimane sighed and she says *Hela batho*, why do they not give me some of that money they will spend on the ground and on gravestones to buy stockings! I have nothing to put on, by my mother.

Over her shoulder I saw the cat with three legs. I pointed with my head. When Chimane looked back and saw it she said *Hm*, even *they* live like kings. The mother-in law found it on a chair and the madam said the woman should not drive it away. And there was no other chair, so the woman went to her room.

Hela!

I was going to leave when I remembered what I wanted to tell Chimane. It was that five of us had collected £1 each to lend her so that she could pay the woman of Alexandra for having done that thing for her. When Chimane's time came to receive money we collected each month and which we took in turns, she would pay us back. We were ten women and each gave £2 at a time. So one waited ten months to receive £20. Chimane thanked us for helping her.

I went to wake up Mrs Plum as she had asked me. She was sleeping late this morning. I was going to knock at the door when I heard strange noises in the bedroom. What is the matter with Mrs Plum? I asked myself. Should I call her, in case she is ill? No, the noises were not those of a sick person. They were happy noises but like those a person makes in a dream, the voice full of sleep. I bent a little to peep through the keyhole. What is this? I kept asking myself. Mrs Plum! Malan! What is she doing this one? Her arm was round Malan's belly and pressing its back against her stomach at the navel, Mrs Plum's body in a nightdress moving in jerks like someone in fits ... her leg rising and falling ... Malan silent like a thing to be owned without any choice it can make to belong to another.

The gods save me! I heard myself saying, the words sounded like wind rushing out of my mouth. So this is what Dick said I would find out for myself!

No one could say where it all started; who talked about it first; whether the police wanted to make a reason for taking people without passes and people living with servants and working in town or not working at all. But the story rushed through Johannesburg that servants were going to poison the white people's dogs. Because they were too much work for us: that was the reason. We heard that letters were sent to the newspapers by white people asking the police to watch over the dogs to stop any wicked things. Some said that we the servants were not really bad, we were being made to think of doing these things by evil people in town and in the locations. Others said the police should watch out lest we poison madams and masters because black people did not know right from wrong when they were angry. We were still children at heart, others said. Mrs Plum said that she had also written to the papers.

Then it was the police came down on the suburbs like locusts on a cornfield. There were lines and lines of men who were arrested hour by hour in the day. They liked this very much, the police. Everybody they took, everybody who was working was asked, Where's the poison eh? Where did you hide it? Who told you to poison the dogs eh? If you tell us we'll leave you to go free, you hear? and so many other things.

Dick kept saying It is wrong this thing they want to do to kill poor dogs. What have these things of God done to be killed for? Is it the dogs that make us carry passes? Is it dogs that make the laws that give us pain? People are just mad they do not know what they want, stupid! But when white policeman spoke to him, Dick trembled and lost his tongue and the things he thought. He just shook his head. A few moments after they had gone through his pockets he still held his arms stretched out, like the man of straw who frightens away birds in a field. Only when I hissed and gave him a sign did he drop his arms. He rushed to a corner of the garden to go on with his work.

Mrs Plum had put Monty and Malan in the sitting-room, next to her. She looked very much worried. She called me. She asked me she said Karabo, you think Dick is a boy we can trust? I did not know how to answer. I did not know whom she was talking about when she said we. Then I said I do not know, Madam. You know! she said. I looked at her. I said I do not know what Madam thinks. She said she did not think anything, that was why she asked. I nearly laughed because she was telling a lie this time and not I.

At another time I should have been angry if she lied to me, perhaps. She and I often told each other lies, as Kate and I also did. Like when she came back from jail, after that day when she turned a hose-pipe on two policemen. She said life had been good in jail. And yet I could see she was ashamed to have been there. Not like our black people who are always being put in jail and only look at it as the white man's evil game. Lilian Ngoyi often told us this, and Mrs Plum showed me how true those words are. I am sure that we have kept to each other by lying to each other.

There was something in Mrs Plum's face as she was speaking which made me fear her and pity her at the same time. I had seen her when she had come from prison; I had seen her when she was shouting at Kate and the girl left the house; now there was this thing about dog poisoning. But never had I seen her face like this before. The eyes, the nostrils, the lips, the teeth seemed to be full of hate, tired, fixed on doing something bad; and yet there was something on that face that told me she wanted me on her side.

Dick is all right Madam, I found myself saying. She took Malan and Monty in her arms and pressed them to herself, running her hands over their heads. They looked so safe, like a child in a mother's arm.

Mrs Plum said All right you may go. She said Do not tell anybody what I have asked about Dick eh?

When I told Dick about it, he seemed worried.

It is nothing, I told him.

I had been thinking before that I did not stand with those who wanted to poison the dogs, Dick said. But the police have come out. I do not care what happens to the dumb things, now.

I asked him I said Would you poison them if you were told by someone to do it?

No. But I do not care, he replied.

The police came again and again. They were having a good holiday, everyone could see that. A day later Mrs Plum told Dick to go because she would not need his work any more.

Dick was almost crying when he left. Is Madam so unsure of me? he asked. I never thought a white person could fear me! And he left.

Chimane shouted from the other yard. She said, *Hei ngoana'rona*, the boers are fire-hot eh!

Mrs Plum said she would hire a man after the trouble was over.

A letter came from my parents in Phokeng. In it they told me my uncle had passed away. He was my mother's brother. The letter also told me of other deaths. They said I would not remember some, I was sure to know the others. There were also names of sick people.

I went to Mrs Plum to ask her if I could go home. She asks she says When did he die? I answer I say It is three days, Madam. She says So that they have buried him? I reply Yes Madam. Why do you want to go home then? Because my uncle loved me very much Madam. But what are you going to do there? To take my tears and words of grief to his grave and to my old aunt, Madam. No you cannot go, Karabo. You are working for me you know? Yes, Madam. I, and not your people pay you. I must go Madam, that is how we do it among my people, Madam. She paused. She walked into the kitchen and came out again. If you want to go, Karabo, you must lose the money for the days you will be away. Lose my pay, Madam? Yes, Karabo.

The next day I went to Mrs Plum and told her I was leaving for Phokeng and was not coming back to her. Could she give me a letter to say that I worked for her. She did, with her lips shut tight. I could feel that something between us was burning like raw chillies. The letter simply said that I had worked for Mrs Plum for three years. Nothing more. The memory of Dick being sent away was still an open sore in my heart.

The night before the day I left, Chimane came to see me in my room. She had her own story to tell me. Timi, her boy-friend, had left her – for good. Why? Because I killed his baby. Had he not agreed that you should do it? No. Did he show he was worried when you told him you were heavy? He was worried, like me as you saw me, Karabo. Now he says if I kill one I shall eat all his children up when we are married. You think he means what he says? Yes, Karabo. He says his parents would have been very happy to know that the woman he was going to marry can make his seed grow.

Chimane was crying, softly.

I tried to speak to her, to tell her that if Timi left her just like that, he had not wanted to marry her in the first place. But I could not, no, I could not. All I could say was Do not cry, my sister, do not cry. I gave her my handkerchief.

Kate came back the morning I was leaving, from somewhere very far I cannot remember where. Her mother took no notice of what Kate said asking her to keep me, and I was not interested either.

One hour later I was on the Railway bus to Phokeng. During the early part of the journey I did not feel anything about the Greenside house I had worked in. I was not really myself, my thoughts dancing between Mrs Plum, my uncle, my parents, and Phokeng, my home. I slept and woke up many times during the bus ride. Right through the ride I seemed to see, sometimes in sleep, sometimes between sleep and waking, a red car passing our bus, then running behind us. Each time I looked out it was not there.

Dreams came and passed. He tells me he says You have killed my seed I wanted my mother to know you are a woman in whom my seed can grow ... Before you make the police take you to jail make sure that it is for something big you should go to jail for, otherwise you will come out with a heart and mind that will bleed inside you and poison you ...

The bus stopped for a short while, which made me wake up.

The Black Crow, the club women ... *Hei*, listen! I lie to the madam of our house and I say I had a telegram from my mother telling me she is very very sick. I show her a telegram my sister sent me as if mother were writing. So I went home for a nice weekend ...

The laughter of the women woke me up, just in time for me to stop a line of saliva coming out over my lower lip. The bus was making plenty of dust now as it was running over part of the road they were digging up. I was sure the red car was just behind us, but it was not there when I woke.

Any one of you here who wants to be baptised or has a relative without a church who needs to be can come and see me in the office ... A round man with a fat tummy and sharp hungry eyes, a smile that goes a long, long way ...

The bus was going uphill, heavily and noisily.

I kick a white man's dog, me, or throw it there if it has not been told the black people's law ... This is Mister Monty and this is Mister Malan. Now get up you lazy boys and meet Mister Kate. Hold out your hands and say hallo to him ... Karabo, bring two glasses there ... Wait a bit – What will you chew boys while Mister Kate and I have a drink? Nothing? Sure?

We were now going nicely on a straight tarred road and the trees rushed back. Mister Kate. What nonsense, I thought.

Look Karabo, Madam's dogs are dead. What? Poison. I killed them. She drove me out of a job did she not? For nothing. Now I want her to feel she drove me out for something. I came back when you were in your room and took the things and poisoned them ... And you know what? She has buried them in clean pink sheets in the garden. *Ao*, clean clean good sheets. I am going to dig them out and take one do you want the other one? Yes, give me the other one I will send it to my mother ... *Hei*, Karabo, see here they come. Monty and Malan. The bloody fools they do not want to stay in their hole. Go back you silly fools. Oh you do not want to move eh? Come here, now I am going to throw you in the big pool. No, Dick! No Dick! no, no! Dick! They cannot speak do not kill things that cannot speak. Madam can speak for them she always does. No! Dick...!

I woke up with a jump after I had screamed Dick's name, almost hitting the window. My forehead was full of sweat. The red car also shot out of my sleep and was gone. I remembered a friend of ours who told us how she and the garden man had saved two white sheets in which their white master had buried their two dogs. They went to throw the dogs in a dam.

When I told my parents my story Father says to me he says, So long as you are in good health my child, it is good. The worker dies, work does not. There is always work. I know when I was a boy a strong sound body and a good mind were the biggest things in life. Work was always there, and the lazy man could never say there was no work. But today people see work as something bigger than everything else, bigger than health, because of money.

I reply I say, Those days are gone Papa. I must go back to the city after resting a little to look for work. I must look after you. Today people are too poor to be able to help you.

I knew when I left Greenside that I was going to return to Johannesburg to work. Money was little, but life was full and it was better than sitting in Phokeng and watching the sun rise and set. So I told Chimane to keep her eyes and ears open for a job.

I had been at Phokeng for one week when a red car arrived. Somebody was sitting in front with the driver, a white woman. At once I knew it to be that of Mrs Plum. The man sitting beside her was showing her the way, for he pointed towards our house in front of which I was sitting. My heart missed a few beats. Both came out of the car. The white woman said 'Thank you' to the man after he had spoken a few words to me.

I did not know what to do and how to look at her as she spoke to me. So I looked at the piece of cloth I was sewing pictures on. There was a tired but soft smile on her face. Then I remembered that she might want to sit. I went inside to fetch a low bench for her. When I remembered it afterwards, the thought came to me that there are things I never think white people can want to do at our homes when they visit for the first time: like sitting, drinking water or entering the house. This is how I thought when the white priest came to see us. One year at Easter Kate drove me home as she was going to the north. In the same way I was at a loss what to do for a few minutes.

Then Mrs Plum says, I have come to ask you to come back to me, Karabo. Would you like to?

I say I do not know, I must think about it first.

She says, Can you think about it today? I can sleep at the town hotel and come back tomorrow morning, and if you want to you can return with me.

I wanted her to say she was sorry to have sent me away, I did not know how to make her say it because I know white people find it too much for them to say Sorry to a black person. As she was not saying it, I thought of two things to make it hard for her to get me back and maybe even lose me in the end.

I say, You must ask my father first, I do not know, should I call him?

Mrs Plum says, Yes.

I fetched both Father and Mother. They greeted her while I brought benches. Then I told them what she wanted.

Father asks Mother and Mother asks Father. Father asks me. I say if they agree, I will think about it and tell her the next day.

Father says, It goes by what you feel my child.

I tell Mrs Plum I say, If you want me to think about it I must know if you will want to put my wages up from £6 because it is too little.

She asks me, How much will you want?

Up by £4.

She looked down for a few moments.

And then I want two weeks at Easter and not just the weekend. I thought if she really wanted me she would want to pay for it. This would also show how sorry she was to lose me.

Mrs Plum says, I can give you one week. You see you already have something like a rest when I am in Durban in the winter.

I tell her I say I shall think about it.

She left.

The next day she found me packed and ready to return with her. She was very much pleased and looked kinder than I had ever known her. And me, I felt sure of myself, more than I had ever done.

Mrs Plum says to me, You will not find Monty and Malan.

Oh?

Yes, they were stolen the day after you left. The police have not found them yet. I think they are dead myself.

I thought of Dick ... my dream. Could he? And she ... did this woman come to ask me to return because she had lost two animals she loved?

Mrs Plum says to me she says, You know, I like your people, Karabo, the Africans.

And Dick and Me? I wondered.

Alex la Guma

A Matter of Taste

from *A Walk in the Night and other Stories* (1967)

The sun hung well towards the west now so that the thin clouds above the ragged horizon were rimmed with bright yellow like the split yolk of an egg. Chinaboy stood up from having blown the fire under the round tin and said, 'She ought to boil now.' The tin stood precariously balanced on two half-bricks and a smooth stone. We had built the fire carefully in order to brew some coffee and now watched the water in the tin with the interest of women at a childbirth.

'There she is,' Chinaboy said as the surface broke into bubbles. He waited for the water to boil up and then drew a small crushed packet from the side pocket of his shredded windbreaker, untwisted its mouth and carefully tapped raw coffee into the tin.

He was a short man with grey-flecked kinky hair, and a wide, quiet, heavy face that had a look of patience about it, as if he had grown accustomed to doing things slowly and carefully and correctly. But his eyes were dark oriental ovals, restless as a pair of cockroaches.

'We'll let her draw a while,' he advised. He put the packet away and produced an old rag from another pocket, wrapped it around a hand and gingerly lifted the tin from the fire, placing it carefully in the sand near the bricks.

We had just finished a job for the railways and were camped out a few yards from the embankment and some distance from the ruins of a one-time siding. The corrugated iron of the office still stood, gaping in places and covered with rust and cobwebs. Passers had fouled the roofless interior and the platform was crumbled in places and overgrown with weeds. The cement curbing still stood, but cracked and covered with the disintegration like a welcome notice to a ghost town. Chinaboy got out the scoured condensed-milk tins we used for cups and set them up. I sat on an old sleeper and waited for the ceremony of pouring the coffee to commence.

It didn't start right then because Chinaboy was crouching with his rag-wrapped hand poised over the can, about to pick it up, but he wasn't making a move. Just sitting like that and watching something beyond us.

The portjackson bush and wattle crackled and rustled behind me and the long shadow of a man fell across the small clearing. I looked back and up. He had come out of the plantation and was thin and short and had a pale white face covered with a fine golden stubble. Dirt lay in dark lines in the creases around his mouth and under his eyes and in his neck, and his hair was ragged and thick and uncut, falling back to his neck and around his temples. He wore an old pair of jeans, faded and dirty and turned up at the bottoms, and a torn leather coat.

He stood on the edge of the clearing, waiting hesitantly, glancing from me to Chinaboy, and then back at me. He ran the back of a grimy hand across his mouth.

Then he said hesitantly: 'I smelled the coffee. Hope you don' min'.'

'Well,' Chinaboy said with that quiet careful smile of his. 'Seeing you's here, I reckon I don' min' either.' He smiled at me, 'you think we can take in a table boarder, pal?'

'Reckon we can spare some of the turkey and green peas.'

Chinaboy nodded at the stranger. 'Sit, pally. We were just going to have supper.'

The white boy grinned a little embarrassedly and came around the sleeper and shoved a rock over with a scarred boot and straddled it. He didn't say anything, but watched as Chinaboy set out another scoured milk-tin and lift the can from the fire and pour the coffee into the cups.

'Help yourself, man. Isn't exactly the mayor's garden party.' The boy took his cup carefully and blew at the steam. Chinaboy sipped noisily and said, 'Should've had some bake bread. Nothing like a piece of bake bread with cawfee.'

'Hot dogs,' the white boy said.

'Huh.'

'Hot dogs. Hot dogs go with coffee.'

'Ooh ja. I heard,' Chinaboy grinned. Then he asked: 'You going somewhere, Whitey?'

'Cape Town. Maybe get a job on a ship an' make the States.'

'Lots of people want to reach the States,' I said.

Whitey drank some coffee and said: 'Yes, I heard there's plenty of money and plenty to eat.'

'Talking about eating,' Chinaboy said: 'I see a picture in a book, one time. 'Merican Book. This picture was about food over there. A whole mess of fried chicken, mealies – what they call corn – with mushrooms an' gravy, chips and new green peas. All done up in colours, too.'

'Pass me the roast lamb,' I said sarcastically.

'Man,' Whitey said warming up to the discussion. 'Just let me get to something like that and I'll eat till I burst wide open.'

Chinaboy swallowed some coffee: 'Worked as a waiter one time when I was a youngster. In one of that big caffies. You should've seen what all them bastards ate. Just sitting there shovelling it down. Some French stuff too, patty grass or something like that.'

I said: 'Remember the time we went for drunk and got ten days? We ate mealies and beans till it came out of our ears!'

Chinaboy said, whimsically: 'I'd like to sit down in a smart caffy one day and eat my way right out of a load of turkey, roast potatoes, beet-salad and angel's food trifle. With port and cigars at the end.'

'Hell,' said Whitey, 'it's all a matter of taste. Some people like chicken and othe's eat sheep's heads and beans!'

'A matter of taste,' Chinaboy scowled. 'Bull, it's a matter of money, pal. I worked six months in that caffy and I never heard nobody order sheep's head and beans!'

'You heard of the fellow who went into one of these big caffies?' Whitey asked, whirling the last of his coffee around in the tin cup. 'He sits down at a table and takes out a packet of sandwiches and puts it down. Then he calls the waiter and orders a glass of water. When the waiter brings the water, this fellow says: "Why ain't the band playing?" '

We chuckled over that and Chinaboy almost choked. He coughed and spluttered a little and then said, 'Another John goes into a caffy and orders sausage and mash. When the waiter bring him the stuff he take a look and say: "My dear man, you've brought me a cracked plate." "Hell," says the waiter. "That's no crack. That's the sausage." '

After we had laughed over that one Chinaboy looked westward at the sky. The sun was almost down and the clouds hung like bloodstained rags along the horizon. There was a breeze stirring the wattle and portjackson, and far beyond the railway line.

A dog barked with high yapping sounds.

Chinaboy said: 'There's a empty goods going through here around about seven. We'll help Whitey, here, onto it, so's he can get to Cape Town. Reckon there's still time for some more pork chops and onions.' He grinned at Whitey. 'Soon's we've had dessert we'll walk down the line a little. There's a bend where it's the best place to jump a train. We'll show you.'

He waved elaborately towards me: 'Serve the duck, John!'

I poured the last of the coffee into the tin cups. The fire had died to a small heap of embers. Whitey dug in the pocket of his leather coat and found a crumpled pack of cigarettes. There were just three left and he passed them round. We each took one and Chinaboy lifted the twig from the fire and we lighted up.

'Good cigar, this,' he said, examining the glowing tip of the cigarette.

When the coffee and cigarettes were finished, the sun had gone down altogether, and all over the land was swept with dark shadows of a purple hue. The silhouetted tops of the wattle and portjackson looked like massed dragons.

We walked along the embankment in the evening, past the ruined siding, the shell of the station-house like a huge desecrated tombstone against the sky. Far off we heard the whistle of a train.

'This is the place,' Chinaboy said to Whitey. 'It's a long goods and when she takes the turn the engine driver won't see you, and neither the rooker in the guard's van. You got to jump when the engine's out of sight. She'll take the hill slow likely, so you'll have a good chance. Jus' you wait till I say when. Hell, that sound like pouring a drink!' His teeth flashed in the gloom as he grinned. Then Whitey stuck out a hand and Chinaboy shook it, and then I shook it.

'Thanks for supper, boys,' Whitey said.

'Come again, anytime,' I said, 'we'll see we have a tablecloth.' We waited in the portjackson growth at the side of the embankment while the goods train wheezed and puffed up the grade, its headlamp cutting a big yellow hole in the dark. We ducked back out of sight as the locomotive went by, hissing and rumbling. The tender followed, then a couple of box-cars, then some coal-cars and a flat-car, another box-car. The locomotive was out of sight.

'Here it is,' Chinaboy said pushing the boy ahead. We stood near the train, hearing it click-clack past. 'Take this coal-box coming up,' Chinaboy instructed. 'She's low and empty. Don't miss the grip, now. She's slow. And good luck, pal!'

The coal-car came up and Whitey moved out, watching the iron grip on the far end of it. Then as it drew slowly level with him, he reached out, grabbed and hung on, then got a foothold, moving away from us slowly.

We watched him hanging there, reaching for the edge of the car and hauling himself up. Watching the train clicking away, we saw him straddling the edge of the truck, his hand raised in a salute. We raised our hands too.

'Why ain't the band playing? Hell!' Chinaboy said.

Ahmed Essop

The Hajji

from *Contrast* 6 (3) 1970

When the telephone rang several times one evening and his wife did not attend to it as she usually did, Hajji Hassen, seated on a settee in the lounge, cross-legged and sipping tea, shouted: 'Salima, are you deaf?' And when he received no response from his wife and the jarring bell went on ringing he shouted again: 'Salima, what's happened to you?'

The telephone stopped ringing abruptly. Hajji Hassen went on sipping tea in a contemplative manner, wondering where his wife had disappeared. Since his return from Mecca after the pilgrimage, he had discovered novel inadequacies in her, or perhaps saw the old ones in a more revealing light. One of her salient inadequacies was never to be around when he wanted her. She was either across the road confabulating with her sister, or gossiping with the neighbours, or away on a shopping spree. And now, when the telephone had gone on assaulting his ears, she was not in the house. He took another sip of the strongly spiced tea to stifle the irritation within him.

When he heard the kitchen door open he knew that Salima had entered. The telephone burst out again in a metallic shrill and the Hajji shouted for his wife. She hurried to the phone.

'Hullo ... Yes ... Hassen ... Speak to him? ... Who speaking? ... Caterine? ... Who Caterine? ... Au-right ... I call him.'

She placed the receiver down gingerly and informed her husband in Gujarati that a woman named 'Caterine' wanted to speak to him. The name evoke no immediate association in his memory. He descended from the settee and squeezing his feet into a pair of crimson sandals, went to the telephone.

'Hullo ... Who? ... Catherine? ... No, I don't know you ... Yes ... Yes ... Oh ... now I remember ... Yes ...'

He listened intently to the voice, urgent, supplicating. Then he gave his answer:

'I am afraid I can't help him. Let the Christians bury him. His last wish means nothing to me ... Madam, it's impossible ... No ... Let him die ... Brother? Pig! Pig! Bastard!' He banged the receiver onto the telephone in explosive annoyance.

'O Allah!' Salima exclaimed. 'What words! What is this all about?'

He did not answer but returned to the settee, and she quietly went to the bedroom.

Salima went to bed and it was almost midnight when her husband came into the room. His earlier vexation had now given place to gloom. He told her of his brother Karim who lay dying in Hillbrow. Karim had cut himself off from his family and friends ten years ago; he had crossed the colour line (his fair complexion and grey eyes serving as passports) and gone to cohabit with a white woman. And now that he was on the verge of death he wished to return to the world he had forsaken and to be buried under Muslim funeral rites and in a Muslim cemetery.

Hajji Hassen had of course rejected the plea, for a good reason. When his brother had crossed the colour line, he had severed his family ties. The Hajji at that time had felt excoriating humiliation. By going over to the white herrenvolk, his brother trampled on something that was vitally part of him, his dignity and self-respect. But the rejection of his brother's plea involved a straining of the heartstrings and the Hajji did not feel happy. He had recently sought God's pardon for his sins in Mecca, and now this business of his brother's final earthly wish and his own intransigence was in some way staining his spirit.

The next day Hassen rose at five to go to the mosque. When he stepped out of his house in Newtown the street lights were beginning to pale and clusters of houses to assume definition. The atmosphere was fresh and heady, and he took a few deep breaths. The first trams were beginning to pass through Bree Street and were clanging along like decrepit but yet burning spectres towards Johannesburg City Hall. Here and there a figure moved along hurriedly. The Hindu fruit and vegetable hawkers were starting up their trucks in the yards, preparing to go out for the day to sell to suburban housewives.

When he reached the mosque the Somali muezzin in the ivory-domed minaret began to intone the call for prayers. After prayers he remained behind to read the Koran in the company of two other men. When he had done the sun was shining brilliantly in the courtyard among the flowers and the fountain with its goldfish.

Outside his house he saw a car. Salima opened the door and whispered,

'Caterine'. For a moment he felt irritated, but realizing that he might as well face her he stepped boldly into the lounge.

Catherine was a small woman with firm fleshy legs. She was seated cross-legged on the settee, smoking a cigarette. Her face was almost boyish, a look that partly originated in her auburn hair which was cut very short, and partly in the smallness of her head. Her eyebrows, firmly pencilled, accentuated the grey-green glitter of her eyes. She was dressed in a dark grey costume.

He nodded his head at her to signify that he knew who she was. Over the telephone he had spoken with aggressive authority. Now, in the presence of the woman herself, he felt a weakening of his masculine fibre.

'You must, Mr Hassen, come to see your brother.'

'I am afraid I'm unable to help,' he said in a tentative tone. He felt uncomfortable; there was something so positive and intrepid about her appearance.

'He wants to see you. It's his final wish.'

'I have not seen him for ten years.'

'Time can't wipe out the fact that he's your brother.'

'He is a white. We live in different worlds.'

'But you must see him.'

There was a moment of strained silence.

'Please understand that he's not to blame for having broken with you. I am to blame. I got him to break with you. Really you must blame me, not Karim.'

Hassen found himself unable to say anything. The thought that she could in some way have been responsible for his brother's rejection of him had never occurred to him. He looked at his feet in awkward silence. He could only state in a lazily recalcitrant tone:

'It is not easy for me to see him.'

'Please come, Mr Hassen, for my sake, please. I'll never be able to bear it if Karim dies unhappily. Can't you find it in your heart to forgive him and to forgive me?'

He could not look at her. A sob escaped from her, and he heard her opening her handbag for a handkerchief.

'He's dying. He wants to see you for the last time.'

Hassen softened. He was overcome by the argument that she had been responsible for taking Karim away. He could hardly look on her responsibility as being in any way culpable. She was a woman.

'If you remember the days of your youth, the time you spent together with Karim before I came to separate him from you, it will be easier for you to pardon him.'

Hassen was silent.

'Please understand that I'm not a racialist. You know the conditions in this country.'

He yielded. He excused himself and went to his room to change. After a while he set off for Hillbrow in her car.

He sat beside her. The closeness of her presence, the perfume she exuded stirred currents of feeling within him. He glanced at her several times, watched the deft movments of her hands and legs as she controlled the car. Her powdered profile, the outline taut with a resolute quality, aroused his imagination. There was something so businesslike in her attitude and bearing, so involved in reality (at the back of his mind there was Salima, flaccid, cowlike and inadequate) that he could hardly refrain from expressing his admiration.

'You must understand that I'm only going to see my brother because you have come to me. For no one else would I have changed my mind.'

'Yes, I understand. I'm very grateful.'

'My friends and relatives are going to accuse me of softness, of weakness.'

'Don't think of them now. You have decided to be kind to me.'

The realism and commonsense of the woman's words! He was overwhelmed by her.

The car stopped at the entrace of a building in Hillbrow. They took the lift. On the second floor three white youths entered and were surprised at seeing Hassen. There was a separate lift for non-whites. They squeezed themselves into a corner, one actually turning his head away with a grunt of disgust. The lift reached the fifth floor too soon for Hassen to give a thought to the attitude of the three white boys. Catherine led him to apartment 65.

He stepped into the lounge. Everything seemed to be carefully arranged. There was her personal touch about the furniture, the ornaments, the paintings. Catherine went to the bedroom, then returned soon and asked him in.

Karim lay in bed, pale, emaciated, his eyes closed. For a moment Hassen failed to recognise him: ten years divided them. She placed a chair next to the bed for him. He looked at his brother and again saw, through ravages of illness, the familiar features. Catherine sat on the bed and rubbed Karim's hand to wake him. After a while he began to show signs of consciousness. She called him tenderly by his name. When he opened his eyes he did not recognise the man beside him, but by degrees, after she had repeated Hassen's name several times, he seemed to understand. He stretched out a hand and Hassen took it, moist and repellent.

A sense of nausea swept over him, but he could not withdraw his hand as his brother clutched it firmly.

'Brother Hassen, please take me away from here.'

Hassen's affirmative answer brought a smile to his lips.

Catherine suggested that she drive Hassen back to Newtown where he could make preparations to transfer Karim to his home.

'No, you stay here. I will take a taxi.' And he left the apartment.

In the corridor he pressed the button for the lift. He watched the indicator numbers succeeding each other rapidly, then stop at five. The doors opened – and there they were again, the three white youths. He hesitated. The boys looked at him tauntingly, their eyes aglitter with cynical humour. Then suddenly they burst into laughter, coarse, raw, deliberately brutish.

'Come into the parlour,' one of them said.

'Come into the Indian parlour,' another said in a cloyingly mocking voice.

Hassen looked at them, annoyed, hurt. Then something snapped within him and he stood there, transfixed. They laughed at him in a raucous chorus as the lift doors shut.

He remained immobile, his dignity clawed. Was there anything so vile in him that the youths found it necessary to maul that recess of self-respect within him? 'They are whites,' he said to himself in bitter justification of their attitude.

He would take the stairs and walk down the five floors. As he descended he thought of Karim. Because of him he had come here and because of him he had been insulted. The enormity of the insult bridged the gap of ten years when Karim had spurned him, and diminished his being. Now he was diminished again!

He was hardly aware that he had gone down five floors when he reached ground level. He stood still, expecting to see the three youths again. But the foyer was empty and he could see the reassuring activity of street life through the glass panels. He quickly walked out as though he would regain in the hubbub of the street something of his assaulted dignity.

He walked on, structures of concrete and glass on either side of him, and it did not even occur to him to take a taxi. It was in Hillbrow that Karim had lived with the white woman and forgotten the existence of his brother; and now that he was dying he had sent for him. For ten years Karim had lived without him. O Karim! The thought of the youth he had loved so much during the days they had been together at the Islamic Institute, a religious seminary governed by ascetics and bearded fanatics, brought the tears to his eyes and he stopped against a shop-window and wept. A few pedestrians looked at him. When the shopkeeper came outside to see the weeping man, Hassen, ashamed of himself, wiped his eyes and walked on.

He regretted his pliability in the presence of the white woman. She had come unexpectedly and had disarmed him with her presence and subtle talk. A painful lump rose in his throat as he set his heart against forgiving Karim. If his brother had had no personal dignity in sheltering behind his white skin, trying to be what he was not, he was not going to allow his moral worth to be depreciated in any way.

When he reached central Johannesburg he went to the station and took the train. In the coach with the non-whites he felt at ease and regained his self-possession. He was among familiar faces, among people who respected him. He felt as though he had been spirited away by a perfumed well-made wax doll, but had managed with a prodigious effort to shake her off.

When he reached home Salima asked him what had been decided and he answered curtly, 'Nothing.' But feeling elated after his escape from Hillbrow he added condescendingly, 'Karim left on his own accord. We should have nothing to do with him.'

Salima was puzzled, but she went on preparing supper.

Catherine received no word from Hassen and she phoned him. She was stunned when he said:

'I'm sorry but I am unable to offer any help.'

'But ...'

'I regret it. I made a mistake. Please make some other arrangements. Goodbye.'

With an effort of will he banished Karim from his mind. Finding his composure again he enjoyed his evening meal, read the paper and then retired to bed. Next morning he went to mosque as usual, but when he returned home he found Catherine there again. Angry that she should have come, he blurted out:

'Listen to me, Catherine. I can't forgive him. For ten years he didn't care about me, whether I was alive or dead. Karim means nothing to me now.'

'Do you find it so difficult to forgive him?'

'Don't talk to me of forgiveness. What forgiveness when he threw me aside and chose to go with you? Let his white friends see to him, let Hillbrow see to him.'

'Please, please, Mr Hassen, I beg you ...'

'No, don't come here with your begging. Please go away.'

He opened the door and went out. Catherine burst into tears. Salima comforted her as best she could.

'Don't cry Caterine. All men hard. Dey don't understand.'

'What shall I do now?' Catherine said in a defeated tone. She was an alien in the world of the non-whites. 'Is there no one who could help me?'

'Yes, Mr Mia help you,' replied Salima.

In her eagerness to clutch at any straw, she hastily moved to the door. Salima followed her and from the porch of her home directed her to Mr Mia's. He lived in a flat on the first floor of an old building. She knocked and waited in trepidation.

Mr Mia opened the door, smiled affably and asked her in.

'Come inside, lady; sit down ... Fatima,' he called to his daughter, 'bring some tea.'

Mr Mia was a man in his fifties, his bronze complexion partly covered by a neatly trimmed beard. He was a well-known figure in the Indian community. Catherine told him of Karim and her abortive appeal to his brother. Mr Mia asked one or two questions, pondered for a while and then said:

'Don't worry, my good woman. I'll speak to Hassen. I'll never allow a Muslim brother to be abandoned.'

Catherine began to weep.

'Here, drink some tea and you'll feel better.' He poured tea. Before Catherine left he promised that he would phone her that evening and told her to get in touch with him immediately should Karim's condition deteriorate.

Mr Mia, in the company of the priest of the Newtown mosque, went to Hassen's house that evening. They found several relatives of Hassen's seated in the lounge (Salima had spread the word of Karim's illness). But Hassen refused to listen to their pleas that Karim should be brought to Newtown.

'Listen to me, Hajji,' Mr Mia said. 'Your brother can't be allowed to die among the Christians.'

'For ten years he has been among them.'

'That means nothing. He's still a Muslim.'

The priest now gave his opinion. Although Karim had left the community, he was still a Muslin. He had never rejected the religion and espoused Christianity, and in the absence of any evidence to the contrary it had to be accepted that he was a Muslim brother.

'But for ten years he has lived in sin in Hillbrow.'

'If he has lived in sin that is not for us to judge.'

'Hajji, what sort of man are you? Have you no feeling for your brother?' Mr Mia asked.

'Don't talk to me about feeling. What feeling had he for me when he went to live among the whites, when he turned his back on me?'

'Hajji, can't you forgive him? You were recently in Mecca.'

This hurt him and he winced. Salima came to his rescue with refreshments for the guests.

The ritual of tea-drinking established a mood of conviviality and Karim was forgotten for a while. After tea they again tried to press Hassen into forgiving his brother, but he remained adamant. He could not now face Catherine without looking ridiculous. Besides he felt integrated now; he would resist anything that negated him.

Mr Mia and the priest departed. They decided to raise the matter with the congregation in the mosque. But they failed to move Hassen. Actually his resistance grew in inverse ratio as more people came to learn of the dying Karim and Hassen's refusal to forgive him. By giving in he would be displaying mental dithering of the worst kind, a man without an inner fibre, decision and firmness of will.

Mr Mia then summoned a meeting of various religious dignitaries and received the mandate to transfer Karim to Newtown without his brother's consent. Karim's relatives would be asked to care for him, but if they refused Mr Mia would take charge.

Karim's relatives refused to accept him. They did not want to offend Hassen, and they also felt that he was not their responsibility.

Mr Mia phoned Catherine and informed her of what had been decided. She agreed that it was best for Karim to be amongst his people during his last days. So Karim was brought to Newtown in an ambulance hired from a private nursing home and housed in a neat little room in a quiet yard behind the mosque.

The arrival of Karim placed Hassen in a difficult situation and he bitterly regretted his decision not to accept him into his own house. He first heard of his brother's arrival during the morning prayers when the priest offered a special prayer for the recovery of the sick man. Hassen found himself in the curious position of being forced to pray for his brother. After prayers several people went to see the sick man, others offered help. He felt an alien and as soon as the opportunity presented itself he slipped out of the mosque.

In a mood of intense bitterness, scorn for himself, hatred of those who had decided to become his brother's keepers, infinite hatred for Karim, Hassen went home. Salima sensed her husband's mood and did not say a word to him.

In his room he debated with himself. In what way should he conduct

himself so that his dignity remained intact? How was he to face the congregation, the people in the streets, his neighbours? Everyone would
soon know of Karim and smile at him half-sadly, half-ironically, for
having placed himself in such a ridiculous position. Should he now
forgive the dying man and transfer him to his home? People would laugh
at him, snigger at his cowardice, and Mr Mia perhaps even deny him the
privilege; Karim was now his responsiblity. And what would Catherine
think of him? Should he go away somewhere (on the pretext of a
holiday) to Cape Town, to Durban? Besides the stigma of being called a
renegade, Karim might take months to die, he might not die at all.

'O Karim, why did you have to do this to me?' he said, moving towards
the window and drumming at the pane nervously. It galled him that a
weak, dying man could bring such pain to him. An adversary could be
faced, one could either vanquish him or be vanquished, with one's
dignity unravished, but with Karim what could he do?

The hours passed by. He paced his room. He looked at his watch; the
time for afternoon prayers was fast approaching. Should he expose
himself to the congregation? 'O Karim! Karim!' he cried, holding on to
the burglar-proof bar of his bedroom window. Was it for this that he had
made the pilgrimage – to cleanse his soul in order to return into the
penumbra of sin? If only Karim would die he would be relieved of his
agony. But what if he lingered on? What if he recovered? Were not
prayers being said for him? He went to the door and shouted in a raucous
voice: 'Salima!'

But Salima was not in the house. He shouted again and again, and his
voice echoed hollowly in the rooms. He rushed into the lounge, into the
kitchen, he flung the door open and looked into the yard.

Several hours passed. He drew the curtains and lay on his bed in the
dark. Then he heard the patter of feet in the house. He jumped up and
shouted for his wife. She came hurriedly.

'Salima, Salima, go to Karim, he is in a room in the mosque yard. See
how he is, see if he is getting better. Quickly!'

Salima went out. But instead of going to the mosque, she entered her
neighbour's house. She had already spent several hours sitting beside
Karim. Mr Mia had been there as well as Catherine. She had wept.

After a while she returned from her neighbour. When she opened the
door her husband ran to her. 'How is he? Is he very ill? Tell me quickly?'

'He is very ill. Why don't you go and see him?'

Suddenly, involuntarily, Hassen struck his wife in the face.

'Tell me, is he dead? Is he dead?' he screamed.

Salima cowered in fear. She had never seen her husband in this raging temper. What had taken possession of the man? She retired quickly to the kitchen. Hassen locked himself in the bedroom.

During the evening he heard voices. Salima came to tell him that several people, led by Mr Mia, wanted to speak to him urgently. His first impulse was to tell them to leave immediately; he was not prepared to meet them. But he had been wrestling with himself for so many hours that he welcomed a moment when he could be in the company of others. He stepped boldly into the lounge.

'Hajji Hassen,' Mr Mia began, 'please listen to us. Your brother has not long to live. The doctor has seen him. He may not outlive the night.'

'I can do nothing about that,' Hassen replied, in an audacious, matter-of-fact tone that surprised him and shocked the group of people.

'That is in Allah's hand,' said the merchant Gardee. 'In our hands lie forgiveness and love. Come with us now and see him for the last time.'

'I cannot see him.'

'And what will it cost you?' asked the priest who wore a long black cloak that fell about his sandalled feet.

'It will cost me my dignity and my manhood.'

'My dear Hajji, what dignity and what manhood? What can you lose by speaking a few kind words to him on his deathbed? He was only a young man when he left.'

'I will do anything, but going to Karim is impossible.'

'But Allah is pleased by forgiveness,' said the merchant.

'I am sorry, but in my case the circumstances are different. I am indifferent to him and therefore there is no necessity for me to forgive him.'

'Hajji,' said Mr Mia, 'you are only indulging in glib talk and you know it. Karim is your responsibility, whatever his crime.'

'Gentlemen, please leave me alone.'

And they left. Hassen locked himself in his bedroom and began to pace the narrow space between bed, cupboard and wall. Suddenly, uncontrollably, a surge of grief for his dying brother welled up within him.

'Brother, brother!' he cried, kneeling on the carpet beside his bed and smothering his face in the quilt. His memory unfolded a time when Karim had been ill at the Islamic Institute and he had cared for him and nursed him back to health. How much he had loved the handsome youth!

At about four in the morning he heard an urgent rapping. He left his room to open the front door.

'Brother Karim dead,' said Mustapha, the Somali muezzin of the mosque, and he cupped his hands and said a prayer in Arabic. He wore a black cloak and a white skull-cap. When he had done he turned and walked away.

Hassen closed the door and went out into the street. For a moment his release into the street gave him a feeling of sinister jubilation, and he laughed hysterically as he turned the corner and stood next to Jamal's fruit-shop. Then he walked on. He wanted to get away as far as he could from Mr Mia and the priest who would be calling upon him to prepare for the funeral. That was no business of his. They had brought Karim to Newtown and they should see to him.

He went up Lovers' Walk and at the entrance of Orient House he saw the night-watchman sitting beside a brazier. He hastened up to him, warmed his hands by the fire, but he did this more as a gesture of fraternisation as it was not cold, and he said a few words facetiously. Then he walked on.

His morbid joy was ephemeral, for the problem of facing the congregation at the mosque began to trouble him. What opinion would they have of him when he returned? Would they not say: He hated his brother so much that he forsook his prayers, but now that his brother is no longer alive he returns. What a man! What a Muslim!

When he reached Vinod's Photographic Studio he pressed his forehead against the neon-lit glass showcase and began to weep.

A car passed by filling the air with nauseous gas. He wiped his eyes, and looked for a moment at the photographs in the showcase; the relaxed, happy, anonymous faces stared at him, faces whose momentary expressions were trapped in celluloid. Then he walked on. He passed a few shops and then reached Broadway Cinema where he stopped to look at the lurid posters. There were heroes, lusty, intrepid, blasting it out with guns; women in various stages of undress; horrid monsters from another planet plundering a city; Dracula.

Then he was among the quiet houses and an avenue of trees rustled softly. He stopped under a tree and leaned against the trunk. He envied the slumbering people in the houses around him, their freedom from the emotions that jarred him. He would not return home until the funeral of his brother was over.

When he reached the Main Reef Road the east was brightening up. The lights along the road seemed to him to be part of the general haze. The buildings on either side of him were beginning to thin and on his left he saw the ghostly mountains of mine sand. Dawn broke over the city and when he looked back he saw the silhouettes of tall buildings bruising the sky. Cars and trucks were now rushing past him.

He walked for several miles and then branched off onto a gravel road and continued for a mile. When he reached a clump of bluegum trees he sat down on a rock in the shade of the trees. From where he sat he could see a constant stream of traffic flowing along the highway. He had a stick in his hand which he had picked up along the road, and with it he prodded a crevice in the rock. The action, subtly, touched a chord in his memory and he was sitting on a rock with Karim beside him. The rock was near a river that flowed a mile away from the Islamic Institute. It was a Sunday. He had a stick in his hand and he prodded at a crevice and the weather-worn rock flaked off and Karim was gathering the flakes.

'Karim! Karim!' he cried, prostrating himself on the rock, pushing his fingers into the hard roughness, unable to bear the death of that beautiful youth.

He jumped off the rock and began to run. He would return to Karim. A fervent longing to embrace his brother came over him, to touch that dear form before the soil claimed him. He ran until he was tired, then walked at a rapid pace. His whole existence precipitated itself into one motive, one desire, to embrace his brother in a final act of love.

He reached the highway and walked as fast as he could, his heart beating wildly, his hair dishevelled. He longed to ask for a lift from a passing motorist but could not find the courage to look back and signal. Cars flashed past him, trucks roared in pain.

When he reached the outskirts of Johannesburg it was nearing ten o'clock. He hurried along, now and then breaking into a run. Once he tripped over a cable and fell. He tore his trousers in the fall and found his hands were bleeding. But he was hardly conscious of himself, wrapped up in his one purpose.

He reached Lovers' Walk, cars growling at him angrily; he passed Broadway Cinema, rushed towards Orient House, turned the corner at Jamal's fruit-shop. And stopped.

The green hearse, with the crescent moon and stars emblem, passed by; then several cars with mourners followed, bearded men, men with white skull-caps on their heads, looking rigidly ahead like a procession of puppets, indifferent to his fate. No one saw him.

Perseus Adams

A True Gruesome

from *New South African Writing* (circa 1970)

When Dawn Vermaak first asked Eric Featherstone to come out with her
he hesitated before accepting the invitation and even after he had given
his answer he felt more than a little uneasy about it. For Dawn had just
turned thirteen years old and Eric Featherstone – apart from being
thirty-two years old – was also her history teacher.

But the difference in ages and the fact that he was the girl's teacher
were not the only reasons for his feeling somewhat apprehensive about
his acceptance. In spite of his university degree and his eight years'
teaching experience, Eric Featherstone had a deeply-rooted conviction
that he was one of life's failures, one of those people doomed to misfortune whenever they embark on any act of initiative or enterprise.
This conviction had not happened suddenly but had grown from a series
of disappointments over the years – partly from his job and partly
through his marriage which had ended three years earlier with his wife
running away with another man. Recently it was confirmed in his own
mind by a conversation he had overheard when members of the staff
were discussing him.

'He's too soft,' Mr Beardsley who taught arithmetic and coached
rugby had said.

'Too friendly with the kids – no sense of discipline.' That had been the
scornful censuring voice of Mr Lindsay who was Dawn's geography
teacher.

'Why doesn't he move out – get a less demanding job like a clerk in a
bank or an insurance office?' Beardsley had gone on to say.

'Even bad teachers usually manage to put *something* across to the
pupils in their classes – they inspire them with some completely private
interest or obsession of their own, but one cannot imagine that character
inspiring anyone to feel anything except boredom or contempt.'

'At least one cannot say he has not been aptly named,' Lindsay had replied. 'A personality with the effect of a feather and as airtight to real living as a stone. Can't imagine how he ever got married in the first place.'

'Well it didn't take long before she realised her mistake, did it?'

And as usual Miss Gregg, Dawn's pretty blonde English teacher, had stuck up for him.

'I think you're both being very cruel – he's really a very sensitive person and the children really love him. He tells them all sorts of interesting stories ...'

'Stories' – Lindsay snorted, irritated by her sympathy. 'No wonder they don't know any history. It's probably the only way he has of keeping them quiet.'

Eric Featherstone had gone away then, not wanting to hear any more.

He stood now at the bus-stop in the suburb where Dawn and he both lived, and waited for her to arrive. He recalled how she had made the invitation and his own mixed feelings upon hearing it. For Dawn was a quiet, reserved child who, as far as he knew, had no close friends. Someone had mentioned her name one day in the staffroom and the comments had been mostly negative. 'She's like a clam – just to get her to speak is an arduous business,' one had said. Beardsley had said he could not remember who she was and Miss Gregg had said she was very introverted but that her compositions were excellent.

It was at the end of the last period of the day that Dawn, strangely confident and with eyes shining, had approached the table and asked the history teacher:

'Have you ever been to Moore's farm?'

'No-o.' He had smiled at her gently, absent-mindedly. 'Where is it?'

'It's in Walmer – not far from where you stay. I would like to show it to you – it's very beautiful – there are hills and streams and one can be all alone and I have a secret place ... Will you come?'

He had been grateful that she had waited until the others had gone before she asked him. After a brief moment of conflict he had given her the answer she sought, remembering his own shyness and loneliness when he was her age and how he, too, had had 'a secret place'. But, as he waited for her to come, the sun shining brightly, the birds singing happily, the people hurrying out to do their Saturday morning shopping, he began to feel uneasy once again. Suppose their meeting and going away together were observed by someone from the school? Walmer was like a small village and, while the people seemed friendly enough, he knew that the Beardsleys and Lindsays would be only too glad to make the most of any unfavourable gossip about him. Well, let them. What he was doing was being done from a heart free of any intentions other than an act of friendship towards a lonely girl. If they did not like it, they could lump it.

It was seven minutes after nine when she came to him. As far as her features went, she was what kind people would call 'homely' – except for her eyes. These were dark and doe-soft and made you think of moss and mulberries. She looked much older than she was, partly because she was tall for her age, but mostly because of a rare poise, a self-possessed dignity. The rhythm of her movements was quieter, deeper than her classmates', who mostly swung in a sharp pendulum between gawkiness and animal grace. Her hair hung down over her shoulders in two brown plaits and she wore a yellow dress that had no sleeves.

'I am sorry I'm late; shall we go?'

They walked together, the girl slightly in front, down a long avenue that bisected the bus-route road and lay at a ninety-degree angle to it. They walked in silence for a few minutes and then she said:

'I told my mother I was going to visit a school-friend. Grown-ups, especially mothers, don't like people of my age to make friends with someone much older.'

'I know,' he said.

'They don't understand about many things – grown-ups, I mean,' she added.

He smiled. 'I agree with you.'

'Of course, you're different,' she said, noticing his smile and sensing the reason for it.

'Am I?'

'Of course, or I wouldn't have asked you.'

The houses began to thin out now and the tarred avenue became a rough corrugated track that seemed to slope abruptly downwards about eighty yards ahead.

'Can anyone go and visit Moore's farm?' he asked her.

'No – I have special permission from the owner.'

'Won't he object to my coming too?'

'No; in any case, he won't be there. He never comes out on a Saturday.'

Soon they reached the point where the track descended. They stood on the brim of a huge, roughly circular hollow in the middle of which a hill, some several hundred feet tall reposed in fiercely green serenity, making the teacher think of psalms and prophets and the ambushes of Zulu impis. On the eastern side was a thickly wooded kloof where, he was told by his young companion, the Baakens River flowed; and on all sides there was evidence of a spacious bird-singing wilderness. Moore's farm began in a valley at their feet and its northern boundary was a fence that cut the crown of the hill in the middle. The air they breathed now was fresh and clean – it seemed to come from an untapped spring and he felt suddenly glad that he had come.

They went down the track that stopped at a rushing stream with a frail-looking suspension bridge over it. The stream was about fifteen feet wide and Dawn went first, the teacher waiting until she had reached the other side before gingerly making his way across. Seeing his caution, she laughed and he was glad that she did; the sound was like pure silver water and it rose up as the voice of a talented soloist sometimes does from the choir in full song surrounding it; an effect that seals rather than detracts from its harmony.

'You're now in Moore's farm.'

Bars of shadow and sunlight alternated as they followed a grassy path past a huddle of sheds; Africans in a blanketed group smoking long-stemmed pipes who gazed at them long and silently as they passed; grazing cows that did the same without stopping their chewing. A dog streaked towards them, a silver arrow in a crescendo of barks, the hail of his indignation changing to a joyful storm of welcome as he recognised Dawn, the furiously wagging tail putting you beyond doubt as to his pleasure as he circled wildly about. Being a faithful watch-dog, he followed them a short distance only and then returned. A mealie-field dropped behind them; several platoons of cabbages, strawberries; and when a beehive that looked like a postbox and made a sound like a dynamo had done the same, they found they had reached the bottom of the hill. Here there were tall trees with thick undergrowth and the dishevelled playfulness of the nearby river. Gaunt lines infiltrated by music.

He was beginning to pant now and asked her, 'Are we going to climb all the way to the top?'

'Not all the way if you don't want to, but my secret place is up here – and you do want to see it, don't you?'

There was a note of anxiety, of an unstated hope that he would not refuse in her voice, and, though he was not looking forward to the climb, he hastened to reassure her.

'Of course I do. I just wanted to know where we were heading.'

About half an hour of trudge, sweat and climb later, he joined her, leaning against a shelf of rock that curved in a half-moon around the entrance to a shallow cave about three-quarters of the way up the hill. Even through the discomfort of heaving lungs, of having to gulp to catch his breath, the sight beneath stirred him with its breadth and height and superb indifference to the schemes and designs of men.

He knew without being told that this was her secret place and thought to himself – she has chosen well – this is a secret place worth having. The two of them stood quite close and looked down without speaking. As their bodies restored their balances, the woodland silences, punctuated agreeably only by chirruping insects and the call of a shrike or sombre bulbul, moved even further within them both, till the wounds of the past became less harsh and the shape of the future not quite so daunting in the shadow it threw.

Eventually he spoke: 'Do you come here often?'

'As often as I can. I think I'm the only one who knows about this place – you can't really see it till you are right on top of it. ... It's peaceful, isn't it?'

'It's magnificent.'

And then he looked at her and thought about her, and she blushed, feeling him do so. Why am I thirty-two and why is she thirteen? he asked himself and grew sad. They seemed so right for each other – and then he wondered if things would be different if the gap between their birth-dates had been smaller or if they lived in a society where their going together did not have to be kept a secret. I must prize every moment of our togetherness here for it must end soon and the chance of another outing is doubtful, considering the risks involved.

After a while she asked him if he would like to climb the remaining distance to the top. ('You can see my home from there ...') and he agreed. They left the cave and climbed slowly, a clump of trees shutting out the view until they reached the long grass that fell like a boy's fringe over the forehead of the hill. On the summit, she pointed out her home, a white matchbox at the very end of a road parallel with the one they had walked down. Then they returned to an open space between some bushes and lay down a few feet apart and looked up at the sky. The girl studied a ladybird as it moved up the stem of a flower and the teacher, watching her, felt himself become part of the insect's world, a world where the skyscrapers were paper-thin and green and trembled in a breeze.

How blue the sky was – and the sun just right - not too warm ... If only life could always be like this. The breeze increased slightly and stirred the long grass to restless sighs and sibilant caresses as if the earth was gently, tremulously kissing the throat of the morning. Dawn, half emerging from her dream-laced idleness, began to peel the bud she had plucked from one of the Red Disas. She did not strip it roughly, impatiently, as most children would, he observed, but very delicately, as if it held an uncovered star.

Suddenly she asked him, 'Do you like Mr Lindsay?'

He considered her question in silence for a few moments and then said: 'I don't know him very well. They say he's a good geography teacher – do you like him?'

'No,' she said, cupping her hand around the open bud as if it were a candle that might go out – 'No. He's a Grudging and I don't like Grudgings.'

'A Grudging?'

'I divide people into four main groups: Grudgings, Gleesons, Gruesomes and Eternals.'

'A Grudging –'

'Grudgings are sheep that butt other sheep. They want to be Gruesomes but they can't. Gleesons are people who are content to be sheep and nothing else. They sort of drift along and do what the rams – the leader sheep – say they should do. Gruesomes are the best really. They are people who are truly different. They make their own world inside themselves if they cannot get away to a secret place. They're anti-Gleeson but they don't really bother too much about them. What they have to watch out for are the Grudgings who are jealous of them.'

'And Eternals?'

'Serious, rather sinister people without a sense of humour. They preach a lot.'

He smiled as he considered her divisions. Then asked: 'What do you class me as?'

'You're a Gruesome like me but you worry about it.' After a thoughtful pause she added, 'A Gruesome that worries too much about being a Gruesome soon becomes a Gleeson.'

'You're a wonderful girl. Do you know that?'

'No, not really. I'm a Gruesone and we are few, that's all.'

'Why do you choose such a name for a type you think highly of? – You know that gruesome means horrible, don't you?'

'Yes, I know, but the others usually think of us as airy-fairy people and I wanted a word that meant the opposite to this because they don't really know us, do they?'

'No,' he said wonderingly. 'No. I don't suppose they do.' As one o'clock drew near, Dawn jumped up. 'I will have to go now – are you coming?'

They descended hand in hand till they arrived at the farm dwellings when they became aware of the world they were returning to and the narrow views and suspicions it harboured, and let go. But the rapport between them did not die – if anything, it was confirmed by the act. On the town side of the suspension bridge they stopped. A path veered to the left and the rough track to the right.

'This path is a short cut to my home,' she said.

'Will I see you here again?' he asked her.

'Yes, but we had better not go together – we'll be seen and then –'

'Then the Gleesons and Grudgings will close in on us,' he smiled.

'Not to mention the Eternals,' she returned, and smiled too, her eyes big and soft, expressing her thanks to him.

'Come whenever you feel like it and if you see me we can talk and I'll show you other places almost as good as my secret place –'

You already have, he thought as she went away from him. After about fifteen yards she stopped and called down, 'Saturday morning is the best time . . .' He nodded and returned her farewell wave.

On the following Wednesday, at first recess in the staffroom Miss Gregg made the excited announcement that she had just been give a wonderful definition of love by one of the pupils.

'Love!' snorted Mr Lindsay. 'What do they know about love?'

'The person concerned must know about it because it's such a true description in just a few words. I had given them a kind of free association test . . . you know, when you say certain words and they have to write down the first thing they think of upon hearing the word.'

'A bit risky, isn't it?' Beardsley asked her, but sounded, Eric Featherstone noticed, more than a little interested.

'Not with standard six.'

'Well, let's hear, what was it?'

'Love is two people alone on a mountain,' Miss Gregg said triumphantly.

'What's wonderful about it?' Lindsay asked her sceptically. A typical Grudging, Eric thought. No doubt he would favour a more horizontal definition.

'But don't you see,' Miss Gregg said, her voice expressing amazement at his lack of comprehension – 'that's exactly what love is. In a few words she's captured so much of the experience, the sense of awe, the feeling of vulnerability . . .'

'I think it's a very good definition,' Beardsley said surprisingly. 'Who made it?'

'Dawn Vermaak – you know, that quiet one you didn't even remember was in your class.'

'Dawn Vermaak!' Lindsay exploded. 'She doesn't know a thing about mountains – in the last exam when they had to fill in things on a map, she put the Drakensberg somewhere over the equator . . .'

'She may not know about mountains but she knows about love,' Miss Gregg said firmly. 'It's one of the best short definitions of the subject I have ever heard – what do you think, Mr Featherstone?'

'I think,' he said, 'it's really memorable – a definition only a true Gruesome could have made.' And his voice was proud and sinewed with so much fierce tenderness that the others stared and one or two wondered if they would not have to reclassify the previous assessments they had made of him.

A.C. Jordan

The Turban

from *Tales from Southern Africa* ... (1973)

It came about, according to some tale, that there was a man named Nyengebule. This man had two wives, and of these two, it was only the head wife who bore him children. But Nyengebule's *ntandanekazi* (favourite wife) was the junior one, because she was younger, livelier and more attractive than the head wife. Nyengebule's in-laws by the junior wife were very fond of him, all of them. He was a warm-hearted and generous man. The women especially – his sisters-in-law including his wife's brothers' wives – used to be delighted when he paid them a visit. They would crowd round him and listen to the amusing stories he had to tell and also to demand the gifts to which they were entitled. These Nyengebule never failed to bring, but because he knew he was the favourite *mkhwenyethu* (brother-in-law), he delighted in teasing the women before producing the gifts because he had had to leave home at short notice, or because he had lost the bag that contained them on his way, or because his wife had offended him in one way or another just before he left home, and he had decided to punish her by not bringing her people any gifts. Then he would sit listening and smiling as the women coaxed and cajoled him, calling him by the great praises of his clan and by his personal ones. But in the end the gifts always came out, each one of them accompanied by an appropriate spoken message of flattery to the receiver. Nyengebule was very popular with the friends and neighbours of his in-laws too, because he was a great entertainer, a great leader of song and dance. When ever there was a *mgidi* (festival) at his in-laws, the whole neighbourhood used to look forward to his coming, because things became lively as soon as he arrived.

Nyengebule's in-laws were sad that their daughter could not bear this man children. In the early years of this marriage, they tried everything they could to doctor her, and when they were convinced that she was barren, they suggested that one of the younger sisters should be taken in marriage by Nyengebule so that she could bear children for her sister. Nyengebule's own people supported this and urged him, reminding him that, by virtue of the *khazi* (bride-tribute) he had already given for the woman who turned out to be barren, he could marry one of the younger sisters without giving any more cattle. But Nyengebule kept on putting this off. To his own people he stated quite openly that he did not desire to do such a thing, that he did not see the need for it because he had enough children by his head wife, and because he loved his junior wife even though she bore him no children. To his senior in-laws he spoke more tactfully, because he knew that it would hurt them if he stated that it made no difference to him whether or not there were children by his marriage with their daughter. So he asked them to give him time. With his brothers-in-law he treated the matter as a joke.

'Oh, get away, you fellows!' he said on one occasion. 'I know you will be the first to hate me if I do this, because it will deprive you of the opportunity to extort cattle from some other fellow who would have to give some cattle for the girl you offer me.'

Everyone present laughed at this. But one of the senior brothers-in-law pressed him. Then Nyengebule said he wanted time to decide which one of his growing sisters-in-law would get on well with his wife as a co-wife. But when the girls he promised to choose from reached marriageable age, he had some other excuse for his delay. At last there came a time when the in-laws decided never to raise the matter again. Nyengebule was happy with their daughter, and the best thing to do was to leave it to these two to raise the matter, if and when they should desire such an arrangement.

One day there came an invitation to Nyengebule and his junior wife. There was going to be a great festival at his in-laws, on such and such a day and he was invited to be present with his wife. With great delight these two made all the necessary preparations. Two days before the day of departure, it occurred to the wife that on her return from these festivities she would be too tired to go gathering firewood, and that it would be wise to gather sufficient wood now, to last her some time after her return. She mentioned this to her co-wife, who decided she might as well go and gather some wood too.

The two women left home early the following morning. When they entered the woods, they separated, each one taking her own direction to find, cut, and pick dry wood and pile it to make her own bundle. But they kept in touch all the time, ever calling to each other to find out if things were going well. The final calls came when each one thought her bundle was big enough, and the two came together to sit and rest before carrying the firewood home. This was early in the afternoon.

While they were sitting there, there was a chirrup! chirrup! The junior wife was the first to hear it and she immediately recognised it as the call of the honeybird. She looked about, and saw this tiny bird fluttering about, now towards her, now away from her, and then towards her and away again.

'The honeybird!' she said and sprang up to follow it.

The honeybird led her on and on, chirruping as it went, until it came to a bees' nest. As soon as she saw this the woman called out to tell her co-wife what she had 'discovered'. The head wife came immediately, and the two gathered the honeycombs and piled them on a patch of green grass while the honeybird fluttered about hopefully. When they had finished, they picked up all the honey, except one comb that they left for the bird, and returned to the place where they had left their bundles of wood, and they sat down and ate together.

As they ate, the head wife took two pieces at a time, ate one and laid the other aside. She did this until they finished. It was only when she saw the head wife packing together what she had been laying aside that the junior wife became aware of what had been happening.

'Oh!' she said. 'I didn't think of that. Why didn't you tell me to put some aside too?'

In reply the head wife said, 'You know why you didn't think of it? It's because you have no children. It's only a woman who has children who remembers that she must lay something aside as she eats.'

The junior wife made no reply to this, and the two picked up their bundles and carried them home.

Nyengebule had been busy all day setting things in order. As far as his side of the preparations was concerned, everything that he intended to take with him to this festival was ready. Even the large fat gelded goat he was going to give as a son-in-law's customary contribution to the festival had already been chosen and fastened to the gatepost, so that it should be ready to lead away the following morning. Now he was waiting until his wives returned so that he should announce to his head wife formally that he and the junior wife would leave at cock-crow, and also to give orders to his boys as to what had to be done by this one and by that one while he was away.

As soon as his wives had entered their respective houses and seen to the few things that usually need straightening up when a wife has been away from her house the whole day, Nyengebule went to the house of his head wife and made this announcement and gave the orders to the boys. His head wife listened very carefully as he gave orders to the boys, and when he had finished, she went over them all, taking one boy after the other:

'Have you heard then, So-and-so? Your father wants you to do this and that while he is away. And you, So-and-so, have you heard what your father says? He wants you to do this, and this, and that.'

After this, she brought out the honey. She took some combs and served them up to her husband in a plate made of clay, and the rest she gave to her children.

'So you women discovered bees today!' said Nyengebule as he gratefully received his share.

'Yes,' said his wife. 'It was *Nobani* (So-and-so) who discovered them. She was drawn by the honeybird.'

'Well done!' said Nyengebule. 'But aren't you going to have any yourself?'

'No, thank you. I had enough in the woods.'

So Nyengebule ate his share and finished it. Then, thanking his head wife for the honey, he said goodbye to them all and went to the junior house. He was looking forward to a much bigger feast of honey. If his head wife had so much to give him, certainly his *ntandanekazi* must have laid aside much more for him, especially as it was she who had 'discovered'. There were no children to share the honey with, and he and his *ntandanekazi* would enjoy the honey together, just the two of them.

He found his junior wife busy with her packing. The evening meal was not yet ready. Nyengebule did not say anything about the honey, because he thought his *ntandanekazi* wanted to give him a pleasant surprise. Maybe she would produce the honey just before the evening meal. But when the food was ready, his wife served it up to him and said nothing about the honey. After the meal, she removed the dishes and washed them and put them away. Now, surely, the honey was coming? But the woman resumed her packing, paying particular attention to each ornament before deciding whether to take it with her or not. She would pick this one up and add it to her luggage, and then replace it by another one. Now and again she would find something wrong with the beads of this or that necklace and pull them out and reset them. She would dig out some ornament that she had not worn for a long time and compare it with one that she had acquired recently, taking long to make up her mind which one was more suitable than the other for this occasion. This went on and on until everyone else had gone to sleep and the whole village was quiet.

When at last she was satisfied that her luggage contained everything she would require for the festivities, the woman yawned and looked at her husband.

'I think we had better sleep now if we mean to leave at cock-crow,' she said.

'Sleep? Isn't there something you've forgotten to give me?'

'Something to give you?'

'Yes! Where's all the honey you brought me?'

'I didn't bring you any honey.'

'You're playing!'

'In truth, I didn't bring you any honey. If you think I'm playing, look for yourself. I forgot really.'

'You forgot? You forgot *me*? What is it that you remember then, if you forget *me*?'

Before she could reply, Nyengebule grabbed a heavy stick and in his anger he struck her hard. The blow landed on her left temple, and she fell to the ground. Terrified at this sight, Nyengebule flung the stick away and ran across the hut and bent over her body, calling her softly by name. Weakly her eyes opened, and then they closed, never to open again.

Nyengebule burst out of the hut, his first impulse being to shout for help, but no sooner had he run out than he retreated into the hut on tiptoe, frightened by the peace and silence of the night. He knelt by his wife's body and touched her here, here and there. Dead! His *ntandanekazi* dead? Yes, quite dead! What is he going to do? He cannot call anyone in here now. He must bury her before dawn. Yes, he must bury her alone. He is lucky too that everyone knows that he should be away at cock-crow. He must bury her and leave at cock-crow as arranged. Then his head wife and the children and all the neighbours will think she has gone with him.

He took a shovel and a long digging-rod and crept out to dig the grave. When he had finished he returned to the hut and looked around. That luggage! That luggage of his wife's! That must be buried with her. He carried the woman's body and laid it in the grave. Then he brought the luggage and laid it beside her body. He covered the body with earth and removed every trace he could find of this night's happenings. But there was one thing he had not noticed. The turban his wife had been wearing that evening had dropped on the ground between the house and the grave.

Nyengebule returned to his house, but not to sleep. What must he do now? Can he still go to his in-laws? Yes, that he must, because if he and his wife do not turn up, the in-laws will know there's something wrong and send someone to come and see what it is. But he has never gone to such festivities alone. His wife has always gone with him. How is he going to explain her absence this time? It will not sound good to his in-laws to say their daughter is ill, for how could he leave her alone then? What is more, they might do what they have always done when their daughter was reported ill – send one of her younger sisters to come and look after her and her husband. But go he must, for this is the only way he can find time to decide what to do. He will leave at cock-crow as arranged. Then he will try to be as he has always been until the festivities are over. Then what? Then what?

'*Kurukuku-u-u-u-ku*' crowed the cocks. Nyengebule crept out of bed and picked up his bags. He tiptoed out of the hut and fastened the door. He spoke softly to the goat as he approached it, in case it should make a noise and rouse his dogs as well as those of his neighbours. But the goat did not give him the least trouble. It was willing to be unfastened and led away.

Nyengebule travelled fast, like one who was running away from something. The goat did not handicap him because his boys had trained it for purposes of riding. Sometimes he led it by the rope, and sometimes he drove it before him.

Early in the afternoon, he had to leave the straight road by which he had been travelling most of the time and take a turn, walking along a path that led straight to his in-laws. Nyengebule stood for a while at this point, undecided whether to take the turn to his in-laws or continue along the straight road, going he knew not where. At last he took the turn. He had taken only a few paces when a honeybird appeared. It fluttered a little ahead of him and led him the way he was going, but the calls it made were not those that a honeybird makes when it leads a person to a bees' nest:

UNyengebul' uyibulel' intandanekazi,
Ibonisel' iinyosi, yaphakula,
Yatya, yalibal' ukumbekela;
Uyiselele kunye nezivatho zomgidi,
Akasibon' isankwane sisiw' endleleni.

Nyengebule has killed his favourite wife,
She discovered bees and gathered honey,
She ate and forgot to leave him a share;
He buried her together with her festival clothes,
And saw not the turban dropping on the way.

Nyengebule was startled. Did these words really come from that bird? And where had this bird gone to now? It had vanished. He went on. The bird appeared again and repeated its actions and song, but before he could do anything about it, it had vanished. But now he made up his mind what to do if it could come again. He would throw a stick at it and kill it. The honeybird appeared a third time and repeated its actions and song. Nyengebule let fly his stick and hit it, breaking one of its wings. The bird vanished, but the broken wing fluttered a little and then fell at his feet, no longer a honeybird's wing but the turban worn by his wife at the time he killed her.

He let it lie there for a while and stood looking at it. His *ntan-danekazi's* turban! Can he leave it there? It should have been buried with her. He must keep it until he can find an opportunity to do this. He picked it up and put it into the bag that contained the gifts for his in-laws.

As soon as he came in sight of his in-laws', the married women came out to welcome him with the shrills and ululations that announce the arrival of anyone who comes driving an animal for slaughter to such festivals. As soon as Nyengebule reached the *nkundla* (courtyard), his brothers-in-law relieved him of the goat, and their wives continued to sing his people's praises as they led him to the hut set aside for him and his wife. In no time, the sisters-in-law came crowding in this hut.

'But where's our sister?' they asked.

'So she hasn't arrived yet?' asked Nyengebule.

'No, she hasn't arrived. When did she leave home?'

'I left a little earlier than she because of the goat I had to bring with me. But she was almost ready when I left, and I thought she would be here before me because she was going to take a short cut and wasn't handicapped like me. She should be here soon.'

They brought him water so that he could wash, and immediately after, some food and beer to make him the jolly *mkhwenyethu* they knew he could be.

The festival was to open on the following day, and therefore the in-laws and their closest friends were busy with the final preparations. The women were straining those quantities of beer that must be ready for the next day, and the men were chopping wood and slaughtering oxen and goats. All the people working at these assignments were already keyed up for the festival. There was plenty of meat and beer for them, and there were far more people than work to do. Therefore most of them were practising the songs and dances with which they intended to impress the guests expected. Nyengebule's arrival therefore caused a great deal of excitement. Now that he had come, they could be sure that they would more than measure up to the famous expert singers and dancers with whom they would have to compete during these festivities. They were sure that this great singer and dancer had added something to his store since they last met him, and they were eager to learn these new things before 'that great day of tomorrow'. So, even before Nyengebule had finished eating and drinking, there were loud, impatient calls from his brothers-in-law and their friends to the *mkhwe* to 'come to the men'. But his sisters-in-law were not prepared to let him go until they had fed him, and until they knew what gifts he had brought them. For some of these gifts might be dainty ornaments that would just be suitable for the festivities.

At last, two of his brothers-in-law went to him.

'On your feet, *mkhwe!*' they said. 'These wives and sisters of ours can get their gifts later. Get up and come to the men.'

So saying, they lifted him up and carried him away, amid the amused protests of his sisters-in-law, as against the shouts of triumph from the onlookers to whom Nyengebule was being carried. As soon as he arrived, the men greeted him with his praises and with song and dance, and invited him to join them. Many of the less busy women in the courtyard cheered, and in no time the place was crowded with onlookers of all ages.

The sisters-in-law, however, remained in the hut, more curious to know what gifts they were getting than to join the admiring crowds. 'I wonder what gift he has brought me this time, and what naughty things he is going to say when he gives it to me!' thought each one. After all, he was their favourite *mkhwenyethu*, and if he should discover at some time that while he was dancing in the courtyard they opened the bag of gifts just to have a look, of course he would pretend to be offended, but in fact he would be delighted. So thought the sisters-in-law, and they pulled out the bag of gifts and opened it. When a little bird's wing flew out of the bag and fluttered above their heads towards the roof, there were screams of delight, for everyone thought this was just one of the *mkhwenyethu's* endless pranks. But the next moment, the women huddled together, horrified by the song of the honeybird:

Nyengebule has killed his favourite wife,
She discovered bees and gathered honey,
She ate and forgot to leave him a share;
He buried her together with her festival clothes,
And saw not the turban dropping on the way.

The women watched the wing speechlessly as it came down, down, down, until it landed on the floor and became a turban that they all knew very well.

Shouts and cheers in the courtyard! Shrills and ululations in the courtyard! Hand-clapping, song and drums in the courtyard! Admiration and praises for Nyengebule in the courtyard! Few of the onlookers, and none of the dancers, have noticed that the sons of this house

– Nyengebule's brothers-in-law and their cousins – are quietly being
called away, one by one, from this rejoicing. To the few who have noticed
this, nothing is unusual about *imilowo* (those of the family) occasionally
withdrawing quietly to hold council about the running of a big festival of
this nature.

Nyengebule was just beginning to teach a new song when two of his
in-laws' elderly neighbours came to tell him that he was wanted by his
in-laws. Up to this moment, he had not met his parents-in-law, and he
assumed that he was being requested to go to the great hut and present
himself formally. But when he indicated to the two elders that he would
have to go to his hut and change his dress before meeting his parents-in-
law, one of them said, 'There's no need for that. It's over there that you
are wanted.' The elder was pointing higher up the slope, to an old, high-
walled stone building – the most prominent building among the ruins of
what used to be the home of the forebears of Nyengebule's in-laws.

The elders walked a few paces alongside him, and then they stopped
and once again pointed out the building to which he had to go. Who
wanted him? he wondered. Maybe his brothers-in-law needed his help
about something or other? Maybe they expected so many guests that
they thought they could prepare this old building for the overflow? But
when he reached the door, the place was so quiet that he did not expect to
find anyone inside.

He pushed the door open without knocking, and he felt cold in the
stomach when he entered. Here were all his in-laws – his parents-in-law,
his wife's father's brothers and their wives, his wife's father's sisters and
their husbands, his wife's mother's brothers and their wives, his wife's
mother's sisters and their husbands, his brothers-in-law and their wives,
his wife's cousins and their wives or husbands, his sisters-in-law – all of
them standing, silent, solemn. In the centre of the building there was a
newly dug grave. On the piles of earth that came out of the grave was the
bag containing the gifts he had brought his sisters-in-law. Next to this
lay the body of the large fat gelded goat he had brought as his contribution to the festival. No one acknowledged his hoarse, half-whis-
pered greetings. Instead, his father-in-law pointed a finger at the bag of
gifts.

'Open that,' was all he said.

Nyengebule lifted up the bag and opened it, but he dropped it again,
his knees sagging a little. The wing of the honeybird had flown out and
was fluttering above the heads of those present, singing its song. When
it finished, it dropped at Nyengebule's feet and became his dead wife's
turban. Nyengebule gave it one look and then raised his head to look at
his father-in-law for the next order. But the father-in-law turned his

face away from him and signalled his eldest sister, a married woman. She stepped forward, lifted the bag of gifts, and cast it into the grave. The father-in-law signalled his two eldest sons. They stepped forward, lifted the dead goat, and cast it into the grave. Once more the father-in-law signalled, and this time all his sons and brother's sons stepped forward and closed in on Nyengebule. All the women covered their faces, but the men looked on grimly, noting every little detail of what was happening. They noted with silent admiration that Nyengebule did not shudder when these men laid their hands on him. They noted that he did not wince when some of the men bound his feet together and sat on his legs, while others stretched out his arms sideways and sat on them. They noted that he did not groan when his two senior brothers-in-law raised his head and twisted his neck.

Four men jumped into the grave and stood ready to receive his limp body from their kinsmen. Everyone was looking now. As the four men laid him carefully on his back beside his rejected gifts, everyone saw the wing of the honeybird fluttering over the grave. As soon as the four men had done their solemn duty and climbed out of the grave, everyone saw the wing of the honeybird landing on the chest of the dying man and becoming his dead wife's turban. Everyone saw Nyengebule's arms moving weakly and rising slowly, slowly, slowly from his sides to his chest. The women sobbed when they saw his hands closing on the turban and pressing it to his heart.

His brothers-in-law and their cousins brought shovels and took their places round the grave. They lifted their first shovelfuls, but before throwing the earth onto his motionless body, they paused just for one moment and bowed their heads, for they noticed that the turban was still pressed to the heart of the dead man.

Peter Wilhelm

Lion

from *L M and Other Stories* (1975)

Towards the end of summer, everything poised for decay, the final bold
shapes tottering under parabolas of hot straining insects, a lion was observed wandering across the rich farmlands to the north-west of Johannesburg: only miles from the city, a golden shape barred by trees
fringing mapped-out regions of cultivation and order, crossing the
thrusting highways in vast lopes that evaded destruction by the thun-
dering, astonished traffic.

There was no formal record of the lion, so he sprang into the city's
awareness fully extant, fused out of the shining air; and the first pre-
monitory twitches of fear manifested themselves in the dreams of the
inhabitants of Sandown, Bryanston, Houghton, all the green suburbs
with women beside blue swimming pools with drinks at 11 a.m. The
pounce, the yellow teeth, the cavernous dark jaws, the feral rush through
the flowering shrubbery – it was all there, a night-time code.

Posses of police and farmers – guns out and oiled, trusty – walked
through the high grass and weeds, stung by immature maize stalks,
looking. They had dogs with them who cringed and whimpered, showing
their own calcium-charged fangs, white and somehow delectable like the
tips of asparagus. They and the children who ran after them shrieking
with terror and breathlessness, black and white tumbled together in the
mordant adventure, were all on a hampered search; the skills of tracking
were forgotten, they could only go by the obvious. Members of the press
went along too, with flushed faces and cameras.

At an early stage it was decided that, given the high price of lions on
the international zoo market, the animal would not, when found, be
killed: anaesthetic darts would be used to stun it first, then it would be
lifted into a cage and transported to a convenient central point for the
disposition of lions.

They followed a trail of kills, day after day, puffing and lagging. Here they found a dog contemptuously munched and discarded; there a mournful heifer, brown licked eyes startled by death, a haunch ripped open – purple and blue ravines, Grade A waste spoiled for the abattoir and the hungry steakhouses.

The heavy, overripe rains had given a lush feel to the fields, spreading green paint over growth, and wild flowers and weeds hammered into the air from uncultivated edges. Fruit fell into mud with sodden plops; irrigation ditches and small streams throbbed, the water corded and waxy. It had been a superb year, a harvest of a year, and the granaries and exchequer were loaded. So the lion penetrated a structure of assent and gratitude with a dark trajectory: his streaming mane, a Tarzan image, cast gaunt shadows on the end of the commercial year.

The boots of the hunters stuck in the mud; they were like soldiers going over the top in 1916, sent into barbed wire and indeterminate sludge by drunken generals; they floundered; the brims of their hats filled with rain; their pants soaked through like those of terrified schoolboys. They made no headway.

Inexorably, champing at the livestock, the lion ate his way towards the northern suburbs of the city, past roadhouses and drive-in cinemas showing documentaries on wild life and the adventures of Captain Caprivi.

The frequency of dreams involving lions and lion-like beings increased significantly among the inhabitants of the green park-like suburbs of the city. The thud of tennis balls against the netting of racquets lost its precision: the shadow was there, in the tennis court, in the cool waves of the swimming pool, in the last bitter juices of the evening cocktail, tasting of aniseed.

The lion came down.

The farmers – who grew plump chickens for the frozen food ranges of the great supermarkets, and poppies for certain anniversaries – were furious at the terroristic incursion. It blighted their reality, shaming them. They woke to fences offensively broken, to minor household animals sardonically slaughtered, not even used for a snack on the road.

The lion behaved precisely like a lion; each animal was decisively killed; there was never any maiming, inadvertent or intentional; his great jaws crunched down on bone and splintered through domesticity.

He took a roving way toward the city: first directly south through well-manured farmlands, then tracing a stream westwards away from the sprawl of concrete and glass – sniffing at it, perhaps, and choosing to skirt.

He seemed to vanish, back into the diminishing lights of early autumn, back into the air, his lithe yellowish body no longer even glimpsed at a distance by the frenzied posses, watched from behind earth walls by large-eyed farm-hands, and howled at by dogs with their black testicles in the dust.

The pressure abruptly diminished like that in a garden hose when the tap is turned commandingly to the left.

Something like silence descended, mote-like and uneasy. The lion had gone away; there had never been a lion; the lion had been a hypnagogic hallucination.

Then he killed a man, most savagely tearing out his guts next to a road, and pin-pointed on a map the kill showed that the westward drift had been temporary and that the lion had in reality resumed coming back. He had followed a stream away from the city, now he was coming back on the opposite bank: all he had done was seek out a place to cross.

Until the occurrence of the first human death, the press and other communications media had adopted an editorial stance towards the lion in which a certain light-heartedness had been mandatory. There had been jibes at authority's inability to find the beast, or even trace its origins. Now, as telephones began to ring incessantly with queries from troubled householders as to the lion's progress, and a sermon was preached in which the light of Christianity was set favourably against the unplumbed blackness of the wilderness and its denizens, the newspapers realised that public opinion was turning against the lion, and they adopted a harder editorial approach: the lion must be shot, or at least swiftly captured, before there were more deaths.

The dead man was reported to be a Bantu male called Samuel Buthelezi, a distant relation of the Zulu Royal family.

It emerged that the followers had in fact passed the lion, going west when he was coming east; he had been asleep on a rock, or in a warm bowl of sand, sunning himself invisibly.

And so the feeling arose that the search had to be made by professionals. A former professional game hunter was accordingly brought out of retirement to put the affair on a more scientific or knowing footing. However, it was impossible to search by night, which was too preponderantly blank to make for ease of vision, silence of movement, or comfort of heart; and so the lion continued to get away. His getting away became the present tense of the searchers and they began to feel he was invincible, that he took devious routes with prior awareness of topography and demography; and when a day or so passed without reports of a kill they indulged in grotesque fantasies – remarking that the lion must be dead in a ditch, or whimpering in a cave with a thorn in his foot. Any of a dozen possibilities, and impossibilities, presented themselves according to the number of searchers involved.

The former professional game hunter was an alcoholic; he drank himself into a stupor and issued contradictory orders.

Small units of the army and air force were summoned to help in the search; it was reasoned that the experience would aid them in tracing terrorists in hostile terrain. Platoons of young men in green and khaki camouflage uniform – bayonets ready at the tips of their rifles – moved lumpily over hills and through lower muddy regions looking for the lion, their boots mired indescribably. In the air fighter and reconnaissance jets flashed from one edge of the horizon to the other, ceaselessly photographing. A helicopter, normally used for the control of traffic and the detection of illegally cultivated marijuana, also chopped its way through the search pattern.

The first white person to be killed by the lion was Dr Margaret Brierwood. A graduate in palaeontology, Dr Brierwood had taken her two children to school and was settling down beside the swimming pool of her and her husband's three-acre holding in a wooded area only ten miles from the city centre. In the course of the preceding night the lion had doubled the distance between him and his pursuers, racing along the fringes of a dual highway connecting the cities of Pretoria and Johannesburg. He had failed to make a kill at dawn and was correspondingly nettled at his own inadequacies – a horse had whinnied to freedom because of a misjudged leap – and driven by hunger.

The Brierwoods' estate was surrounded by a low wooden fence, easily hurdled, and the lion sat for some time within the grounds, panting softly, his tail rapidly frisking dust and grass, before moving. He observed the morning activity narrowly, tempted at one point to carry off a black man who swept the floor of the swimming pool with a long vacuum brush. He was deterred by innumerable activities in his immediate environment: a large fly that bit his haunch and made him snap irritably at the air, two birds that made trilling love in overhead leaves, a subtle alteration in the quality of the morning light which stirred inchoate levels of unease in the beast.

The strangeness of the pool – its non-drinking-place aspects – had a dazzling effect on the mind of the lion. It made him indecisive about striking.

Eventually, however, he made his charge – out of the wooded garden, up a grass slope to the pool's verge, then a leap across a tea table – glass shattering, sugar cubes ascending white in the clear air – and a last controlled embrace with Dr Brierwood, his vast paws over her breasts, the talons holding firm, his jaws clamping down on her neck to draw up spouts of blood.

Dr Brierwood had been midway through a paragraph in an article pointing out certain anomalies in a palaeontologist's analysis of recent finds at unexpected levels of the Olduvai Gorge in Kenya. When the intimidating, blood-freezing, total horror of the lion's roar swept over her like a wave of pure death from an opened crypt, she looked up and screamed. The lion dropped down out of the sky to seize her; one finger convulsively jabbed at the place where she had stopped reading; and she felt her bones being crushed with more force than she had ever conceived.

Terrified servants ran for help. Within an hour a cordon of men and weaponry had been set in a ring around the Brierwood estate. For miles in all directions traffic began to slow, to stop, to impact into jarring hooting masses. Thousands of sightseers came from all directions, hampering operations.

At the centre of command was the former professional game hunter, who was half mad from anxiety and gracelessly attempted to defer to anyone in uniform; but orders had been given that he alone was in charge, and as the crisis gained dimension, moving towards a critical moment when something would after all have to be done, he realised that a decision – on something, anything – would have to be taken. He pushed his way through people who shouted into each other's faces and went into a house which instantly transformed into a headquarters. Maps were pinned on walls, markers were moved on boards, grids were established; the military apparatus became dominant, and he realised that a military solution might be inevitable.

To think more clearly the game hunter locked himself in a lavatory and drank.

The lion left the remains of his kill beside the swimming pool and made his way into the woods to sleep. It was a fine autumn morning, holding the last of the summer heat in the bright dappled areas of light under the trees, and soothing and cool in the shade. Drowsiness overcame him and he stretched at his full length to digest Dr Brierwood.

The small, frightened, trigger-happy group which – under the dilatory leadership of the former professional game hunter – finally made its way to the swimming pool and found the dead woman, was incapacitated by the sight. Each registered an atrocity; each felt an impulse to shout, or rescript the terms of the find; inevitably there was a sickly anticipation of retribution and subsequent guilt.

In the judicial inquiry which was later held into the circumstances of the killing, it was considered extraordinary that the grounds of the

Brierwood estate were not fully, immediately searched. No search was made; once Dr Brierwood had been removed the servants were questioned on the movements of the lion, and when two agreed that it had been seen wandering along a stretch of country road north of the estate there was a surge in that direction. The testimony of the servants was instantly accepted: it had a satisfactory emotional content, and the searchers were in any case dazed at the fury that had broken out at the edge of the swimming pool.

On a bed of brown fallen leaves at the outer boundary of the Brierwood estate the lion slept peacefully all day; he moaned softly in his sleep like a dreaming cat, his immense male head on his paws.

By midnight the curious had moved away, and the searchers were bunched together indecisively in a small army camp. A violent electric storm had disrupted communications, and the various groups who were out on the roads and in the fields with torches and guns blundered through wet darkness, seeing nothing, knowing nothing, dead at heart. Damage to an underground telephone cable at two a.m. put several thousand receivers out of order in the area; and this contributed to an impression of profound devastation. There was a universal sense of depression, and sleepers were driven down into grey underworlds where faceless statues intoned meaningless arguments.

Shortly after dawn the lion left the woods, through which horizontal light splintered prismatically. He sniffed the wind and plodded south again, through landscaped terraces and sprawling ranch-style homesteads. Down pine-needle matted lanes and across dew-spotted lawns he padded with no more noise than soft rustlings and the snap of small twigs.

Soon the terrain changed, and taking the easiest way he was beguiled towards the exact heart of Johannesburg along the concrete swathes of the M1 motorway. It was a bright, crisp morning; the sky was enormous, blue to violet at the zenith, streaked with high tufts of cirrus, almost invisible. Ahead, the dark autumnal cone of ash and smoke remained to be burned off the city, dense, dirty but giving a solid emphasis to the tower blocks: an appropriate frame.

He went on through the awakening suburbs, stinging smells of coffee and morning toast, the first cars coughing into life. And then the first cars began to pass him, early motorists staring with incredulity, astonishment, in tumults of weirdness at the apparition. They accelerated around the lion, so that there was an aspect of untampered serenity about his passage.

He walked into Johannesburg, quite alone after a time, since once word had reached the authorities of his route the motorway was closed and for the second time in twenty-four hours traffic choked to a standstill. The lion could hear distant clangour and uproar, meaningless. Soon he began to sniff irritably at acrid fumes and the like, but his entry remained inflexible; he took no offramps, and remained on the left of the road within the speed limit.

By mid-morning he was weary, and stopped, and looked around. This was the city: geometrical mountains advanced into themselves, making no horizon, netting together like stone fronds into an impassivity of yellow, grey, gold, black. He had no sense of distance or perspective and could not see into the new environment.

He roared at it.

His roar echoed back.

He stood at the edge of the motorway, where it swept over old buildings and streets and looked down past John Vorster Square to the Magistrates' Courts and the Stock Exchange, and beyond that to the Trust Bank and the Carlton Centre: the shapes impacted up against his sight.

Below him when he looked again, men and women seethed, their clothing briskly making fresh patterns as they moved around, then settling or resettling into something else.

North and south the motorway spread dully; nothing whatsoever moved; a small wind beat miserably at pieces of brown newspaper gusted over the tar.

He roared at everything.

And, tinnily, a kind of echo came back: but buzzing, inconsequential, intermittent. Far above a small black dot came down at him.

The helicopter, the former professional game hunter.

Suddenly the lion was deafened and shaken by fear: a metal thing jabbered at him only yards away, black grit tossed up by mad winds into his nose. Men with strained white faces spilled out into the motorway, pincered him.

And then, of course, the military solution.

Bessie Head

Life

from *The Collector of Treasures and other Botswana Village Tales*
(1977)

In 1963, when the borders were first set up between Botswana and South
Africa, pending Botswana's independence in 1966, all Botswana-born
citizens had to return home. Everything had been mingled up in the old
colonial days, and the traffic of people to and fro between the two countries had been a steady flow for years and years. More often, especially if
they were migrant labourers working in the mines, their period of set-
tlement was brief, but many people had settled there in permanent
employment. It was these settlers who were disrupted and sent back to
village life in a mainly rural country. On their return they brought with
them bits and bits of a foreign culture and city habits which they had
absorbed. Village people reacted in their own way; what they liked, and
was beneficial to them – they absorbed, for instance, the faith-healing
cult churches which instantly took hold like wildfire – what was harmful
to them, they rejected. The murder of Life had this complicated undertone of rejection.

Life had left the village as a little girl of ten years old with her parents
for Johannesburg. They had died in the meanwhile, and on Life's return,
seventeen years later, she found, as was village custom, that she still had
a home in the village. On mentioning that her name was Life Morapedi,
the villagers immediately and obligingly took her to the Morapedi yard
in the central part of the village. The family yard had remained intact,
just as they had left it, except that it looked pathetic in its desolation. The
thatch of the mud huts had patches of soil over them where the ants had
made their nests; the wooden poles that supported the rafters of the huts
had tilted to an angle as their base had been eaten through by the ants.
The rubber hedge had grown to a disproportionate size and enclosed the
yard in a gloom of shadows that kept out the sunlight. Weeds and grass
of many seasonal rains entangled themselves in the yard.

Life's future neighbours, a group of women, continued to stand near her.

'We can help you to put your yard in order,' they said kindly. 'We are very happy that a child of ours has returned home.'

They were impressed with the smartness of this city girl. They generally wore old clothes and kept their very best things for special occasions like weddings, and even then those best things might just be ordinary cotton prints. The girl wore an expensive cream costume of linen material tailored to fit her tall, full figure. She had a bright, vivacious friendly manner and laughed freely and loudly. Her speech was rapid and a little hysterical but that was in keeping with her whole personality.

'She is going to bring us a little light,' the women said among themselves, as they went off to fetch their work tools. They were always looking 'for the light' and by that they meant that they were ever alert to receive new ideas that would freshen up the ordinariness and everydayness of village life.

A woman who lived near the Morapedi yard had offered Life hospitality until her own yard was set in order. She picked up the shining new suitcases and preceded Life to her own home, where Life was immediately surrounded with all kinds of endearing attentions – a low stool was placed in a shady place for her to sit on; a little girl came shyly forward with a bowl of water for her to wash her hands; and following on this, a tray with a bowl of meat and porridge was set before her so that she could revive herself after her long journey home. The other women briskly entered her yard with hoes to scratch out the weeds and grass, baskets of earth and buckets of water to re-smear the mud walls, and they had found two idle men to rectify the precarious tilt of the wooden poles of the mud hut. These were the sort of gestures people always offered, but they were pleased to note that the newcomer seemed to have an endless stream of money which she flung around generously. The work party in her yard would suggest that the meat of a goat, slowly simmering in a great iron pot, would help the work to move with a swing, and Life would immediately produce the money to purchase the goat and also tea, milk, sugar, pots of porridge or anything the workers expressed a preference for, so that those two weeks of making Life's yard beautiful for her seemed like one long wedding-feast; people usually only ate that much at weddings.

'How is it you have so much money, our child?' one of the women at last asked, curiously.

'Money flows like water in Johannesburg,' Life replied, with her gay and hysterical laugh. 'You just have to know how to get it.'

The women received this with caution. They said among themselves that their child could not have lived a very good life in Johannesburg. Thrift and honesty were the dominant themes of village life and everyone knew that one could not be honest and rich at the same time; they counted every penny and knew how they had acquired it – with hard work. They never imagined money as a bottomless pit without end; it always had an end and was hard to come by in this dry, semi-desert land. They predicted that she would soon settle down – intelligent girls got jobs in the post office sooner or later.

Life had had the sort of varied career that a city like Johannesburg offered a lot of black women. She had been a singer, beauty queen, advertising model, and prostitute. None of these careers were available in the village – for the illiterate women there was farming and housework; for the literate, teaching, nursing, and clerical work. The first wave of women Life attracted to herself were the farmers and housewives. They were the intensely conservative hard-core centre of village life. It did not take them long to shun her completely because men started turning up in an unending stream. What caused a stir of amazement was that Life was the first and the only women in the village to make a business out of selling herself. The men were paying her for her services. People's attitude to sex was broad and generous – it was recognised as a necessary part of human life, that it ought to be available whenever possible like food and water, or else one's life would be extinguished or one would get dreadfully ill. To prevent these catastrophes from happening, men and women generally had quite a lot of sex but on a respectable and human level, with financial considerations coming in as an afterthought. When the news spread around that this had now become a business in Life's yard, she attracted to herself a second wave of women – the beer-brewers of the village.

The beer-brewing women were a gay and lovable crowd who had emancipated themselves some time ago. They were drunk every day and could be seen staggering around the village, usually with a wide-eyed, illegitimate baby hitched on to their hips. They also talked and laughed loudly and slapped each other on the back and had developed a language all their own:

'Boy-friends, yes. Husbands, uh, uh, no. Do this! Do that! We want to rule ourselves.'

But they too were subject to the respectable order of village life. Many men passed through their lives but they were all for a time steady boy-friends. The usual arrangement was:

'Mother, you help me and I'll help you.'

This was just so much eye-wash. The men hung around, lived on the resources of the women, and during all this time they would part with about two rand of their own money. After about three months a tally-up would be made:

'Boy-friend,' the woman would say. 'Love is love and money is money. You owe me money.' And he'd never be seen again, but another scoundrel would take his place. And so the story went on and on. They found their queen in Life and like all queens, they set her activities apart from themselves; they never attempted to extract money from the constant stream of men because they did not know how, but they liked her yard. Very soon the din and riot of a Johannesburg township was duplicated, on a minor scale, in the central part of the village. A transistor radio blared the day long. Men and women reeled around drunk and laughing and food and drink flowed like milk and honey. The people of the surrounding village watched this phenomenon with pursed lips and commented darkly:

'They'll all be destroyed one day like Sodom and Gomorrah.'

Life, like the beer-brewing women, had a language of her own too. When her friends expressed surprise at the huge quantities of steak, eggs, liver, kidneys, and rice they ate in her yard – the sort of food they too could now and then afford but would not dream of purchasing – she replied in a carefree, off-hand way: I'm used to handling big money.' They did not believe it; they were too solid to trust to this kind of luck which had such shaky foundations, and as though to offset some doom that might be just around the corner they often brought along their own scraggy, village chickens reared in their yards, as offerings for the day's round of meals. And one of Life's philosophies on life, which they were to recall with trembling a few months later, was: 'My motto is: live fast, die young, and have a good-looking corpse.' All this was said with the bold, free joy of a woman who had broken all the social taboos. They never followed her to those dizzy heights.

A few months after Life's arrival in the village, the first hotel with its pub opened. It was initially shunned by all the women and even the beer-brewers considered they hadn't fallen *that* low yet – the pub was also associated with the idea of selling oneself. It became Life's favourite business venue. It simplified the business of making appointments for the following day. None of the men questioned their behaviour, nor how such an unnatural situation had been allowed to develop – they could get all the sex they needed for free in the village, but it seemed to fascinate them that they should pay for it for the first time. They had quickly got to the stage where they communicated with Life in shorthand language:

'When?' And she would reply: 'Ten o'clock.' 'When?' 'Two o'clock.' 'When?' 'Four o'clock,' and so on.

And there would be the roar of cheap small talk and much buttock slapping. It was her element and her feverish, glittering, brilliant black eyes swept around the bar, looking for everything and nothing at the same time.

Then one evening death walked quietly into the bar. It was Lesego, the cattle-man, just come in from his cattle-post, where he had been occupied for a period of three months. Men built up their own, individual reputations in the village and Lesego's was one of the most respected and honoured. People said of him: 'When Lesego has got money and you need it, he will give you what he has got and he won't trouble you about the date of payment ...' He was honoured for another reason also – for the clarity and quiet indifference of his thinking. People often found difficulty in sorting out issues or the truth in any debatable matter. He had a way of keeping his head above water, listening to an argument and always pronouncing the final judgement: 'Well, the truth about this matter is ...' He was also one of the most successful cattle-men with a balance of R7 000 in the bank, and whenever he came into the village he lounged around and gossiped or attended village kgotla meetings, so that people had a saying: 'Well, I must be getting about my business. I'm not like Lesego with money in the bank.'

As usual, the brilliant radar eyes swept feverishly around the bar. They did the rounds twice that evening in the same manner, each time coming to a dead stop for a full second on the thin, dark concentrated expression of Lesego's face. There wasn't any other man in the bar with that expression; they all had sheepish, inane-looking faces. He was the nearest thing she had seen for a long time to the Johannesburg gangsters she had associated with – the same small, economical gestures, the same power and control. All the men near him quietened down and began to consult with him in low earnest voices; they were talking about the news of the day which never reached the remote cattle-posts. Whereas all the other men had to approach her, the third time her radar eyes swept round he stood his ground, turned his head slowly, and then jerked it back slightly in a silent command:

'Come here.'

She moved immediately to his end of the bar.

'Hullo,' he said, in an astonishingly tender voice and a smile flickered across his dark, reserved face. That was the sum total of Lesego, that basically he was a kind and tender man, that he liked women and had been so successful in that sphere that he took his dominance and success for granted. But they looked at each other from their own worlds and came to fatal conclusions – she saw in him the power and maleness of the gangsters; he saw the freshness and surprise of an entirely new kind of woman. He had left all his women after a time bacause they bored him, and like all people who live an ordinary humdrum life, he was attracted to that undertone of hysteria in her.

Very soon they stood up and walked out together. A shocked silence fell upon the bar. The men exchanged looks with each other and the way these things communicate themselves, they knew that all the other appointments had been cancelled while Lesego was there. And as though speaking their thoughts aloud, Sianana, one of Lesego's friends commented: 'Lesego just wants to try it out like we all did because it is something new. He won't stay there when he finds out that it is rotten to the core.'

But Sianana was to find out that he did not fully understand his friend. Lesego was not seen at his usual lounging-places for a week and when he emerged again it was to announce that he was to marry. The news was received with cold hostility. Everyone talked of nothing else; it was as impossible as if a crime was being committed before their very eyes. Sianana once more made himself the spokesman. He waylaid Lesego on his way to the village kgotla:

'I am much surprised by the rumours about you, Lesego,' he said bluntly. 'You can't marry that woman. She's a terrible fuck-about!'

Lesego stared back at him steadily, then he said in his quiet, indifferent way: 'Who isn't here?'

Sianana shrugged his shoulders. The subtleties were beyond him; but whatever else was going on it wasn't commercial, it was human, but did that make it any better? Lesego liked to bugger up an argument like that with a straightforward point. As they walked along together Sianana shook his head several times to indicate that something important was eluding him, until at last with a smile, Lesego said: 'She has told me all about her bad ways. They are over.'

Sianana merely compressed his lips and remained silent.

Life made the announcement too, after she was married, to all her beer-brewing friends: 'All my old ways are over,' she said. 'I have now become a woman.'

She still looked happy and hysterical. Everything came to her too easily, men, money, and now marriage. The beer-brewers were not slow to point out to her with the same amazement with which they had exclaimed over the steak and eggs, that there were many women in the village who had cried their eyes out over Lesego. She was very flattered.

Their lives, at least Lesego's, did not change much with marriage. He still liked lounging around the village; the rainy season had come and life was easy for the cattle-men at this time because there was enough water and grazing for the animals. He wasn't the kind of man to fuss about the house and during his time he only made three pronouncements about the household. He took control of all the money. She had to ask him for it and state what it was to be used for. Then he didn't like the transistor radio blaring the whole day long.

'Women who keep that thing going the whole day have nothing in their heads,' he said.

Then he looked down at her from a great height and commented finally and quietly: 'If you go with those men again, I'll kill you.'

This was said so indifferently and quietly, as though he never really expected his authority and dominance to encounter any challenge.

She hadn't the mental equipment to analyse what had hit her, but something seemed to strike her a terrible blow behind the head. She instantly succumbed to the blow and rapidly began to fall apart. On the surface, the everyday round of village life was deadly dull in its even, unbroken monotony; one day slipped easily into another, drawing water, stamping corn, cooking food. But within this there were enormous tugs and pulls between people. Custom demanded that people care about each other, and all day long there was this constant traffic of people in and out of each other's lives. Someone had to be buried; sympathy and help were demanded for this event – there were money loans, new-born babies, sorrow, trouble, gifts. Lesego had long been the king of this world; there was, every day, a long string of people, wanting something or wanting to give him something in gratitude for a past favour. It was the basic strength of village life. It created people whose sympathetic and emotional responses were always fully awakened, and it rewarded them by richly filling in a void that was one big, gaping yawn. When the hysteria and cheap rowdiness were taken away, Life fell into the yawn; she had nothing inside herself to cope with this way of life that had finally caught up with her. The beer-brewing women were still there; they still liked her yard because Lesego was casual and easy-going and all that went on in it now – like the old men squatting in corners with gifts: 'Lesego, I had good luck with my hunting today. I caught two rabbits and I want to share one with you ...' – was simply the Tswana way of life they too lived. In keeping with their queen's new status, they said:

'We are women and must do something.'

They collected earth and dung and smeared and decorated Life's courtyard. They drew water for her, stamped her corn, and things looked quite ordinary on the surface because Lesego also liked a pot of beer. No one noticed the expression of anguish that had crept into Life's face. The boredom of the daily round was almost throttling her to death and no matter which way she looked, from the beer-brewers to her husband to all the people who called, she found no one with whom she could communicate what had become an actual physical pain. After a month of it, she was near collapse. One morning she mentioned her agony to the beer-brewers: 'I think I have made a mistake. Married life doesn't suit me.'

And they replied sympathetically: 'You are just getting used to it. After all it's a different life in Johannesburg.'

The neighbours went further. They were impressed by a marriage they thought could never succeed. They started saying that one never ought to judge a human being who was both good and bad, and Lesego had turned a bad woman into a good woman which was something they had never seen before. Just as they were saying this and nodding their approval, Sodom and Gomorrah started up all over again. Lesego had received word late in the evening that the new born calves at his cattle-post were dying, and early the next morning he was off again in his truck.

The old, reckless wild woman awakened from a state near death with a huge sigh of relief. The transistor blared, the food flowed again, the men and women reeled around dead drunk. Simply by their din they beat off all the unwanted guests who nodded their heads grimly. When Lesego came back they were going to tell him this was no wife for him.

Three days later Lesego unexpectedly was back in the village. The calves were all anaemic and they had to be brought in to the vet for an injection. He drove his truck straight through the village to the vet's camp. One of the beer-brewers saw him and hurried in alarm to her friend.

'The husband is back,' she whispered fearfully, pulling Life to one side.

'Agh,' she replied irritably.

She did dispel the noise, the men, and the drink, but a wild anger was driving her to break out of a way of life that was like death to her. She told one of the men she'd see him at six o'clock. At about five o'clock Lesego drove into the yard with the calves. There was no one immediately around to greet him. He jumped out of the truck and walked to one of the huts, pushing open the door. Life was sitting on the bed. She looked up silently and sullenly. He was a little surprised but his mind was still distracted by the calves. He had to settle them in the yard for the night.

'Will you make some tea,' he said. 'I'm very thirsty.'

'There's no sugar in the house,' she said. 'I'll have to get some.'

Something irritated him but he hurried back to the calves and his wife walked out of the yard. Lesego had just settled the calves when a neighbour walked in, he was very angry.

'Lesego,' he said bluntly. 'We told you not to marry that woman. If you go to the yard of Radithobolo now you'll find her in bed with him. Go and see for yourself that you may leave that bad woman!'

Lesego stared quietly at him for a moment, then at his own pace as though there were no haste or chaos in his life, he went to the hut they used as a kitchen. A tin full of sugar stood there. He turned and found a knife in the corner, one of the large ones he used for slaughtering cattle, and slipped it into his shirt. Then at his own pace he walked to the yard of Radithobolo. It looked deserted, except that the door of one of the huts was partially open and one closed. He kicked open the door of the closed hut and the man within shouted out in alarm. On seeing Lesego he sprang cowering into a corner. Lesego jerked his head back indicating that the man should leave the room. But Radithobolo did not run far. He wanted to enjoy himself so he pressed himself into the shadows of the rubber hedge. He expected the usual husband-and-wife scene – the irate husband cursing at the top of his voice; the wife, hysterical in her lies and self-defence. Only Lesego walked out of the yard and he held in his hand a huge, blood-stained knife. On seeing the knife Radithobolo immediately fell to the ground in a dead faint. There were a few people on the footpath and they shrank into the rubber hedge at the sight of that knife.

Very soon a wail arose. People clutched at their heads and began running in all directions crying yo! yo! yo! in their shock. It was some time before anyone thought of calling the police. They were so disordered because murder, outright and violent, was a most uncommon and rare occurrence in village life. It seemed that only Lesego kept cool that evening. He was sitting quietly in his yard when the whole police force came tearing in. They looked at him in horror and began to thoroughly upbraid him for looking so unperturbed.

'You have taken a human life and you are cool like that!' they said angrily. 'You are going to hang by the neck for this. It's a serious crime to take a human life.'

He did not hang by the neck. He kept that cool, head-above-water indifferent look, right up to the day of his trial. Then he looked up at the judge and said calmly: 'Well, the truth about this matter is, I had just returned from the cattle-post. I had had trouble with my calves that day. I came home late and being thirsty, asked my wife to make me tea. She said there was no sugar in the house and left to buy some. My neighbour, Mathata came in after this and said that my wife was not at the shops but in the yard of Radithobolo. He said I ought to go and see what she was doing in the yard of Radithobolo. I thought I would check up about the sugar first and in the kitchen I found a tin full of it. I was sorry and surprised to see this. Then a fire seemed to fill my heart. I thought that if she was doing a bad thing with Radithobolo as Mathata said, I'd better kill her because I cannot understand a wife who could be so corrupt . . .'

Lesego had been doing this for years, passing judgement on all aspects of life in his straightforward, uncomplicated way. The judge, who was a white man, and therefore not involved in Tswana custom and its debates, was as much impressed by Lesego's manner as all the village men had been.

'This is a crime of passion,' he said sympathetically. 'So there are extenuating circumstances. But it is still a serious crime to take a human life so I sentence you to five years imprisonment . . .'

Lesego's friend, Sianana, who was to take care of his business affairs while he was in jail, came to visit Lesego still shaking his head. Something was eluding him about the whole business, as though it had been planned from the very beginning.

'Lesego,' he said, with deep sorrow. 'Why did you kill that fuckabout? You had legs to walk away. You could have walked away. Are you trying to show us that rivers never cross here? There are good women and good men but they seldom join their lives together. It's always this mess and foolishness . . .'

A song by Jim Reeves was very popular at that time: *That's What Happens When Two Worlds Collide*. When they were drunk, the beer-brewing women used to sing it and start weeping. Maybe they had the last word on the whole affair.

Joel Matlou

Man Against Himself

from *Staffrider* 2 (4) 1979

We must work before the sun goes down. The life of a man is very heavy in his bones and his future is a deep unknown grave.

One day when I was alone, struggling to get money, and far away from my home where no one lives or grows, I met a man from Zululand called Dlongolo. He told me to try for work at the offices of Rustenburg Platinum Mine (RPM) in Bleskop, eight kilometres from where I was living.

The following day I went to the offices of RPM. I found work. The man who hires labourers was a Black man with three missing upper teeth. I was told to come on Monday. Before I left the premises I saw the sportsground, the mine hospital, a bar, a café, trucks, vans, buses and a compound with many rooms and toilets. But I left because I was sleeping at the hostel in Rustenburg and my home was in Mabopane, Odi.

On Monday morning I returned to the offices with others. At about 9.30 a.m. our passes were taken and looked into. They told me to fill in the forms they gave me in Ga-Rankuwa. So, with the little money that I had, I arrived in Ga-Rankuwa and my forms were filled in, but I was surprised when they told me to pay R1 for the forms. I paid it and left. So I was short of money for the train back to Rustenburg. I had only 85 cents in my pocket, and the journey would cost R1.10. It was 9.30 a.m. and the train left Ga-Rankuwa at 10.00 a.m. I was far from the station and I lost hope of catching the train. I thought of begging for money, but decided I was too young to beg.

My second plan was that I should sleep somewhere in Ga-Rankuwa and at about 4 a.m. I would walk to the station of Wolhuterskop where

my 85 cents would be enough for the train. At about 8 p.m. I chose
myself a toilet to sleep in at a certain school in Ga-Rankuwa, Zone 4. I
went into the toilet at night but it was very dark inside. There were lights
all over Ga-Rankuwa roads. I walked slowly to the back of the toilets
where I found a big stone. I sat on it trying not to think of dangerous
snakes under the stone. At midnight I heard barking dogs. All the people
in Ga-Rankuwa were asleep. At about 3 a.m. I heard cars hooting all over
Ga-Rankuwa. I thought I was in danger. But those cars belonged to
newspapers and were calling for their employees. And there were two
buses hooting. I though they were staff buses for drivers. People started
to walk on the roads then, to catch trains and buses to Pretoria and
Rosslyn. At about 5.15 a.m. I felt cold. I was wearing a shirt, a jersey,
trousers, and shoes without socks. The sun rose and I left Ga-Rankuwa
early so that I could catch the 11.30 a.m. train at Wolhuterskop. I ran
until De Wild were I started to walk and beg a lift to Brits or Rustenburg.

On the road to Brits I saw a Black man sitting on the white government
stone indicating bridges. I greeted him and he greeted me. As I passed he
called, and stood up. He begged 20 cents from me. With shame I told
him my story and showed him the forms I'd filled out in Ga-Rankuwa.
He was wearing sandals, black trousers, a red 'hemp',[1] a black jersey and
a scarf. He had a camera in his hand. I continued to tell him my story. I
told him to beg a lift to Brits, where he was going. A truck carrying sand
arrived and we stopped it for a lift. The driver took us to Brits. We got off
at the bus rank. He asked me to accompany him to the pass office for a
reference book. At the pass office we saw convicts cutting grass and
sweeping the pass office floors. He was given a duplicate and we departed.

I started to run through the town until I was outside Brits. The station
of Wolhuterskop was very far and there were no short cuts so I used the
main roads, like a car. I was tired and felt like a convict on the run. I could
not imagine what was going to happen. My stomach was empty. As I
was walking on the tar road I met two beautiful girls aged about eighteen
to twenty. I am twenty-three. They were carrying boxes with dirty dust
coats inside. I greeted them and asked for the Wolhuterskop station. One
of the girls, speaking Pedi, told me that it was not so far away. The second
girl asked where I was from. I told her that our factory van broke down
near Brits, and I was reporting back to work. She asked where I worked
and I told her at the United Tobacco Company in Rustenburg, about
which I knew nothing really. We parted. Not far from the station I met a
traffic inspector resting under the plantation trees. He greeted me nicely
and I also accepted his greetings. I thought to myself that my road was
now open because I had got a greeting from a White traffic inspector.

That was nearly true and nearly false beause I could never have imagined what was going to happen after my struggles. At the station there was a queue for tickets. My ticket cost 75 cents to Bleskop where Rustenburg Platinum Mine offices are, so I had 10 cents left. I bought myself a half brown bread costing 7 cents at the nearest café, and sat under the trees on the grass where I ate the bread alone. I drank some water and my stomach was full like a strong man. The train arrived, so I boarded it but my mind and future were still missing without hopes. My heart was very heavy as I got on to the train so I thought of my motto: 'If the Lord gives you a burden, he will also provide help to carry it, and in the whole world there are so many people who pray for a new life.'

When I arrived at Bleskop I wondered where I would sleep that night. I just took a stroll until 7.30 p.m., back to Bleskop station. There were a few people going home from the mines. And I started to breathe softly without fearing. There was a big waiting-room in which many people were asleep and I too slept there. People from the mines were playing records with their gumba-gumba.[2] Bleskop was very quiet but gumba-gumba men were blasting records the whole night until 2.30 in the morning, when they boarded the Pretoria train. I was left with the others who were going to the mines the next day.

After the gumba-gumba men left, Bleskop station became quiet. When the sun rose over the mountains of Pretoria, we set off for the Rustenburg Platinum Mine, some wearing blankets. The mine was where we were going to buy our lives with blasted rocks.

We arrived at the offices which were still closed, and sat on the grass. Mine people were training on the sportsground. Some were jumping and singing in the mine hall in the mine language, 'sefanagalo'.[3] At 7.30 a.m. the ambulance arrived at high speed, its top lamp flashing. It stopped near the door of the mine hospital. Two people and the driver got out without speaking. Their faces were in sorrow. From the back came six people in mine clothes, with their head lamps still on. They off-loaded two coffins and carried them into the mine hospital. I shivered like the branches of a tree. My motto was still in my mind but I thought that I had seen Mabopane for the last time, and my parents, relatives and friends too.

At 8 a.m. the offices opened. We were called and our passes were taken from us. At 9 a.m. we collected our passes and the Black officer told us that there was work at Swartklip. They gave us tickets to Swartklip which cost R1.35, single.

When we arrived at Swartklip we were shown to empty rooms and given plates for food. Then we saw a film which ended at 10 p.m. Back in our rooms we slept well, with police guarding us with kieries.

On Friday morning the man known as Induna woke us at 5 a.m. He told us to report at the labour office as soon as possible. We did so. At the labour office our passes were taken. At about 9.30 a.m. a Black man in white clothes told us to follow him. We were led to a big house with many rooms and beds, which looked like a hospital. We were taken to a room where there was a chair, a desk and a scale ending in 200 kg. There we met another man, all in white, who had many files in his hands, where our names were already written. They told us to undress. We were checked from toes to head for wounds, then weighed. When the doctor produced a big needle and injected us near the heart to kill shocks when we went underground, I felt I was fighting for my dear beautiful life. Late on Friday we returned to the labour offices. We were given three days' tickets for food at the compound and shown a film.

On Sunday at about 7.30 p.m., after my meal, I tried to find an empty tin and get a little chaechae, which is what mageu[4] is called on the mines. Joel! Joel Matlou! someone called out to me. I looked at the people sleeping on the grass, and saw a man with a tape recorder. 'Come here, come here,' he said. I moved slowly towards him. He stood up and said, 'Joel, what do you want here?' When I recognised him I was so happy that I kissed him. It was Joseph Masilo of Mabopane who was now living in Moruleng, Rustenburg. We were at school together at Ratshetlho Higher Primary in Mabopane seven years ago. We started questioning one another about our reasons for being on the mine. I told him I had taken the job because I needed money fast, to pay off a big instalment.

'How do you come here?' I asked him.

'Suffering brought me,' he said. 'In two weeks' time I complete my ticket and get paid.'

'Couldn't your people or relatives and friends help you settle your accounts?' I asked.

'It is difficult to reach relatives and friends. Are you married?'

'No,' I replied. 'I will think first before I marry. Mines do not have girls. Where and how often do you get to have a girl near you here at mines?'

'This place is a jail,' said Joseph. 'No girls around here and you must have respect for yourself until your sentence is finished. Stop asking me silly questions. All the people here have troubles.'

We parted and arranged to meet the following day.

I was so very happy to meet my best friend after seven years. My heart was open and all things were going well.

On Monday morning we went to the labour offices. There were three compounds, A, B and C. A compound is called Union Section. B is called Entabeni and C is called Hlatini. They are far away from each other. The officer told us we would be transferred to C compound, Hlatiti. We fetched all our belongings and the mine bus took us to Hlatini compound. There were many people in Hlatini. Some were drinking beers, playing ball, running and playing tape recorders. A big man with a bald head took us to a room called 'School Mine'. In that room we found chairs and a big white board. We were told to sit down quietly and listen. Then all the windows and doors of the room were closed. We were shown a television film of a man teaching new labourers how to build and pack wood and another film on First Aid.

Then a Black man wearing a black dust coat, with a missing left eye, called us to the office. He gave us cards, then called us one by one to take boots, belts and iron (copper) hats. Then we were given numbers. A young man came running with a plastic bag containing small numbers. The numbers were on small pieces of iron 200 mm long and 100 mm wide. My number was 3281. That was on Tuesday.

There were twenty little windows, like those at which people buy tickets for buses or trains. There you got your lamp and battery for work when you produced your number. My number was 3281, and my window number was eight. We were told to report at the windows at 6 a.m. for work.

Back at the compound we enjoyed our mine meal, saw a film and went to sleep. At 5 a.m. we were woken by a loudspeaker. We got our lamp and battery and were taken to a big office where we were ordered to sit down on the floor. We were still to see and learn more.

A White man introduced himself as Mr Alfred Whitefield from Northam, Rustenburg. He spoke English, Tswana and Sefanagalo but not Afrikaans. He said: *'Umtheto wase* mine *uthi, aikhona wena sebenzisa umlilo lapha kalo* mine. *Aikhona wena hlala phanzi banye ba sebenza. Vuka umtheto wa* boss boy. *Sebenzisa a ma* toilets *a se* mine. *Aikona choncha. Sebenzisa* umine Bank *ku beka imali yakho.'* [The law of the mine says: Do not make fire here in the mine. Do not sit down while others are working. 'Wake up!' is the law of the boss boy. Use the mine toilets. Do not steal. Use the mine bank to save your money.] Those were the words which I still remember from Mr A. Whitefield.

Before we went to work under the soil of Africa, we were given a hand belt with a number on it. It was a blue belt. My number was 2256731.

At 7.15 a.m. the boss boy took us to the lift. As it went down my ears went dead and I saw dark and light as we passed other levels. The levels go from 6 to 31. The lift stopped at 28 level. There I saw lights, small trains *(makalanyane)*, a tool room, a workshop, toilets, a power station, big pipes, drinking water, a telephone and so on.

The boss boy gave us a small book which had twenty-four pages.

Every day he tore out one page from it. When it was empty you get your pay and a new book.

We gave our tickets to the boss boy then walked for one hour to the end of the shaft. The mine shaft was very hot. I was wearing a shirt and trousers. The sweat ran off me like water. There were three tunnels. The small trains, the *makalanyana*, had red lights on the back and front indicating danger. Before the blasting, small holes were drilled in the walls and a man referred to as a chessa-boy put explosives into them. After the blasting we found broken pipes, the ventilator on the ground, bent rails, a cracked wall and other damage. The blast gave us heavy work. The *makalanyane* and its trucks were called to collect all stones. You can find a stone weighing 200 kg far from the blast.

A Zulu from King Williamstown was digging *mosele* (water concrete) when part of the ventilator fell on him and his left leg was trapped under it. The boss called us and we lifted the ventilator to take out the trapped man. His leg was broken and bloody. Four men carried him to the lift and an ambulance was called.

Water leaked from the top of the walls. Sometimes small stones fell on us. In another section of the tunnel were people called Loaders *(Malaisha)*. My boots were full of water. The time for clocking out started to roll round, so we followed our boss boy to the station. We switched off our lamps while we waited in the queue because at the station there were electric lights. We were wet like fishes and ugly like hippos. Some were sitting and resting with empty stomachs. There were two lifts running up and down, taking people out of the shaft. When one was underground, the other was on the surface, off-loading. After twenty minutes, the lift arrived. The guard opened the door and we flowed in. The notice on the door said the lift took only twenty people. But we were packed like fishes in a small can. At level 6 the guard opened the door and we came out, one by one, as the door is very small. We gave our officer the lamps and he gave us back our numbers.

There was no time or chance to prove yourself: who you are and what you want. I did not wash my clothes or bath because I did not have soap and other clothes to put on. All I did was eat and sleep on the grass and listen to the music from the loudspeaker at the office of Hlatini compound (C).

I had already lost hope of going back to Pretoria where I belonged. I could not even imagine that my girl-friend was thinking about me. Life was so bad; for me life was a little piece of stone. Washing, bathing, cutting nails, dressing in clean clothes and reading newspapers was far from me. It could be about 640 000 miles far from me.

The mine injection makes you forget about your parents, relatives and friends, even your girl-friend. The injection makes you think only about work underground. After three weeks underground I was part of that world.

In the yard of Hlatini compound there was coal and wood and in the rooms was only one stove. If it was cold you could make a fire or cook your own favourite food. The bar and shop were in the yard.

The days went on and on until my ticket said twenty-three days. One month ends on day twenty-four. Then we'd get our money. When my ticket said twenty-four days, I was working underground for the last time. My last day underground went so fast. On the twenty-fifth day I went to the paymaster to get my money. I was told to come back after six days. This was bad news. Waiting for my six days to end, I slept in the bush every night because I did not want to go underground. My main wish was to escape. During my last six days in the lonely bush I came across many dead cattle killed by Pondos and Basotho because these nations like meat. I also saw old shafts and old machines, so I used to enjoy myself going underground using ropes and chains. The shafts were very dark. During my wanderings I saw people ploughing their lands and growing crops. I also came across a slum known as Mantserre near the big mountain, far from the Hlatini compound, where there were schools, shops and churches. In the bush I met some wild animals like springboks, hares and impalas, as well as partridges. I even met people riding bicycles from the mines to Mantserre slum on the narrow paths.

I wore my mine clothes during this time as I didn't want to show people that I wasn't working. When I returned to the mine I took off my mine clothes and wore my own dirty ones. I was so happy to know that tomorrow was pay day. I met young men at Hlatini playing records and singing. I joined in though I didn't know them. My meal was so good that I ate like a pig and drank chaechae like a drunkard. What I did not know was that I was on the verge of a complete mental breakdown. My last night at Hlatini was very long and terrible. It harboured demons, but it also symbolised escape from dangerous falling rocks to the gentle air of Pretoria City.

At 3.30 a.m. a loudspeaker woke up the people as usual. I was left alone in the room, waiting for 9 a.m., for my pay. I decided to steal clothes, tape recorders and radios but God refused to allow it. Music was playing on the loudspeakers. To me things seemed to be changing; even the birds were singing a chorus which I didn't understand. The hours went by and at 8.30 a.m. people started to queue for pay. I joined them. After an hour the paymaster arrived, police guarding him with revolvers. Each of us was asked for a number, and fingerprints were taken. They gave me a pay slip which had two parts. At a second window they took one part and I was left with the pay slip with my thumb print on it. At the third window they took my pay slip and gave me the money which a policeman counted so that they would not rob me. The money was ninety-six rand. It was for my own work. I risked my life and reason for it.

I went out of the main gates at Hlatini to escape to Northam station. I pretended to be counting my money at the gate so that the police guards would not realise that I was running away. I did not finish counting: I just thrust it into my empty pocket and walked out of the main gate towards the bush to free myself. That time life was not endless but everlasting. The earth was once supposed to be flat. Well, so it is, from Hlatini to Northam. That fact does not prevent science from proving that the earth as a whole is spherical. We are still at the stage that life itself is flat – the distance from birth to death. Yet the probability is that life, too, is spherical and much more extensive and capacious than the hemisphere we know.

The black dots in my eyes turned brown, like a dagga[5] smoker or a dreamer. I felt like a political asylum-seeker, running to Tanzania. To get to Northam I had to cross two compounds. I ran like hell until I crossed A and B compounds. Then I ran to catch the 10.30 train from Northam to Rustenburg. Two Black men, and a White man on a tractor, looked at me, surprised. Far from the ploughing men I crossed a ditch in which a half-eaten impala lay. Birds were singing, animals roaring. At 8 p.m. cars passed me, one after another and I started to fear for my life. I hid under small bridges or in the long grass. At 9 p.m. I saw small yellow lights and I realised that it must be the station. My feet were aching and swollen and bloody.

At the station there was a café where I bought chips and a half brown and sat on the grass to eat it. After buying a ticket to Rustenburg, I found a small piece of paper on the grass. I took it to the toilets, wet it and washed my face with it. I even bought vaseline to smear on my dirty face. My face looked like that of a real man, but not my clothes.

The train arrived at 10.30 p.m. People looked at me. Some of them were laughing instead of crying blood. After I arrived in Rustenburg I went to the shops. People were laughing at my dirty clothes, even White people. The shopkeeper thought I was a robber, so I showed him my pay slip. I bought a three-piece suit, a blue shirt, black and red socks and a Scotch tie. It cost me seventy-one rand and I was left with only twenty-two rand. I couldn't arrive home with dirty clothes, so I decided to buy my pride with my suffering.

I changed my clothes at the Rustenburg station toilets and put the old ones in a paper bag. I was really a gentleman. People, mostly girls, asked for the time when they saw me, just for pleasure. I had a *Rand Daily Mail* newspaper in my right hand, and walked like a president. I was smelling of new clothes.

Suffering taught me many things.

I recall a poem which is a plea for me:

I don't like being told
This is in my heart, thinking
That I shall be me
If I were you
I but not you
But you will not give me a chance
I am not you
Yet you will not let me be
You meddle, interfere in my affairs as if they were yours
And you were not me
You are unfair, unwise
That I can be you, talk act and think like you
God made me
For God's sake, let me be me
I see your eyes but you don't see your eyes
I cannot count your fingers because you see them all
Act yourself and I will act myself, not being told but doing it oneself.

Suffering takes a man from known places to unknown places. Without suffering you are not a man. You will never suffer for the second time because you have learned to suffer.

I am grateful to Mr Dlongolo who told me about mine work and that it was a fast way of making money.

It was Friday and most of the people on the train were students and mine workers going home to Pretoria and the Transkei. Everyone was happy. Even I was happy. If suffering means happiness I am happy. The 1.35 p.m. train pulled out and I sat reading the *Rand Daily Mail*. The train stopped at all stations: Colombia, Turfground, Maroelakop, Bleskop, Marikana, Wolhuterskop, Brits West, Beestekraal, Norite, Stephanus and Taljaardshoop, when it left the Republic of Bophuthatswana and crossed into South Africa. On the train people sold watches, apples, socks, liquor, shoe laces, lip ice and so on. When I saw the beautiful girls I thought of my own beautiful sweetheart, my bird of Africa, sea water, razor: green-coloured eyes like a snake, high wooden shoes like a cripple; with soft and beautiful skin, smelling of powder under her armpits like a small child, with black boots for winter like a soldier, and a beautiful figure like she does not eat, sleep, speak or become hungry. And she looks like an artificial girl or electric girl. But she was born of her parents, as I was. She is Miss Johanna Mapula Modise of Mabopane who was born during a rainy day. As I am Mr Joel Medupe Matlou of Mabopane and I was also born during a rainy day. Mapula and Medupe is our gift from God. So, we accepted these names by living together.

The train arrived in Ga-Rankuwa on time. I bought some groceries and took a taxi to Mabopane. From there I went straight home where I met my mother and young brothers. They were happy and I was happy with them. The following morning I visited my girl-friend.

She cried when she saw me, silently looking down on the soil of Africa. I did not tell her I had worked on the mine. I said I had got a job in Johannesburg.

'Why didn't you tell me that you were going to work in Johannesburg? You didn't even write to me. You just sat there and forgot me,' she said.

'One of my friends took me to Johannesburg where he found me work. So there was no chance, I just left,' I lied to her.

Back on Mabopane's dusty roads again I looked like a real gentleman. Many people were happy to visit me as they knew I was a peace lover and didn't drink or smoke. There was nothing which worried me. I had thought that getting back to Mabopane's dusty roads would lead me to suffer, but eating alone was almost more than I could bear. I learned to forget yesterdays and to think of tomorrows. Each morning in the township, I said to myself: 'Today is a new life.' I overcame my fear of loneliness and my fear of want. I am happy and fairly successful now and have a lot of enthusiasm and love for life. I know now that I shall never again be afraid of sleeping under a tree alone, regardless of what life hands me. I don't have to fear blasting. I know now that I can live one day at a time and that every day is a time for a wise man.

1. *hemp* shirt
2. *gumba-gumba* record-player
3. *sefanagalo* pidgin
4. *mageu* (non-alcoholic) drink
5. *dagga* marijuana

Christopher Hope

Learning to Fly

from *Private Parts and Other Tales* (1980)

Long ago, in the final days of the old regime, there lived a colonel who held an important job in the State Security Police and his name was Rocco du Preez. Colonel du Preez was in charge of the interrogation of political suspects and because of his effect on the prisoners of the old regime he became widely known in the country as 'Window jumpin' ' du Preez. After mentioning his name it was customary to add 'thank God', because he was a strong man and in the dying days of the old regime everyone agreed that we needed a strong man. Now Colonel du Preez acquired his rather strange nickname not because he did any window jumping himself but rather because he had been the first to draw attention to this phenomenon which affected so many of the prisoners who were brought before him.

The offices of State Security were situated on the thirteenth floor of a handsome and tall modern block in the centre of town. Their high windows looked down on to a little dead-end street far below. Once this street had been choked with traffic and bustling with thriving shops. Then one day the first jumper landed on the roof of a car parked in the street and after that it was shut to traffic and turned into a pedestrian shopping mall. The street was filled in and covered over with crazy paving and one or two benches set up for weary shoppers. However, the jumpings increased. There were sometimes one or two a week and several nasty accidents on the ground began to frighten off the shoppers.

Whenever a jump had taken place the little street was cordoned off to allow in the emergency services: the police, the undertaker's men, the municipal workers brought in to hose down the area of impact which was often surprisingly large. The jumpings were bad for business and the shopkeepers grew desperate. The authorities were sympathetic and erected covered walk-ways running the length of the street leaving only the central area of crazy pavings and the benches, on which no one had ever been known to sit, exposed to the heavens; the walk-ways protected by their overhead concrete parapets were guaranteed safe against any and all flying objects. But still trade dwindled as one by one the shops closed, and the street slowly died and came to be known by the locals, who gave it a wide berth, as the 'landing field'.

As everyone knows, window jumpings increased apace over the years and being well placed to study them probably led Colonel Rocco du Preez to his celebrated thesis afterwards included in the manual of psychology used by recruits at the Police College and known as du Preez's Law. It states that all men, who brought to the brink, will contrive to find a way out if the least chance is afforded them and the choice of the means is always directly related to the racial characteristics of the individual in question. Some of du Preez's remarks on the subject have come down to us, though these are almost certainly apocryphal, as are so many tales of the final days of the old regime. 'Considering your average white man,' du Preez is supposed to have said, 'my experience is that he prefers hanging – whether by pyjama cord, belt, strips of blanket; providing he finds the handy protuberance, the cell bars, say, or up-ended bedstead, you'll barely have turned your back and he'll be up there swinging from the light cord or some other chosen noose. Your white man in his last throes has a wonderful sense of rhythm – believe me, whatever you may have heard to the contrary – I've seen several Whites about to cough it and all of them have been wonderful dancers. Your Indian, now, he's something else, a slippery customer who prefers smooth surfaces. I've known Asians to slip and crack their skulls in a shower cubicle so narrow you'd have sworn a man couldn't turn in it. This innate slitheriness is probably what makes them good businessmen. Now, your Coloured, per contra, is more clumsy a character altogether. His hidden talent lies in his amazing lack of co-ordination. Even the most sober rogue can appear hopelessly drunk to the untrained eye. On the surface of things it might seem that you can do nothing with him; he has no taste for the knotted strip of blanket or the convenient bootlace; a soapy bathroom floor leaves him unmoved – yet show him a short, steep flight of steps and he instinctively knows what to do. When it comes to Africans I have found that they, perverse as always, choose another way out. They are given to window jumping. This phenomenon has been very widespread in the past few years. Personally, I suspect its roots go back a long way, back to their superstitions – i.e. to their regard for black magic and witchcraft. Everyone knows that in extreme instances your average blackie will believe anything; that his witch-doctors will turn the white man's bullets to water; or, if he jumps out of a window thirteen stories above terra firma he will miraculously find himself able to fly. Nothing will stop him once his mind's made up. I've seen up to six Bantu jump from a high window on one day. Though the first landed on his head and the others saw the result they were not deterred. It's as if despite the evidence of their senses they believed that if only they could practise enough they would one day manage to take off.'

'Window jumpin'' du Preez worked in an office sparsely furnished with an old desk, a chair, a strip of green, government-issue carpet, a very large steel cabinet marked 'Secret' and a bare, fluorescent light in the ceiling. Poor though the furnishings were, the room was made light and cheerful by the large windows behind his desk and nobody re- members being aware of the meanness of the furnishings when Colonel du Preez was present in the room. When he sat down in his leather swivel chair behind his desk, witnesses reported that he seemed to fill up the room, to make it habitable, even genial. His reddish hair and green eyes were somehow enough to colour the room and make it complete. The eyes had a peculiar, steady glint to them. This was his one pecu- liarity. When thinking hard about something he had the nervous habit of twirling a lock of the reddish hair, a copper colour with gingery lights, in the words of a witness, around a finger. It was his only nervous habit. Since these were often the last words ever spoken by very brave men, we have to wonder at their ability to register details so sharply under terrible conditions; it is these details that provide us with our only glimpse of the man, as no photographs have come down to us.

It was to this office that three plainclothes men one day brought a new prisoner. The charge-sheet was singularly bare: it read simply, 'Mphahlele ... Jake. Possession of explosives'. Obviously they had got very little out of him. The men left closing the door softly, almost rever- ently, behind them.

The prisoner wore an old black coat, ragged grey flannels and a black beret tilted at an angle which gave him an odd, jaunty, rather continental look, made all the more incongruous by the fact that his hands were manacled behind him. Du Preez reached up with his desk ruler and knocked off the beret revealing a bald head gleaming in the overhead fluorescent light. It would have been shaved and polished, du Preez guessed, by one of the wandering barbers who traditionally gathered on Sundays down by the municipal lake, setting up three-legged stools and basins of water and hanging towels and leather strops for their cutthroat razors from the lower branches of a convenient tree and draping their customers in large red and white check clothes, giving them little hand mirrors so that they could look on while the barbers scraped, snipped, polished and gossiped away the sunny afternoon by the water's edge beneath the tall bluegums. Clearly Mphahlele belonged to the old school of whom there were fewer each year as the fashion for Afro-wigs and strange woollen bangs took increasing hold among younger Blacks. Du Preez couldn't help warming to this just a little. After all, he was one of the old school himself in the new age of trimmers and ameliorists. Mphahlele was tall, as tall as du Preez and, he reckoned, about the same age – though it was always difficult to tell with Africans. A knife scar ran from his right eye down to his collar, the flesh fused in a livid welt as if a tiny mole had burrowed under the black skin pushing up a furrow behind it. His nose had been broken too, probably as the result of the same township fracas, and had mended badly turning to the left and then sharply to the right as if unable to make up its mind. The man was obviously a brawler. Mphahlele's dark brown eyes were remarkably calm – almost to the point of arrogance, du Preez thought for an instant, before dismissing the absurd notion with a tiny smile. It shocked him to see an answering smile on the prisoner's lips. However he was too old a hand to let this show.

'Where are the explosives?'

'I have no explosives,' Mphahlele answered.

He spoke quietly but du Preez thought he detected a most unjustifiable calm amounting to confidence, or worse, to insolence, and he noted how he talked with special care. It was another insight. On his pad he wrote the letters MK. The prisoner's diction and accent betrayed him: Mission Kaffir. Raised at one of the stations by foolish clergy as though he was one day going to be a white man. Of course, the word 'kaffir' was not a word in official use any longer. Like other names at that time growing less acceptable as descriptions of Africans: 'native', 'coon' and even 'Bantu', the word had given way to softer names in an attempt to respond to the disaffection springing up among black people. But du Preez, as he told himself, was too old a dog to learn new tricks. Besides, he was not interested in learning to be more 'responsive'. He did not belong to the ameliorists. His job was to control disaffection and where necessary to put it down with proper force. And anyway, his notes were strictly for his own reference, private reminders of his first impressions of a prisoner, useful when, and if, a second interview took place. The number of people he saw was growing daily and he could not expect to keep track of them all in his head.

Du Preez left his desk and slowly circled the prisoner. 'Your comrade who placed the bomb in the shopping centre was a bungler. There was great damage. Many people were killed. Women and children among them. But he wasn't quick enough, your friend. The blast caught him too. Before he died he gave us your name. The paraffin tests show you handled explosives recently. I want the location of the cache. I want the make-up of your cell with names and addresses as well as anything else you might want to tell me.'

'If the bomb did its business then the man was no bungler,' Mphahlele said.

'The murder of women and children – no bungle?'

Mphahlele shrugged. 'Casualties of war.'

Du Preez circled him and stopped beside his right ear. 'I don't call the death of children war. I call it barbarism.'

'Our children have been dying for years but we have never called it barbarism. Now we are learning. You and I know what we mean. I'm your prisoner of war. You will do whatever you can to get me to tell you things you want to know. Then you will get rid of me. But I will tell you nothing. So why don't you finish with me now? Save time.' His brown eyes rested briefly and calmly on du Preez's empty chair, and then swept the room as if the man had said all he had to say and was now more interested in getting to know that notorious office.

A muscle in du Preez's cheek rippled and it took him a moment longer than he would have liked to bring his face back to a decent composure. Then he crossed to the big steel cabinet and opened it. Inside was the terrible, tangled paraphernalia of persuasion, the electric generator, the leads and electrodes, the salt water for sharpening contact and the thick leather straps necessary for restraining the shocked and writhing victim. At the sight of this he scored a point; he thought he detected a momentary pause, a faltering in the steady brown eyes taking stock of his office, and he pressed home the advantage. 'It's very seldom that people fail to talk to me after this treatment.' He held up the electrodes. 'The pain is intense.'

In fact, as we know now, the apparatus in the cabinet was not that actually used on prisoners – indeed, one can see the same equipment on permanent exhibition in the National Museum of the Revolution. Du Preez, in fact, kept it for effect. The real thing was administered by a special team in a soundproof room on one of the lower floors. But the mere sight of the equipment, whose reputation was huge among the townships and shanty towns, was often enough to have the effect of loosening stubborn tongues. However, Mphahlele looked at the tangle of wires and straps as if he wanted to include them in his inventory of the room and his expression suggested not fear but rather – and this du Preez found positively alarming – a hint of approval. There was nothing more to be said. He went back to his desk, pressed the buzzer and the plainclothes men came in and took Mphahlele downstairs.

Over the next twenty-four hours 'Window jumpin' ' du Preez puzzled over his new prisoner. It was a long time before he put his finger on some of the qualities distinguishing this man from others he'd worked with under similar circumstances. Clearly, Mphahlele was not frightened. But then other men had been brave too — for a while. It was not only bravery, one had to add to it the strange fact that this man quite clearly did not hate him. That was quite alarming: Mphahlele had treated him as if they were truly equals. There was an effrontery about this he found maddening and the more he thought about it, the more he raged inside. He walked over to the windows behind his desk and gazed down to the dead little square with its empty benches and its crazy paving which, with its haphazard joins where the stones were cemented one to the next into nonsensical, snaking patterns, looked from the height of the thirteenth story as if a giant had brought his foot down hard and the earth had shivered into a thousand pieces. He was getting angry. Worse, he was letting his anger cloud his judgement. Worse still, he didn't care.

Mphahlele was in a bad way when they brought him back to du Preez. His face was so bruised that the old knife scar was barely visible, his lower lip was bleeding copiously and he swayed when the policemen let him go and might have fallen had he not grabbed the edge of the desk and hung there swaying. In answer to du Preez's silent question the interrogators shook their heads. 'Nothing. He never said *nothing*.'

Mphahlele had travelled far in the regions of pain and it had changed him greatly. It might have been another man who clung to du Preez's desk with his breath coming in rusty pants; his throat was choked with phlegm or blood he did not have the strength to cough away. He was bent and old and clearly on his last legs. One eye was puffed up in a great swelling shot with green and purple bruises, but the other, he noticed with a renewed spurt of anger, though it had trouble focusing, showed the same old haughty gleam when he spoke to the man.

'Have you any more to tell me about your war?'

Mphahlele gathered himself with great effort, his one good eye flickering wildly with the strain. He licked the blood off his lips and wiped it from his chin. 'We will win,' he said 'soon.'

Du Preez dismissed the interrogators with a sharp nod and they left his presence by backing away to the door, full of awe at his control. When the door closed behind them he stood up and regarded the swaying figure with its flickering eye. 'You are like children,' he said bitterly, 'and there is nothing we can do for you.'

'Yes,' said Mphahlele, 'we are your children. We owe you everything.'

Du Preez stared at him. But there was not a trace of irony to be detected. The madman was quite plainly sincere in what he said and du

Preez found that insufferable. He moved to the windows and opened them. It was now that, so the stories go, he made his fateful remark. 'Well, if you won't talk, then I suppose you had better learn to fly.'

What happened next is not clear except in broad outline even today, the records of the old regime which were to have been made public have unaccountably been reclassified as secret, but we can make an informed guess. Legend then says that du Preez recounted for his prisoner his 'theory of desperate solutions' and that, exhausted though he was, Mphahlele showed quickening interest in the way out chosen by white men – that is to say, dancing. We know this is true because du Preez told the policemen waiting outside the door when he joined them in order to allow Mphahlele to do what he had to do. After waiting a full minute, du Preez entered his office again closing the door behind him, alone, as had become customary in such cases, his colleagues respecting his need for a few moments of privacy before moving on to the next case. Seconds later these colleagues heard a most terrible cry. When they rushed into the room they found it was empty.

Now we are out on a limb. We have no more facts to go on. All is buried in obscurity or say, rather, it is buried with du Preez who plunged from his window down to the landing field at the most horrible speed, landing on his head. Jake Mphahlele has never spoken of his escape from Colonel 'Window jumpin' ' du Preez. All we have are the stories. Some firmly believe to this day that it was done by a special magic and Mphahlele had actually learnt to fly and that the colonel on looking out of his window was so jealous at seeing a black man swooping in the heavens that he had plunged after him on the supposition, regarded as axiomatic in the days of the old regime, that anything a black man can do, a white man could do ten times better. Others, more sceptical, said that the prisoner had hidden himself in the steel cabinet with the torture equipment and emerged to push du Preez to hell and then escaped in the confusion you will get in a hive if you kill the queen bee. All that is known for sure is that du Preez lay on the landing field like wet clothes fallen from a washing line, terribly twisted and leaking everywhere. And that in the early days of the new regime Jake Mphahlele was appointed chief investigating officer in charge of the interrogation of suspects and that his work with political prisoners, especially white prisoners, was soon so widely respected that he won rapid promotion to the rank of colonel and became known throughout the country as Colonel Jake 'Dancin' ' Mphahlele, and after his name it was customary to add 'thank God', because he was a strong man and in the early days of the new regime everyone agreed we needed a strong man.

Bheki Maseko

Mamlambo

from *Staffrider* 5 (1) 1982

Mamlambo is a kind of snake that brings fortune to anyone who accommodates it. One's money or livestock multiplies incredibly.

This snake is available from traditional doctors who provide instructions regarding its exploitation. Certain necessities are to be sacrificed in order to maintain it. Sometimes you may have to sacrifice your own children, or go without a car or clothes. It all depends on the instructions of the doctor concerned.

The duties involved are so numerous that some people tend to forget some of them. A beast must be slaughtered from time to time, and failing to comply with the instructions results in disaster. It is said that this monster can kill an entire family, always starting with the children and leaving its owner for last.

Getting rid of this fortune snake is not an easy task when one has had enough of luck and sacrificing. Some say a beast must be slaughtered, then the entire carcass must be enfolded with the skin and thrown away. This is done in the presence of an indigenous doctor who performs the necessary ritual to the end.

Someone will come along, pick up a shiny object, and Mamlambo is his. There are many things about this monster.

Here is an account of how Sophie acquired Mamlambo and what happened to her:

Sophie Zikode was a young, pretty, ebony-faced woman with a plump and intact, moderate body. Ever since she came to stay in the Golden City to work as a domestic servant, she never had a steady boy-friend. The man who lasted longer than any other was Elias Malinga, who was from Ermelo. He was the first man she met when she came to Johannesburg and he was the only man she truly loved.

She was so obsessed with love that she readily abandoned any posses-

sions or habits that Elias disliked. In spite of the priority his children and
wife in Ermelo enjoyed, she was still prepared to marry Elias Malinga
without the slightest intention of disrupting his marriage during their
love affair.

One day, after a quarrel, Elias went away and never came back again.
She phoned his place of employment to be told by a friend of Elias that he
(Elias) had had enough of her. She never heard from him ever again.

After Elias, Sophie never again had a steady boy-friend. They all deserted her after two or three months. But it no longer hurt. The only
name that haunted her day and night was Elias.

Ever since Elias left her she had never loved anybody else. All she
wanted now was a husband she could be loyal to. But she just could not
find one. Then along came Jonas, a tall, well-built Malawian who was
much more considerate than any of the other men.

For the first time in her young life a thought came into her mind: She
must consult a traditional doctor for help. She wanted to keep Jonas
forever. She must see Baba Majola first thing in the morning.

The following morning Sophie visited Baba Majola, who was a street
cleaner. The old man listened sympathetically to her problem while he
swept rubbish out of a gutter. He told her to return at four in the afternoon. Sophie was there on time.

Baba Majola gave her some smelly, sticky stuff in a bottle. He told her
to rub her whole body with it before the boy-friend came, and to put it
under the pillow when they sleep. The poor girl agreed amicably.

She did exactly as she had been told to do. She felt guilty as the atmosphere became tense in the little room.

They ate in silence as the clock on the small table ticked away, disturbing the deep silence. Jonas was not his usual self today. He was quiet
in a strange manner.

They were sleeping for some minutes when Jonas felt something
peculiar under the pillow. It felt cold and smooth.

'Sophie, Sophie,' he called, shaking her gently. 'What is this under
the pillow?'

Sophie had felt the strange object soon after they had climbed into bed.
But she had been scared to ask Jonas what it was.

'I don't know,' she replied, pretending to be sleepy. 'Switch on the
light, let's have a look.'

With a trembling hand Jonas fumbled for the switch. 'Gosh, what a
big snake!'

Jonas was the first to jump out of bed. Sophie followed. They fiddled
with the door until it was open and ran into the brightly-lit street.

Semi-naked, they knocked at the servant's door of a house in the neighbourhood to wake up a friend of Sophie's. Sophie's friend was very stunned to find them in that manner.

Quickly they explained the situation and together they went back to Sophie's room. Through the window they could see the snake, lying across the bed. Sophie was very scared, but Jonas – Christ! – Jonas, he could hardly speak.

Realising that things were bad, Sophie decided to tell the whole truth. She told Jonas she did it 'because I wanted to keep you forever'. They decided to go to a traditional doctor who stayed a few streets away.

They knocked and, after waiting awhile, the doctor answered. He opened the door but quickly closed it again. They heard him say: 'Wait outside there. I can sense something melancholy.'

They could hear the indigenous doctor saying something in a strange language, and the smell of burning muti came to them in full force.

He began to moan, as if speaking to gods in a faraway land. He then opened the door and enquired what their problem was. Sophie retold her story.

'Oh, my girl. What you have in your room is Mamlambo,' he shuddered.

'What? Mamlambo!' cried Sophie. 'Oh God, what have I done to deserve such punishment? What big sin have I committed to be punished in this manner?' Tears streamed continuously down her cheeks.

'Crying won't solve the problem, my dear girl,' intervened the doctor in broken Zulu. 'The only solution is to get rid of the snake, and I need your co-operation to do that. I'll give you a suitcase to take to your room, and the snake . . .'

'What!' cried Sophie. 'Must I go back to that room again? Oh, no, not me, I'm sorry.'

'The choice is yours, my girl. You either keep it or get rid of it. The sooner the better, because if you don't it will be with you wherever you go. It is your snake. The witch-doctor was tired of it, so he transferred it to you. So you are duty bound to transfer it to someone else or keep it.'

'Transfer it to someone else! Oh no! Why don't we throw it into the river or somewhere?' Sophie grumbled.

'You can't. Either you transfer it, or you keep it. Do you want my help or what?' asked the doctor in a businesslike manner.

'Yes.' Sophie agreed, in a tired voice, eyeing her friend, Sheila, and the timid Jonas, with the 'I hate to do it' look.

The traditional doctor took a large suitcase from the top of the wardrobe, put some muti inside and burnt it. He moaned again, as if speaking to gods they could not see. He chanted on in this manner for what seemed like ages.

'You'll take this suitcase to your room and put it next to your bed. The snake will roll itself into the suitcase.' He saw that Sophie was doubtful so he added: 'It's your snake. It won't harm you.' He continued: 'You will then go to a busy place and give it to someone. That you will figure out for yourself.'

They all went back to Sophie's room. The big snake was still there. Having told herself to 'come what may,' Sophie tiptoed into the room and put the suitcase next to the bed.

Slowly, as if it were smelling something, the snake lifted its head, slid into the suitcase and gathered itself into a neat coil.

Her mind was obsessed with Johannesburg Station, where she would give Mamlambo to someone for good. She walked quickly towards the taxi rank, impervious to the weight of the suitcase.

She did not want to do this to anyone, but she had no option.

Remembering that taxis were scarce after eight, she quickened her pace. She saw a few police cars patrolling the area, probably because of the high rate of housebreaking, she thought.

It was while she was day-dreaming at the bus-stop that she realised the car at the traffic lights was a patrol car headed in her direction. Should she drop the suitcase and run? But they had already seen her and she would not get far. How will she explain the whole thing to the police? Will they believe her story? The news will spread like wildfire that she's a witch! What would Elias think of her?

'What are you doing here at this time?' asked the passenger policeman.

'I'm waiting for a taxi, I'm going to the station,' answered Sophie, surprised that her voice was steady.

'We don't want to find you here when we come back,' commanded the policeman, eyeing the suitcase. The car screeched away.

She was relieved when the taxi appeared. The driver loaded the suitcase in the boot asking what was so heavy. She simply told him it was groceries.

There were two other passengers in the taxi who both got off before the taxi reached the city.

'Are you going to the station?' enquired the driver inquisitively.

'No, I'm going to the bus terminus,' Sophie replied indifferently.

'I know you are going to the station and I'm taking you there,' insisted the man.

'You can't take me to the station,' said Sophie, indignant. 'I'm going to Main Street, next to the bus terminus.'

Ignoring her, he drove straight to the station, smiling all the way.

When they reached the station he got out of the car and took the suitcase from the boot.

Sophie paid him and gestured that she wanted her suitcase. But the man ignored her.

'To which platform are you going? I want to take you there.'

'I don't want your help at all. Give me my suitcase and leave me alone,' she urged, beginning to feel really hot under the collar.

'Or are you going to the luggage office?' mocked the man, going towards the brightly-lit office.

Sophie was undecided. Should she leave the suitcase with this man and vanish from the scene? Or should she just wait and see what happened? What was this man up to? Did he know what was in the suitcase, or was he simply inquisitive? Even if she bolted, he would find her easily. If only she had brought someone with her!

Suddenly she was overwhelmed by anger. Something told her to take her suitcase from the man by force. He had no business to interfere in her affairs. She went straight into the office, pulled the suitcase from between the man's legs and stormed out.

Stiff-legged, she walked towards the station platform, feeling eyes following her. She zigzagged through the crowds, deaf to the pandemonium of voices and music blaring from various radios. She hoped the taxi driver wasn't following her but wouldn't dare look back to see.

'Hey you, girl! Where do you think you're going?' It was the voice of the taxi driver.

She stopped dead in her tracks, without turning. She felt a lump in her throat and tears began to fall down her cheeks. She was really annoyed. Without thinking, she turned and screamed at the man.

'What do you want from me? What on earth do you want?'

With his worn-out cap tipped to the right and his hands deep in his khaki dustcoat pockets, the smiling man was as cool as ever. This angered Sophie even more.

'You are running away and you are trying to erase traces,' challenged the taxi driver indifferently, fingering his cap time and again.

'What's the matter?' asked a policeman, who had been watching from a distance.

'This man has been following me from the bus rank and is still following me. I don't know what he wants from me,' cried Sophie.

'This woman is a liar. She boarded my taxi and she's been nervous all the way from Kensington. I suspect she's running away from something. She's a crook,' emphasised the taxi driver looking for approval at the crowd that had gathered around them.

'You are a liar! I never boarded your taxi and I don't know you. You followed me when I left the bus rank.' Sophie wept, tears running freely down her cheeks.

'Let her open the suitcase – let's see what's inside.' Sheepish Smile went for the suitcase.

'All right. All right.' The policeman intervened. 'Quiet, everybody. I do the talking now. Young man,' he said, 'do you know this woman?'

'I picked her up at Kens ...'

'I say, do you know her?'

'Yes, she was in my taxi ...'

'Listen, young man,' said the policeman, beginning to get angry. 'I'm asking you a straightforward question and I want a straightforward answer. I'm asking you for the last time now. I-say-do-you-know-this-woman?' He pointed emphatically at Sophie.

'No, I don't know her,' replied Sheepish Smile reluctantly, adjusting his cap once again.

'Did she offend you in any manner?'

'No,' he replied, shamefaced.

'Off you go, then. Before I arrest you for public disturbance,' barked the policeman, pointing in the direction from which the man had come. Then he turned to Sophie.

'My child, go where you are going. This rascal has no business to interfere in your affairs.'

Relieved, she picked up her suitcase, thanked the policeman and walked towards platform fourteen, as the policeman dispersed the people and told them to mind their own business.

* * *

Platform fourteen. The old lady grew impatient. What's holding him? she thought. She came bi-monthly for her pension pay and each time the taxi dropped them on the platform, her son would go to the shop to buy food for the train journey home. But today he was unusually long in coming back.

These were the thoughts going through her mind when a young, dark, pretty woman approached her.

'Greetings, Gogo,' said the young woman, her cheeks producing dimples.

'Greetings, my child,' answered the old lady, looking carefully at this young pretty woman who was a symbol of a respectable makoti.

'When is the train to Durban departing?' asked Sophie, consulting her watch.

'At ten o'clock.'

The conversation was very easy with the loquacious old lady. The cars and people on the platform increased.

'Excuse me, Gogo, can you look after my luggage while I go to the shop? I won't be long.'

'O.K., O.K., my child,' agreed the old lady, pulling the suitcase nearer.

She quickly ascended the steps. By the time she reached the top she was panting. To her surprise and dismay, here was Elias shaking hands with another man. They chatted like old friends who hadn't seen each other for a long time.

Sophie stood there confused. Fortunately Elias's back was turned on her and the place was teeming with people. She quickly recovered and mingled with the crowd. Without looking back she zigzagged through the crowded arcade.

She was relieved when she alighted from the bus in Kensington. She had nearly come face-to-face with Elias Malinga. Fortunately he was cheerfully obsessed with meeting his friend. She was scared all the way to the bus terminus, but more so for the taxi driver. Now something else bothered her. The old lady? Who was she? Sophie felt as if she knew, or had at least seen the woman somewhere. She searched into the past, but couldn't locate it.

What will happen to the suitcase? Will the old lady take it?

And Elias? What was he doing there? She suddenly felt hatred for Elias. He had never pitied her, and it was worse when she phoned his place of employment, to be a laughing-stock to his friends. She became angry with herself to have allowed her life to be dominated by love that brought no peace or happiness, while Jonas was there giving all the love and kindness he possessed. For the first time she fell in love with Jonas. But will he still accept her? If only he could ask her to marry him. She would not do it for the sake of getting married. She would be marrying a man she truly loved.

Jonas and the Nyasa doctor were seated on the bed when Sophie came in. Sophie was surprised to see all Jonas's belongings packed up.

'Are you leaving me, Jonas?' Sophie whispered in a shaky voice.

'No, darling. My father wants me back in Malawi because he can no longer handle the farm by himself. And I would be very happy to take you along with me.'

'But I don't have a passport. How can I go to Malawi without one? And besides, my parents won't know where I am.'

'We are in fact not going today. We will negotiate with your parents next Saturday,' said Jonas, pointing at the doctor who sat quietly on the bed, nodding time and again.

* * *

It was a cool, sunny Saturday when the doctor took Sophie and Jonas to Jan Smuts Airport in his small car. Sophie was going to board a plane for the first time in her life. Jonas had made many trips to see his ailing father, who wanted him to take over the farm. For a long time Jonas had ignored his father's pleas for him to take over the running of the farm. But now he had finally relented.

Through the car window Sophie watched the people moving leisurely in and out of shops. The trees lining Bezuidenhout Valley Avenue and the flowers in the Europeans' gardens looked beautiful and peaceful as they fluttered in the cool morning air. It was as if she were seeing this part of Johannesburg for the first time.

They couldn't identify Baba Banda (the doctor) among the crowd that stood attentively on the balcony, as they stared through the plane window.

The flying machine took off and the crowd waved cheerfully. Sophie felt that it was taking her away from the monster that had terrified her a few days ago.

The buildings below became smaller as the airplane went higher, until the undersurface turned into a vast blue sky.

She wondered where, in one of those houses, was Mamlambo. But could never guess that it had become the property of Elias. Yes, after Elias had chatted to his friend, he went back to his mother.

'Whose case is this, Mama?'

'A young girl's. She asked me to look after it for her until she returned. But I don't know what's happened to her.'

'Well, if she doesn't come back, I'll take it.'

Njabulo S. Ndebele

Death of a Son

from From South Africa: Triquarterly 69 (1987)

At last we got the body. Wednesday. Just enough time for a Saturday funeral. We were exhausted. Empty. The funeral still ahead of us. We had to find the strength to grieve. There had been no time for grief, really. Only much bewilderment and confusion. Now grief. For isn't grief the awareness of loss?

That is why when we finally got the body, Buntu said: 'Do you realise our son is dead?' I realised. Our awareness of the death of our first and only child had been displaced completely by the effort to get his body. Even the horrible events that caused the death: we did not think of them, as such. Instead, the numbing drift of things took over our minds: the pleas, letters to be written, telephone calls to be made, telegrams to be dispatched, lawyers to consult, 'influential' people to 'get in touch with', undertakers to be contacted, so much walking and driving. That is what suddenly mattered: the irksome details that blur the goal (no matter how terrible it is), each detail becoming a door which, once unlocked, revealed yet another door. Without being aware of it, we were distracted by the smell of the skunk and not by what the skunk had done.

We realised something too, Buntu and I, that during the two-week effort to get our son's body, we had drifted apart. For the first time in our marriage, our presence to each other had become a matter of habit. He was there. He'll be there. And I'll be there. But when Buntu said: 'Do you realize our son is dead?' he uttered a thought that suddenly brought us together again. It was as if the return of the body of our son was also our coming together. For it was only at that moment that we really began to grieve; as if our lungs had suddenly begun to take in air when just before, we were beginning to suffocate. Something with meaning began to emerge.

We realised. We realised that something else had been happening to us, adding to the terrible events. Yes, we had drifted apart. Yet, our estrangement, just at that moment when we should have been together, seemed disturbingly comforting to me. I was comforted in a manner I did not quite understand.

The problem was that I had known all along that we would have to buy the body anyway. I had known all along. Things would end that way. And when things turned out that way, Buntu could not look me in the eye. For he had said: 'Over my dead body! Over my dead body!' as soon as we knew we would be required to pay the police or the government for the release of the body of our child.

'Over my dead body! Over my dead body!' Buntu kept on saying.

Finally, we bought the body. We have the receipt. The police insisted we take it. That way, they would be 'protected'. It's the law, they said.

I suppose we could have got the body earlier. At first I was confused, for one is supposed to take comfort in the heroism of one's man. Yet, inwardly, I could draw no comfort from his outburst. It seemed hasty. What sense was there to it when all I wanted was the body of my child? What would happen if, as events unfolded, it became clear that Buntu would not give up his life? What would happen? What would happen to him? To me?

For the greater part of two weeks, all of Buntu's efforts, together with friends, relatives, lawyers and the newspapers, were to secure the release of the child's body without the humiliation of having to pay for it. A 'fundamental principle'.

Why was it difficult for me to see the wisdom of the principle? The worst thing, I suppose, was worrying about what the police may have been doing to the body of my child. How they may have been busy prying it open 'to determine the cause of death'?

Would I want to look at the body when we finally got it? To see further mutilations in addition to the 'cause of death'? What kind of mother would not want to look at the body of her child? people will ask. Some will say: 'It's grief.' She is too grief-stricken.

'But still ...,' they will say. And the elderly among them may say: 'Young people are strange.'

But how can they know? It was not that I would not want to see the body of my child, but that I was too afraid to confront the horrors of my own imagination. I was haunted by the thought of how useless it had been to have created something. What had been the point of it all? This body filling up with a child. The child steadily growing into something that could be seen and felt. Moving, as it always did, at that time of day when I was all alone at home waiting for it. What had been the point of it all?

How can they know that the mutilation to determine 'the cause of death' ripped my own body? Can they think of a womb feeling hunted? Disgorged?

And the milk that I still carried. What about it? What had been the point of it all?

Even Buntu did not seem to sense that that principle, the 'fundamental principle', was something too intangible for me at that moment, something that I desperately wanted should assume the form of my child's body. He still seemed far from ever knowing.

I remember one Saturday morning early in our courtship, as Buntu and I walked hand-in-hand through town, window-shopping. We cannot even be said to have been window-shopping, for we were aware of very little that was not ourselves. Everything in those windows was merely an excuse for words to pass between us.

We came across three girls sitting on the pavement, sharing a packet of fish and chips after they had just bought it from a nearby Portuguese café. Buntu said: 'I want fish and chips too.' I said: 'So seeing is desire.' I said: 'My man is greedy!' We laughed. I still remember how he tightened his grip on my hand. The strength of it!

Just then, two white boys coming in the opposite direction suddenly rushed at the girls, and, without warning, one of them kicked the packet of fish and chips out of the hands of the girl who was holding it. The second boy kicked away the rest of what remained in the packet. The girl stood up, shaking her hand as if to throw off the pain in it. Then she pressed it under her armpit as if to squeeze the pain out of it. Meanwhile, the two boys went on their way laughing. The fish and chips lay scattered on the pavement and on the street like stranded boats on a river that had gone dry.

'Just let them do that to you!' said Buntu, tightening once more his grip on my hand as we passed on like sheep that had seen many of their own in the flock picked out for slaughter. We would note the event and wait for our turn. I remember I looked at Buntu, and saw his face was somewhat glum. There seemed no connection between that face and the words of reassurance just uttered. For a while, we went on quietly. It was then that I noticed his grip had grown somewhat limp. Somewhat reluctant. Having lost its self-assurance, it seemed to have been holding on because it had to, not because of a confident sense of possession.

It was not to be long before his words were tested. How could fate work this way, giving to words meanings and intentions they did not carry when they were uttered? I saw that day, how the language of love could so easily be trampled underfoot, or scattered like fish and chips on the pavement, and left stranded and abandoned like boats in a river that suddenly went dry. Never again was love to be confirmed with words. The world around us was too hostile for vows of love. At any moment, the vows could be subjected to the stress of proof. And love died. For words of love need not be tested.

On that day, Buntu and I began our silence. We talked and laughed, of course, but we stopped short of words that would demand proof of action. Buntu knew. He knew the vulnerability of words. And so he sought to obliterate words with acts that seemed to promise redemption.

On that day, as we continued with our walk in town, that Saturday morning; coming up towards us from the opposite direction, was a burly Boer walking with his wife and two children. They approached Buntu and me with an ominously determined advance. Buntu attempted to pull me out the way, but I never had a chance. The Boer shoved me out of the way, as if clearing a path for his family. I remember, I almost crashed into a nearby fashion display window. I remember, I glanced at the family walking away, the mother and the father each dragging a child. It was for one of those children that I had been cleared away. I remember, also, that as my tears came out, blurring the Boer family and everything else, I saw and felt deeply what was inside of me: a desire to be avenged.

But nothing happened. All I heard was Buntu say: 'The dog!' At that very moment, I felt my own hurt vanish like a wisp of smoke. And as my hurt vanished, it was replaced, instead, by a tormenting desire to sacrifice myself for Buntu. Was it something about the powerlessness of the curse and the desperation with which it had been made? The filling of stunned silence with an utterance? Surely it ate into him, revealing how incapable he was of meeting the call of his words.

And so it was, that that afternoon, back in the township, left to ourselves at Buntu's home, I gave in to him for the first time. Or should I say I offered myself to him? Perhaps from some vague sense of wanting to heal something in him? Anyway, we were never to talk about that event. Never. We buried it alive deep inside of me that afternoon. Would it ever be exhumed? All I vaguely felt and knew was that I had the keys to the vault. That was three years ago, a year before we married.

The cause of death? One evening I returned home from work, particularly tired after I had been covering more shootings by the police in the East Rand. Then I had hurried back to the office in Johannesburg to piece together on my typewriter the violent scenes of the day, and then to file my report to meet the deadline. It was late when I returned home, and when I got there, I found a crowd of people in the yard. They were those who could not get inside. I panicked. What had happened? I did not ask those who were outside, being desperate to get into the house. They gave way easily when they recognised me.

Then I heard my mother's voice. Her cry rose well above the noise. It turned into a scream when she saw me. 'What is it, mother?' I asked, embracing her out of a vaguely despairing sense of terror. But she pushed me away with an hysterical violence that astounded me.

'What misery have I brought you, my child?' she cried. At that point, many women in the room began to cry too. Soon, there was much wailing in the room, and then all over the house. The sound of it! The anguish! Understanding, yet eager for knowledge, I became desperate. I had to hold onto something. The desire to embrace my mother no longer had anything to do with comforting her; for whatever she had done, whatever its magnitude, had become inconsequential. I needed to embrace her for all the anguish that tied everyone in the house into a knot. I wanted to be part of that knot, yet I wanted to know what had brought it about.

Eventually, we found each other, my mother and I, and clasped each other tightly. When I finally released her, I looked around at the neighbours and suddenly had a vision of how that anguish had to be turned into a simmering kind of indignation. The kind of indignation that had to be kept at bay only because there was a higher purpose at that moment: the sharing of concern.

Slowly and with a calmness that surprised me, I began to gather the details of what had happened. Instinctively, I seemed to have been gathering notes for a news report.

It happened during the day, when the soldiers and the police that had been patrolling the township in their Casspirs began to shoot in the streets at random. Need I describe what I did not see? How did the child come to die just at that moment when the police and the soldiers began to shoot at random, at any house, at any moving thing? That was how one of our windows was shattered by a bullet. And that was when my mother, who looked after her grandchild when we were away at work, panicked. She picked up the child and ran to the neighbours. It was only when she entered the neighbor's house that she noticed the wetness of the blanket that covered the child she held to her chest as she ran for the sanctuary of neighbours. She had looked at her unaccountably bloody hand, then she noted the still bundle in her arms, and began at that moment to blame herself for the death of her grandchild . . .

Later, the police, on yet another round of shooting, found people gathered at our house. They stormed in, saw what had happened. At first, they dragged my mother out, threatening to take her away unless she agreed not to say what had happened. But then they returned and, instead, took the body of the child away. By what freak of logic did they hope that by this act their carnage would never be discovered?

That evening, I looked at Buntu closely. He appeared suddenly to have grown older. We stood alone in an embrace in our bedroom. I noticed, when I kissed his face, how his once lean face had grown suddenly puffy.

At that moment, I felt the familiar impulse come upon me once more, the impulse I always felt when I sensed that Buntu was in some kind of danger, the impulse to yield something of myself to him. He wore the look of someone struggling to gain control of something. Yet, it was clear he was far from controlling anything. I knew that look. Had seen it many times. It came at those times when I sensed that he faced a wave that was infinitely stronger than he, that it would certainly sweep him away, but that he had to seem to be struggling. I pressed myself tightly to him as if to vanish into him; as if only the two of us could stand up to the wave.

'Don't worry,' he said. 'Don't worry. I'll do everything in my power to right this wrong. Everything. Even if it means suing the police!' We went silent.

I knew that silence. But I knew something else at that moment: that I had to find a way of disengaging myself from the embrace.

Suing the police? I listened to Buntu outlining his plans. 'Legal counsel. That's what we need,' he said. 'I know some people in Pretoria,' he said. As he spoke, I felt the warmth of intimacy between us cooling. When he finished, it was cold. I disengaged from his embrace slowly, yet purposefully. Why had Buntu spoken?

Later, he was to speak again, when all his plans had failed to work: 'Over my dead body! Over my dead body!'

He sealed my lips. I would wait for him to feel and yield one day to all the realities of misfortune.

Ours was a home, it could be said. It seemed a perfect life for a young couple: I, a reporter; Buntu, a personnel officer at an American factory manufacturing farming implements. He had travelled to the United States and returned with a mind fired with dreams. We dreamed together. Much time we spent, Buntu and I, trying to make a perfect home. The occasions are numerous on which we paged through *Femina, Fair Lady, Cosmopolitan, Home & Garden, Car*, as if somehow we were going to surround our lives with the glossiness in the magazines. Indeed, much of our time was spent window-shopping through the magazines. This time, it was different from the window-shopping we did that Saturday when we courted. This time our minds were consumed by the things we saw and dreamed of owning: the furniture, the fridge, TV, video-cassette recorders, washing machines, even a vacuum cleaner and every other imaginable thing that would ensure a comfortable modern life.

Especially when I was pregnant. What is it that Buntu did not buy, then? And when the boy was born, Buntu changed the car. A family, he would say, must travel comfortably.

The boy became the centre of Buntu's life. Even before he was born, Buntu had already started making enquiries at white private schools. That was where he would send his son, the bearer of his name.

Dreams! It is amazing how the horrible findings of my newspaper reports often vanished before the glossy magazines of our dreams, how I easily forgot that the glossy images were concocted out of the keys of typewriters, made by writers whose business was to sell dreams at the very moment that death pervaded the land. So powerful are words and pictures that even their makers often believe in them.

Buntu's ordeal was long. So it seemed. He would get up early every morning to follow up the previous day's leads regarding the body of our son. I wanted to go with him, but each time I prepared to go he would shake his head.

'It's my task,' he would say. But every evening he returned, empty-handed, while with each day that passed and we did not know where the body of my child was, I grew restive and hostile in a manner that gave me much pain. Yet Buntu always felt compelled to give a report on each day's events. I never asked for it. I suppose it was his way of dealing with my silence.

One day he would say: 'The lawyers have issued a court order that the body be produced. The writ of *habeas corpus*.'

On another day he would say: 'We have petitioned the Minister of Justice.'

On yet another he would say: 'I was supposed to meet the Chief Security Officer. Waited the whole day. At the end of the day they said I would see him tomorrow if he was not going to be too busy. They are stalling.'

Then he would say: 'The newspapers, especially yours, are raising the hue and cry. The government is bound to be embarrassed. It's a matter of time.'

And so it went on. Every morning he got up and left. Sometimes alone, sometimes with friends. He always left to bear the failure alone.

How much did I care about lawyers, petitions and Chief Security Officers? A lot. The problem was that whenever Buntu spoke about his efforts, I heard only his words. I felt in him the disguised hesitancy of someone who wanted reassurance without asking for it. I saw someone who got up every morning and left not to look for results, but to search for something he could only have found with me.

And each time he returned, I gave my speech to my eyes. And he answered without my having parted my lips. As a result, I sensed, for the first time in my life, a terrible power in me that could make him do anything. And he would never ever be able to deal with that power as long as he did not silence my eyes and call for my voice.

And so, he had to prove himself. And while he left each morning, I learned to be brutally silent. Could he prove himself without me? Could he? Then I got to know, those days, what I'd always wanted from him. I got to know why I have always drawn him into me whenever I sensed his vulnerability.

I wanted him to be free to fear. Wasn't there greater strength that way? Had he ever lived with his own feelings? And the stress of life in this land: didn't it call out for men to be heroes? And should they live up to it even though the details of the war to be fought may often be blurred? They should.

Yes it is precisely for that reason that I often found Buntu's thoughts lacking in strength. They lacked the experience of strife that could only come from a humbling acceptance of fear and then, only then, the need to fight it.

Me? In a way, I have always been free to fear. The prerogative of being a girl. It was always expected of me to scream when a spider crawled across the ceiling. It was known I would jump onto a chair whenever a mouse blundered into the room.

Then, once more, the Casspirs came. A few days before we got the body back, I was at home with my mother when we heard the great roar of truck engines. There was much running and shouting in the streets. I saw them, as I've always seen them on my assignments: the Casspirs. On five occasions they ran down our street at great speed, hurling tear-gas canisters at random. On the fourth occasion, they got our house. The canister shattered another window and filled the house with the terrible pungent choking smoke that I had got to know so well. We ran out of the house gasping for fresh air.

So, this was how my child was killed? Could they have been the same soldiers? Now hardened to their tasks? Or were they new ones being hardened to their tasks? Did they drive away laughing? Clearing paths for their families? What paths?

And was this our home? It couldn't be. It had to be a little bird's nest waiting to be plundered by a predator bird. There seemed no sense to the wedding pictures on the walls, the graduation pictures, birthday pictures, pictures of relatives, and paintings of lush landscapes. There seemed no sense anymore to what seemed recognisably human in our house. It took only a random swoop to obliterate personal worth, to blot out any value there may have been to the past. In desperation, we began to live only for the moment. I do feel hunted.

It was on the night of the tear-gas that Buntu came home, saw what had happened, and broke down in tears. They had long been in the coming...

My own tears welled out too. How much did we have to cry to refloat stranded boats? I was sure they would float again.

A few nights later, on the night of the funeral, exhausted, I lay on my bed, listening to the last of the mourners leaving. Slowly, I became conscious of returning to the world. Something came back after it seemed not to have been there for ages. It came as a surprise, as a reminder that we will always live around what will happen. The sun will rise and set, and the ants will do their endless work, until one day the clouds turn gray and rain falls, and even in the townships, the ants will fly out into the sky. Come what may.

My moon came, in a heavy surge of blood. And, after such a long time, I remembered the thing Buntu and I had buried in me. I felt it as if it had just entered. I felt it again as it floated away on the surge. I would be ready for another month. Ready as always, each and every month, for new beginnings.

And Buntu? I'll be with him, now. Always. Without our knowing, all the trying events had prepared for us new beginnings. Shall we not prevail?

Gcina Mhlope

The Toilet

from *Sometimes When it Rains – Writings by South African Women*
(1987)

Sometimes I wanted to give up and be a good girl who listened to her
elders. Maybe I should have done something like teaching or nursing as
my mother wished. People thought these professions were respectable,
but I knew I wanted to do something different, though I was not sure
what. I thought a lot about acting ... My mother said that it had been a
waste of good money educating me because I did not know what to do
with the knowledge I had acquired. I'd come to Johannesburg for the December holidays after writing my matric exams, and then stayed on,
hoping to find something to do.

My elder sister worked in Orange Grove as a domestic worker, and I
stayed with her in her back room. I didn't know anybody in Jo'burg
except my sister's friends whom we went to church with. The Methodist
church up Fourteenth Avenue was about the only outing we had together. I was very bored and lonely.

On weekdays, I was locked in my sister's room so that the Madam
wouldn't see me. She was at home most of the time: painting her nails,
having tea with her friends, or lying in the sun by the swimming pool.
The swimming pool was very close to the room, which is why I had to
keep very quiet. My sister felt bad about locking me in there, but she had
no alternative. I couldn't even play the radio, so she brought me books,
old magazines, and newspapers from the white people. I just read every
single thing I came across: *Fair Lady*, *Woman's Weekly*, anything. But
then my sister thought I was reading too much.

'What kind of wife will you make if you can't even make baby clothes,
or knit yourself a jersey? I suppose you will marry an educated man like
yourself, who won't mind going to bed with a book and an empty
stomach.'

We would play cards at night when she knocked off, and listen to the radio, singing along softly with the songs we liked.

Then I got this temporary job in a clothing factory in town. I looked forward to meeting new people, and liked the idea of being out of that room for a change. The factory made clothes for ladies' boutiques.

The whole place was full of machines of all kinds. Some people were sewing, others were ironing with big heavy irons that pressed with a lot of steam. I had to cut all the loose threads that hang after a dress or a jacket is finished. As soon as a number of dresses in a certain style were finished, they would be sent to me and I had to count them, write the number down, and then start with the cutting of the threads. I was fascinated to discover that one person made only sleeves, another the collars, and so on until the last lady put all the pieces together, sewed on buttons, or whatever was necessary to finish.

Most people at the factory spoke Sotho, but they were nice to me – they tried to speak to me in Zulu or Xhosa, and they gave me all kinds of advice on things I didn't know. There was this girl, Gwendolene – she thought I was very stupid – she called me a 'bari' because I always sat inside the changing room with something to read when it was time to eat my lunch, instead of going outside to meet guys. She told me it was cheaper to get myself a 'lunch boy' – somebody to buy me lunch. She told me it was wise not to sleep with him, because then I could dump him anytime I wanted to. I was very nervous about such things. I thought it was better to be a 'bari' than to be stabbed by a city boy for his money.

The factory knocked off at four-thirty, and then I went to a park near where my sister worked. I waited there till half-past six, when I could sneak into the house again without the white people seeing me. I had to leave the house before half-past five in the mornings as well. That meant I had to find something to do with the time I had before I could catch the seven-thirty bus to work – about two hours. I would go to a public toilet in the park. For some reason it was never locked, so I would go in and sit on the toilet seat to read some magazine or other until the right time to catch the bus.

The first time I went into this toilet, I was on my way to the bus stop. Usually I went straight to the bus stop outside the OK Bazaars where it was well lit, and I could see. I would wait there, reading, or just looking at the growing number of cars and buses on their way to town. On this day it was raining quite hard, so I thought I would shelter in the toilet until the rain had passed. I knocked first to see if there was anyone inside. As there was no reply, I pushed the door open and went in. It smelled a little – a dryish kind of smell, as if the toilet was not used all that often, but it was quite clean compared to many 'Non-European' toilets I knew. The floor was painted red and the walls were cream white.

It did not look like it had been painted for a few years. I stood looking around, with the rain coming very hard on the zinc roof. The noise was comforting – to know I had escaped the wet – only a few of the heavy drops had got me. The plastic bag in which I carried my book and purse and neatly folded pink handkerchief was a little damp, but that was because I had used it to cover my head when I ran to the toilet. I pulled my dress down a little so that it would not get creased when I sat down. The closed lid of the toilet was going to be my seat for many mornings after that.

I was really lucky to have found that toilet because the winter was very cold. Not that it was any warmer in there, but once I'd closed the door it used to be a little less windy. Also the toilet was very small – the walls were wonderfully close to me – if felt like it was made to fit me alone. I enjoyed that kind of privacy. I did a lot of thinking while I sat on that toilet seat. I did a lot of day-dreaming too – many times imagining myself in some big hall doing a really popular play with other young actors. At school, we took set books like *Buzani KuBawo* or *A Man for All Seasons* and made school plays which we toured to the other schools on weekends. I loved it very much. When I was even younger I had done little sketches taken from the Bible and on big days like Good Friday, we acted and sang happily.

I would sit there dreaming . . .

I was getting bored with the books I was reading – the love stories all sounded the same, and besides that I just lost interest. I started asking myself why I had not written anything since I left school. At least at school I had written some poems, or stories for the school magazine, school competitions and other magazines like *Bona* and *Inkqubela*. Our English teacher was always so encouraging; I remembered the day I showed him my first poem – I was so excited I couldn't concentrate in class for the whole day. I didn't know anything about publishing then, and I didn't ask myself if my stories were good enough. I just enjoyed writing things down when I had the time. So one Friday, after I'd started being that toilet's best customer, I bought myself a notebook in which I was hoping to write something. I didn't use it for quite a while, until one evening.

My sister had taken her usual Thursday afternoon off, and she had delayed somewhere. I came back from work, then waited in the park for the right time to go back into the yard. The white people always had their supper at six-thirty and that was the time I used to steal my way in without disturbing them or being seen. My comings and goings had to be secret because they still didn't know I stayed there.

Then I realised that she hadn't come back, and I was scared to go out again, in case something went wrong this time. I decided to sit down in front of my sister's room, where I thought I wouldn't be noticed. I was reading a copy of *Drum Magazine* and hoping that she would come back soon – before the dogs sniffed me out. For the first time I realised how stupid it was of me not to have cut myself a spare key long ago. I kept on hearing noises that sounded like the gate opening. A few times I was sure I had heard her footsteps on the concrete steps leading to the servant's quarters, but it turned out to be something or someone else.

I was trying hard to concentrate on my reading again, when I heard the two dogs playing, chasing each other nearer and nearer to where I was sitting. And then, there they were in front of me, looking as surprised as I was. For a brief moment we stared at each other, then they started to bark at me. I was sure they would tear me to pieces if I moved just one finger, so I sat very still, trying not to look at them, while my heart pounded and my mouth went dry as paper.

They barked even louder when the dogs from next door joined in, glared at me through the openings in the hedge. Then the Madam's high-pitched voice rang out above the dogs' barking.

'Ireeeeeene!' That's my sister's English name, which we never use. I couldn't move or answer the call – the dogs were standing right in front of me, their teeth so threateningly long. When there was no reply, she came to see what was going on.

'Oh, it's you? Hello.' She was smiling at me, chewing that gum which never left her mouth, instead of calling the dogs away from me. They had stopped barking, but they hadn't moved – they were still growling at me, waiting for her to tell them what to do.

'Please Madam, the dogs will bite me,' I pleaded, not moving my eyes from them.

'No, they won't bite you.' Then she spoke to them nicely, 'Get away now – go on,' and they went off. She was like a doll, her hair almost orange in colour, all curls round her made-up face. Her eyelashes fluttered like a doll's. Her thin lips were bright red like her long nails, and she wore very high-heeled shoes. She was still smiling; I wondered if it didn't hurt after a while. When her friends came for a swim, I could always hear her forever laughing at something or other.

She scared me – I couldn't understand how she could smile like that but not want me to stay in her house.

'When did you come in? We didn't see you.'

'I've been here for some time now – my sister isn't here. I'm waiting to talk to her.'

'Oh – she's not here?' She was laughing, for no reason that I could see.

'I can give her a message – you go on home – I'll tell her that you want to see her.'

Once I was outside the gate, I didn't know what to do or where to go. I walked slowly, kicking my heels. The street lights were so very bright! Like big eyes staring at me. I wondered what the people who saw me thought I was doing, walking around at that time of the night. But then I didn't really care, because there wasn't much I could do about the situation right then. I was just thinking how things had to go wrong on that day particularly, because my sister and I were not on such good terms. Early that morning, when the alarm had gone for me to wake up, I did not jump to turn it off, so my sister got really angry with me. She had gone on about me always leaving it to ring for too long, as if it was set for her, and not for me. And when I went out to wash, I had left the door open a second too long, and that was enough to earn me another scolding.

Every morning I had to wake up straight away, roll my bedding and put it all under the bed where my sister was sleeping. I was not supposed to put on the light although it was still dark. I'd light a candle, and tiptoe my way out with a soap dish and a toothbrush. My clothes were on a hanger on a nail at the back of the door. I'd take the hanger and close the door as quietly as I could. Everything had to be ready set the night before. A washing basin full of cold water was also ready outside the door, put there because the sound of running water and the loud screech the taps made in the morning could wake the white people and they would wonder what my sister was doing up so early. I'd do my everything and be off the premises by five-thirty with my shoes in my bag – I only put them on once I was safely out of the gate. And that gate made such a noise too. Many time I wished I could jump over it and save myself all that sickening careful-careful business!

Thinking about all these things took my mind away from the biting cold of the night and my wet nose, until I saw my sister walking towards me.

'Mholo, what are you doing outside in the street?' she greeted me. I quickly briefed her on what had happened.

'Oh Yehovah! You can be so dumb sometimes! What were you doing inside in the first place? You know you should have waited for me so we could walk in together. Then I could say you were visiting or something. Now, you tell me, what am I supposed to say to them if they see you come in again? Hayi!'

She walked angrily towards the gate, she turned to me with an impatient whisper.

'And now why don't you come in, stupid?'

I mumbled my apologies, and followed her in. By some miracle no one seemed to have noticed us, and we quickly munched a snack of cold chicken and boiled potatoes and drank our tea, hardly on speaking terms. I just wanted to howl like a dog. I wished somebody would come and be my friend, and tell me that I was not useless, and that my sister did not hate me, and tell me that one day I would have a nice place to live ... anything. It would have been really great to have someone my own age to talk to.

But also I knew that my sister was worried for me, she was scared of her employers. If they were to find out that I lived with her, they would fire her, and then we would both be walking up and down the streets. My eleven rand wages wasn't going to help us at all. I don't know how long I lay like that, unable to fall asleep, just wishing and wishing with tears running into my ears.

The next morning I woke up long before the alarm went off, but I just lay there feeling tired and depressed. If there was a way out, I would not have gone to work, but there was this other strong feeling or longing inside me. It was some kind of pain that pushed me to do everything at double speed and run to my toilet. I call it my toilet because that is exactly how I felt about it. It was very rare that I ever saw anybody else go in there in the mornings. It was like they all knew I was using it, and they had to lay off or something. When I went there, I didn't really expect to find it occupied.

I felt my spirits really lifting as I put on my shoes outside the gate. I made sure that my notebook was in my bag. In my haste I even forgot my lunchbox, but it didn't matter. I was walking faster and my feet were feeling lighter all the time. Then I noticed that the door had been painted, and that a new window pane had replaced the old broken one. I smiled to myself as I reached the door. Before long I was sitting on that toilet seat, writing a poem.

Many more mornings saw me sitting there writing. Sometimes it did not need to be a poem; I wrote anything that came into my head – in the same way I would have done if I'd had a friend to talk to. I remember some days when I felt like I was hiding something from my sister. She did not know about my toilet in the park, and she was not in the least interested in my notebook.

Then one morning I wanted to write a story about what had happened at work the day before; the supervisor screaming at me for not calling her when I'd seen the people who stole two dresses at lunch time. I had found it really funny. I had to write about it and I just hoped there were enough pages left in my notebook. It all came back to me, and I was smiling when I reached for the door, but it wouldn't open – it was locked!

I think for the first time I accepted that the toilet was not mine after all ... Slowly I walked over to a bench nearby, watched the early spring sun come up, and wrote my story anyway.

Zoë Wicomb

Ash on my Sleeve

from *You Can't Get Lost in Cape Town* (1987)

Desmond is a man who relies on the communicative powers of the hand-shake. Which renders my hand, a cluster of crushed bones, inert as he takes a step back and nods approvingly while still applying the pressure. He attempts what proves impossible in spite of my decision to co-op-erate. That is to stand back even further in order to inspect me more thoroughly without releasing my hand. The distance between us cannot be lengthened and I am about to point out this unalterable fact when his smile relaxes into speech.

'Well what a surprise!'

'Yes, what a surprise,' I contribute.

It is of course no longer a surprise. I arranged the meeting two months ago when I wrote to Moira after years of silence between us, and yes-terday I telephoned to confirm the visit. And I had met Desmond before, in fact at the same party at which Moira had been struck by the eloquence of his handshake. Then we discussed the role of the Student Represent-ative Council, he, a final year Commerce student, confidently, his voice remaining even as he bent down to tie a shoe-lace. And while I floun-dered, lost in subordinate clauses, he excused himself with a hurried, 'Back in a moment.' We have not spoken since.

'You're looking wonderful, so youthful. Turning into something of a swan in your middle age hey!'

I had thought it prudent to arrange a one-night stay which would leave me the option of another if things went well. I am a guest in their house; I must not be rude. So I content myself with staring at his jaw where my eyes fortuitously alight on the tell-tale red of an incipient pimple. He releases my hand. He rubs index finger and thumb together, testing an imagined protuberance, and as he gestures me to sit down the left hand briefly brushes the jaw.

It always feels worse than it looks, he will comfort himself, feeling its enormity; say to himself, the tactual never corresponds with the appearance of such a blemish, and dismiss it. I shall allow my eyes at strategic moments to explore his face then settle to revive the gnathic discomfort.

Somewhere at the back of the house Moira's voice has been rising and falling, flashing familiar stills from the past. Will she be as nervous as I am? A door clicks and a voice starts up again, closer, already addressing me, so that the figure develops slowly, fuzzily assumes form before she appears: '... to deal with these people and I just had to be rude and say my friend's here, all the way from England, she's waiting ...'

Standing in the doorway, she shakes her head. 'My God Frieda Shenton, you plaasjapie, is it really you?'

I grin. Will we embrace? Shake hands? My arm hangs foolishly. Then she puts her hands on my shoulders and says, 'It's all my fault. I'm hopeless at writing letters and we moved around so much and what with my hands full with children I lost touch with everyone. But I've thought of you, many a day have I thought of you.'

'Oh nonsense,' I say awkwardly. 'I'm no good at writing letters either. We've both been very bad.'

Her laughter deals swiftly with the layer of dust on that old intimacy but our speech, like the short letters we exchanged, is awkward. We cannot tumble into the present while a decade gapes between us.

Sitting before her I realise what had bothered me yesterday on the telephone when she said, 'Good heavens man I can't believe it ... Yes of course I've remembered ... OK, let me pick you up at the station.'

Unease at what I now know to be the voice made me decline. 'No,' I said. 'I'd like to walk, get to see the place. I can't get enough of Cape Town,' I gushed. For her voice is deeper, slowed down eerily like the distortion of a faulty record player. Some would say the voice of a woman speaking evenly, avoiding inflection.

'I bet,' she says, 'you regretted having to walk all that way.'

She is right. The even-numbered houses on the left side of this interminable street are L-shaped with grey asbestos roofs. Their stoeps alternate green, red and black, making spurious claims to individuality. The macadamised street is very black and sticky under the soles, its concrete edge of raised pavement a virgin grey that invites you to scribble something rude, or just anything at all. For all its neat edges, the garden sand spills on to the pavement as if the earth were wriggling in discomfort. It is the pale porous sand of the Cape Flats pushed out over centuries by the Indian Ocean. It does not portend well for the cultivation of prize-winning dahlias.

I was so sure that it was Moira's house. There it was, a black stoep inevitably after the green, the house inadequately fenced off so that the garden sand had been swept along the pavement in delicately waved watermark by the previous afternoon's wind. A child's bucket and spade had been left in the garden and on a mound of sand a jaunty strip of astroturf testified to the untameable. I knocked without checking the number again and felt foolish as the occupier with hands on her hips directed me to the fourth house along.

Moira's is a house like all the others except for the determined effort in the garden. Young trees grow in bonsai uniformity, promising a dense hedge all around for those who are prepared to wait. The fence is efficient. The sand does not escape; it is held by the roots of a brave lawn visibly knitting beneath its coarse blades of grass. Number 288 is swathed in lace curtains. Even the glass-panelled front door has generously ruched lengths of lace between the wooden strips. Dense, so that you could not begin to guess at the outline approaching the door. It was Desmond.

'Goodness me, ten, no twelve years haven't done much to damage you,' Moira says generously.

'Think so Moi,' Desmond adds. 'I think Frieda has a contract with time. Look, she's even developed a waistline', and his hands hover as if to describe the chimerical curve. There is the possibility that I may be doing him an injustice.

'I suppose it's marriage that's done it for us. Very ageing, and of course the children don't help,' he says.

'It's not a week since I sewed up this cushion. What do the children do with them.' Moira tugs at the loose threads then picks up another cushion to check the stitiching.

'See,' Desmond persists, 'a good figure in your youth is no guarantee against childbearing. There are veins and sagging breasts and of course some women get horribly fat; that is if they don't grow thin and haggard.' He looks sympathetically at Moira. Why does she not spit in his eye? I fix my eye on his jaw so that he says, 'Count yourself lucky that you've missed the boat.'

Silence. And then we laugh. Under Desmond's stern eye we lean back in simultaneous laughter that cleaves through the years to where we sat on our twin beds recounting the events of our nights out. Stomach-clutching laughter as we whispered our adventures and decoded for each other the words grunted by boys through the smoke of the braaivleis. Or the tears, the stifled sobs of bruised love, quietly, in order not to disturb her parents. She slept lightly, Moira's mother, who said that a girl cannot keep the loss of her virginity a secret, that her very gait proclaims it to the world and especially to men who will expect favours from her.

When our laughter subsides Desmond gets a bottle of whisky from the cabinet of the same oppressively carved dark wood as the rest of the sitting-room suite.

'Tell Susie to make some tea,' he says.

'It's her afternoon off. Eh ...' Moira's silence asserts itself as her own so that we wait and wait until she explains, 'We have a servant. People don't have servants in England, do they? Not ordinary people, I mean.'

'It's a matter of nomenclature I think. The middle classes have cleaning ladies, a Mrs Thing, usually quite a character, whom we pretend to be in awe of. She does for those of us who are too sensitive or too important or intelligent to clean up our own mess. We pay a decent wage, that is for a cleaner, of course, and not to be compared with our own salaries.'

Moira bends closely over a cushion, then looks up at me and I recall a photograph of her in an op-art mini-skirt, dangling very large black and white earrings from delicate lobes. The face is lifted quizzically at the photographer, almost in disbelief, and her cupped hand is caught in movement perhaps on the way to check the jaunty flick-ups. I cannot remember who took the photograph but at the bottom of the picture I recognise the intrusion of my right foot, a thick ankle growing out of an absurdly delicate high-heeled shoe.

I wish I could fill the ensuing silence with something conciliatory, no something that will erase what I have said, but my trapped thoughts blunder insect-like against a glazed window. I who in this strange house in a new Coloured suburb have just accused and criticised my hostess. She will have seen through the deception of the first-person usage; she will shrink from the self-righteousness of my words and lift her face quizzically at my contempt. I feel the dampness crawl along my hairline. But Moira looks at me serenely while Desmond frowns. Then she moves as if to rise.

'Don't bother with tea on my account,' I say with my eye longingly on the whisky, and carry on in the same breath, 'Are you still in touch with Martin? I wouldn't mind seeing him after all these years.'

Moira's admirers were plentiful and she generously shared with me the benefits of her beauty. At parties young men straightened their jackets and stepped over to ask me to dance. Their cool hands fell on my shoulders, bare and damp with sweat. I glided past the rows of girls waiting to be chosen. So they tested their charm – 'Can I get you a lemonade? Shall we dance again?' – on me the intermediary. In the airless room my limbs obeyed the inexorable sweep of the ballroom dances. But with the wilder Twist or Shake my broad shoulders buckled under a young man's gaze and my feet grew leaden as I waited for the casual enquiry after Moira. Then we would sit out a dance chatting about Moira and the gardenia on my bosom meshed in maddening fragrance our common interest. My hand squeezed in gratitude with a quick goodnight, for there was no question about it: my friendship had to be secured in order to be considered by Moira. Then in the early hours, sitting cross-legged on her bed, we sifted his words and Moira unpinned for me the gardenia, crushed by his fervour, when his cool hand on my shoulder drew me closer, closer in that first held dance.

Young men in Sunday ties and borrowed cars agreed to take me with them on scenic drives along the foot of Table Mountain, or Chapman's Peak where we looked down dizzily at the sea. And I tactfully wandered off licking at a jumbo ice-cream while they practised their kissing, Moira's virginity unassailable. Below, the adult baboons scrambled over the sand dunes and smacked the bald bottoms of their young and the sun-licked waves beckoned at the mermaids on the rocks.

Desmond replies, 'Martin's fallen in love with an AZAPO woman, married her and stopped coming round. Shall we say that he finally lost interest in Moi?'

The whisky in his glass lurches amber as he rolls the stem between his fingers.

'Would you like a coke?' he asks.

I decline but I long to violate the alcohol taboo for women. 'A girl who drinks is nothing other than a prostitute,' Father said. And there's no such thing as just a little tot because girls get drunk instantly. Then they hitch up their skirts like the servant girls on their days off, caps scrunched into shopping bags, waving their Vaaljapie bottles defiantly. A nice girl's reputation would shatter with a single mouthful of liquor.

'The children are back from their party,' Moira says. There is a shuffling outside and then they burst in blowing penny whistles and rattling their plastic spoils. Simultaneously they reel off the events of the party and correct each other's versions while the youngest scrambles on to his mother's lap. Moira listens, amused. She interrupts them, 'Look who's here. Say hallo to the auntie. Auntie Frieda's come all the way from England to see you.' They compose their stained faces and shake hands solemnly. Then the youngest bursts into tears and the other two discuss in undertones the legitimacy of his grievance.

'He's tired,' Desmond offers from the depths of his whisky reverie, 'probably eaten too much as well.'

This statement has a history, for Moira throws her head back and laughs and the little boy charges at his father and butts him in the stomach.

'Freddie, we've got a visitor, behave yourself hey,' the eldest admonishes.

I smile at her and get up to answer the persistent knock at the back door which the family seem not to hear. A man in overalls waiting on the doorstep looks at me bewildered but then says soberly, 'For the Missus,' and hands over a bunch of arum lilies which I stick in a pot by the sink. When I turn round Moira stands in the doorway watching me. She interrupts as I start explaining about the man.

'Yes, I'll put it in the children's room.'

I want to say that the pot is not tall enough for the lilies but she takes them off hurriedly, the erect spadices dusting yellow on to the funnelled white leaves. Soon they will droop; I did not have a chance to put water in the pot.

I wait awkwardly in the kitchen and watch a woman walk past the window. No doubt there is a servant's room at the far end of the garden. The man must be the gardener but from the window it is clear that there are no flowers in the garden except for a rampant morning glory that covers the fence. When Moira comes back she prepares grenadilla juice and soda with which we settle around the table. I think of alcohol and say, 'It's a nice kitchen.' It is true that sunlight sifted through the lace curtains softens the electric blue of the melamine worksurfaces. But after the formality of the sitting room the clutter of the kitchen comes as a surprise. The sink is grimy and harbours dishes of surely the previous day. The grooved steel band around the table top holds a neat line of grease and dust compound.

'Yes,' she says, 'I like it. The living room is Desmond's. He has no interest in the kitchen.'

And all the while she chops at the parsley, slowly chops it to a pulp. Then beneath the peelings and the spilled contents of brown paperbags she ferrets about until she drags out a comb.

'Where the hell are the bay leaves?' she laughs, and throws the comb across the worksurface. I rise to inspect a curious object on the windowsill from which the light bounces frantically. It is a baby's shoe dipped into a molten alloy, an instant sculpture of brassy brown that records the first wayward steps of a new biped. I tease it in the sunlight, turning it this way and that.

'Strange object,' I say, 'whose is it?'

'Ridiculous hey,' and we laugh in agreement. 'Desmond's idea,' she explains, 'but funnily enough I'm quite attached to that shoe now. It's Carol's, the eldest; you feel so proud of the things your child does. Obvious things, you know, like walking and talking you await anxiously as if they were man's first steps on the moon and you're so absurdly pleased at the child's achievement. And so we ought to be, not proud I suppose, but grateful. I'm back at work, mornings only, at Manenberg, and you should see the township children. Things haven't changed much, don't you believe that.'

She picks up the shoe.

'Carol's right foot always leaned too far to the right and Desmond felt that that was the shoe to preserve. More character, he said. Ja,' she sighs, 'things were better in those early days. And anyway I didn't mind his kak so much then. But I'd better get on otherwise dinner'll be late.'

I lift the lace curtain and spread out the gathers to reveal a pattern of scallops with their sprays of stylised leaves. The flower man is walking in the shadow of the fence carrying a carrier-bag full of books. He does not look at me holding up the nylon lace. I turn to Moira bent over a cheese grater, and with the sepia light of evening streaming in, her face lifts its sadness to me, the nut-brown skin, as if under a magnifying glass, singed translucent and taut across the high cheekbones.

'Moira,' I say, but at that moment she beats the tin grater against the bowl.

So I tug at things, peep, rummage through her kitchen, pick at this and that as if they were buttons to trigger off the mechanism of software that will gush out a neatly printed account of her life. I drop the curtain still held in my limp hand.

'What happened to Michael?' she asks.

'Dunno. There was no point in keeping in touch, not after all that. And there is in any case no such thing as friendship with men.' I surprise myself by adding, 'Mind you, I think quite neutrally about him, even positively at times. The horror of Michael must've been absorbed by the subsequent horror of others. But I don't, thank God, remember their names.'

Moira laughs. 'You must be kinder to men. We have to get on with them.'

'Yes,' I retort, 'but surely not behind their backs.'

'Heavens,' she says, 'we were so blarry stupid and dishonest really. Obsessed with virginity, we imagined we weren't messing about with sex. Suppose that's what we thought sex was all about: breaking a mem-brane. I expect Michael was as stupid as you. Catholic, wasn't he?'

I do not want to talk about Michael. I am much more curious about Desmond. How did he slip through the net? Desmond scorned the methods of her other suitors and refused to ingratiate himself with me. On her first date Moira came back with a headache, bristling with secrecy no doubt sworn beneath his parted lips. We did not laugh at the way he pontificated, his hands held gravely together as in prayer to prevent interruptions. Desmond left Cape Town at the end of that year and I had in the meantime met Michael.

There was the night on the bench under the loquat tree when we ate the tasteless little fruits and spat glossy pips over the fence. Moira's fingers drummed the folder on her lap.

'Here,' she said in a strange voice, 'are the letters. You should just read this, today's.'

I tugged at the branch just above my head so that it rustled in the dark and overripe loquats fell plop to the ground.

'No, not his letters, that wouldn't be right,' I said. And my memory skimmed the pages of Michael's letters. Love, holy love that made the remembered words dance on that lined foolscap infused with his smell. I could not, would not, share the first man to love me.

'Is he getting on OK in Durban?' I asked

'Yes, I expect he still has many friends there. I'm going up just after the finals and then perhaps he'll come back to Cape Town. Let's see if we can spit two pips together and hit the fence at the same time.'

So we sat in the dark, between swotting sessions, under the tree with yellow loquats lustrous in the black leaves. Perhaps she mimicked his Durban voice, waiting for me to take up the routine of friendly mockery. I try in vain to summon it all. I cannot separate the tangled strands of conversation or remembered letters. Was it then, in my Durban accent, that I replied with Michael's views about the permanence and sanctity of marriage?

'Ja-ja-ja,' Moira sighs, pulling out a chair. And turning again to check a pot on the stove, her neck is unbecomingly twisted, the sinews thrown into relief. How old we have grown since that night under the loquat tree, and I know that there is no point in enquiring after Desmond.

'Do you like living here?' I ask instead.

'It's OK, as good as anything.'

'I was thinking of your parents' home, the house where I stayed. How lovely it was. Everything's so new here. Don't you find it strange?'

'Ag Frieda, but we're so new, don't we belong in estates like this? Col-oureds haven't been around for that long, perhaps that's why we stray. Just think, in our teens we wanted to be white, now we want to be full-blooded Africans. We've never wanted to be ourselves and that's why we stray ... across the continent, across the oceans and even here, right into the Tricameral Parliament, playing into their hands. Actually,' and she looks me straight in the eye, 'it suits me very well to live here.'

Chastened by her reply I drum my fingertips on the table so that she says gently, 'I don't mean to accuse you. At the time I would have done exactly the same. There was little else to do. Still, it's really nice to see you. I hope you'll be able to stay tomorrow.' Her hand burns for a moment on my shoulder.

It is time for dinner. Moira makes a perfunctory attempt at clearing the table then, defeated by the chaos, she throws a cloth at me.

'Oh God, I'll never be ready by seven.'

I am drawn into the revolving circle of panic, washing down, screwing lids back on to jars, shutting doors on food that will rot long before discovery. Moira has always been hopeless in a kitchen so that there is really no point in my holding up the bag of potatoes enquiringly.

'Oh stick it in there,' and with her foot she deftly kicks open a dank cupboard where moisture tries in vain to escape from foul-smelling cloths. In here the potatoes will grow eyes and long pale etiolated limbs that will push open the creaking door next spring.

Her slow voice does not speed up with the frantic movements; instead, like a tape mangled in a machine, it trips and buzzes, dislocated from the darting sinewy body.

The children watch television. They do not want to eat, except for the youngest who rubs his distended tummy against the table. We stand in silence and listen to the child, 'I'm hungry, really hungry. I could eat and eat.' His black eyes glint with the success of subterfuge and in his pride he tugs at Moira's skirt, 'Can I sit on your knee?' and offers as reward, 'I'll be hungry on your knee, I really will.'

Something explodes in my mouth when Desmond produces a bottle of wine, and I resolve not to look at his chin, not even once.

'I've got something for you girls to celebrate with; you are staying in tonight, aren't you? Frieda, I promise you this is the first Wednesday night in years that Moira's been in. Nothing, not riots nor disease will keep her away from her Wednesday meetings. Now that women's lib's crept over the equator it would be most unbecoming of me to suspect my wife's commitment to her Black culture group. A worthy affair, affiliated to the UDF you know.' The wine which I drink too fast tingles in my toes and fingertips.

'So how has feminism been received here?' I ask.

'Oh,' he smiles, 'you have to adapt in order to survive. No point in resisting for the sake of it, you have to move with the times ... but there are some worrying half-baked ideas about ... muddled women's talk.'

'Actually,' Moira interjects, 'our group has far more pressing matters to deal with.'

'Like?' he barks.

'Like community issues, consciousness raising,' but Desmond snorts and she changes direction. 'Anyway, I doubt whether women's oppression arises as an issue among whites. One of the functions of having servants is to obscure it.'

'Hm,' I say, and narrow my eyes thoughtfully, a stalling trick I've used with varying success. Then I look directly at Desmond so that he refills my glass and takes the opportunity to propose a toast to our reunion. This is hardly less embarrassing than the topic of servants. The wine on my tongue turns musty and mingles with the smell of incense, of weddings and christenings that his empty words resurrect.

Desmond is in a co-operative mood, intent on evoking the halcyon days of the sixties when students sat on the cafeteria steps soaking up the sun. Days of calm and stability, he sighs. He reels off the names of contemporaries. Faces struggle in formation through the fog of the past, rise and recede. Rita Jantjes detained under the Terrorism Act. 'The Jantjes of Lansdowne?' I ask.

'It's ridiculous of them to keep Rita. She knows nothing; she's far too emotional, an obvious security risk,' Moira interjects.

'No,' Desmond explains, 'not the Lansdowne Jantjes but the Port Elizabeth branch of the family. The eldest, Sammy, graduated in Science the year before me.'

I am unable to contribute anything else, but he is the perfect host. There are no silent moments. He explains his plans for the garden and defers to my knowledge of succulents. There will be an enormous rockery in the front with the widest possible variety of cacti. A pity, he says, that Moira has planted those horrible trees but he would take over responsibility for the garden, give her a bit more free time, perhaps I didn't know that she has started working again?

Moira makes no effort to contribute to the conversation so diligently made. She murmurs to the little one on her knee whose fat fingers she prevents from exploring her nostrils. They giggle and shh-ssht each other, marking out their orbit of intimacy. Which make it easier for me to conduct this conversation. Only once does he falter and rub his chin but I avert my eyes and he embarks smoothly on the topic of red wine. I am the perfect guest, a deferential listener. I do not have the faintest interest in the production of wine.

When we finish dinner Desmond gets up briskly. He returns to the living room and the children protest loudly as he switches off the television and puts on music. Something classical and rousing, as if he too is in need of revival.

'Moi,' he shouts above the trombones, 'Moi, the children are tired, they must go to bed. Remember it's school tomorrow.'

'OK,' she shouts back. Then quietly, 'Thursdays are always school-days. But then Desmond isn't always as sober as I'd like him to be.'

She lifts the sleeping child from her lap on to the bench. We rest our elbows on the table amongst the dirty dishes.

'He gets his drink too cheaply; has shares in an hotel.' Moira explains how the liquor business goes on expanding, how many professional people give up their jobs to become liquor moguls.

'Why are the booze shops called hotels? Who stays in them? Surely there's no call for hotels in a Coloured area?'

'Search me, as we used to say. Nobody stays in them, I'm sure. I imagine they need euphemisms when they know that they grow rich out of other people's misery. Cheap wine means everyone can drown his sorrows at the weekends, and people say that men go into teaching so that they have the afternoons to drink in as well. I swear the only sober man to be found on a Saturday afternoon is the liquor boss. The rest are dronkies, whether they loaf about on street corners in hang-gat trousers or whether they slouch in upholstered chairs in front of television sets. And we all know a man of position is not a man unless he can guzzle a bottle or two of spirits. It's not surprising that the Soweto kids of '76 stormed the liquor stores and the shebeens. Not that I'd like to compare the shebeen queen making a miserable cent with the Coloured 'elite' as they call themselves who build big houses and drive Mercedes and send their daughters to Europe to find husbands. And those who allow themselves to be bought by the government to sit in Parliament ...'

She holds her head. 'Jesus, I don't know. Sometimes I'm optimistic and then it's worth fighting, but other times, here in this house, everything seems pointless. Actually that wine's given me a headache.'

I stare into the dirty plate so hard that surely my eyes will drop out and stare back at me. Like two fried eggs, sunny-side-up. Then I take her hand.

'Listen, I know a trick that takes headaches away instantly.' And I squeeze with my thumb and index finger deep into the webbed V formed by the thumb of her outstretched hand. 'See? Give me the other hand. See how it lifts?' Like a child she stares in wonderment at the hand still resting in mine.

The back door bursts open and Tillie rushes in balancing on her palm a curious object, a priapic confection.

'Look,' she shouts, 'look isn't it lovely? It's the stale loaf I put out for the birds and they've pecked it really pretty.'

The perfectly shaped phallus with the crust as pedestal has been sculpted by a bird's beak. Delicately pecked so that the surface is as smooth as white bread cut with a finely serrated knife. We stare wanly at the child and her find, then we laugh. Tears run down Moira's face as she laughs. When she recovers her voice is stern. 'What are you doing outside at this hour? Don't you know it's ten o'clock? Where's Carol?

Carol bursts in shouting. 'Do you know what? There are two African men in the playhouse, in our playhouse, and they've got sleeping bags. Two grown-ups can't sleep in there! And I went to tell Susie but she won't open the door. She spoke to me through the window and she said it's time to go to bed. But there's other people in her room. I heard them. And Susie shouldn't give people my sleeping bag.'

Moira waves her arm at Carol throughout this excited account, her finger across her lips in an attempt to quieten the child.

'Ssht, ssht, for God's sake, ssht,' she hisses. 'Now you are not to prowl around outside at night and you are not to interfere in Susie's affairs. You know people have problems with passes and it's silly to talk about such things. Daddy'll be very cross if he knew that you're still up and messing about outside. I suggest you say nothing to him, nothing at all, and creep to bed as quietly as you can.'

She takes the children by the hands and leads them out of the room. Moments later she returns to carry off the little one sleeping on the bench. I start to clear the table and when she joins me she smiles.

'Aren't children dreadful? They can't be trusted an inch. I clean forgot about them, and they'll do anything not to go to bed. When adults long to get to bed at a reasonable hour which is always earlier than we can manage ... Of course sleep really becomes a precious commodity when you have children. Broken nights and all that. No,' she laughs, looking me straight in the eye, 'I can't see you ever coping with children.'

The dishes are done. There is a semblance of order which clearly pleases Moira. She looks around the kitchen appreciatively then yawns. 'We must go to bed. Go ahead, use the bathroom first. I'll get the windows and doors shut. Sleep well.'

I have one of the children's bedrooms. For a while I sit on the floor; the little painted chair will not accommodate me, grotesque in the Lilliputian world of the child. Gingerly I lay my clothes across the chair. It is not especially hot, but I open the window. For a while. I lie in my night-dress on the chaste little bed and try to read. The words dance and my eyes sting under heavy lids. But I wait. I stretch my eyes wide open and follow a mad moth circling the rabbit-shaped lamp by the side of the bed. I start to the mesmerising scent of crushed gardenia when the book slips and slips from under my fingers. In this diminutive world it does not fall with a thud. But I am awake once more. I wait.

Ernst Havemann

A Farm at Raraba

from *Bloodsong and Other Stories of South Africa* (1987)

My late dad was a magnificent shot. One time when we were hunting in the Low Veld and had paused for a smoke, there was the yelp of a wild dog, and a troop of impala came bounding over the tall grass. Opposite us, three hundred yards off, was a stony ridge like a wall, six feet high. You would think those buck would avoid it, but no, they went straight at it. One after the other, without pausing or swerving, they leapt over it. They cleared it by three or four feet. I tell you, friend, it was a beautiful sight. You can't beat Nature for beauty, eh.

By the time the first two impala were over the ridge, late Dad was ready, and as the next one leapt, Dad got him. In mid-air. Same with the next one, and the next, and the next. And the next. And the next. That was six buck, one after the other.

Do you know, the wild dogs chasing those buck didn't pause for the impala that late Dad had killed. They didn't even react to the shots. They just followed one particular buck that they had marked, and we saw them pull it down a couple of minutes later. You've got to hand it to Nature; she knows what she's doing.

But the most wonderful thing was when we got to the dead impala. Four of them were piled one on top of the other, neatly, like sacks in a store. Late Dad had shot each of them through the heart, at exactly the same point in its leap. The other two had been a bit slow. Late Dad had got each of them in the shoulder. If you can't get a head or a heart shot, the next best is the shoulder, because there's a lot of bone there, and if you hit bone it brings a creature down. It can't run, you see. The worst place is behind the heart, because then your bullet goes through a lot of soft entrails, eh. A gut-shot animal will sometimes run a couple of miles before it drops and you may never find it. When I hear of fellows shooting like that, it makes me want to put a slug into their guts and see how they would like to die that way.

Those impala were a bit of a problem. We only had a licence for two and we only had the two mules we were riding. But God sent the ravens to Elijah, eh, so he sent us this Hottentot, Khamatjie. He worked crops on a share on the same farm as late Dad, but he was luckier with his farming – they lived on the smell of an oil rag, those bastards. I don't mean 'bastard' in a nasty way. I just mean there was a white father or grandfather, you understand. Well, thank God, this Khamatjie pitches up with his Ford pick-up and a mincing machine, because he thought he would shoot a zebra. Nobody wants to eat zebra, but when it's sausage it's lovely; you call it beef or koodoo or eland. Late Dad and Khamatjie and I made impala sausages for two days.

In front of other white people Dad always treated Khamatjie like dirt, but otherwise he was very respectful, because he was always borrowing money from Khamatjie and getting drunk with him. He said Khamatjie didn't mind supplying the brandy so long as he could say he drank with a white man.

The training late Dad gave me in bushcraft and using a rifle came in pretty handy when I was on the border of South-West, doing my army service. The call-up interrupts a man's career, if he's got a career, but a fellow that hasn't had army has missed an experience – the outdoor life, learning about musketry and map reading and section leading, and who's what in these little frontline states, and the tribes and the various movements in Angola and Caprivi and Botswana. The big thing, though, is the campanionship. Until you've marched with four hundred other chaps, all in step, all singing 'Sarie Marais' or 'Lili Marlene' or 'You can do with your loo loo what you will' – until you've sat with five or six buddies in an ambush, not daring to take a breath in a case a guerrilla gets you – until you've done things like that, you don't know what loving your land and your folk is.

Out there, in the bundu, the action is sort of clean, like they say it was in North Africa when we were fighting Rommel in late Dad's war. Not like shooting little black schoolgirls in the bum from inside an armoured car. How brave does a fellow have to be for that? I wonder what these township heroes would do if they were faced with Swapo guerrillas like my lot were.

Because I was keen and liked the bush, eh, I got to be a sergeant, and they gave me six munts they had scratched up in Damaraland, and sent us off across the border into Angola. An intelligence probe, they said. Just these six munts, and me, and an intelligence corporal named Johan. He had had a course of interrogation training and his main job was to train these munts to get information out of prisoners. Scary stuff, man. You've got to hate a person to do it properly, or just hate people, eh.

Our first ten days on patrol yielded nothing. Then on the eleventh day, I had left Johan and the munts to fix our bivvie for the night while I went ahead for a looksee, at a big granite outcrop about two miles ahead. Just before I got to it there were shots from our camp, then some answering shots, then silence. I hid and waited quietly. After five minutes I saw four Swapies, running for all they were worth, along the side of a kopje half a mile away. They disappeared behind a dune, then bunched up on the big granite outcrop before the first Swapie launched himself off it to cross a crevasse. By that time I was ready, and I got him as he jumped. The next one was too close behind to stop, and I dropped him and number three as fast as it takes to press the trigger. The last one in the bunch pulled back, but I was quick and ready. I hit him, too. I heard the bullet ricochet off the rock, so I reckoned he was probably only wounded.

I was sure the first three would be dead, and I thought, Late Dad, look at that! Three in mid-air! And they're not impala, Dad. They're Royal Game.

Do you know about Royal Game? Late Dad told me, in the old days, before we became the Republic, anything that you were not allowed to shoot, because it was rare or useful, like tickbirds or ibises or oribi, was called Royal Game. Kids in those days believed it was because these birds or animals were reserved for the Royal Family to shoot. Fancy Prince Charles potting away at a flock of egrets or an iguana, eh! So Dad and his friends called desert natives Royal Game, because they are wild but you're not allowed to shoot them, see?

Like I told you, man, I can't bear to think of a gutshot animal, lying in pain for hours. I felt the same way about this guerrilla, but I was on edge too. They say a wounded lion or buffalo is the most dangerous game in the wild, because he stalks the hunter. A wounded munt guerrilla must be worse, because he's got more IQ, eh, so I circled very cautiously round the granite rock. When I got opposite the crevasse I could see three bodies, one on top of the other, quite still. At eight hundred yards, three in three shots, it's a satisfaction, man.

And there, thank God, was guerrilla number four, just round the corner. He was standing upright in a narrow cleft in the rock, with one foot apparently stuck, and he was gripping his left bicep. A pressure point, I supposed. Through my field glasses I could see his left sleeve was a thick mat of blood. So all I had got was his arm. I found myself making excuses, thinking I had been slow because I used a peepsight. Late Dad always shot over open sights; he reckoned a sniper's eye aimed his hand, like a cowboy with a pistol, or a kid with a catapult.

The guerrilla's rifle was wedged above his head. For safety's sake I put a bullet into it. That left him unlikely to do much damage. When I edged my way closer I saw his leg was held fast in a crack, so he really was stuck and helpless. He was one of those yellow Hottentot types, with spaces between his peppercorns of hair, about my age but as wrinkled as a prune. These Kalahari natives go like that by the time they're twenty: it's the sun or glands, I don't know. He was wearing a cast-off Cuban tunic.

I climbed up the rock and looked down on him, trying to remember the few words of local lingo I had picked up from my men, but when he heard me he said in Afrikaans, 'Good day, my baas.'

I was pleased, I can tell you. It meant I could interrogate him myself and, as he was our first prisoner, it would show Johan and my black soldiers that I was one step ahead of them, and it wasn't for nothing I was a sergeant.

The guerrilla bowed his head and pointed with his good hand. 'If you are going to shoot, make it two shots, please, so that I will be properly dead.'

'I don't shoot tethered goats,' I said.

After a moment or two he looked up. 'Can the goat have some water?'

'First, talk.'

'Yes, I talk, baas. What would baas like to talk about?'

I interrogated him, in the way we had been instructed, using trick questions and repetitions. In case he was lying or hiding anything I prodded his wounded arm once or twice. He bore it as if he had it coming to him, but he didn't appear to keep information back, and when his voice cracked I passed down my water bottle.

His name was Adoons, which is a jokey way of saying Adonis. It is what one calls a pet baboon. The farmer his family had worked for called him that. Eventually his own family stopped using the native name his father gave him and almost forgot it. It seemed to belong to someone else, Adoons said.

He had been a hunters' guide and a shepherd. When his family was pushed off the farm – for sheep stealing, it seemed – he joined the guerrillas who were fighting for Namibian independence. He had only the vaguest idea what the fighting was about. He knew it was against whites, but he had never heard of Namibia. Not surprising, when you think that there is no such place. He called it 'South-West,' just like we do. He moved from one guerrilla band to another, depending on how he liked the band's leader, and how much food or loot was available. His present band was under an Ndebele refugee from Zimbabwe. They were supposed to report to a General Kareo, but they had never seen him. I carefully recorded it all in my field notebook.

When I had done with questions, I sat back and lighted a cigarette. At the sound of the match he looked up. Smoking alone or drinking alone is not something a decent man wants to do; it's like making love alone, late Dad used to say. I gave Adoons the cigarette and lighted another one for myself.

He exhaled till his chest was flat, and then inhaled the smoke to fill his lungs. He held it for a long time before letting it out and saying, 'Thank you, baas. Baas is a good man.'

He smoked in deep gulps, keeping his head down. When he finished the cigarette he looked up. 'Why didn't baas shoot when I was full of smoke?'

'I told you I don't shoot jackal bait,' I said.

'I can see baas is a good man, but if baas's men find me here, they will do bad things to me. Perhaps it will take three days.'

'I will tell them you have already talked.'

'They will not care. They will torture me to make a game. My people will do it, too, if they catch one of your black soldiers. This is not Sunday school, my baas.'

'We don't torture prisoners,' I replied angrily. I knew he would not believe me.

'What will baas do with me?'

The fact was I didn't know what the hell I could do with Adoons. Once he has been interrogated, a native prisoner is worthless – worse, he would be a danger. He would have to be fed and guarded, and if he escaped he could give the enemy all sorts of valuable information. We didn't keep prisoners, except white men and Cubans: you can exchange or use them for propaganda.

As if sharing my problem, he said, 'Has baas perhaps room for another shepherd on baas's farm?'

'I haven't got a farm and if I wanted a shepherd I would not employ a bloody Hottentot rebel.'

'It is near sunset. Baas will go soon, before it gets dark. And when baas goes the hyenas will come. A hyena can bite right through a man's leg. A living man's leg.'

I looked down at his skinny leg disappearing into the rock cleft, then climbed down and looked at his imprisoned foot. All I had to do was untie the laces and manipulate his ankle to get his foot out, leaving the boot behind. Then I gave the empty boot a kick and it came loose, too. Adoons wriggled till he found a purchase for his toes and raised himself a few inches.

'Give me your hand, Hottentot,' I said. 'I'll pull you out.'

He put up his hand. I took him by the wrist and he clasped my wrist. With unexpected agility he braced his feet against the side of the cleft and scrambled up. I threw him his boot. When he stood up to catch it, his tunic opened to reveal a pistol loose in a leather holster on a broad, stylish belt round his waist.

He smiled shamefacedly. 'I took it from the policeman who arrest me for stealing sheep.'

'Is it loaded?'

'Oh, yes. Five bullets. I used one to learn to shoot it, but I've never fired it since. One has to be close to a man.'

'You could have shot me.'

'Yes, my baas. The pistol was stuck fast, like me, but when you were asking all those questions and leaning down to hear what I was saying, the barrel was pointing straight at you.'

'Why didn't you shoot?'

'If baas was dead I would still be stuck in that rock with no one to help me before the soldiers or the hyenas came.'

His wounded arm had been banged as he made his way up. It now began to bleed through the clot, not actively but *clthip, clthip, clthip.* Since I carried three field dressings, I could spare one. I dusted the antiseptic powder that came with it on Adoon's wound, bandaged it, and gave him one of the painkiller pills we were issued with.

'I would be a good shepherd for you. It is easy to work well for a kind master. Anyone can see baas will give good food, and a hut with a proper roof, and no sjambok whippings. Except for cheeky young men who have been to school.'

'Come on, we must find a shelter for the night,' I said. I didn't like the thought of the hyenas he had talked about.

'These pills are good. The pain is quiet. Baas is like a doctor, eh? A sheep farmer has to be a doctor. I am very good with karakul ewes at lambing time. Baas knows, for the best fur you must kill the lambs as soon as they are born. Stillborn lambs are better. Their skins shine like black nylon with water spilled on it. It's messy, clubbing and skinning the little things without damaging the pelts. It's sad to hear all those ewes baa-ing. The meat is only fit for cows and vultures. But the rich ladies want the pelts before they get woolly.'

He pointed out an overhanging rock twenty yards away. 'Shall we spend the night there? Out of the dew, and it's open only on one side.'

As we moved, I picked up dry sticks for kindling, but he put his hand on my arm. 'If the soldiers see me in the firelight, or my people see baas, they will shoot.'

I felt foolish and amateur.

'The dead men have clothes. Shall I fetch some?'

'We'll go together,' I said. I wasn't going to get myself ambushed.

We went round the rock to the little cliff where the bodies lay. He whistled in admiration. 'Baas shoots like a machine. These dead Ovambos look as if they've been arranged with a forklift truck.' He added proudly, 'I can drive a forklift. I learned on the sheep ranch.'

We collected a couple of goatskins, a bush shirt with only a small blood patch, a water bottle, and a haversack of boiled ears of corn. There were three rifles. I grabbed two and took the bolts out of them. Adoons had already taken possession of the third. He grinned mischievously as he worked the bolt and demonstrated how he could use the rifle by tucking its butt under his sound arm.

'Now we can help each other, eh, baas. Like that bird that sits in a crocodile's mouth and cleans bits of meat out from between the crocodile's teeth. The crocodile does not eat him.'

We settled down close together under the overhang and had an ear of corn each, and a pull from my hip flask. My dear old ma gave it to me when I was leaving for the border. 'When you put it to your lips, it is your old momma kissing you,' she said. I wondered what she would say if she knew she was kissing a Swapie Hottentot, too.

'Angora goats pay better than karakul sheep in the Dry Veld,' Adoons said. 'When I am the head shepherd, baas will give me a few sheep of my own. I will have a woman with buttocks that stick out so much you can use them for a step-ladder. Ai! What fat yellow legs that woman has!' He sucked his breath in lasciviously. 'Baas will have white girls in town but on the farm now and then a bushman girl. Ai, what a surprise he gets when he finds that the girl has an apron!' He described in detail the strip of skin some bushman women have hanging down from their gashes, and how some bushmen have an erection all the time, just like in the rock paintings.

I got sleepy and he shook me. 'No sleep tonight,' he said. 'Listen.' There were sounds of animals round the bodies. 'Better we talk. Also it is good for a man and his mate to chat, isn't it?'

'I thought you fellows didn't want white men to have farms,' I said. 'You want all the land for yourselves.'

'Oh, yes. Yes, that's right. General Kareo says I will have a farm of my own. And a hundred sheep.'

'Why stop at a hundred? Why not a thousand? Be a big boss. Make people call you "*Mr* Adoons." '

'How will I look after a thousand animals? I can't even count past twenty sheep without taking stones out of one pocket and putting them

in the other. No, not a thousand. Unless – unless bass was my foreman.'
He laughed like a drunkard. 'If my people win the war, will baas be my
foreman? Please. Baas could have the big farmhouse and a motor car.
Baas need not call me "baas", just "Mr Adoons". Everything my
foreman wants to do, he can do. Will my foreman be angry if some of the
shepherds hide away when the police visit?'

'If your lot were the government, they would be your policemen.'

'Policemen are policemen. Dogs' turds. Always after passes.'

'Your lot say there won't be passes anymore.'

'No passes! If people don't have passes, how can you trace a stock
thief? What will we do if bad Ovambo kaffirs steal my karakuls?'

'That's your problem. Perhaps you'll have to get fierce German guard
dogs.'

'Oh, yes. That's a clever idea. My foreman will always find a way.
Now, let's talk of nice things, not problems. What is baas's name?'

'Martinus.'

'That is a friendly name for a foreman. In the evenings, after the
shepherds have done their work and the sheep and goats are in their
thorn kraals, Mr Adoons and foreman Martinus will sit together and talk
and look at the veld. Ai, it's pretty country, between Platberg and the
Boa River. Short sweet grass and big flat-crown thorn trees for shade.
Animals eat the pods in the winter. There are eland and kudu and impala
and bushpigs, but enough grass for karakul sheep too.'

'Sounds all right,' I said.

'In the kloof there are wild bees and baboons. Ai, those baboons!
When a baboon finds a marula tree where the plums have fermented, he
gets as drunk as a man. Ai, those drunk baboons! The leopards eat only
baboons, never sheep.'

'Any water?'

'Water! There is the Boa River and big freshwater pans full of barbel
and eels and ducks, and widow birds with long black tails like church
deacons, and spur-wing geese on the mud flats. The place is called
Raraba. We shall sit and drink buchu brandy and talk. Or just sit silent,
like old friends do.'

'What the hell would you and I find to talk about?'

'Ai, pals' talk. About the grazing and the government and women and
hunting and what happens after you die. I suppose baas knows lots of
Jesus stories.'

'I don't like buchu,' I said.

'Do you like the kind of brandy called Commando? They say it is
good.'

'Klipdrif is the best kind.'

'Then we will have Klipdrif, Martinus.'

'If it's hot and dry, one could irrigate a few acres for a vineyard,' I said.

'Does Martinus know about wine?'

'My grandfather used to make wine with grapes from his backyard.'

'Ai, but this is lucky! So Foreman Martinus would grow grapes and make sweet wine. They say if you give a girl a bottle of that red Cape wine, her legs open before the bottle is finished. But I like brandy better.'

'Me too,' I said.

'Sometimes we will give a bottle of wine to the old people, too. On Mr Adoons's farm the labourers can stay even when they are too old to work. And when the rations are given out, the old people get meat and mealie-meal, too, just like the others. Is that right, Martinus?'

'If the baas says so,' I said.

At first light we stretched and scouted. There was no activity. Adoons tore a sleeve out of a dead guerrilla's shirt; I made a sling and tied his wounded arm against his chest. He kept a grip on the rifle all the time.

I offered him my flask, and we each took a swallow. He handed me one of the two ears of corn left in the haversack, and pointed south. 'Foreman Martinus must walk that way. I will go north.'

'Good luck, Mr Adoons. I'll come and visit you at your farm at Raraba after the war, and see if you still need a foreman.'

'Ai, Martinus,' he said, 'we will drink and talk, eh. Ai, how we will talk!' He knocked his rifle barrel against mine, like clinking a glass, and set off.

I slid behind the rock where I could watch him without exposing myself. Late Dad used to say if you trust a Hottentot you might as well wear a cobra for a necklace; so I kept my crossed hairs on him, expecting him to whirl round any moment and loose off, or to disappear behind a boulder or thick shrub and perhaps circle round to take me in the rear. However, he walked very deliberately up the hill, and did not dodge behind trees or rocks like an experienced veld man would, nor did he look back to see what I was doing.

When he reached the top of the kopje he stood for some moments silhouetted against the sky and waved his gun. Challenging me to shoot? When he disappeared over the top, I quickly shifted to another position a couple of hundred yards away so that if he crawled round to the side of the kopje I would be ready for him. By sun-up nothing had happened, so I decided he was on his way to find his band. He would probably keep the field dressing I put on his arm and pretend that he had shot a South African soldier.

I found my chaps easily enough – I told them I could have shot three or four of them if I had been a guerrilla – and sent them to see what they could find on the Swapies I had shot; even those fellows sometimes have letters or helpful papers.

You would think a man's second-in-command would want to say a warm word about the marksmanship. The blackies were impressed, but Johan said, 'You shouldn't have shot to kill, Sarge. We're not in the humane hunting business, you know. A dead Swapie is nafi, isn't he?' He liked showing off his intelligence jargon, like using 'nafi' to mean 'not available for interrogation.'

I shut up about Adoons. My blackies might have been able to pick up his trail and perhaps find him before he rejoined his lot, especially if his wound started bleeding again. Then, if they roughed him up a bit, he could hardly avoid giving the whole story away, and that would mean a court martial for me, wouldn't it?

We eventually caught a few Swapies. I did not like Johan's attitude, but he was right – a dead prisoner is nafi – so I shot for the leg and told the men to do the same. I stood by with a sub-machine-gun at the ready during the interrogations in case any of the prisoners knew about me and Adoons. Fortunately, none did.

When I finished my army I took my discharge there in South-West and went to have a look at the Platberg area and especially Raraba.

It is nice country, if you like desert, and a man could pick up a thousand hectares cheap from fellows who are getting cold feet about the UN. Also the market for Persian lamb – that's karakul – is looking up again, now that Greenpeace has stopped women from buying baby seal. Some sheep ranchers say they would send Greenpeace a donation if it wasn't for the currency restrictions.

I followed the Boa River up to Platberg. The river runs against the mountain cliffs, so there is no space in between for a farm. I thought I must have misunderstood Adoons.

That evening there was a drunk lying asleep in the gutter outside the hotel. The doorman laughed when I bent down to shake the man.

'Leave him, mister,' he said. 'He's happier in Raraba.'

It turns out that is what the Hottentots around there call a lullaby, a dreamland that is too nice to be real. At first I was disappointed. Then I thought, Just as well. Suppose a man had a nice sheep ranch, and then one day a bloody old yellow Hottentot pitched up and said, 'Martinus, old friend, do you remember your baas, Mr Adoons? I've brought a bottle of Klipdrif brandy. That's the kind you like, isn't it? Let us sit and drink and talk pal's talk.'

It would be embarrassing, eh.

Ivan Vladislavic

Journal of a Wall

from *Missing Persons* (1989)

31 May

I have a feeling that I am starting this too late.

It is hardly three weeks since he started the wall – but already he has laid the foundations. That is not too much to catch up, perhaps. But it would have been pleasantly symmetrical to have begun on the same day, to have taken up my pen as he took up his trowel.

I should have foreseen it all. I had a sense, when they delivered the bricks, that something in which I would have a part was beginning. If I had not been watching from behind the curtains in my lounge, like a spy, perhaps it would have been clear to me that I was meant to be more than an observer.

They brought the bricks almost three weeks ago. Saturday 11 May, as I look at my calendar. I was watching the cricket on television when I heard the truck stop across the road. The engine revved for several min-utes – I suppose the driver had gone in to check whether he was at the right address – and that's why I went to investigate.

When I looked out through the curtains he was crossing the lawn with a man wearing blue overalls. His wife was watching from the veranda.

The bricks were packed incongruously in huge plastic bags, very strong plastic, I suppose. He went straight up to the truck, put one foot on the rear wheel and hoisted himself up. He took out a pocket-knife and cut a slit in the plastic, put his finger in to touch the bricks. He held his hand there for a minute, as if he was taking a pulse. Then he put his eye to the slit. It took a long time before he was satisfied. I had an inkling then that something important was beginning. I should have fetched a pen and started recording immediately. I would have had the details now, those all-important beginning moments. Already the memories are fading: I can't remember when she went back inside, for instance, but I don't think that she watched the unloading.

He supervised that task himself. It didn't take long. I wished that the bricks weren't wrapped in plastic; then they could have been passed along a chain of sure hands from the back of the truck to a corner of the garden. Instead the driver of the truck operated a small crane mounted just behind the cab, and the man directed him to pile the bags of bricks one on top of the other on the pavement. I remember at least that there were nine bags. When that was over he went inside – it was probably then that I noticed she was gone – and returned with a pen to sign the delivery papers.

After the truck had gone he went straight back into the house. I was surprised. I expected him to examine the bricks again. But apparently he was satisfied.

I returned to the television set. The game was over. I watched for a while, hoping to get the final score. But I was restless. The news came on. It was Michael de Morgan. He told us there was unrest in the townships again. He showed us a funeral crowd being dispersed with tear-gas. A bus burned in the background. Then a camera in a moving car tracking along the naked faces of houses, and children peeling away from the vehicle like buck in the game reserve. A cloud of black smoke from a supermarket. Soldiers. Some people hurling bricks into the burning bus.

The following scenes may upset some viewers, Michael de Morgan said gently.

I switched off the set. I was upset enough.

I went back to the window. It was almost dark outside, the house across the road a blue shadow. But the front door was open, and in the glow from the lounge I could see him reclining in an easy chair on the veranda, with his feet up on a table, drinking a beer.

The pile of bricks was another dark shape in the twilight. From the way in which he was sitting, with his legs swung to one side, I would say that he was watching over them. He looked as if he was going to stay there all night. Or perhaps he was trying to decide what to build. Or had already decided and could see the final product, with each brick in place.

I was restless that evening, and upset and depressed. I drank too much. The room wanted to spin. That impulse came to me through the bed-springs, just a gentle tremor at first, but the walls of the house held fast. I put one foot on the floor, trying to weigh it down. Then it came again, the room trying to twist itself free from the rest of the house, rip up its tap-root and ascend into the sky. Plaster powder rained down on me as cracks chased through the walls and ran themselves into corners. Then the rafters cracked like ribs and the room began to turn. The whole place rattled and groaned, spun faster and faster, and then rose slowly like an ancient flying-machine, ripping roof-tiles like fingernails, tearing the sinew of electrical wiring, bursting the veins of waterpipes, up into the night sky.

I went to look through the bedroom window. The city was spread out below me like a map, but I couldn't get my bearings. There was my house, with its gaping wound. I felt a wind on my neck, and when I looked up I saw the ceiling drift away. The night, effervescent with stars, poured in.

I sat down on the end of my bed. The bricks began to peel away from the walls in squadrons and they flew down to my neighbour's house and assembled themselves into barbecues and watch-towers and gazebos and rondawels and bomb shelters. When all the walls had unravelled completely I was left floating on the raft of the floor, dragged by the currents of the sky this way and that, until the boards all rotted away below me and I sank down into my bathroom and got sick.

I woke up very late on Sunday morning, feeling terrible. It was several hours before I could bring myself to get up and take a shower. The room had fitted itself back into the house imperfectly, with the doors and windows in the wrong places, and the floors were awash with books, broken glass, clockwork, clothing, kindling. I decided to put off tidying up until after breakfast – which was lunch, actually.

While I was eating I suddenly remembered my neighbour's bricks, and rushed to the lounge window. I was surprised and hurt to discover that he had already started work without me. He was digging a trench along the boundary of his property, where the fence used to be. The fence posts were still there, but the wire itself lay in a huge buckled roll on the front lawn. A wall! Of course.

After some minutes of watching him I hit on a plan for getting a closer view of the building operations. I strolled to the shop, bought the Sunday paper, and then took a slightly longer route which would take me past his house on my way home. It worked perfectly. I stopped to tie my shoe-laces, which I had cunningly loosened before I rounded the corner, so that I could get a good look at the trench and, indeed, at him. Fortunately, he was working with his back to me.

The trench seemed to me inordinately deep – although I must say that I have never actually built a wall myself – eighteen inches or more. And at least two foot across. It was possible that he was planning to build an extremely thick, high wall of the kind that is fairly common in our suburb, in which case the foundations would have to be secure. But I was more inclined to think that he was simply an amateur. He didn't look as if he had built a wall before either.

Frankly, he was a disappointment to me. It was the first time I had really seen him from close range. Indeed, until the day before it would be true to say that I had never seen him. He was simply the driver of a car or the pusher of a lawn-mower. My first real glimpse of him, swinging up onto the truck, had convinced me that he was strong, seasoned, capable. Now I saw how wrong I was. He had taken off his shirt (it hung limply on one of the fence posts) and his back was pale and flabby. His neck was burnt slightly red. He was wearing long pants, which looked clean and ironed, not at all like work pants. What bothered me most was the way in which he swung the pick; there was no conviction in it at all. I wished that I could get a look at his hands.

Of course, I probably didn't think all this in the time it takes to tie a shoe-lace: it is more likely that I simply observed and then thought about it all later, as I read my newspaper and in a deck-chair in the front garden.

I spent the better part of the afternoon watching him from behind the paper. He never looked my way once. He worked very slowly, but steadily, and by five o'clock, when it had become quite cool and almost time for me to go in, he had finished the trench. He put on his shirt and fetched her out of the house to review the day's achievements. He seemed very pleased with himself: he even sprang into the hole and did a little jig for her, and that made me like him more. And she put her arm around his shoulders when they went back in, and that made me proud of her too.

I waited for a few minutes, thinking that they would perhaps come out onto the veranda for sundowners, but the door remained closed, and eventually I also had to go in. Nothing happened for a week. I had hoped that he would not do any more building while I was away at work. I noted with relief that he was waiting for the following weekend. The week dragged.

Once or twice during the week I saw him inspecting the trench after work, probably checking for subsidence; and once or twice when my evening strolls took me past the trench I too was able to make a quick examination. It seemed to be holding up well. On those occasions I also managed to get a closer look at the bricks. He seemed to have forgotten about them. I admired that in him – his patience, his faith. It is possible, of course, that he inspected the bricks late at night after I had gone to sleep, but I doubt it.

Their habits seemed to be fairly steady. He usually came in at about five-thirty and put the car straight in the garage. They didn't go out much. They would watch television every night until about ten-thirty and then retire to bed. The television was on from about six, and so I presumed that either they ate as soon as he came in from work or they took their meals in front of the set.

I speculated about the programmes they watched. Did the news upset them ? I for one was finding the news depressing – full of death and de-struction. Who would build amid these ruins? I used to stand behind my curtain and look across at their lounge window, flickering blue as a screen. What on earth were they shoring up?

On the following Saturday (this would have been the 18th of May) I was up early, early enough to see the building sand delivered. Would that I had been ready with pen and paper to describe how the mountain of fine white sand slid from the back of the tip-truck, and the great cloud of dust that boiled up and hung over the houses.

I knew when I saw that perfect dune, white as flour, spilling over the kerb and the pavement, that the foundations would be laid that day. He materialised out of the dust-storm, wearing a blue T-shirt this time but the same pants (fortunately starting to look a little grubby and crumpled) and carrying a spade and a bucket of water. He stood for a while staring into the dust as if waiting for instructions. Then he set to, separating a pile of the sand and shovelling it onto a sheet of corrugated-iron. He seemed a little more lively this morning. I was pleased. There was quite a spring in his step as he went off to the garage.

The combined haze of the dust-cloud and the net curtain behind which I was standing was making it very difficult for me to see what was going on. By this time a sense was growing in me that it was very important to catch every detail, although I was still blind to the fact that I should have been writing it all down as it happened.

There he was returning with a bag of cement on his shoulder. I could see him quite clearly for a while but then he was back in the haze.

I paced my lounge, searching for an excuse to get closer to him. The one I finally found was a little obvious perhaps, but he generally seemed to take no notice of me, so I decided to chance it. I pulled my car out of the garage, fetched a bucket of water, and started to wash the wind-screen. By now the dust had settled somewhat, and I was surprised to see her coming into view. She was sitting on a kitchen chair, and wearing a pale-pink dressing-gown. She was holding a book, and at first I thought she was reading. Then it seemed to me that she was reading out instruc-tions. As I watched he measured out a quantity of cement in a tin and sprinkled it over the sand. He looked at her. She spoke again. He mixed the sand and the cement with the spade and shaped it into a dam.

Jesus! I said to myself, they're following a recipe.

Then I realised with a start that I was staring. I quickly dipped my sponge in the water and sloshed it over the roof of the car. Schooled my arm to keep rubbing as I watched.

When he had finished the mixing he put the cement in a wheelbarrow and carried it to the beginning of the trench. She walked with him, reading all the way, and watched over him as he tipped the cement into the trench and smoothed it with a length of wood.

And so it went. After the third trip she went inside – presumably he had memorised the procedure – and I did not see her again that day. When he broke for lunch so did I. When I heard the spade clattering on the corrugated-iron again a half-hour later I went back to washing the car.

He worked as doggedly laying the foundations as he had done digging the trench, and I found my admiration for him growing. After a whole day of washing my car I was exhausted; he neither slackened nor speeded up as he approached the end of the trench, just worked on at the same relentlessly steady pace. He seemed to me to be a remarkable example of soldiering on. I needed to take a leaf out of his book. I thanked him silently as he set to cleaning the wheelbarrow and the spade with meticulous care.

I resolved to try and follow his example in the week ahead. It would be at least a week before the building proper could being; the foundations would have to settle. He would be patient, and so would I.

On the Monday evening after he had laid the foundations I saw him come home from work. After he had put the car in the garage and closed the door I expected him to walk down to the building-site for some kind of inspection. But he went straight inside. It made me feel a little foolish, as if I was letting the side down. I put the whole thing out of my mind. Yet I was waiting for the weekend with a growing sense of anticipation.

So I was immediately uneasy when he parked the car in the driveway on Friday evening, instead of putting it in the garage as usual. He hurried inside. Surely they weren't planning to go out? I had specifically decided to get an early night so that I would be fresh for the next day's building, and I expected him to do the same.

I was alarmed when he came out just a few minutes later carrying a suitcase. He put it in the boot and went back inside. Could it be true? Would they go away on such an important weekend? It was inconceivable. I brought a bottle over to the window and poured myself a large Scotch. There he was, coming out again. He went to the car and started cleaning the windscreen. Then I knew it was true. I finished the drink, poured another one. Perhaps they were going to the drive-in? With a suitcase? No ... He went back inside. The lights in the house went out one by one. Then they both came out of the front door. She was wearing a nightie and large pink slippers and carrying a suitcase, a smaller version of the one he had put in the boot. They left the hallway light burning. He took the case from her and they walked to the car. How could they do this to me!

I quickly opened the curtains, switched the light on, and stood in the centre of the window, one hand holding the bottle of Scotch and the other pressed against the glass. I stared hard at them, took a long swig from the bottle. The car still hadn't moved. Then she got out and went back inside. Going to check that the taps are off, I thought. The swines. She was back very quickly, carrying a book and something in a brown paper bag. She got in and he switched the interior light on. They both looked at the book. Now the car started, the tail-lights glowed red in the dusk, the car was reversing, they were driving away.

The inside of the car was a warm, light bubble. I saw his profile, and beyond it her face, as soft and ripe as a fruit. She was looking at him, or perhaps at me, and I wondered what she thought of me, weeping at my post, holding my pickled tongue in one cupped palm and the bloodied bayonet in the other.

I finished the Scotch and went for a walk. Oh, I walked all over the place, staring into the blank faces of walls, peering into the blind eyes of windows, shouting obscenities into the leafy ears of hedges. I made the dogs bark. I rattled gates and banged on doors. I put the fear of the devil into the whole suburb. Those sleeping houses, their gigantic gasping and snoring, their tossing and turning. I waded through drifts of dry leaves in the culverts. I left my footprints in flowerbeds. I beat their welcome mats against their front doors until their gardens choked on the dust of ten thousand five o'clock feet. The breeze smelt of formalin. Everything was covered in wax and powdered and pinned. I brought back a newspaper billboard that said THREE MORE DIE IN UNREST and it was easy to believe in unrest and death with the rattle of leaves in the throats of the drains, the letterboxes choked with pamphlets, the bottles of milk souring on the doorsteps.

I forgave them.

I went over just after midnight, in an overcoat, in a balaclava. I shone my torch along the length of the trench: it was looking good. In a few places the earth had subsided, and I cleared it with my hands, and swept up a few dry leaves.

I brought back with me a brick.

I put it on my desk, on an embroidered cloth, and turned the fluorescent lamp on it. It was an extraordinary brick. It looked so heavy, as if it had been hewn from solid rock in the quarries of some not yet discovered planet. It was reddish brown, with a cracked, cratered surface, and it was still warm to the touch. It looked as if it would plummet through the desk, the floor, sink down into the earth as if it were water.

Yet the more I looked at it, the more it looked like a familiar object. After a long time of watching it, it began to look like a loaf of bread, hot from the oven, steaming, fermenting inside.

I could hardly sleep that night with its hard presence in the house, its bubbling and hissing. But I eventually sank into the mottled depths of a dreamless sleep.

In the morning the brick had cooled. Its surface had hardened to a stiff crust.

I was tempted to keep it as some sort of memento. But by late afternoon I had begun to resent its stony silence, its impenetrable skin, and I resolved to return it to the pile as soon as it grew dark. I wanted to maintain some connection with it, however, so I marked each of its impassive faces with a small dot of white paint, and put it in the oven to dry.

When it was dark I took the brick over concealed in a folded newspaper which I carried under my arm. On the pavement I was suddenly tempted to explore the house and the back garden. The front lawn lay spread like a huge welcome mat, inviting me into the nooks and crannies of their private spaces. But I was afraid: someone could see me and mistake me for a burglar. So I returned the brick to its pile and carefully folded the plastic wrapper over it.

I was just turning back towards my own house when I spotted the letters, jutting like a tongue from the letterbox. I looked around quickly. There was no one in sight. I was bold enough to take the letters onto their veranda and skim through them in the light from behind the frosted panes of the front door. There were three letters. One was addressed to The Householder. The other two were addressed to Mr G.B. Groenewald. I returned the letters to the box and scurried home with my discovery.

Mr and Mrs Groenewald returned from their outing on Sunday evening. I was overjoyed to see them. I wanted them to know that I had taken good care of everything in their absence, so I flashed my lounge light in a cryptic morse of welcome and affection. No answering signal came. I suspect that they were tired from their journey and went straight to bed.

The week that followed was uneventful: we were all waiting for the weekend. Then today – yes, it is the 31st of May today – I finally realised what I had to do: I had to write it all down. I have laid my own foundations, and from now on it will be brick for word, word for brick. Tomorrow the building begins. I must have a good night's sleep.

1 June

7.15 a.m.
I have made my arrangements; I have pen and paper, I have a chair in front of the window. I set it all up last night. This morning I was up at six. Showered, shaved, put on my work clothes. Now I am waiting for us to begin.

8.30 a.m.
Here he comes. He is wearing the blue check and the trousers. He pauses on the top step of the veranda, looks out over his kingdom. Ah, if he knew that I was watching he wouldn't stretch in that bone-cracking way. He goes to the garage. He looks quite energetic, although a shadow of sleep drags across the lawn behind him. He opens the garage door, goes into the twilight. Comes out pushing the wheelbarrow loaded with a bag of cement, a spade, a box of tools. Goes to the beginning of the trench. Drags the piece of corrugated iron over, shovels sand onto it.

Let me leave him to mix while I describe briefly the sky behind him: It is a flat sky, like faded blue canvas. It could be dangling from the top of my window frame. At the bottom the canvas is notched raggedly by the roofs of the houses. A slight breeze comes up and the canvas sways: a black edge opens up between it and the houses, closes again as the breeze drops.

He has mixed the cement. He leaves it to set, pushes the barrow to the pile of bricks. He slits the plastic with one long, sure pass of the pocket-knife. There are beads of moisture on the plastic and they run to rivers as he peels it back from the wound. His hand goes in. Comes out with a brick. He weights it in his hand, turns it to look at it from all angles, puts it in the wheelbarrow. Reaches for another. If I had binoculars perhaps I would be able to tell, even at this distance, which brick is mine.

The wheelbarrow is full. He pushes it to the beginning of the trench. He takes a ball of string from the tool-box, stretches a length between the first fence post and the second, checks it with a spirit level. When he stands the string cuts him just below the knee. Surely that is too low? He kneads the cement with the back of the spade. He takes up his trowel. He goes down on his knees in the trench. He reaches for a brick. Weighs it. His hands go down into the earth. Damn! I can't see what he's doing. I've missed the laying of the first brick!

10.30 a.m.
He works incredibly slowly. As if there were only one place in the whole bloody wall where any particular brick will fit.

He has laid three courses so far, and has just started the fourth. This is the first course I can see clearly. He weighs each brick in his hand. Then he settles it on its dollop of cement, shuffles it in, taps it with the handle of the trowel, slices off the oozing cement, taps it again. Sometimes he starts over, scraping the surface clean, putting the brick aside and choosing another. I cannot see why. They look the same to me.

I wonder where she is? I expected her to be there for the first brick.

I should go over and speak to him. It would be simple. Perhaps he would welcome some discussion. I would suggest, for example, that he make the wall slightly higher: what good is a wall if one can see over it? I would also advise him to wear a hat – I could offer to lend him one of mine. He's not used to the sun.

I could tell him how interested I am in his project. That would surprise him. If I told him about my own plan to document the whole process and showed him the work I had done so far, perhaps he would let me bring a chair over and sit right there, where I could record smells, noises; perhaps he would answer a few questions about his motivations, and even listen to some constructive criticism.

On the other hand my interest could affect him badly. Perhaps I should let him carry on unhindered for a while, until we have a clearer picture of the road ahead.

12.30 p.m.
I am pleased to note that he has moved the string to shoulder height. But now he is going inside, probably for lunch.

2.45 p.m.
I don't know whether I will be able to keep this up. He loves this wall, every brick of it, but he loves it so passionlessly, with a love so methodical and disciplined, that it might as well be loathing.

He has loved his wall up to shoulder height, brick by careful brick, and now he fetches a step-ladder and the wall goes higher. He checks each course with the spirit-level, and then stands back to look at his work.

It is very boring to watch.

5.00 p.m.

He has finished work for the day. The wall is about two metres high. He has filled in the panel between the first two fence posts. Unless he speeds up considerably, I estimate that it will be several months before the wall is completed.

They are sitting now on the veranda. She came out a few minutes ago and put two beers on the table. Came down to inspect the wall. I couldn't see her response, because she looked at it from the inside, as if that was the more important side. But she seemed to say something to him, because he spoke and listened and then smiled. Then she went back to the veranda and sat in the other chair. They raised their glasses to one another and I raised mine too and clinked it against the window-pane.

2 June

It is Sunday evening. He has finished another panel. This morning he uprooted the second fence post and strung the marker between the wall and the third post.

I think that I have caught up with him only to become bored.

He is a machine. His hands repeat themselves – brick after brick after brick they open and shut like pliers. His flabby muscles contract and relax in a predictable rhythm.

I think I dislike him. Why must he weigh each brick and toss it over in his hand? Why must he tap each brick with the handle of the trowel, twice on one side, three times on the other, and once solidly in the middle, before he is satisfied? The man has no imagination. I can see already that his wall will be just another wall. An ordinary coincidence of bricks and mortar, presentably imperfect. It won't fall down, but then it won't fly either. He'll probably put plaster over his careful bricks and paint it green and people will think it was bought in a shop.

29 June

Today the wall finally passed the half-way mark. For the first time I can no longer see them as they drink their customary beer. I have resolved to speak to them before they disappear entirely.

30 June

I am writing this from the Cafe Zurich. I simply had to get out. I had to get away from them. I have delayed recording the events of yesterday evening because I needed time to calm down. I was so angry – and it will become clear that I had every reason to be – that I was sure my observations would seem spiteful and unfair.

But I think that I now have sufficient emotional distance from the incident to put it down objectively, as it happened.

During the course of yesterday afternoon, watching another panel of bricks edging up into the air, obscuring the house, I had become worried about the Groenewalds. More specifically, I had become worried about our relationship. There they were, celebrating the crossing of the half-way line, but hidden behind their wall. Here I was, celebrating the same occasion, but hidden behind my curtain. And just fifty metres or so separating us.

I began to regret my reticence. They were nice people, I knew. He was solid and reliable and purposeful. She was quiet and sweet and sensitive. They were my kind of people. If only I had broken the ice earlier. Now there was so much ground to be made up. Yet, at the same time, even though they were unaware of it, we had so much in common. The wall. They knew it from one side, I knew it from the other. I began to see it not so much as a barrier between us, but as a meeting-point. It was the thin line between pieces in a puzzle, the frontier on which both pieces become intelligible. Or perhaps it was like those optical puzzles in which you see the profile of a beautiful young woman or an old hag, but never both at the same time. I tossed these analogies around in my head, hoping to arrive at one I could share with them, an opening line I could call to them as I emerged from around the wall and took my first real steps into their lives. Eventually I decided to take a cup instead and ask for some sugar.

They were on the veranda, as I thought, drinking beer. They looked up as I crossed the lawn, suspiciously perhaps, although I couldn't see their expressions clearly in the blue gleam that the TV set in the lounge threw on them.

'Good evening Mr Groenewald, Mrs Groenewald,' I called, approaching them at a pace I thought they would appreciate, neither too fast nor too slow. 'I wonder if you could help me?'

He rose from his chair, put the beer on the table, and took one step to the edge of the veranda. She sat back in her chair and crossed her legs.

I stopped just below him but I spoke to her. 'I'm making a trifle and, you know how it is, I've run out of sugar for the custard. Could you spare me a bit, just until tomorrow?'

She rose quickly, took the cup from my hand, and went into the house. I took a few steps after her, drawn by the flickering blue of her retreating back, but he stepped towards the door, as if to block my path.

I was disappointed. I had hoped to gain access to the house, to measure their space against my imaginings. I heard the familiar fanfare announcing the six o'clock news. If only he would invite me in to watch the news with them: that would give us many opportunities to discuss the state of the country, the newest trouble spots, local and abroad, and get to know one another.

But he made no move. I realised quickly that the more important opportunity was right in my hands – to discuss the wall with its maker. She, after all, had as little to do with the wall as a trowel or a piece of string. It was just as well she had left us alone.

I turned slightly, so that my pose suggested that I was watching the wall.

'I've been following your progress with interest,' I said. 'Perhaps you have seen me? I live right across from you.'

'No,' he said.

'It's a fine wall,' I went on undaunted. After all, hadn't they been invisible to me for months, even years (I couldn't remember whether they had moved in before or after me). 'A very fine wall indeed. A little high perhaps. A little forbidding.'

'I would make it higher,' he said, 'but there are municipal regulations.'

I began to feel uneasy. He hadn't invited me to sit, so I perched on the edge of the veranda.

'Have you built a wall before?' I asked

'Many times,' he said. 'More times than I care to remember.'

That threw me. I was going to say that he was doing a good job, for a first attempt. But perhaps I would never have reached that line anyway, for it struck me then, with a sense of loss, that I couldn't see my house at all from this side. It had vanished completely. The sky above the wall was a blank, moronic space, as high as the stars. There was nothing in it that would provide comfort to a human heart, that would fill a human eye. The world beyond the wall was empty: there was not even a world there. Perhaps my house would be visible from the veranda? I stood, hoping to find a way up. But he had moved, while I was musing, to the top of the steps, and was looking back over his shoulder through the open window at the flickering television screen. The curtains were open. You could see right in. I moved towards the steps.

Just then she came out with the cup of sugar. She handed it down to me. It was very full and a few grains spilled onto my fingers.

'I'll replace it tomorrow. Thank you,' I said.

'Please don't bother,' she replied.

I had to leave. The lawn seemed vast. I crossed towards the hard edge of the wall, behind which the world was slowly materialising again. I had an extraordinary sense as I walked, somewhat stiffly, with the sugar trickling onto my fingers, that no eyes were on me. No one was watching me. I wanted to look back, but I couldn't. I couldn't confirm such an obvious insult.

I was mad as hell. I was in my lounge, where everything was still the same. I was mad as could be. I smashed up a chair. Still the rage wouldn't leave me. I smashed up a table. Then I started to feel better, pacing around among the splinters with a bottle of Scotch in my hand. Who the hell did they think they were, treating me like a dog? Who the fuck were they anyway? Lunatics, blind people, fat slobs, smug shit-houses.

I should have gone right into their house and smashed up a few things. That would have been perfect, with the news in the background. I would have shown them unrest and rioting and burning, in three dimensions. I would have given them wanton destruction of private property. I would have given them hell in the eye-level oven, and stonings with the bric-a-brac from the room divider. And then I would have left them uneasy calm after yesterday's violence.

But was it all worth it?

I sat down in the surviving chair and thought about it more carefully. They were such perverse people. What were they planning to do behind that ridiculous wall? Volkspele? Nude braaivleises? Secret nocturnal rituals accessible only to people in helicopters?

Fuck them. I had to tidy up.

17 August

The wall is almost finished.

I have not been thinking about it much. Of course, since the unfortunate incident with the sugar I've had to avoid them, to spare us all embarrassment. I have been going to work early and coming in late – and always careful to avert my gaze. Yet, out of the corner of my eye, as it were, I've watched the wall edge malevolently towards the end of the trench. There is not much space left for it to cross: scarcely a metre. That will be done next weekend and the betrayal will be complete.

I am no longer interested in them. They have blurred into the background out of which they came. But, for the sake of symmetry, I have decided to record the end of it all, the laying of the final brick. It seems necessary. Then I can be done with this journal.

24 August

He is almost finished. He is building the last panel from the garden side.

I have watched him slowly obliterated by his wall. Now all I can see is a pair of hands reaching up.

I imagine that she is there with him, holding a bottle of champagne. No doubt I will see the cork flying up to the stars.

But is there cause for celebration? No. Is there reason for building when things are falling down? No. Is there reason for drinking beer when people are starving? Probably not. Do two people and a bottle of champagne make sense when citizens are pitched against soldiers, when stones are thrown at tanks? Does private joy make sense in the face of public suffering?

There he begins the last course of bricks. How bored I am with the tired repetition of gesture. How bored I am with the familiar shapes of words. How bored I am with this journal. It's just a wall. That must be clear by now. Even a child could see it. And the words that go into it like bricks are as bland and heavy and worn as the metaphor itself.

He lays the last brick. But I have the last word.

THE END

Later that same evening:

I am writing simply because I cannot sleep. And the reason I cannot sleep is that those bastards across the road are having a party. A wall-warming, I suppose. The music is too loud. And the buzzing of voices! They have strung coloured lights in the trees. Candles are burning in paper bags on top of the wall. I would phone the police, but I have already smashed the telephone.

I would gather to me, if I could, the homeless and the hungry, the persecuted, the pursued, the forgotten, those without friends and neighbours, to march around the wall. We would be blowing paper trumpets left over from office parties, and banging on cake tins, and raising up a noise to wake the dead and bring the wall tumbling down.

8 September

Today there was something new attached to the wall: a FOR SALE notice.

17 September

Today a SOLD notice.

2 November

Today they left.

I went across and stood on the pavement to watch their household effects being put into the truck. It is all as I expected: the knotty pine, the wicker, the velveteen, the china, the cotton print, the plastic, the glass, the stainless-steel, the beaten copper.

I stood right next to the truck with my hands on my hips. I dared them to meet my eye but they seemed not to notice me, or not to care. They put a few boxes on the back seat of the car and they followed the pantechnicon. I watched until they disappeared.

The wall looked ashamed of itself.

9 November

The new people have moved in. They are simply people carrying boxes and banging doors. Good.

Today the municipality pruned all the trees in our suburb. The sky has opened up. The wall turns its back on the street. It is a beautiful sunny day. I must get out.

And I must remember to take a stroll past the wall some time and see if I can spot my brick.

David Medalie

The Shooting of the Christmas Cows

from *The Shooting of the Christmas Cows* (1990)

A good Impressionist painting is a memory as well as a vision. The painter is simultaneously the begetter of impressions and the recorder of their afterglow. That is what softens the mists, blurs the vineyards and canals, and makes tremulous the sunrises. To efface without excluding is the aim of the Impressionist painter. Most acts of memory do not accomplish that very fine balance; that is why they are inartistic.

This probably seems like some sort of preamble, but it is not meant to be. I am trying to recall what I can of the shooting of the Christmas Cows.

I remember that I awoke even earlier than necessary that morning, and that great feelings of excitement coincided with my waking moments. The excitement was like a squirming ball of kittens that I hugged to my chest and squeezed, if only to make them wriggle the more. My bedroom had been redecorated yet again, several weeks previously, this time in apricot and white, and the sunlight sidled in through the white lace curtains. This was a sun in immediate post-solstice prime, heady and lingering-long with the unleashed length of its African December days. The dressing-table and the headboard of the bed, which had been painted a fresh apricot colour, glowed now as if sunlight were not light but syrup. My rag dolls were arranged, as always, at the foot of the bed. On the dressing-table was a tiny porcelain figurine which Mother had given me for Christmas the year before. It was a milk-maid walking with her pail: her long skirt lay unruffled about her stockings, and her little feet seemed poised for skipping or effortless movement.

That bedroom was more important to Mother than it was to me. She loved it, even though she changed it so frequently, and even now I can see her, tall and brusque, arranging everything in it with deft movements of her hands, creating with undeniable craftmanship a sanctuary pristine. That bedroom was a dove egg lying in the heart of a flower. I would as soon have untidied anything in it as I would have sworn at the teacher at school, or thrown something at her. I maintained that room with dutiful reverence.

After the last redecoration, Mother surveyed the refurbished sanctum with evident satisfaction. She said. 'There, it's perfect. I have made it beautiful for my little girl, haven't I?'

That morning I dressed swiftly and carefully, putting on one of my newest summer dresses and, brushing my hair with swift strokes, I put it back with what we used to call an Alice band. I ran into Mother's room and woke her, gently but insistently. When she opened her eyes, I said, 'Let's go now, it's late.'

She glanced swiftly at her wrist-watch with her slightly narrowed blue eyes, and then shook her head. Mother always moved from sleep to full alertness without any intermediate period of sleepiness or languor. When she spoke, her voice was characteristically decisive: 'It's not late, it's far too early. They'll still be eating breakfast. It's not polite to arrive too early.'

I told her that Annemarie had said that I should come as early as possible, for we could spend only the morning together. I did not add that Annemarie had said that if I did not arrive early in the morning, I would miss the shooting of the Christmas cows. This I deliberately suppressed, for I did not want Mother to ask, with her peremptory voice, 'What do you mean? What is she talking about? The shooting of *what*?'

I would simply not have been able to answer. I had not the faintest notion what Christmas cows were, and why or how one shot at them. I had not been able to bring myself to ask this of the blissfully and energetically self-confident Annemarie. I merely knew that it was something I could not bear to miss.

While Mother dressed, I sat on the edge of her bed and waited. The sight of her, her sleek dark hair, her capable, faintly sallow hands, and her precise movements, aroused in me – as always – an emotion verging on awe. There was something so wordlessly hat-lifting about her, about her beige or cream skirts, her long leather boots, and her crocodile-skin handbags.

We ate a rather hurried breakfast and, before long, we were seated in the car, heading out of town to the farm where Annemarie and her family lived. Mother drove a steel-grey Jaguar. With its curious, elongated shape, and its unusual head-lamps, it looked like a gigantic bullet wearing pince-nez. Inside there were sheepskin seat-covers, and the dashboard gleamed with mysterious knobs and dials. The engine always seemed to hum dutifully, but Mother worked the gears as if she were scolding it for tardiness.

Within minutes we passed out of town, and sped along the open road. On either side of us were tall maize plants on the verge of coming into seed. Here and there one or two early plants had already done so, and they held their lone golden sprigs aloft. They were gawky green summer princesses, and the boldest amongst them waved the banners of fertility. There was an almost tactile sense of growth and dampness and process. It was a day bound by that process to the preceding day, and to the day that would come afterwards. The next day was the Day of Nativity itself, but a maize field in late December is too preoccupied with growth to pay much attention to birth and rebirth.

My impatience notwithstanding, we soon reached the turnoff to the farm. A large sign with the letters R.B. JOOSTE – WELGEVONDEN stood at the point where the tarred road and the gravel road met. There were rows of bluegum trees on either side of the gravel road, which lay between them like a long trail of scrambled eggs. Even in the still morning air, the blue-green leaves of the trees moved faintly. Bluegum trees seem always to have devoted their lives to eradicating stasis and symmetry. When they are still, they never seem wholly motionless, and when they are straight, they are never wholly perpendicular. They grow in uneven spurts, and they even die erratically, with a slow, gangrenous browning of each waving arm.

As we neared the house, I felt again the sensation of barely controlled excitement. Characteristically, my bladder stirred: like a well on a dark night, it could not fail to reflect the dangling of the stars.

Annemarie had unaccountably befriended me towards the end of that year, after ignoring me entirely for about ten months. Her company was sought after by the other children in the class; mine was not. Consequently, her befriending of me had the quality of a rich man's bestowing charity on one less fortunate than himself: the riches of the former are brought more sharply into focus because of what they mean to the latter. Nevertheless, I was elated when Annemarie accepted me as her friend. Then she said, 'Come and spend the day before Christmas with us on the farm. Come early, so that you can be there for the shooting of the Christmas cows. Ask your mother today.'

I obtained Mother's consent, omitting all mention of Christmas cows. We had been invited elsewhere for lunch, so it was agreed that Mother would fetch me towards noon.

Mother said, 'Annemarie? You never mentioned her before.'

I said, 'She's a new friend. She lives on a farm, on the Morgenzon road. We've passed it often – she says it's by those bluegums. It's not far.'

Mother said, 'All right. If it's convenient for her parents.'

Apparently it was, and so now the car swept along the gravel driveway to the farmhouse, with a sound as of steel teeth chewing something. The phrase murmured persistently amongst my thoughts: The Shooting of the Christmas Cows. The Shooting of the Christmas Cows. The rhythmical quality itself was suggestive. Perhaps it was all an esoteric pre-Christmas family ritual in which the Jooste family participated. Perhaps it was something peculiar to Afrikaans-speaking families. Perhaps they all shot Christmas cows today, just as they would eat delectable Christmas dishes tomorrow.

Annemarie was waiting impatiently for me outside the house, dancing excitedly from one foot to another, her pigtails whipping animatedly about her head. 'At last,' she muttered to me, but she greeted Mother with the meticulous politeness of rural Afrikaner children. Her father appeared at the back door. He walked slowly towards us, throwing me into a state of alarm. I had met him only once before and, although he seemed kind, he made me nervous. He greeted Mother with slow courtesy, shaking her slender hand with his own large, reddish one. He shook my hand too, and patted me on the head in an avuncular way. 'So, Estelle,' he said, 'you've come to spend the morning with us on the farm?'

I muttered, 'Yes, Oom. Thank you, Oom.'

Shyness lay upon my tongue like aphasia, and I studied my feet, not as if I'd never seen them before, but as if I never expected to see them again. The shyness from which I suffered was too raw to be called self-consciousness. It consisted of an unremitting desire to eradicate, somehow, the attention of all adults except Mother – and attention which not even benevolence could soften.

Mr Jooste invited Mother in for a cup of coffee. She declined, saying that she was pressed for time. She would call for me in a few hours, she said, and Annemarie's father inclined his head, simultaneously managing to suggest that he wished that she could stay longer, but that to demur would be impolite. Then Mother bent to kiss me, reminded me redundantly to behave myself, replaced the sunglasses on her nose, and was gone almost before the scent of her perfume had faded.

As soon as the car swept out of the driveway, Annemarie said, 'You're just in time. The boys are waiting down there. Come, quickly!'

Tugging at my hand, she led me to a small paddock a short distance from the farmhouse, where at least forty black men and youths were gathered. Some were lounging about, and others stood laughing and talking animatedly. Several very small children were there too, and they chased one another with cries of delight, while some older boys stood on the outskirts of the crowd, each holding a large plastic bag or hessian sack. The paddock was bounded by a tall wooden fence, and we clambered onto it – Annemarie with agility, myself with slow doggedness – and sat on top of it, with our legs dangling over the side. I felt the splintery texture of the wood through my thin summer dress, and I smelt the pitch with which the wood had been treated. It was dirtying my dress, I felt certain, and Mother's disapproval sounded in my ears, but there seemed little that could be done without imperilling Annemarie's good opinion of me, and so I ignored it as best I could.

One or two of the men greeted Annemarie, '*Sawubona, Nonna.*'

She responded to each greeting with nonchalant familiarity, '*Yebo*, Petrus. *Yebo*, Timothy. *Kunjani?*'

One man greeted me too, but I averted my face and pretended not to hear, for I didn't know the correct responses, those assured phrases which Annemarie produced so effortlessly.

There was a young man with a huge grin, which divided his face into mouth and eyes as the peeling of an orange divides the fruit into orange rind and orange proper. Throwing his shapeless hat into the air, he shouted suddenly, 'Heppie Krismass! Heppie Krismass!'

Laughing good-humouredly, the others took up the cry: 'Heppie Krismass! Heppie Krismass!'

Annemarie's jaws worked as she chewed on several long blades of grass. Her legs were brown and wiry, and covered with scratches and little scabs. She drummed with her bare heels against the wooden fence. I asked, 'Is this where the Christmas cows are shot?'

She said, 'Oh, yes. Pa deals it out here too. I've seen it every year since I was five. It's very exciting. You'll see.'

At this point, two cows were driven into the paddock by a young boy. Unperturbed by the large crowd, they immediately began cropping the grass, wrapping their tongues around the desired clump, and then pulling at it with ripping sounds. They were angular as only aged cows in poor condition can be. Their bodies were a mass of ridges and hollows and balloonings, like a landscape distorted by floods and droughts. Annemarie explained that they were both – or rather had been – dairy cows. the large one was a Friesland cow, with distinctive black-and-white markings. Her udder was grossly misshapen, one half strangely distended and considerably longer than the other half. Lopsided and flaccid, it swung between her legs as she walked. The other cow was a Jersey. She was a great deal smaller than the Friesland, and golden-dappled in colour, with huge protruding eyes like luminously convex pools.

Not long after the two cows had made their appearance, Mr Jooste and his son Hendrik – Annemarie's elder brother – were seen approaching the paddock. A large rifle was strapped to Mr Jooste's shoulder. The crowd renewed their cry with gusto, 'Heppie Krismass ! Heppie Krismass !'

Mr Jooste responded by letting off a shot into the air which produced hoots of laughter. Everything that occurred or was said seemed to enhance the general feeling of merriment and festivity. Annemarie laughed too, thumping energetically with her heels against the fence. Mr Jooste said something, and everyone laughed again. I asked Annemarie what he had said, and she replied, 'Oh, he says they've been drinking already, although it's not Christmas yet.'

I turned to look at Annemarie's brother. Hendrik Jooste was about sixteen years old, a lanky youth with short-cropped hair. He was twisting the lapels of his shirt. Whereas his sister was incorrigibly voluble, Hendrik always seemed to be reluctant to speak at all. When he did, it was as if he had first to rearrange pebbles in his cheeks, or as if his taciturnity was caused by his Adam's apple interfering, in some way, with the progress of sound.

Mr Jooste called Annemarie to him, and a long, vehement conversation ensued, which I was too far away to follow. Annemarie protested about something, gesticulated, pointed towards me, threw up her hands, and threatened with her expressive lower lip to set one of her tearful tantrums in motion. Finally, it seemed that her father relented, for she nodded vigorously, leaped into the air, and came skipping back to me. She greeted me with a broad grin somewhat lacking in teeth – Annemarie had been bankrupting the tooth fairy of late – and took me to a point a short distance away from the paddock, where, by standing on a mound of earth, we had a good view of the proceedings. She said, 'Pa says we can stay. We have to watch from here and not go any nearer. Pa says it's on condition that if you get scared and want to go to the house, you have to say so at once, and I have to take you without any argument and stay with you. He says I must remember that you're not used to all this. But you won't get scared, will you? There's nothing to be scared of. You don't want to go to the house, do you? We'll miss everything.'

I said, 'No.'

Annemarie thereupon ran about in circles, no doubt to express her approbation, as well as her general excitement. She hummed 'Silent Night, Holy Night' as she ran.

A young black man, standing a little apart from the others, was gazing at us. He did not avert his eyes when I looked at him, nor did he offer a greeting. His head was closely shaven, and he wore a dirty-looking green jacket and faded checked trousers. His gaze was neither curious nor hostile – merely direct and impassive. When Annemarie danced about, he smiled faintly, but not in a complicit or indulgent way. I asked Annemarie who he was. She said – loudly enough for him to hear that we were talking about him – 'Simon Mhlangu. He's only been here a few months. He works at the dairy. Pa says he works hard and doesn't shirk like most of the young men, or come to milk drunk on the weekends, but Pa says he's too sour and unfriendly, and not respectful enough.'

Mr Jooste could now be heard ordering everyone to stand well back, and yelling at some young boys who were wrestling on the grass, and who did not hear him at first. We could see everything that went on without having to crane our necks very much. We were almost in the middle of the crowd. A man standing next to me began to rummage in his pocket, and took out a large pocket-knife, the blade of which he wiped ceremoniously on a tuft of grass. I watched as Annemarie's father raised the rifle to his shoulder and aimed it at the large Friesland cow. A strange quiet descended: the uproarious children stood silently, the scuffling of the bags and sacks against the ground ceased, and even Mr Jooste's sheep-dog lay down and was motionless except for the flickering of its ears. The only sound was the distant stirring of the leaves of the bluegum trees, sighing – not *with* the wind, as is usual – but *at* the wind.

Then we heard a crack which sounded different from the shot which Mr Jooste had let off earlier in jest. It was like the sound a whip makes when a ringmaster cracks it.

The cow simply dropped. She fell suddenly and heavily, and emitted a loud grunt of apparent discomfort as she hit the ground. Her legs were folded under her in a splayed sort of way, and blades of grass still dangled from her mouth. The instant after she fell, several of the men leapt forward, with knives brandished, and the company at large stirred, like a leg shaking and stretching to free itself of a 'pins and needles' sensation. The men who had come forward pushed the jerking body of the cow onto its side, and one seized the head by the horns and bent it backwards, while another began to saw at the throat with a pocket-knife. There was a gurgling sound – clearly audible from where we stood – and then I saw a thick red stream that gushed onto the kikuyu grass and sprayed the faces and clothes of those men who didn't jump away in time, and there was a sound as of the sudden emptying of subterranean drains. The legs continued to kick furiously all the while, with a regular rather than a spasmodic movement, as if desperately trying to rid the body of an ever-tightening net. Annemarie had stood transfixed with rapt attention, and now turned to me with a shining face, and said, 'Pa says it's dead before it hits the ground, because it's been shot through the brain. It's just the nerves that make it kick like that. They cut the throat so that the blood can run out, and then the meat tastes better. Did you see how well Pa shoots?'

I nodded, but did not speak. Fixing me with a baleful look, she asked. 'You don't want to go back to the house, do you?'

I replied that I didn't. She turned back to the spectacle below us with evident relief.

The contortions of the curiously animate dead cow – so much like the twitching of a lizard's discarded tail – finally ceased. The gushing of blood from the hole in the throat slowed down to a slow dripping. The men drew back, and waited for the other cow to be shot. Mr Jooste now did something which surprised everyone. With deliberate and rather grand ceremoniousness, he turned to Hendrik, who stood beside him, and handed the gun over to him. Then he stepped back himself. As his son took the gun from him – his face pale and drawn – cheers and cries of encouragement rose up from the crowd, 'Yebo, Kleinbaas. Nguwe, Kleinbaas. Yebo.'

Annemarie danced on the spot with renewed excitement. She said, 'Oh, look. Hendrik is going to shoot. It'll be the first time. Hendrik is going to shoot.'

The second cow had paid little attention to the death of the first. Hendrik studied her for some moments before he raised the gun to take aim. When he did so, the near-palpable silence returned. It contrasted profoundly with the raucous cries of a minute or two earlier: death imminent, it seemed, was anticipated with silence; death achieved was greeted with noisy jubilation.

This time, when the sharp crack of the rifle was heard, a hoarse, bellowing sound rose, which ceased momentarily, and then began again. No one moved. The sound grew steadily louder. The Jersey cow was running in crazed and flailing circles around the paddock. She shook her head from side to side, and her tongue hung from her mouth as she emitted that great cry. Hendrik reloaded frantically, and fired again. This time he missed completely. The cow was still reeling, and long streams of saliva were dripping from her mouth and tongue. The blind sound of her cry continued throughout. Still the crowd of men and youths remained motionless, as if attempting to ignore politely the unwitting nakedness of someone.

Hendrik now seemed to be pleading with his father to take the gun from him. Mr Jooste – if my reading of the dumbshow was correct – refused and pointed towards the cow. Hendrik's face was very white as he raised the gun to take aim once more. Even Annemarie's tawny little body had not moved an inch. Annemarie's brother fired again, and this time the cow dropped to the ground. This was greeted by a loud cheer, and even more men than previously ran forward to help with the throat-cutting. Mr Jooste and his son both turned away, and, without any further exchange of words, returned to the house. Annemarie pulled me towards the paddock, saying, 'Come, now we must watch the skinning and cutting up.'

The adult men had spontaneously divided themselves into two groups, and were gathered now about the two carcasses. The young man who had beamed and grinned at us so impressively when we arrived, was now performing an energetic dance, slapping his hands against his gum-boots, and accepting good-naturedly the railing of the others. Simon Mhlangu, the dour young man, had betrayed no emotion whatsoever during the shooting of the cows. Now he was the first to begin skinning one of the carcasses, his head bowed with concentration, and transluscent droplets of sweat glistening on his forehead.

First, a long cut was made in the skin, all the way along the cow's underside. Then, with much laboured exertion, the men peeled off the skin by pressing with their fists at the place where the skin and the shiny grey-pink flesh were joined. Finally the cow's skin remained joined only to her backbone and her head, and she lay on her own skin, with her feet in the air. Even the huge udder of the Friesland cow was stripped of its skin, revealing a fatty, yellowish mass. The heads of the cows lay, blood-bespattered, and attached only tenuously to the rest of the carcass. The bulging eyes of the Jersey cow were dull now, like dusty black leather. Annemarie lifted the bottom lip away with her finger, and showed how the cow's teeth were worn to the gums and, in several places, missing entirely. That was how one knew, she explained, that the cow was very old. 'Her teeth are a mess. Did you ever see such a mess?' she asked and looked at me to see how well I was responding to all this. I merely shook my head. She evidently wanted to find some way of thanking me for not making her go back to the house, for she giggled in a conspiratorial way, and said, 'Maybe she didn't brush her teeth in the right way, like Miss Fourie said we must.' It was a circuitous way of re-affirming our friendship, which was, after all, a thing of the classroom, but I did not respond to that either.

They were using an axe to split the breastbone of the other cow, and splinters of bone flew about in the air for some moments. Numerous pairs of bloodied hands, unhurried but purposeful, busied themselves about the carcasses. From time to time, someone would get up to wipe off the worst of the blood against the long kikuyu grass. Some of the men began to sing, a repetitive song of choruses without verses, which moved amongst them with a slow, regular movement, like someone on a garden swing.

It was hot, and there were swarms of flies. They settled on the car-casses and, in particular, on the voluminous stomachs as they were lifted out onto the grass, leaving exposed a great cavern, dark red and ribbed with white bone. The huge stomachs were glossy-grey in colour, and the seemingly endless intestinal coils lay spread out on the grass with them. They split the stomachs open, and emptied them of their contents, which were mounds of wet green matter, overwhelmingly pungent. I took a few steps backwards at this point, but Annemarie remained unper-turbed.

Pieces of meat were rapidly being detached from the carcasses and borne off to the far end of the paddock, where they were laid in a neat row. Haunches lay with the hoof still attached, and there were pieces of the rib-cage, where the long white bones showed through like a section of corrugated-iron roofing. The skins were folded up, the heads were put to one side, and someone was sent to the house to tell Mr Jooste that the meat was ready for distribution.

He soon arrived with Hendrik, as before, in tow. Hendrik looked less pale, but not very much more at ease. Together they inspected the rows of meat. Once or twice, Mr Jooste ordered a regrouping of the pieces, or the cutting into two of a piece that he considered too large. Then he opened a large black book which he carried under his arm, and began to call out the names of the men, putting a tick next to their names after they had come forward and made their selection. Each man, after choosing the chunk of meat he wanted, called forward one of the youths or little boys, who would put it into his plastic bag or hessian sack. Some chose silently, and returned wordlessly to the assembled crowd. Others said, '*Dankie, my baas. Baie dankie.*'

The names of the older men were called first. When the younger men were called, several pieces of meat that were appreciably larger than the rest still remained. Mr Jooste now intervened when the men made their selections, directing them to take this piece or that. Simon Mhlangu's name was called, and he moved purposefully towards a large haunch, and lifted it up by the hoof. Mr Jooste said, 'No, no. Not that one. Here take one of these.'

Simon Mhlangu did not answer. He remained clutching the meat by the hoof, and stared unblinkingly ahead of him. Annemarie's father said, 'What's the matter with you? I said take this one.'

Still the black man made no movement. Speaking slowly and thickly, he said. 'I want this one.'

In a voice of rising irritation, Mr Jooste said, 'Have you got a wife? *Unomfazi wena?*' Simon Mhlangu shook his head. The farmer replied, 'then you must take a small piece. The big pieces are for the men with families.'

Still clutching the meat, Simon Mhlangu said, 'I work hard. I take this one.'

'I'm not going to stand here all day and argue with you,' the farmer said. 'You take a small piece or you get nothing.'

Several of the other men uttered what seemed like warnings or remarks intended to dissuade the dour young man, but he lifted the haunch even higher, and said something in Zulu. It was almost unbearably hot now. The sun stood high, like a golden monocle on the limitless blue eye of the sky. Flies settled on the piece of meat, even as he held it up into the air. 'You take a small piece', Mr Jooste repeated, 'or you get no meat for Christmas. That's the end of the story.'

Simon Mhlangu hurled the haunch of meat at Mr Jooste. It landed, with a slurpy sort of thud, on the grass in front of the farmer's feet.

In a low voice, Mr Jooste said, 'Get off this farm. You get off this farm. Tomorrow, if you're still on the farm, I call the police. Do you understand me? Now go.'

Turning to go, Simon Mhlangu spat on the ground in front of him. He said, 'I go. I go. I work hard for you all year, you must not tell me what to take. I must take the piece I want.' He strode away, fixing his gaze on Annemarie and me as he left. His eyes were baleful and red-flecked, and he made me want to look away, although I didn't.

Mr Jooste turned to Hendrik and, in a clearly audible voice, said, 'That's the trouble with them. You give them something and they behave as if it's their right.'

The handing-out of the meat continued without further incident. At the end, there were a few small pieces of meat left over, and Mr Jooste gave them to those whom he felt had perhaps not received a sufficiently large share, or who had distinguished themselves in some way during the course of the year. The young boys ran a race, which provoked much interest, and the winner and runner-up were each given one of the heads. Then Mr Jooste fired the rifle into the air, and said, 'Happy Christmas. All right, that's it. Happy Christmas. You must all be back at work on Thursday.'

We turned to go back to the house, and at that point I saw Mother's car pulling up in the driveway in a skein of whitish dust. As soon as we were close enough to catch a glimpse of her, I broke away from Annemarie and her father and brother, and ran towards Mother. I flung myself against her with some force, and cried harsh sobs into the folds of her skirt. When Mother asked me what the matter was, I didn't answer. 'Tell me what it is,' she said, but I merely continued to cry. Mother said, 'Mr Jooste, may I know what is going on?'

Mr Jooste addressed a few low words to Annemarie. A part of her indignant response was audible: 'But she *didn't*! She never said she wanted to go back to the house. I *asked* her. She never said a word.' Her father then turned to us and said, 'I am afraid we have succeeded in upsetting your daughter, but without intending to in any way. We allowed her to watcch the shooting of the cows, and perhaps we should not have done so. But she showed no sign of being upset until she saw you. I am truly sorry about it.'

There was silence for a few moments, and then Mother said, 'The *what*?' The *shooting of cows*? You made her watch the shooting of cows. How *dare* you subject her to that? I've never heard of such a thing in my life. Is that how you look after children that have been placed in your care?'

Mr Jooste answered, 'I do look after children who have been placed in my care, as you put it. I cannot guess what they are thinking or feeling if they don't say anything. I have apologised for allowing her to become upset. That is all I can say about it.'

My sobs had diluted themselves to a steady sniffle by now. I still held Mother's dress, but no longer buried my face in it. She looked down at me and said, 'Get in the car.'

She too got in, with a great slamming of the door. She started the car up with a toss of her head, and again I heard the wheels crushing the gravel beneath them, as we hurtled away from the farmhouse. I continued to sniffle all the way back to town.

On the way home, I had a mental picture, secret and organic like a flower growing in a cave. It was of Mother's car, entirely dismantled and broken up into little pieces. The pieces were laid out in a row on the grass. First I thought, 'They can't put it together again.' And then I thought, 'But nobody can eat it. Nobody can eat any of it.'

E. M. Macphail

Annual Migration

from *New Contrast* (1991)

Esther likes to leave at the end of summer, well before the first cold nights of the highveld winters. She returns after the early thunderstorms have begun and the jacaranda trees no longer stand in mauve pools of their own making. She stopped going to Europe when her children went to live in the States. But no matter what others may have to say she had met quite a few interesting, as well as friendly, people.

Esther is quite short. Although she isn't fat there is a roundness to her. When she accepts a second slice of cake, she always says with a conspiratorial smile: 'I eat too much. I must go on a diet.' She has neat hands which she uses prettily. They are smooth and white and surprisingly free of the brown smudges which litter her face. She speaks with a strong accent and can talk Russian, French, Italian and Yiddish.

Esther's daughter lives in Houston and her son in New York. After she'd stayed with him the first time her son gave her a book called *How to be a Jewish Mother* and told her to read it carefully. Later on she gave the book to Mrs Ginsberg who, Esther thought, could make better use of it than she could.

It had been a mistake to greet Mrs Ginsberg that first time. Esther, about to walk over to the shops, had stood in the entrance while the chauffeur held open the rear door of the big black car and the maid carried the handbag. She waited while Mrs Ginsberg moved slowly out through the heavy glass security doors on which is etched the name of the building. The hall porter made sure the double doors were firmly closed after they had passed through. All she had said, as she came alongside Mrs Ginsberg, was, 'Have a good day.' She hadn't meant anything by it. You heard it all the time in the States. Mrs Ginsberg turned around. 'What did you say?' she asked. So Esther repeated, 'Have a good day,' and she smiled the second time. But Mrs Ginsberg wanted to know why

she must have a good day that day. Which is what happens when you
only mean to be friendly. It didn't mean you wanted to be friends for the
rest of your life. Mrs Ginsberg had told her to sit in the back with her
even though Esther said she wanted the exercise. But Mrs Ginsberg said,
'It is too hot for walking. The wind will blow your hair. Also they are
snatching handbags.' When she asked, 'Are you shy because you haven't
got a car?' Esther gave in and sat beside her. By the time the chauffeur
parked as near to Woolworth's as he could, they each knew that the
other's children had left the country.

Esther said she went to visit her family at the beginning of May and,
although they would like her to stay longer, she always returned home
in the spring.

Every year Mrs Ginsberg's daughter brought her three children from
Australia and her son-in-law would come when he wasn't so busy. At
first when he was both working and studying at the university he
couldn't make it but it would be easier when he had his own business. He
was a lawyer. He had a very good brain.

'... and in Manhattan my son has his own apartment. New York is
called the Big Apple and it is very stimulating intellectually,' Esther said,
and added, 'It is good for the mind.'

Esther always stops off in New York first. Her unmarried son settled
there after his sister had written telling him about the opportunities for
dentists. She told him a guy could make a stack if he was prepared to
work hard, like after hours and especially at the weekends. New Yorkers
never seemed to go to bed. The movies even started at midnight and all
night long there were people in the streets. So why shouldn't they have
their teeth fixed at night? But how was Esther to know that his
apartment was also the rooms and the nurse his girl-friend? And there is
a new nurse every year. Who would want to stay for more than three
days if you have to wait until the last patient leaves before you can go to
bed on the convertible couch in the waiting room? And even with the
police sirens, the honking of fire engines and helicopters buzzing you
heard everything as well as that year's nurse telling her son to choose
between herself and that goddam *yenta*.

'My three grandchildren have more intellectuality than any other
children I know. When they were born I could tell they were special because their toes were curled up or not curled up — I can't remember
which — two hours after birth yet.' Mrs Ginsberg paused to take breath.
'... and now they must go to the school for children with special gifts.'
    '... New York has so much to give: the theatre, the latest foreign

films, the restaurants ... out of this world. And the shops ... fantastic.'
Esther rolled her eyeballs back and lifted both hands, palms outward with
spread fingers.

There was so much to remember about that first visit. There had been
the suitcase which friends advised Esther to take empty because the
shopping in the States — especially New York — was outstanding. But
she had been a whole month in Houston and her daughter still hadn't
found the time to take her to the shops. When the summer school
holidays started there was even less time. Her daughter never seemed to
sit down.

'And all of my grandchildren are fantastic artistic. And the little one
plays the violin yet. And, shame, it's nearly as big as her. And can you
believe it also, they are very good at netball,' Mrs Ginsberg said.
    'After the New York crowds and the theatre and everything it is good
to settle down in Houston and take things easy. Even if my unmarried
son wants me to stay longer. But I can't wait to see my grandchildren.
They scream with excitement when I arrive and they unpack all the presents.'

It is going on for three years since Esther and Mrs Ginsberg became
friends.
    After the long flight home Esther always hopes she will have a few
days to rest. But the servants talk and Mrs Ginsberg phones at once to
say it only seems the other day that she left. And is her son in New York
married yet.
    On her last trip to the States, Esther found out about telephone re-
corders and as soon as she returned she had one installed. Now it saves
her having to think up on-the-spot excuses for not going to the shops or
having coffee or listening to Mrs Ginsberg's youngest granddaughter
play the violin.
    How Esther had longed for the first letter after the family left. When
all the farewell parties were over and they were packed up at last and
ready to go, her daughter vowed she would write as soon as they arrived.
At the airport she comforted Esther and made her promise she would
visit them within a year. She told Esther's maid, who had also come to
say goodbye, to take care of her mother. Almost exactly a year after they
had gone, Esther herself was at Jan Smuts, leaving to visit the States for
the first time. She had wondered if her daughter's husband would be
more friendly than he used to be. Perhaps the thousands of kilometres
between them would have made a difference.

Right from the beginning Esther insisted on helping.

'Of course I know how to use a vacuum cleaner.'

'I never saw you use one when I lived at home.'

'So I can read the instructions,' Esther had answered.

She told her daughter not to rush back after taking the children to school. But rather to have coffee with her friends like she used to. But how was she to know that liquid detergent was not meant for dish-washers? Still, it hadn't taken the two of them long to mop up the foam before it reached the new rugs.

'... and it will save having to wash the floor,' Esther said.

'I never bloody wash the floor unless I bloody have to.'

There had been only one morning that Esther remembered being able to persuade her daughter to have a cup of tea. She had patted the seat next to her and they sat together on the settee.

'I would have taken the little ones to Bible studies if I wasn't nervous about driving on the wrong side of the road.' Esther sipped her tea and added, 'You must rest more. You're looking much older than when you left. You musn't neglect yourself.'

'What do you mean?'

'You know men are very quick to notice when their wives don't take care of themselves. You used to have your hair done every week at home.'

Her daughter hadn't answered. But Esther knew it was best for her to hear certain things from her mother.

She sighed. 'You know that girl of mine is getting lazier and lazier.'

'How?' her daughter asked.

'Well she doesn't make pudding as often as she used to. She thinks she can get away with just putting some fruit on the table.'

Accepting another slice of cake, Esther said, as she always does, 'I eat too much. I must go on a diet.'

She smiled as if making a joke.

All of a sudden her daughter had jumped up on the Chesterfield and let loose a long drawn-out scream.

'What is the matter? What is it?' Esther shouted. She had wondered if it was one of those goggas that used to upset her so.

'Is it a Parkview prawn?'

'Don't you know that life isn't just diets and hair and servants?' her daughter had shrieked.

Then, in the sudden silence, Esther asked if it was that time of the month. But the bellowing started again and, like a cow's, it was broken up by moments of quiet which had made Esther wonder if her daughter was beginning to pull herself together. But each time she stood up to help her down from the settee, she screamed, 'Leave me alone, leave me. *Voetsak.*'

Mrs Ginsberg's daughter still lives in Sydney and still brings her children to visit their granny every year. And her daughter's husband is making so much he can come for a month. First class. So there is plenty of time for him and her daughter to go to Botswana, the Kruger Park and the ones in Natal and Namibia. But the kids would only get restless so they must stay with their old granny. And if the weather is good at the Cape, their parents can fit in a few days there as well. Esther agrees that children can't be cooped up all day in a flat, even a penthouse yet. And, of course, they would get fed up being driven around by the chauffeur. She asks why she doesn't send them to the public library. But Mrs Ginsberg says they are never allowed to go anywhere on their own. They might get into trouble. One hears all the time what can happen. Esther says that the librarian will look after them. She has seen this already the first time she was in Houston.

Esther had found the library by accident. When she wasn't able to calm her daughter, she ran outside to find someone who might know what to do. She had seen a car backing into a parking bay just up the street, and she ran towards it, calling, 'Help. Please help me.' But as she came level, the driver changed his mind and drove off quickly. She pressed the bells on two different gates and, although she thought she saw a curtain move in one window, nobody answered. She ran through the little park in the middle of the next block, which was a mistake, because not only was there nobody in it, but she must have taken the wrong exit out of it. Suddenly, there had been so many people in a street which she didn't recognise. Each time she had tried to stop somebody, the person would look at her as if she was speaking a foreign language. If they were old, they shook their heads. If they were young, they looked her up and down and turned away. Perhaps it was her slippers. As she had stood wondering how to find her way back, she noticed an arrow above the words LENDING, READING and REFERENCE LIBRARY. Inside the building, with its high domed ceiling, the sudden shutting out of the traffic noises, as well as the SILENCE notice, made Esther pause. Instead of rushing, she had tiptoed over to the desk labelled INFORMATION.

The librarian had shown her how to find her way back on the street directory. Coming into the house quietly, she was relieved to find that the bellowing had stopped. She sat in her bedroom and listened to what the calm and very controlled voice said on the kitchen telephone. Americans don't use 'bloody' as a swear word and when Esther returns home it always surprises her to hear it so often. The voice had said, 'My mother must not stay in this bloody house any bloody longer. She must bloody fuckoff.' The voice had paused for a moment and then said, 'She talks about home all the time. She insists on helping and she just makes one bloody fuckup after another.' Again there was a pause. 'No of course she's not here.' Esther's shoulders relaxed and when the back door had banged, she had known that her grandchildren would be picked up from Bible studies in good time.

Once Esther has recovered from the long flight home — this last time she had hardly more than three hours' sleep — she phones Mrs Ginsberg and they arrange to have tea together. She always brings her something from the States. Once it was the book that Esther's son gave her about the irritating ways of Jewish mothers. This time it is a small Statue of Liberty with a black face.

The librarian in Houston had given Esther several brochures. One was about the Salvation Army, which claimed they never turned anyone away. She recalled seeing at home, at Christmas time, a woman in a bonnet, standing at the corner, shaking a tambourine, while a uniformed man played the bugle. Another pamphlet interested her more. The organisation described one of its activities as providing accommodation suitable for women, on their own, in strange towns. She had read on: 'The YWCA operates hotels and residences — one of its first objects is to provide safe, inexpensive and decent places for women to live — summer camps, programs of education and recreation, all without regard to the economic, racial or religious conditions of participants.'

Mrs Ginsberg has such a lot to tell Esther whenever she returns from the States. The Australian family will be arriving shortly and Mrs Ginsberg is glad their stay always coincides with Esther's return. She adds, 'And it looks as if they will be lucky with the weather. It is always perfect when they come. I don't know how they arrange it.'

'When I leave my grandchildren in Houston they ask every year why I don't stay with them for ever and ever.'

Mrs Ginsberg is very keen to hear if there are any signs of Esther's son getting married.

'Will you have your grandchildren to stay all the time?' Esther asks.

Mrs Ginsberg says, but of course they will stay with their granny who loves them so much. And this time she will tell the chauffeur to bring his children to play often.

The Houston librarian and Esther have become great friends. He says her grandchildren are the best behaved children he has ever had in his library. She keeps an eye on them in the afternoons while he tells her about his difficulties. How, in the school holidays, the mothers drop their children off with him. But even though he hires extra help in the summer, they can't stop them from fighting. Once he locked the doors and wouldn't allow them in. This was during the mayoral election and his action was called discriminatory by one of the political parties. Since then, he has never shut anyone out of his library. Esther doesn't mind listening. She feels she owes it to him. As soon as she sees her grandson starting to fidget, she sits down and reads the books they have chosen. And not just once. They only leave when neither of the children can think of another question to ask.

During the rest of that first time with her Houston family, Esther hadn't been able to help because of her back. It was for this reason, too, that when their annual holiday came up, she had asked if they would excuse her. And her son-in-law said, before they left, to be sure not to answer the front door and not on any account to go to the little park on the next block.

It had seemed a pity not to visit Boston while she had the opportunity. Also, it was a good chance to find out more about the YWCA, and Esther decided to go by Amtrak rather than fly. One could see more from a train. She remembers she had no trouble finding the place. It always surprises her how easy it is to get a cab in the States, while at home she has to book a taxi in advance. Right from stepping into the entrance – one could hardly have called it a foyer – she knew it was the right place to stay while deciding where to spend the winter months away from home in future. Esther can't remember exactly when her son and daughter first started telling her what was best for her. But now that she herself knows, she spends three nights in New York and two weeks in Houston. By moving from one Y to another she has found what suits her best. And it is Canada where, in Victoria, British Columbia, she rents a room and bath for four months every year. Her foreign travel allowance is enough and she meets others, like herself, who enjoy the concerts in the summer. She attends lectures, meets people from all over the place, sometimes even makes new friends. When they ask her where she learned to speak so many languages, she tells them she is a real wandering Jewess.

Deena Padayachee

The Finishing Touch

from *The Finishing Touch* (1992)

The shebeen was full of raucous people having a great old time. But Satha noticed that his friend Muthu didn't look too happy. The old man had come into the shebeen a few minutes before and simply plopped down into a chair. He had taken his first drink in one gulp and was now staring at his empty glass like a zombie. That wasn't like Muthu, ruminated Satha, not like Muthu at all. Satha went over to Muthu and focused bleary eyes glassily on his friend. He asked him why he was looking so depressed.

'That Trishen's robbing me blind, man.'

'He's running your Shakas hardware shop for you, eh, Muthu?'

'Ja, and the money he's bringing in isn't 'nough to pay the bleddy rent!'

'But why for you renting that small shop when you own a nice, big hardware store next to your house?'

'It's for the licence – I run my big business on that small business' licence.'

'Ja,' Satha nodded sympathetically, 'I suppose it's difficult for our people to get a licence for a business?'

'Ja, man. Where a coolie like me's gonna get a licence from the Wurropean man?'

'Ja, that's true ... white people don't like giving us business licences, pity, man.'

'Ja,' commented Muthu, 'Europeans don't like competition from us Indians.'

Satha contemplated Muthu's morose face for a while. Then he said, 'Why you don't change your name? You know, to white people's name?'

'What! Can't do dat!'

'But can, man. Look my cousin-brother, his name's Jaybalan ... white people call him Jesse. He change his surname from Appadu to Appolos. That's a Greek name. When he write letter now to white man, the white man think him foreign-white man. He now getting top-class foreign-white treatment! You know foreign-whites getting best treatment in our country?'

'But he can only do this when he's writing to somebody?'

'Ja, but man, he getting lot privileges with letters ... because they thinking him one *witou*, not a bloody coolie!'

'But that must have been long ago?'

'No man, it's happening now. Yay! You go, change name from Coopoosamy to something important sounding. Now what I heard that Major Tate calling you? What was it, let me see ... Cooper, that's it, COOPER!'

'Go 'way man, you mad!'

'How then you gonna get licence? That Trishen's getting fat. You wasting time, money on that Shakas shop. You can't be two places one time. You got to look after one shop, man.'

'Ja, but the white man will never let me get a white man's name. Besides I'm not Christian.'

'Look, you Tamil, you always Tamil. This white name's just to bluff the *witous*. White name don't make you Christian. My cousin Jaybalan, he not Christian just because white people call him Jesse.'

'Ja, but I don't know, my family always had Indian name. What are my relatives gonna think?'

'Your relatives, they not clever like you. If they had half your brains they'd make money like you, and they too would have English names. What use our Indian names? Only get us into trouble.'

Muthu suddenly looked serious and sober, 'Ja, but it's like spitting on our ancestors, our culture; our names are symbolic of everything that gives us a rich heritage, our identity ...'

'Addah, man, what you talking? What's in a name? One name's as good as another. And you know for the white man we're nothing. We just non-whites. He know nutting 'bout our culture, 'bout us. We nothing for him. At least when we use his name we might get somewhere ... you not cross when the white customers call you Michael or Cooper?'

'No I'm not cross. But I donno, Satha, fifty years I been Muthusamy Coopoosamy, now suddenly you want me to be become Michael Cooper ... I don't know whether I can adjust to it.'

'For more than twenty years the white people kept name Michael for you. All you doing is making the thing legal, that's all.'

'Hell, I don't know ...'

'You'll adjust, man, we Indians know lot 'bout 'dapting. We good at it. The white man, he always closing the front door and we always finding the back door, the side door ...'

'Heck, Satha, I feel lousy 'bout this; these damn white people ... they name us like they name their cats and dogs and now we add insult to injury by going one step farther and making their 'pet-names' legal ...'

Satha was not to be put off, 'Well, you might feel bad about it, but man, it serves a higher purpose. It's gonna help your upliftment.'

Muthu looked away from Satha. For a few moments he became oblivious to the noise around him. He stared into space, much as he did when he played chess, and pondered what Satha had said. In a crazy way it made sense. It was not the first time he had been forced to eat humble pie in order to get ahead. And it was the kind of tactic that had helped people like him to survive.

'We make it by using the opportunity, seizing the initiative, not by sitting on our backsides and letting events overwhelm us! Sometimes it paid to sacrifice the Bishop and gain the Queen,' he reflected to himself. A gleam came into his eyes.

Satha noticed the change in Muthu's face, 'Look,' he said, I got one lawyer friend. He tell you.'

The lawyer confirmed Satha's story. Muthu thought about the matter for a few more weeks but there was no hope of getting his hardware licence through a normal application. It was a big thing changing his name, yet he had got used to being called Michael and Cooper. Even his friends and most of the Africans and Indians were calling him by these names. His wife didn't object and he had no children. He thought she actually liked the white name and often called him Michael. It was becoming the vogue for Indians to have shortened English names like Pat for Pathmanandan or Terence for Thenageran. Muthu felt very afraid and nervous, but he decided to put his faith in God and do what was necessary. He had very little land – certainly not enough to farm and survive on. So he had set up a hardware store in a *bundu* when other people thought that he was mad to do so. But he had stocked what the farmers had wanted and his prices were keen. He had behaved with humility and the white farmers had not felt threatened. It was to their advantage to buy from him rather than go to the distant white town and buy hardware.

So Muthu made the long journey to the Department of Indian Affairs in Tegwhite to change his name. He was directed through a maze of offices (and was often given wrong directions by irritable clerks) till he finally arrived at the section that handled many things, including name-changes. The waiting area was empty. The only person in the front office was an Indian clerk who was busy writing at his desk. The man noticed the sheepish-looking, badly dressed Indian come into the office but he continued writing. There were no seats in the reception area and there was just the one solitary desk behind the counter. A plastic name-plate on the desk proclaimed, 'Ahmed Mayet'. Muthu could see a closed door at the back of Ahmed's open office. The fancy brass name-plate had emblazoned on it: SENIOR SUPERVISOR and below it in elegant capitals: MR BALLARD. Muthu stood respectfully for a minute thinking that the important-looking clerk had noticed him. After another minute Muthu gave a discreet cough. Ahmed ignored the lone, dark man. Then a white man entered the office. Ahmed put on a warm, welcoming, obsequious smile and said, as he stood up: 'Good afternoon, Mr Nicholson, sir! Can I help you, sir?'

'Hello, Ahmed! Yes, I'm just going to see Mr Ballard.' The white man was already entering Ahmed's office through the swing-door. Ahmed's smile widened and Mr Nicholson urbanely breezed through into Mr Ballard's office after barely a knock and calling out of his name.

'Eh, excuse me, sir,' Muthu asked.

But Ahmed acted as if Muthu was not there. The old man didn't know what to do. He needed help from the clerk, and he couldn't afford to get upset, so he waited meekly. Finally, after a further two minutes Ahmed stopped writing and deigned to cast an imperial glance at what looked at him to be a country-bumpkin.

'Ja?' he barked, his hand still holding his pen.

'Please, sir,' said Muthu in a plaintive tone as if he was back at school, 'I want to change ... to change my name.' Muthu was hunched forward in his shabby clothes clenching his hat in his hands.

He looked thoroughly servile. Ahmed grinned to himself. This was going to be an amusing day after all!

'Ja, well, what is your name now?'

'Muthu, sir, Muthusamy Coopoosamy.'

'So, what are you going to change your name to? Poo-poo or Coopoo?' Ahmed grinned.

'No Sir.' Years of bureaucratic rudeness and insults had largely inured Muthu to any minor attacks launched by second-rate front office clerks. With great dignity, as if he was already a white man, Muthu said, 'I want to become, eh ... I want to be called ... I mean ...'

'Yes man, out with it. What's going to be your new name?'

'Michael, sir. Michael Cooper!' Even Muthu couldn't believe he had so much effrontery.

'What?' Ahmed said, his eyes bulging. His pale face turned a shade of pink and he pushed his glasses back. This coal-black coolie wanted a white man's name. Everybody knew that lots of coolies were crazy but this ...!

Ahmed had some white blood in him and he felt that he was more entitled to take on a white man's name than this, this ... But he had stuck to his own name. Now here was a coolie with the gall ...

He struggled to maintain his composure and asked, 'Why do you want a white man's name?'

'Oh no sir, it's not that, it's not that at all; it's just that I got a business and my European customers, they always call me Mike or Michael. My name Muthusamy ... well, it's difficult for white people to say. Then, all the white people they calling me Cooper instead of Coopoosamy. Me, I'm thinking, Michael Cooper is a nice-sounding name ... and it's not wrong, because the clever white people ... they're already calling me like that. So I thought nice to make it legal on the passbook.' Muthu had spoken earnestly and respectfully and Ahmed had listened attentively.

'Really? Well, I don't know about this. Why aren't you proud to be an Indian and have a nice Indian name? You can change your name if you want, but change it to an Indian name. Otherwise the white people, they might get suspicious.'

'Begging pardon, sir, but this way I make things easy for the white man ... and this is the white man's country.' Ahmed shook his head ... the tricks the coolies got up to: they were too much. He had heard the Europeans say that you couldn't keep them down no matter what you did. They were too cunning, that was the trouble, said the Europeans.

And he knew that the new laws allowed people to change their names to just about anything. That was bad. Soon you'd have a whole lot of subversives changing their names to that of seditious people like Mandela or Gandhi. This reform business was really getting out of hand. The non-whites really didn't seem to know their place anymore and 'elevated' non-whites like himself who were so indispensable to the white baas were coming increasingly under pressure.

Reluctantly he pushed the necessary forms across to Muthu and told him to advertise the name change in the white daily newspaper three times in three weeks.

Muthu felt as if he was walking on air when he left the office. 1969 might be a lucky year after all.

Two months after the advertisements appeared in the paper and after he had personally handed the application forms to Ahmed, Muthu had still not been given official notification of the name change. He went in to see Ahmed. Ahmed found it difficult to ignore the bumbling old man completely and after only two minutes he spoke to him.

'Yes?'

'Please sir, when will I be informed of my name change? It's gone more than two months now. There haven't been any objections to my name change, have there, sir?'

'No, there haven't been any objections but you must be patient, Coo-poo-sammy, these things take time. Many important Government Departments must be notified of this thing you want to do. My supervisor, Mr Ballard, is a very busy man. The government can't be hurried, you know. You must be very grateful that we allowed you to do all these things.' Ahmed didn't think it was right that a grand thing like a white man's name should come easily to a coolie.

But Muthu was getting a bit irritated now. (Almost like a white man, he reflected to himself with mild surprise.)

'But sir,' he remonstrated, 'I have filled in all the forms and I have advertised as you instructed at great personal expense and nothing's happened.'

Ahmed looked at the Indian with astonishment. Was the fellow completely barmy? Did he think that a white man's name made him even slightly into a white man? The old man was even speaking with a degree of confidence that was not there before and he stood a lot straighter. He was actually looking Ahmed in the eye. This was a coolie who needed to be kept in his place! He had not passed the Cooper file across to Mr Ballard. Now he wondered idly whether he ever should?

'You must go home and wait, Mr Coo-poo-sammy,' he said sternly. 'Patience. Patience is a virtue that certain races will do well to imbibe,' he added in the same tone of voice that he had heard the Europeans use when they said that sort of thing. The blank bureaucratic wall was impenetrable. Muthu left.

However three weeks later, Muthu was finally summoned to appear before Supervisor Ballard. Dressed impeccably (after all, he was going to see a white man this time) by Satha in a new three-piece suit and tie, old man Muthu presented himself at the Indian Affairs office. Nowadays he brought a book along that he was studying, so that he could keep himself busy while Ahmed made him wait. The book was *Learn To Speak English Properly*.

He arrived ten minutes early for his appointment but Ahmed only allowed him to see the European half an hour later.

Trying to look as harmless as possible, Muthu entered the office and stood respectfully at attention till the white man decided to look at him. It was a very large, very untidy office full of files and books all thrown higgledy-piggledy all over the place. After about a minute the official cast a scalding look at Muthu as if he was a horrible filthy mess and curtly addressed him from his sitting position.

'Now what's all this about you wanting to change your name to a ...?' Ballard couldn't bring himself to say it.

He was a big, hairy, fat man with a huge beer belly that made him look many months pregnant. His brown safari suit bulged in an unseemly manner over his abdomen. His hair was an unruly brown thatch. Ballard was not yet fifty and had lived the good life in what had been a model colony. But now things were changing ... as was personified by this ebony, cringing little toad. The awful expression on the pink man's face was thoroughly intimidating. This was a cold, hostile wall that Muthu was facing, somehow worse than Ahmed outside. At least with Ahmed you felt that beyond all the crude harassment was a fellow-being with at least some feeling, that the silly superciliousness was in a sense childish playfulness. But this ... this was a cruel monster. Muthu thought that the official could quite easily issue a decree for him to lose his business or be kicked out of his home without so much as a twinge of his Christian conscience.

He waited for the supervisor to complete the sentence, but then he finally said, 'Sir, I'm not trying to be difficult. I serve the white people, sir. They call me Cooper. Mr Tate is a rich farmer, sir, he told me Cooper is a nice name for me, sir. With respect, sir I'm not trying to be a cheeky coolie, sir.' Muthu had rehearsed his defense many times at home and he felt quite pleased with his delivery. Even Mr Stevenson, the author of the English book, might have been satisfied, reflected Muthu.

'Well, I don't know about that ...' Ballard glared at the uncomfortable-looking coolie and remembered that he had named his dog, Caesar. Well, what was wrong with the name Cooper for a coolie? It was a good Anglo-Saxon name and perhaps it was all part of the march of Western Culture. The Amercian Negroes had lost all their own names and languages. Perhaps that was the destiny of the Indians too. Besides whatever name the coolies used, they were still coolies. Muthu had known that he would be treated provocatively, but as he had planned, he kept cool.

With a great deal of effort he suppressed the anger welling up within him and continued in an even voice, 'I beg your pardon, sir, but I have a letter from Major Tate, sir.'

'Really?' Ballard was surprised. The Indian handed the Supervisor the letter. Ballard opened the sealed envelope. It was neatly typed and stated:

TO WHOM IT MAY CONCERN

I have known Muthusamy Coopoosamy for the last thirty years. During that time he has rendered valuable service to the local European farming community through his hardware and poultry businesses. He has often served us even on Sundays. During that time he has become known to the local farmers as Michael and at times has been referred to as Michael Cooper. He has always been of a co-operative disposition and I am sure that a name change will merely legalise what has become a statement of fact.

It was signed with a large flourish by the Major. Ballard was impressed. This was the right sort of coolie, then; not one of your agitators. And it seemed the ape was serious about this name-change thing. Ballard played with his little beard, enjoying the feeling of the fur and the sense of sexual power he always revelled in when he tormented a non-white, much like a cat playing with a cockroach. Suddenly he transfixed the Indian with his cold 'white man' look and said imperiously, 'You may go.'

Muthu slid out of the office feeling very inferior, very stupid and a real nuisance. Why had he let Satha talk him into this crazy thing?

After another month, Muthu came into Ahmed's waiting room. This time after only a minute, Ahmed said, with just a touch of irritation, 'Yes?' Muthu was tired of everything: coming here, being treated like a pest, everything. But he had spent good money on this thing and it was only right that he got what he had paid for. After all, what he was doing was not against the white man's law. Muthu didn't say anything. He just looked with a haggard expression on his face at the clerk.

Ahmed stood up, threw his pen down on his desk and said, 'Ah, Mr Coo-poo-samy! We've got to know you well!' He grinned at the old man and came over to the counter. He leaned over and said in a confidential, conspiratorial tone, 'You know, old man, the trouble with us Indians (Ahmed's heart almost gave a lurch when he said this. He didn't really think of himself as an Indian, well not the ordinary kind of Indian anyway) is that we tend to work very hard on doing something like building a fine temple, but we lack the finishing touch. What the white people call *finesse*. You know, an Indian will sweat blood to build a house, but he won't spend a rand on getting his grass verge cut ... Indians will build a magnificent Temple but they'll pay the priest peanuts. An Indian will study hard and qualify as a doctor but he'll talk like a motor-mechanic. Now people like us, you know what I mean,' Ahmed winked a few times at the old man and gave a conspiratorial grin, 'who try for something better with our lives ...' Muthu's face feigned ignorance. Ahmed continued, 'Oh, come on now, you know what I mean. We are birds of a feather, you and I. You trying to take on a white man's name like Cooper of all things, and me here ... well if you want a white man's name, you better learn to be a little like him ...'

'You mean this *finesse* thing?'

'Precisely, old man, precisely!' Who said you couldn't teach an old dog new tricks, thought Ahmed. 'Look here Muthu,' he growled, 'you don't look stupid to me. (Well not completely stupid, cogitated Ahmed.) But things haven't come right for you, because you haven't put the "finishing touch" to this thing!'

'Finishing touch, sir?'

'Yes, man; the "finishing touch" – a bit of gravy; you know what I mean, some butter on the toast, a bit of grease on the ...'

Ahmed looked knowingly at the Indian. For a few moments Muthu was puzzled but then suddenly the devious expression on the clerk's face made sense. 'Have to learn to be a little like the white man,' thought Muthu. 'Is there anything in particular you would like, sir, I mean in the way of gravy?'

'Well, I happen to know that Mr Ballard likes chicken *biryani* ... and his mouth absolutely waters for *dhall-roti* ... Now if you could see your way clear to ...'

'Oh, certainly sir, most stupid of me sir! I have a little poultry-farm I run on the side, sir, do you think Mr Ballard, and you, would like some eggs too, sir?' Ahmed's face was one big wolfish grin.

Satha and his friend were drinking, and why not? This time they had good reason: they had something to celebrate!

'Mr Cooper, sir, now that you have Trishen in your big shop and under your thumb, are you going to squeeze?'

'Like a white man, Satha, like a white man! With *finesse*, Satha, with loads of ice-cold, decorous *finesse*!'

'Ice-cold *what*?'

'Decorous finesse, Satha, decorous finesse. It means to handle something carefully ... with a fine, delicate touch. I'm reading all the books the white people read, Satha. They can't stop us doing that.'

'Really, Mu, I mean Michael.' Satha's eyes were bloodshot and bulging. He was really impressed. He gripped his drink tightly in his left hand and stared at Mr Cooper.

'Yes, man, and I listen to them very carefully when they talk, the white people. Don't you think that I am beginning to sound like them now?'

'Mr Cooper, sir, I think you are.'

'And I've enrolled in a Speech and Drama class … you just wait and see; soon, when I talk to you on the phone you won't be able to make out that Mr Cooper is anything but a dyed-in-the-wool Englishman.'

'Died in the *what*?'

Michael grinned. 'A pukka Englishman, Satha. A real, honest-to-goodness English bull-dog!'

'Ja man, that's true; that's how you sound.' Michael gave his friend a benign look of self-assured superiority much like that he had so often seen the whites give the non-whites.

'Well, let's celebrate now, eh, Mike. These days you even drinking like a *witou*!' He held up his drink with a flourish, 'Here's to your new name, Michael, here's to your hardware licence, to the Licensing Bureau, to Capitalism, here's to …'

Michael clicked glasses with Satha: 'To the Indian Affairs bums … to Western Civilisation, to Free Enterprise, and Satha …?'

'Yes, my friend?'

'Here's to the Finishing Touch!'

Liz Gunner

The Mandela Days

from *Soho Square V* (1992)

So we took him at dead of night and wrapped him in the skin of the beast we had slaughtered for him. We left our place, quietly, so that the dogs of our neighbours wouldn't bark, and we went a distance with him, putting the body in the open truck and driving with no headlights to the forest, the gum-trees at Stamford, not so far from the sea where the old king had crossed the water into exile after the war with the English.

Sipho had brought a spade. We didn't want to throw him into the forest like a dog. He was our son, our kinsman, my child. So we took spades and dug him a grave, not deep because it would attract suspicion even in this time of killing and dying, and it would take time.

We gave him a shallow grave, our Njomane, our young son who had followed the wrong path and gone with the enemy. Brave, like the old Njomane –

You who went away for years
But in the fourth year we saw you again!

Our young one, following where we told him not to go.

The skin of the beast was stiff, like his young body and they fitted awkwardly into the hole, deep enough for dogs not to sniff and for the stench of decay to be lost. So we threw earth over him and his wrong ways, asking in our hearts, *How could you follow a stranger from another nation,*

go with people who burnt and killed and looted and turned children against their elders and make them dance mad dances learnt in the countries to the north?

Follow a stranger who had spent long years in jail far away in the south, a man who knew nothing of our lives here, our ways.

Singing their mad songs which made you wild with reckless joy –

Tambo, Mandela, Sisulu, Slovo we have never seen them.

Our son, why did you do this?

But this is not the end of it. People will know that we lost a son. Women will tell his story and the fearfulness of it. That out of shame or scorn or anger, or was it fear they took his body and threw it to the dogs far away from the homestead, far from the ancestors, and they will never sing his song with the others. They will talk about us in quiet huts at funerals when the women sit alone guarding the body of the mourned one and what we have done will be a sign of the country dying.

Why did he ask so many questions?

Baba, who is Mandela? Why do we sit with so little and the long cars speed up and down the black road? What is the history of our part, before the sugar came? before the whites came?

Better to have had him dull and quiet but still with a smile and the laughter.

Baba, is it true that the old people called it Ematafeni, because it was like a great green plain scattered with cattle and homesteads stretching out as far as the eye could see, when you came down from the hills to the north, from Hlabisa? And they say it was rich with people and cattle and it was Dube territory, and Mjadu territory. Father tell me, is this true? And ourselves, the Mhlongos, the People of the Sun we have been here for long years? Isn't it so?

And you who rush along the black tarred road with the speed of meteors and see only the tattered huts and thin cattle and the limping men, know that you see nothing.

Maureen Isaacson

Holding Back Midnight

from *Holding Back Midnight and Other Stories* (1992)

The night is shooting past. It is bright jet and hot. The air is as smooth as the whisky we sip on the veranda of the old hotel that has become my parents' home. We are safe from the faded neon and slow-moving traffic lights outside. The bubbles of fifty chilled bottles of champagne are waiting to spill as we touch down on the new century. In our own way, we each believe that from that moment on nothing will ever be the same.

Anything could happen at midnight. President Manzwe has said that he has a surprise for us. What can it be?

'Cheers!' shouts my mother. Old opals shine dully against her sagging lobes, her webbed neck. She is flushed, like a dead person who has been painted to receive her final respects.

'Cheers!' echoes her friend Ethel.

Smoke and disillusion have ravaged their voices. Their tongues are too slack to roll an olive pip. They walk slowly among the guests, in silver dresses that were fashionable once. They teeter on sling-back stilettos. They offer salmon and bits of fish afloat on shells of lettuce leaves.

Don't the people at this party ever think about AIDS ? Out there in the real world, they give you cling paper gloves in restaurants lest you should bleed from an unnoticed cut. Waiters wear them. Doctors. Environmentalists, like my husband Leon and me. The lack of sterility makes me queasy tonight.

'What is the time, Dad?' I ask.

'Be patient,' he says.

Hopefully the moment we are waiting for will release him from the grip of history. History is ever-present in my father, like the patterns that shimmer from the chandeliers over the cracked walls. It is trapped in the broken paving outside this hotel where angels of delight once fluttered eyelashes as if they were wings at white men. History hovers, with the ghosts of the illicit couplings that once heated the hotel's shadowy rooms. It is funnelled through my memory.

Here comes my Uncle Otto, ex-Minister of Home Affairs, glass in hand. Looking at his ginger moustache, I am seven years old again. I am sitting on his lap at the bar. Don't tell your mother, he is saying. His hand is on my knee. I feel the closeness of flesh. Angels are rubbing themselves against the men. Men against angels.

'Why angels?' I want to know.

'Because they take the white men to heaven,' says Uncle Otto.

Like the street names that have been removed for their Eurocentricity, my parents and their friends are displaced. They do not understand the new signs. Their silhouettes glide across the garden, outlining their nostalgia. Through the shrill chirp of the crickets, I catch the desolation in the voices. The talk of lifts that no longer work, of the rubbish that piles up. There goes our old dentist Louis Dutoit and his wife Joyce, speaking of 'Old Johannesburg'. For all the world we are still there. Except for Leon and me of course. We could not have married in the old days, him being coloured and all. Doctor Dutoit would not even have filled Leon's teeth.

How graciously they tolerate us now. We have breezed in from our communal plot in the outer limits of the mega-city these people are too afraid to visit.

'Not without an AK-4777 rifle,' my father has said.

Instead they ruminate in this, the last of the shrunken ghettos that began to decline when cheap labour went out. Not for them the spread of shebeens and malls that splash jazz from what used to be poverty-stricken township to the City Hall. The place we now call Soweto City. Connected by skyway and flyway, over the underground, as steady as the steel and the foreign funding on which it runs. Talk about one door closing. The Old Order was not yet cold in its grave and the place was gyrating, like a woman in love.

And the people out there? There are millions of us – living the good life advertised by laser-honed graphics that dazzle the streets. We are fast-living. Street-wise. Natural. We till the land. Our food is organic. See this party dress? It's made of paper. Tomorrow I'll shred it. Recycle later.

I thank heavens for Leon. I envy him his equilibrium. Forgive and forget. That's what he said before we came here tonight. His kind of thinking has helped me cope with the effect my parents have on me.

'Thank the Lord Leon's surname is also Laubscher. Some people will never know,' is all they said when I told them about our marriage.

Dad is the perfect host. But earlier this evening his sentimentality got the better of him when Uncle Otto reminded him of the New Year's Eve parties, five times the size of this one, held at our old house. Foreign diplomats, caviar, black truffles in Italian rice. Now he embraces Ethel. One-two. One-two. He dances a little jig with her on the veranda, cooled by the breeze that fans the palm tree. I squirm, reminded of the way he used to cavort when the hotel was in its prime.

'I'm a miner at heart,' he used to say, insisting that the place was a private sideline of no consequence.

Was anyone fooled into believing it was anything but a thriving business? We had more maids than rooms that needed polishing in our double-storey house. My parents had owned three game farms and four cars. A relic of the Old Regime, my father will never forgive the New Order for destroying his life-style. I am sure that in his dreams he still sells the kisses of angels to those who would cross the forbidden colour line by night, endorse it by day.

'Would you like to dance?' asks Paul Schoeman, once the minister of Law and Order. 'Mona Lisa ...,' sings Nat King Cole. I shuffle. Our feet collide. He holds me close, looks into my eyes and says, 'How can you live in the native township?'

I am unable to persuade old Schoeman that the change has brought with it a downswing in crime. I say all the things my father will not hear. But like Dad he does not grasp a word about redistribution. About progress. How can they when they insist without blinking that English and Afrikaans are still the official languages?

'You talk too much,' he says and pulls me towards him, gripping me so tightly that my left nipple sets off his security panic button, the kind my parents pay a fortune to wear round their necks. A siren wails. Up here on the veranda, men remove the fleshy fingers they have been rolling over their wives' naked, sagging backs. The whites of the wives' eyes show. Paul Schoeman grabs my breast. I scream. I put my hands to my ears. I want to block out the wailing. The barking of the Rottweilers. The jibbering of the guests. Four armed response security guards appear. Their sobriety creates a striking contrast.

They are not amused when my father says, 'False alarm. Who let the dogs out?' Leon is nowhere to be seen.

'Have a snack,' mother offers. It is anchovy, tart and salty.

'Is it nearly time for champagne?' I want to know.

'It won't be long now,' says Dad, as if he were meting out a punishment.

'What is the time?' shouts someone. One minute to midnight, says my watch. My father pours me another whisky.

'Be patient', he commands. Any minute now, I tell myself.

'To the year two thousand!' I shout. 'To the future!'

'There is nothing to look forward to.' Dad's voice is weighed down. Now two of him are saying. 'This is the future.' The thick curl of his cigar smoke throws me back into a time when I believed that he had power over the planets. Now I am starting to believe that my father is actually capable of holding back midnight. I want to call the security guards with their military boots and pistols to return.

'Do you want to see the real danger we face here tonight?' I will ask. Then I will see what they can do about the fear that washes this party like a backward-moving current.

I am standing alone when it happens. The blackness of the sky is spolit as fire crackers explode brightly into two million broken stars. An ethereal chorus resounds above the voice of Nat King Cole, above the marabi jazz that plays on Station Nnwe in the background. As the heavens shift, time dissolves and my rapture rises.

Down below, the profusion of papyrus plants, the beds of lobelia, chrysanthemum and wild hydrangea, the lawn that is overrun with weeds are illuminated by an unearthly light. 'Happy New Year!' Leon embraces me from behind. 'Did you hear what Manzwe said?' he asks.

From a great distance, I hear my father saying that there is still one minute to go.

Biographical Notes

ABRAHAMS, Peter (1918–)
Born in South Africa. Left for England in the forties. Published his novels in England where they were well received. The first black writer after Sol Plaatje to publish a novel. Lives in Jamaica. Publications include a collection of short stories (*Dark Testament*, 1942), eight novels and two autobiographies.

ADAMS, Perseus (1933–)
Born in Cape Town and educated at Sea Point Boys High and U.C.T., Adams taught in Cape Town until 1965, when he left for the Far East. He has two collections of poetry to his name; *The Land at My Door* (1965) and *Grass for the Unicorn* (1975), and has had his poems and short stories published in a number of anthologies.

BOETIE, Dugmore (1920–1966)
He spent his early years in Sophiatown, Johannesburg. His life s a tramp, gaol-bird and con-man is graphically recollected in his autobiographical novel *Familiarity is the Kingdom of the Lost: The Story of a Black Man in South Africa*, edited by Barney Simon and first published in 1969.

BOSMAN, Herman Charles (1905–1951)
Born in the Cape Province, educated in Johannesburg, Bosman qualified as a teacher and took up his first appointment at a farm school in the Marico district near the Bechuanaland (now Botswana) border. He lived in Europe from 1930 to 1939 and, on his return to South Africa, was appointed editor of a Pietersburg weekly. His publications include four collections of short stories (*Mafeking Road, Unto Dust, Jurie Steyn's Post*

Office and *A Bekkersdal Marathon)*, two volumes of *belles-lettres (Cold Stone Jug* and *A Cask of Jerepigo*), poetry and novels.

BROWNLEE, Frank (1875–1951)
Grandson of John Brownlee who came to South Africa as missionary in 1816. Educated at Dale College, King William's Town. Entered government service of the Cape Colony in 1893. Magistrate and native commissioner in the Native Affairs Department at various stations from 1905 to 1933. Became president of the Native Appeal Court, Transvaal and Natal Division in 1933. Publications include a history of the Transkei and work in Afrikaans. Published one novel, *Ntsukumbini – Cattlethief* (1929) and two collections of short stories.

COPE, Jack (1913–1991)
Born in Mooi River, Natal and educated at Durban High School. Journalist: Durban 1931, Fleet Street, London 1935 to 1941. He farmed, worked for a fishing company, lectured, was a journalist on *The Cape Times*. Publications include a biography (*Comrade Bill*, 1943), poems (1948), eight novels and three collections of short stories. Edited *Seismograph* and, with Uys Krige, *The Penguin Book of South African Verse* (1968). Translated, with William Plomer, *Selected Poems* by Ingrid Jonker (1968). Co-founder and editor of *Contrast* and editor of the Mantis Series of Southern African Poets (1973–1977). He spent his last years living in England.

CRIPPS, Arthur Shearly (1869–1952)
Educated at Charterhouse, Trinity College, Oxford and Cuddeston Theological College. Vicar of Ford End, Essex (1894 to 1900). Missionary in Mashonaland (1901 to 1926), missionary in (1915 to 1916), vicar of Ford End (1926 to 1930), missionary in Mashonaland from 1930. Publications include two sociological studies – *The Sabi Reserve* and *An Africa for Africans* – several collections of poetry and short stories and nine novels.

DHLOMO, Rolfes Reginald Raymond (1906–1971)
Born near Pietermaritzburg, Dhlomo is an important figure in black South African literature. He was a freelance writer of some stature, becoming, in 1932, assistant editor of *The Bantu World* and, in 1943, editor of *Ilanga Lase Natal*. His many publications include the novel, *An African Tragedy* (1928).

ESSOP, Ahmed (1931–)
Born in India and came to South Africa with his family in 1934. He has studied at the University of South Africa and worked as a teacher and in the business world. He has published two novels, *The Visitation* (1980) and *The Emperor* (1984), and two collections of short stories, *The Hajji and Other Stories* (1978) and *Noorjehan* (1990).

FITZPATRICK, Sir Percy (1862–1931)
Born in King William's Town, Cape Province, and educated at St Gregory's College near Bath, England. Returned to South Africa in 1884. Prospector at Barberton and editor of *The Barberton Herald* from 1886 to 1889. Travelled in Mashonaland (*Through Mashonaland with Pick and Pen*, 1892) with Lord Randolph Churchill's expedition. He took an active part in the Reform movement in Johannesburg and gave an account of the Kruger regime in *The Transvaal from Within* (1899). Publications include *The Outspan* (1897), *From the Front* (1900), and *Jock of the Bushveld* (1907).

GIBBON, Perceval (1879–1926)
Born in Trelach, Wales, and educated at the Moravian School, Baden. Joined the merchant service, worked as a journalist and war-correspondent. Joined the *Rand Daily Mail* on its foundation in 1902. Publications include a volume of verse, three novels and three collections of short stories.

GLANVILLE, Ernest (1856–1925)
Born in Wynberg, Cape. Educated at St Andrew's College, Grahamstown. One of the first to peg a claim on the diamond fields in 1873. He was war-correspondent for the *Daily Chronicle* in 1879, joined the *Cape Argus* in 1902 and became editor in 1907. Between 1888 and 1923, he published over twenty volumes including novels and short-story collections.

GORDIMER, Nadine (1923–)
Born in the Transvaal. Published her first story ('Come again Tomorrow') in *Forum* at the age of fifteen. Publications include collections of short stories and a number of novels. *Friday's Footprint* (short stories) won the W.H. Smith and Son Literary Award in 1961; *A Guest of Honour* (novel) was awarded the James Black Memorial Prize in 1973, and in the following year *The Conservationist* (novel) shared the Booker Prize. Gordimer has been an influential figure in the Congress of South African Writers. In 1991 she was awarded the Nobel Prize for literature.

GOUDVIS, Bertha (1876–1966)
Born in England. Came to South Africa in 1881. Lived variously in South Africa, Southern Rhodesia and Moçambique working as a hotelier and a journalist. She published *Little Eden*, a novel, in 1949, and a volume of short stories, *The Mistress of Mooiplaas and Other Stories*, in 1956. She also published a play, *The Aliens*, in 1936.

GUNNER, Liz (1944–)
Gunner was born in Columbo, Ceylon. She has lived in the Orange Free State, the Natal Midlands and Northern Natal. She has been a teacher, freelance journalist and has worked for a number of years in higher education in the United Kingdom. She currently teaches African Literature at the School of Oriental and African Studies, University of London. Her publications include *A Handbook for Teaching African Literature* (1984) and – with Mafika Gwala – she has edited and translated a collection of Zulu poetry, *Musho! Zulu Popular Praises* (1991). Her short stories have appeared in the *Arekopaneng Newsletter*, *Staffrider* and *Soho Square V*.

HAVEMANN, Ernst (1918–)
Born in Zululand, where he grew up on a farm speaking Zulu and Afrikaans. He studied at Natal University and during the Second World War served in Libya and Egypt. He then worked in African administration for both the South African Railways and the Province of Natal before practising as a mining engineer. In the 1970s he emigrated to British Columbia, Canada. His collection of stories is entitled, *Bloodsong* (1987).

HEAD, Bessie (1937–1986)
Born in Pietermaritzburg, Natal. She trained as a teacher, worked as a journalist for the magazine *The Golden City Post* in Johannesburg, and then left for a teaching post in Botswana, living there from 1964 until her death. Most of her works focus on life in Botswana and include the novels *When Rain Clouds Gather* (1968), *Maru* (1971) and *A Question of Power* (1973). Her stories have appeared in the volumes *The Collector of Treasures* (1977) and *Tales of Tenderness and Power* (1989).

HOPE, Chrsitopher (1944–)
Born in Johannesburg, but grew up in Pretoria. He studied at the Universities of the Witwatersrand and Natal. He has worked as an underwriter, copywriter, teacher and journalist both in South Africa and England, where he settled in 1975. He has published several volumes of poems

and is a regular book reviewer in journals such as the *Times Literary Supplement* and the *London Magazine*. His novels include *A Separate Development* (1980), *Kruger's Alp* (1984), *The Hottentot Room* (1986) and *Black Swan* (1987). His stories appear in the volume *Private Parts and Other Tales* (1981).

ISAACSON, Maureen (1955–)
Born in Johannesburg and studied at the University of the Witwatersrand. For three years she lived in Sweden. She has worked as a copywriter and journalist. She worked as a researcher on the two volumes *The Fifties People of South Africa* and *The Finest Photos from the Old Drum*. She lives in Johannesburg and works for the *Sunday Star* newspaper.

JACOBSON, Dan (1929–)
Born in Johannesburg, educated at Kimberley Boys' High and the University of the Witwatersrand, Johannesburg. Teacher, journalist, he has taught at universities in the U.S.A. Publications include stories, articles and reviews. Novels include *The Trap*, *Dance in the Sun* and *The Price of Diamonds*. He lives in London.

JORDAN, Archibald Campbell (1906–1968)
Xhosa novelist and critic. Born in Mbokothwana, South Africa, he became professor of African Languages and Literature at the University of Wisconsin Madison, U.S.A., where he later died. Brought up in the Transkei and in Cape Town. Wrote folk-tales, riddles and proverbs which he heard from old people still in touch with oral traditions. His novel, *Ingqumbo Yeminyanya* (The Wrath of the Ancestors) was written in Xhosa as were many of his poems and tales. His critical and historical essays and didactic folk-tales were written in English.

KRIGE, Uys, (1910–1987)
Poet, critic, playwright, short-story writer and translator. Most of his works are in Afrikaans. He won numerous literary prizes. Publications include translations from English, Spanish and French into Afrikaans of poetry and drama, notably Shakespeare. His works in English include *The Way Out* (autobiography), *The Dream and the Desert* (stories) and *Two Lamps* (drama). He co-edited with Jack Cope the influential *Penguin Book of South African Verse* (1968). For many years he lived at Onrus on the Cape coast.

LA GUMA, Alex (1925–1985)
Born and educated in Cape Town, La Guma, the son of a prominent

Communist Party member, spent a lifetime engaged in political opposi-
tion to apartheid. He was an accused in the infamous Treason Trial of the
1950s and served periods of house arrest during the early 1960s. In 1966
he left South Africa and served the African National Congress in the
U.K. and in the Caribbean. His works include the story collection *A
Walk in the Night* (1968) and the novels *And a Threefold Cord* (1964),
The Stone Country (1967), *In the Fog of the Season's End* (1972) and
Time of the Butcherbird (1979).

MACPHAIL, Ella Mary (1922–)
Born near Johannesburg where she now lives. She grew up in various
small towns of the Transvaal and isolated parts of the bushveld. Her
volume of stories is entitled *Falling Upstairs* (1982). Her novels are
Phoebe & Nio (1987) – for which she received the CNA Literary Award –
and *Mrs Chudd's Place* (1993). She is a director of Hippogriff Press,
Johannesburg.

MASEKO, Bheki (1951–)
Born near Newcastle, Natal. He grew up in Soweto. He left school to
work as a truck driver and later in a laboratory at the Chamber of Mines.
He is currently studying for a B.A. Degree through the University of
South Africa. His volume of stories *Mamlambo* appeared in 1991.

MATLOU, Joel (1957–)
Born in Mabopane. Matlou is among a new generation of South African
writers. His first, highly distinctive stories, appeared in *Staffrider*
magazine at the end of the 1970s. His volume *Life at Home and Other
Stories* appeared in 1991. He works as a clerk in a factory in Pretoria.

MATTHEWS, James (1929–)
Educated in Cape Town and lives in Athlone, Cape. Publications include
Cry Rage (volume of poetry, originally banned in South Africa) and *The
Park*, a collection of short stories. A second collection, *Asikwela*, has
been published in Sweden. Has worked variously as newspaper-seller,
messenger, journalist and telephonist.

MEDALIE, David (1963–)
Born in Bethal, Transvaal. Holds English Literature degrees from the
Universities of the Witwatersrand and Oxford. He has taught at the Uni-
versity of Cape Town and is currently lecturing in the English De-
partment at the University of the Witwatersrand. His volume of stories
The Shooting of the Christmas Cows appeared in 1990.

MHLOPE, Gcina (1958–)
Born near Durban, but went to high school in the Transkei. Her first stories and poems were written in Xhosa. She has worked as a writer, actress and storyteller. She has toured extensively outside South Africa and has appeared in many film and theatre roles. She is at present resident director at the Market Theatre, Johannesburg. She has a published play, *Have You Seen Zandile?* (1988) and has had her stories and poems published in a number of magazines and anthologies.

MILLIN, Sarah Gertrude (1890–1968)
Born in Lithuania but, apart from a few months, lived all her life in South Africa. Publications include seventeen novels, including *God's Stepchildren* (1924); biographies – *Rhodes and General Smuts* (two volumes); autobiographies – *The Night is Long* and *The Measure of My Days*; and histories – *The South Africans, South Africa* and *The People of South Africa*. A collection of essays appeared under the title *Men on a Voyage*, and her account of Hitler's war came out in a six-volumed diary published between 1944 and 1948. She wrote a play called 'No Longer Mourn' adapted from her novel, *Mary Glenn*.

MPHAHLELE, Ezekiel (Es'kia) (1919–)
Born in Marabastad, Pretoria, trained at Adam's College, near Durban and then worked as a teacher. He was dismissed from his teaching post in 1952 for his outspoken opposition to the Bantu Education Act. He then worked in Johannesburg for *Drum* magazine before leaving South Africa on an exit permit in 1957. He spent twenty years in exile mainly teaching at various universities in North America and in Africa. In 1977 he returned to South Africa to become the first professor of African Literature in the country at the University of the Witwatersrand. Among his works – many of them originally banned – are two autobiographies – *Down Second Avenue* (1959) and *Afrika, My Music* (1984). He has also written novels and his major collection of stories is *In Corner B* (1967). He has published two influential volumes of essays on South African literature – *The African Image* (1962) and *Voices in the Whirlwind* (1974).

NDEBELE, Njabulo (1948–)
Born in Johannesburg, but grew up in Charterston Location, Nigel, which is the setting of many of his stories. He holds degrees from the Universities of Botswana, Cambridge and Denver. He was Pro-Vice Chancellor of the University of Lesotho until 1991, when he returned to South Africa after a long absence to become Head of the Department of African Literature at the University of the Witwatersrand. He is at

present Vice-Rector of the University of the Western Cape. He is president of the Congress of South African Writers. Ndebele started his writing career as a poet, but is best known for his stories which appeared in the volume, *Fools* (1983). His critical essays, some of the most incisive on South African writing, appeared under the title *Rediscovery of the Ordinary* in 1991.

PADAYACHEE, Deena (1953–)
Born in Durban and grew up in Umhlali, Natal. A graduate of Natal University, Padayachee practises as a medical doctor in Durban. His stories have appeared in journals and anthologies in South Africa and abroad. His story 'The Finishing Touch' won the 1991 Nadine Gordimer Short Story Award. His volume of stories, *What's Love Got To Do With It?* appeared in 1992.

PATON, Alan (1903–1988)
Born in Pietermaritzburg, educated in Natal. Principal of Diepkloof Reformatory from 1935 to 1948. In 1948 his first novel, *Cry the Beloved Country*, was widely acclaimed in Britain, Europe and the U.S.A. This was followed by a second novel, *Too Late the Phalarope*; a collection of short stories, *Debbie Go Home*; and several books on contemporary politics in South Africa. In 1964 his biography of Jan Hofmeyr was published, followed by the autobiographical *Kontakion for You Departed*. A religious book entitled *Instrument of Thy Peace* was followed by a second work of biography on Geoffrey Clayton, Archbishop of Cape Town, *Apartheid and the Bishop*, which won the Central News Agency Literary Award for 1973. He was active in politics, serving as President of the South African Liberal Party – of which he was a founder member – from 1958 until 1968 when the party was disbanded. Honorary degrees have been conferred on him by several universities, including Harvard, Yale, Edinburgh and Natal.

PLOMER, William (1903–1973)
Born in Pietersburg, educated in England, the young Plomer was both farmer and trader, and travelled widely in Greece and Japan. He edited the short-lived, but famous, *Voorslag* magazine with Roy Campbell and Laurens van der Post. He published a life of Rhodes (1933), edited the diary of Kilvert (1938), written several novels (notably, *Turbott Wolfe*, 1925), as well as poetry, short stories and two volumes of autobiography.

SCHREINER, Olive (1855–1920)
The ninth of twelve children born to a German-born missionary and his

English wife in the Eastern Cape. Little formal education but read widely in nineteenth-century history and philosophy. Much of her early life was spent in the Cape and she worked as a governess on isolated farms in the Karoo. Her writing was divided between works of fiction and polemical essays. In 1883 *The Story of an African Farm* was published. Her second novel, *Undine*, was completed in 1876 and published posthumously in 1929. In *Trooper Peter Halket of Mashonaland* (1897) she presented an allegorical account of Cecil John Rhodes and his British South Africa Company. Her uncompleted novel, *From Man to Man* was published posthumously in 1926. She wrote eight short stories and twenty-six allegories or dreams, *Dreams* (1890), *Dream Life and Real Life* (1893) and *Stories, Dreams and Allegories* published in 1923. Polemical works include *The Political Situation* (1896) and *An English South African's View of the Situation* (1899). Other works discuss the position of women, minority groups and the Boer, and the First World War. These essays, including *Woman and Labour*, appear as a collection in *Thoughts on South Africa*, first printed in 1923. Olive Schreiner lived in England and in Europe from 1881 to 1889. She then returned to South Africa where she involved herself in the politics of the time. She died in Wynberg, Cape.

SCULLY, William Charles (1855–1943)
Born in Dublin. Came to South Africa in 1867. Between the ages of thirteen and twenty-one he was a shepherd, diamond-prospector and big game hunter. He entered the Cape civil service in 1876 and retired as Chief Magistrate of Port Elizabeth in 1914. Author of a volume of poetry; three volumes of short stories, *Kafir Stories*, *The White Hecatomb* and *By Veld and Kopje*; several novels, including *Daniel Vanaanda* and *A Vendetta of the Desert*; two volumes of reminiscences; a history of South Africa; and memoirs and descriptions of early Johannesburg and Bushmanland.

SMITH, Pauline (1884–1959)
Born in the Cape Province, the daughter of an English doctor. Her seminal short story, 'The Pain', appeared in *The Adelphi* (Middleton Murry) and received wide notice. A translated and adapted version of the story has appeared on South African television. Other works to receive attention were *The Little Karoo* (1925), *The Beadle* (1926) and *Platkop's Children* (1935).

THEMBA, Can (1924–1968)
Born in Marabastad in the Northern Transvaal. Won the first Mendi

Memorial Scholarship to Fort Hare. Worked in Johannesburg as teacher and journalist on *Drum* and *The Golden City Post*. He left for Swaziland in 1963 and died there in Manzini.

VLADISLAVIC, Ivan (1957–)
Born in Pretoria, but lived much of his life in Johannesburg. He holds degrees from the University of the Witwatersrand and works as a freelance editor. He was closely associated with the magazine *Staffrider* for a number of years, and co-edited the commemorative volume *Ten Years of Staffrider* (1988). He has published a collection of stories *Missing Persons* and a novel *The Folly* (1993).

WICOMB, Zoë (1948–)
Born near van Rhynsdorp in the Cape Province. She has studied at the Universities of the Western Cape, Reading and Strathclyde. She lived for many years in the United Kingdom where she taught literature and cultural studies at institutions of further and higher education. In 1992 she returned to South Africa to teach at the University of the Western Cape. She is on the editorial board of *The Southern African Review of Books*. Her volume of stories, *You Can't Get Lost in Cape Town* appeared in 1987.

WILHELM, Peter (1943–)
Educated in Johannesburg where he lives and works as an economic journalist/editor. His works include the novels, *The Dark Wood* (1977), *Summer's End* (1984) and *The Healing Process* (1988); he has published three volumes of stories – *LM and Other Stories* (1975), *At the End of A War* (1981) and *Some Place in Africa* (1987).

Acknowledgement of Copyright

This editor and publisher would like to express their thanks for permission to reproduce the following stories published in this anthology:

Cosaw Publishing (Pty) Ltd for Deena Padayachee's 'The Finishing Touch'
  Maureen Isaacson's 'Holding Back Midnight'
  Bheki Maseko's 'Mamlambo'
  Joel Matlou's 'Man Against Himself'
Nadine Gordimer for 'A Chip of Glass Ruby' from *Not for Publication*
Liz Gunner for 'The Mandela Days' from *Soho Square*
Hamish Hamilton Ltd for Ernst Havemann's 'A Farm at Raraba' from *Bloodsong*
Sir Rupert Hart-Davis for William Plomer's 'The Child of Queen Victoria'
Human and Rousseau (Edms) Bpk for H C Bosman's 'Birth Certificate' from *A Bekkersdal Marathon*
Dan Jacobson for 'Stop Thief' from *A Long Way from London*
Patricia Reynolds of John Johnson (Authors Agents) Ltd for Bessie Head's 'Life' from *The Collector of Treasures*
T M L Krige for Uys Krige's 'Death of the Zulu' from *The Dream and the Desert*
E M Macphail for 'Annual Migration' from *New Contrast*
Njabulo Ndebele for 'Death of a Son' from *From South Africa – Triquartely 69*
Jonathan Paton for Alan Paton's 'A Drink in the Passage' from *Debbie Go Home*
David Philip Publishers (Pty) Ltd for:
  Jack Cope's 'The Flight' from *The Tame Ox and Other Stories*

Alex La Guma's 'A Matter of Taste' from *A Walk in the Night and Other Stories*

David Medalie's 'The Shooting of the Christmas Cows' from *The Shooting of the Christmas Cows*

Ivan Vladislavic's 'Journal of a Wall' from *Missing Persons*

Can Themba's 'The Will to Die' from *The Will to Die*

Virago Press for Zoë Wicomb's 'Ash on my Sleeve' from *You Can't Get Lost in Cape Town*

Peter Wilhelm for 'Lion' from *L M and Other stories*.

Although every effort has been made to trace copyright holders, this has not always been possible. Should any infringement have occurred, the editor and publisher apologise and undertake to amend these omissions in the event of a reprint.